About the author

Chloe Timms is a writer, mentor, campaigner and podcast
host from the Kent coast. After a career in teaching, Chloe
studied for an MA in Creative Writing at the University
of Kent and won a scholarship at the Faber Academy.
Chloe is passionate about disability rights, having been
diagnosed with the condition Spinal Muscular Atrophy
at 18 months old, and has campaigned on several crucial
issues. In 2022 Chloe launched her podcast Confessions
of a Debut Novelist. *The Seawomen* is her first novel.

Praise for *The Seawomen*:

'Beautifully written . . . a great concept, brilliantly executed'
Sunday Business Post

'A powerful, enchanting novel, with prose so vivid you can taste the salt
in the air on your tongue'
Anna Bailey, bestselling author of *Tall Bones*

'An unsettling and lushly written reimagining of witch trials, exploring
fertility, control and how what we believe can save us – or destroy us.
The Handmaid's Tale meets *The Shape of Water*'
Kirsty Logan, author of *The Gloaming*

'An allegorical love story with echoes of fairytales and told with a
visceral brutality. At its heart it is about whether to believe what we are
told over what we feel to be true'
Kate Sawyer, author of *The Stranding*

'A gripping tale of love and bravery; *The Seawomen* immerses you in its
watery world'
Sophie Ward, author of *Love and Thought Experiments*

'This book sucked me under and held me in its gorgeous, terrifying
embrace. It's a rare treat to read a story so gripping told in such beautiful
prose. Dive in and don't look back'
Zoe Gilbert, author of *Folk*

Chloe Timms

The Seawomen

HODDER

First published in Great Britain in 2022 by Hodder Studio
An imprint of Hodder & Stoughton
An Hachette UK company

This paperback edition published in 2023

1

A CIP catalogue record for this title is available from the British Library

Paperback ISBN 978 1 529 36960 1
eBook ISBN 978 1 529 36958 8

Typeset in Bembo by Hewer Text UK Ltd, Edinburgh
Printed and bound in Great Britain by Clays Ltd, Elcograf S.p.A.

Hodder & Stoughton policy is to use papers that are natural, renewable
and recyclable products and made from wood grown in sustainable
forests. The logging and manufacturing processes are expected to
conform to the environmental regulations of the country of origin.

Hodder & Stoughton Ltd
Carmelite House
50 Victoria Embankment
London EC4Y 0DZ

www.hodder.co.uk

For Mum and Dad

The Untethering

I've got my fingers pushed right into my ears, and the screaming softens. But even with my fingers in, the woman is still making a noise as she's held back, her chin all wet and shiny with spit. She doesn't make any words now, just screams. I spread my tongue against the roof of my mouth and hum, trying to numb out her sound with mine, but the hums tickle air out of my nose and I can still hear everything. I'm humming that bedtime rhyme my grandmother loves to tuck me in with. 'Little Fisherboy Blue'. About the one who caught the Seawoman in a net and boiled her in a pot for supper.

The Keepers have got the screaming woman by the arms and legs now, swinging her up into the air as if her body is a blanket. She's naked, so I can see the yellow-white grip marks on her ankles. She must be cold. I hide my chin inside my fleecy coat. They hold the woman tight because she keeps jerking her body all over the place, like she's a dried-up fish on land. The woman tries biting them. Snarling and snapping. One of the men who isn't carrying her, the one leading them, steps nearer to her. A Minister. I can tell by his shirt. Dark as the sky. He says something, up close to her face like he's breathing on her. He slaps her.

The noise of it gets right under my skin, even though my fingers are still in my ears and I can hear the whooshing of blood. I look down at my boots, mostly hidden by the muddy hem of my skirt, and see the blue peeking out. My grandmother paid extra for the blue laces, because she says blue is a holy colour, God's favourite. She bought them from the supply puffer that comes every Wednesday and blasts its horn so we all know to wait for them in the port and rummage for the things we want to buy.

Someone in the crowd gasps. My grandmother must feel my body shrink, because she puts her hands on my shoulders. She's already told me once.

'Eyes to the front. Don't look away, Esta. It's important.'

The Minister slaps the woman again, and this time she stills. The crowd around us pushes in closer, peering to get a better look. My grandmother leans in too, and I can feel her behind me, her shell shape all curved up because of her bad back. We don't normally walk this far out, not to the jetty at the top of the island. She says it's because of her back and at her speed it would take us hours, but I know that's not the reason. She hates the northernmost part of the island, where the freezing sea roars up so high it might swallow us. That's why she wouldn't stand at the front of the crowd to watch, and pulled me back far enough that the sea spray wouldn't touch us. Instead we're standing on a mound, raised enough to see everything happening below. She wanted me to have a good view. It'll be okay, I keep telling myself, as long as we don't look directly at the water.

The woman is silent now, face starting to go a bit pink where the Minister's hand landed. We're all squeezed, not breathing, just watching. And then, bursting from the woman's chest, comes an animal noise. I press on my ears until they ring. A foot kicks out and flies from their grip. Two more Keepers on the edge of the crowd rush over to help. Kicking and kicking and kicking, her whole body shaking. There's a girl next to me in the crowd who whimpers until she is shushed by her mother. My grandmother presses down on my shoulders and I know what she is trying to tell me: *remember this, this is the important part.*

Another Keeper comes forward when they whistle for him, fingers in their mouths. He hands over a bottle and a cloth to the man who slapped her. The Ministers talk, but it's too low and whispery for any of us to hear, even when I pull my hands away from my ears. The wind drags the sound away from the jetty and carries it across the sea. That's where the woman will be soon. Grandmother's seen this happen a few times, she said, a few. She wouldn't tell me how many. This is the first one I've seen. This important night. The Untethering.

The Minister with the bottle tips some of the liquid onto the cloth and stuffs it into the woman's mouth, holding it down until she coughs. She gasps and retches, struggles, but everything slows, neck slumping, her eyelids closed. They lay her down on the jetty, tying her feet together with a big knotty rope, then her hands. No fighting, no screaming. She grizzles like a baby after a nap. There are girls around me nudging their mothers, pulling on their sleeves with questions. Some have sisters they whisper to. Father Jessop will explain everything. Those are the words of my grandmother I keep repeating. The thought of his smile at the front of church stops me thinking about any more questions.

Everyone here is a girl. Apart from the important ones, like the Keepers, the Ministers and Father Jessop, there aren't any other men here. No dads or brothers. They are allowed to stay at home.

The woman is lifted into the yole and they lay her down in its hull. The sea slops, rocking the boat like a cradle. It's just the right size to fit her. These are old boats; ones too battered to use. Put a fisherman in, my grandmother said, and he'd sink right to the bottom of the sea. Only the Seawomen swim. None of us can. The Keepers use another piece of rope to tie the woman down, wrapping it around the planks that go from one side of the boat to the other. Those are called thwarts. Barrett told me all the special names for parts of a boat. He knows everything about them. I'm not supposed to know about boats, because boats would make me think too much about the sea, and that would be bad, so what he told me, I keep secret. Even from my grandmother.

'Can we go home?' I ask.

'It's not done yet,' she says, patting my head and looking away like she's ignoring me.

The Minister in charge tugs on the ropes before nodding to Father Jessop, standing at the front in the crowd. Quiet and almost hidden the whole time. He steps forward and faces us, the audience, his robes puffing up like a sail in the wind. He holds a golden bell in his hands. The bell used to belong to Father Lambert John, Father Jessop's great-great-great-great-grandfather. Four greats. Father Lambert was one of the settlers who rebuilt this island when God told him to create a new home for good people, away from the corruptions of the world.

He discovered the Seawomen too. We hear stories all the time. Lesson after lesson in school. Back then, when Father Lambert arrived, the Seawomen lived in the water around the island. But when his followers made a home here, the Seawomen saw their devotion and swam up to the shoreline. They called out to the women and the girls, trying to tempt them away from God and lead them into darkness. Father Lambert and his men drove them and their evil away and put rules in place to protect us, to stop them ever returning. We have to be good, my grandmother says, otherwise they'll come again. The darkness too. It crawls into us when we're bad, spreads and spreads until there's nothing of God left. The Seawomen – they can sense it.

Father Lambert lived long ago, hundreds and hundreds of years, and my head hurts to think about it. The bell is kept in the Ministry now, only brought out at special times like this.

Father Jessop rings the bell and it makes a loud wavy sound when he thwacks it against the air, turning every head towards him. The sound reminds me of the birthdays when we cherish new life, and the Festival of the Land when we celebrate our lives here away from evil. When I'm older, I'll be married and the bell will ring then. And when the Eldermothers decide I'm ready for the Lord's duty and my mother-year begins. My grandmother gives my shoulders another squeeze, and I look straight at Father Jessop's long face. He rings the bell twelve times. One solid ring for every month. We are all unmoving, playing statues, waiting for him to begin speaking.

'God chose this island to save us,' he says, 'and we are truly grateful to be given this chance. But we must be aware of the darkness and its servants, the ones who try to lure us away from His righteous path! We must protect this sacred land in the name of Salvation. This woman . . .' he points now to the boat, 'she might look like one of you, but believe me when I tell you this, she has betrayed the word of God! She has the darkness in her. She is one of *them*!'

There's a noise in the crowd, a shuffle, a cooing, a sniffle of fear. Father Jessop is pointing out across the water now, out towards the dark sea, out past the patrol ferries.

'God learnt of her true nature and He showed us. There was fever. Night terrors. That was her! There was a child, shaking and screaming in the night-time. That was her! A neighbour, covered in black and blue marks. A newborn who never made its first cry. That was her! Cattle dying, goats diseased. A small boy fitting and frothing after she met his eye. We have studied her for marks of their making and challenged her on these accusations. She could give us no answers. But the Lord could. He is the only one who can make that judgement. Like every woman, she was given a year. The ultimate test, her one duty. And that too she failed. The Lord stopped her from bringing new life into this world. He showed the one sign we could not ignore. He stopped the spread of evil. Twelve childless, godless months, and God has shown us the truth. We are left with only one choice, to follow Father Lambert John's ruling against followers of the Seawomen. With the Lord's guidance, we send her back to the water with them, where she belongs. Where her body cannot curse this island any more!'

The grown-ups start clapping, and it spreads from one set of hands to the next. The ground shakes with the stamping of feet and I feel like I'm drowning in noise, cheering all around. A group of girls in front of me jump and clap at the same time, and my grandmother shakes my shoulders because I forgot to start clapping, so I join in until my hands sting.

Father Jessop says she's one of *them*, but how can she be when she doesn't even have a tail? I checked.

He smiles, and it makes his eyes disappear. He looks into the crowd, searching for someone, until he spots the woman he's after and beckons her over. A woman with a moon-round belly. She rolls her hand over it and he does the same. The crowd gets louder. I recognise her from Moss Farm, the croft with the four ugly goats that I pass on the way to school.

'Is it your first?' he asks her.

She shakes her head, her chin tucked down like I do when I'm shy. 'My third.'

When she has five children there'll be a big party for all of us. A feast. Music and dancing. Those parties are almost as good as the festival. Children are to be celebrated, Father Jessop says. Our island depends on them. Without our kind, the darkness will rise and all that is good, all that is beautiful, will be destroyed.

Father Jessop smacks his hands together even faster. 'God is with you!' he says, flashing his tongue when he laughs, and sends her back into the crowd.

He brings forward another person. This time it's a man, separated and hidden from the rest of us until now. Short and old and sad. He has a pillowy face, red under the eyes like my grandmother gets in the evening when she says she's been thinking too hard. When a glass sits empty on the table and she mutters my mother's long-gone name like she thinks I can't hear it. But I do. *Maddow. Maddow.*

'Lark . . . Lark, come now,' Father Jessop says. 'We're all here to support you today.'

The man called Lark fists his hands together and nods. We're all clapping softly now, patting.

'Your wife has darkness in her soul. You've heard the accusations, but now we have proof. Her motheryear has passed without a child. She has brought shame onto you, and evil onto the island. The Lord tells us that a woman who avails the Seawomen shall be put to death. We have no choice.'

Lark nods again.

'Have faith in God! Prove to Him your devotion, Lark. Will you rid us all of this ungodly woman? Will you send her back to the seabed and back to the women who have transformed her into something so wretched?'

Lark makes a little noise like a cat at a door. Father Jessop puts his arm around his shoulders and strokes his back. He walks Lark to the jetty where the yole is moored. Another one of Barrett's boat words. Another secret growing black in my belly.

It's the husband's job to untie the last knot and set the boat free. The ceremony means he's free to marry again. For his second wife, a woman of age from a big family is best; there's more chance of a baby if she comes from a strong line. But some men are unlucky, my grandmother explained, some marry godless woman after godless woman and never have any children. They have to come to the jetty several times and send each of their wives out to sea.

Lark stares down at the yole, at the rope he must untie. The patrol ferries chug in waiting, their chuffs of cloud smoking the sky, their lights giving the water between us and them a golden slick. They sit on the border of where our sea meets the dark. To protect us, but today they have another job: to make sure the boat doesn't bob in our sea for hours.

Lark kneels on the dock, unlacing the rope from the hook. He leans in close to the water's edge and pushes on the boat with a pole to send it on its way. Inside the hull, there's movement. The once sleepy woman is trying to pull her hands and feet free but she is weak and the tide is already taking her, dragging her away wave by wave. The cheers start up, too loud for me to hear whether the woman has started screaming again. Lark rises to his feet. He doesn't watch the boat or his wife, the woman who used to be his wife, disappear. He doesn't stay like the rest of us have to and watch her pass the border, watch the patrols give a light-flash signal that we're all safe to go home.

Sometimes, my grandmother said, if the water is very rough, the boat won't last the journey. It won't even reach the patrols. *Capsize.* That's what it's called.

The boat tips to the side and my grandmother grips my hand until her knuckles feel like stones. The woman inside the yole must be shivering, dizzy. A wave pushes the boat forward and pulls it back, like a big breath, and when it lets go, the boat flips, turning upside down. We're silent. Watching, waiting, until we see her body, face down and silent. Drowned.

GIRL

He said: 'Pay heed to the daughters, for they are the weak and the tender, prone to dealings of the dark.' If she lives with devotion and self-control from the moment she takes her mother's breast, she will be saved. Preserve her sweetness, hide her from the rapturous emotions that tempt her away from innocence. Only then, when her fruit grows in servitude, will she fulfil God's purpose and deliver Him the gift of a child.

BEGINNINGS 40:12–15

One

Picture the island now and what do I see? A grey day, the wind crackling, the gulls crying. The land, a turret rising high out of the wild sea, the top of the island – the northern edge – lost in mist. The chapel, the church, the harbour, the peat moors, the knitters and milkers, the gutter women with their knives, fish juices and seawater running up to their elbows. Women clutching their crosses, looking down at their feet, praying for the Lord's protection. They've heard the rumours; they had an inkling all along. The bells of a Sunday service ringing out past the gust-wrecked croft houses, through the fields as the wild sheep chase each other as far as the heather in the north, to the stretches of the island that are worn and crumbled, once ours but claimed by the sea now.

I picture the past, her cottage. Where it all began. What would I have changed? What good is change? It's too late for that now. It's too late for anything.

This island is built on stories. Tales, lore, lies. They have their reasons. To while away the hours, to hide the truth, to soften, to reassure, to explain, to warn, to scare. Everyone on this island has a story, and this is mine.

I am three years old, struggling to keep up with her.

We were walking there, to her cottage on a south-easterly point of the island, a downward slope where the land was carpeted in green and pitted with holes made by field mice and puffins. Around the cottage was a scruff of nettles, a low mist rolling off the spine of the sea. We were caught in the middle of a downpour, a squall of it coming straight from the west, rain so cold it made me forget I was made of flesh and blood, so fast I lost my vision. We were laden with bags and boxes. Nothing in them belonged to me, everything inside was given

11

in sympathy. Wooden blocks, knitted dolls, clothes that other children had outgrown, dresses that would take months to fit me. A large bonnet that had been made especially to cover my scars. We were running for shelter, the horizontal sheets of rain making everything a murky silver. Everything that had once been mine was ash. We stood under the overhang of the white cottage, shaking off the wet, my teeth rattling pebbles. Sarl was her name. My grandmother. I'd like to sever her from my story, but I can't. Our blood is tied, my story is hers. Everything I am started with her, in that damp cottage.

I stared at the blue door, painted for God's appreciation, a cross above it. All the houses across the stretch of the island carried crosses and wreaths, all a message to God for protection and a warning to the sea and the women within in: *stay back*.

Once inside, she took a breath and roughly pulled my coat off my shoulders.

'There. Nothing wrong with a bit of rain.'

I would soon learn she was the type of woman that didn't own an umbrella. If it rained, God meant for us to get wet. Nothing happened on Eden's Isle that wasn't God's doing.

In the cold, my nose started to run, but I was too afraid to move and wipe it. My grandmother's rain-wet fingers stilled my chin. 'Now you're here. And it's time to be brave, isn't it? You're not a baby any more, Esta.'

I was old enough to realise something was missing, something was wrong. *You're not a baby any more*. She'd said that before. I had a memory of it. Somewhere else, another time. After the fire. After the doctor. After the screaming. My cheek waxy. Weeping. Red. Raw. Prodded. Thick with bandages.

'Are you listening? Don't sniff.'

She didn't use the word *dead*, or anything like it, she just told me my parents were gone. Not once did she look like she might cry, that she missed her only daughter.

'It's just the two of us now. You live here. With me. You under-stand? Right here in this cottage. You have a room and a bed and I have mine and you aren't to disturb me. Yes?'

I nodded or blinked. I can't remember if any words left my mouth or if I even understood her, but I understood enough to follow her further into the cottage as she told me every rule I could not break, every blessing we needed to give. It was my first time seeing the cottage, its walls covered in faded patterned paper, and framed paintings from another time, another place. Later I learnt they were pictures that told stories of the past, the glories of the old world and lessons from the Great Book.

At last she took me to a room upstairs. A breathless cupboard with a table blocked against the wall by the bed. On the table she had laid out everything I needed to be her granddaughter. A copy of the Great Book, a collection of Father Lambert John's speeches and lessons, though I couldn't read yet, and a portrait of his wife, Dinah John. I picked it up.

'She's there to watch over you. Remind you how to be.'

Dinah had twelve sons. She recognised the weakness in women, knowing they needed more than just a preacher and a holy book to keep them faithful against the Seawomen. It was her idea to gather the wise women, the ones who knew how to read a woman's soul and confer with the heavens. Who knew when we were ready to carry a child. She called them the Eldermothers.

I looked around the rest of the room. Not a toy or a soft stuffed thing to cuddle at night. The window was small, holding a grey square of the rain outside. This window would tell me how the day was going to be, she said. Good or bad. Our weather was God's temperament, lashing and tumultuous, a rare bleed of sun to make us believe warmth was out there if we worked hard enough. Through the glass I saw a screech of gulls fly further and further away until they were out of sight.

Gone, I thought, that word circling in my skull. But I didn't understand it then. That gone meant forever, my parents dissolving like sand under a wave, like they were never there. My grandmother's empty explanation filled my mouth with questions about what had happened, what my life was, questions too clattering to hold inside all at once. They filled me, overflowing and creeping into the corners of my body. The questions didn't arrive all at once. Not on that first day, in the downpour, or the next when she slammed her hands on the table because I didn't thank God before I sucked oatmeal from a spoon. It happened gradually. The wonderings of how and why. They came to me between her stories of how the island came to be. Of Father Lambert and his wife Dinah, as she read the copies of their diaries to me and the catechism they left behind, the Great Book, explaining how the island needed to be run and the warnings of what would happen if we didn't follow God's word. As she told me bedtime stories of the Seawomen.

She waited until the room was black and all that was between me and the roar of the sea were the walls of my room and a blanket.

'They're out there, in the water,' she said, her voice damp in the whorl of my ear. 'Waiting for us to fail. Waiting to reclaim the island. All they need is sin. Naughty girls. Horrible thoughts. They feed off it.'

They were a mutation of creation, she told me, spawned from abomination, the old world disrupting the natural way of things. A species that could live without land, without men. Everything they were was against God.

She told me stories of women from the island who'd been weak and faithless, who'd let their minds be bewitched. Women who would never reach Salvation. The worse these women were, the more they encouraged the Seawomen closer to the island. Her stories always ended the same way.

'And they'll come for you too. If you turn your back on God.'

I tried to find quiet times of the day, when we had just prayed together in candlelight, the edges of her mood melted, to ask questions about my parents. These were the times when she was sober, calmest, when I was praying how she wanted, kneeling together, legs almost touching, when she would let me say *Dear God* and *Amen*, when her voice was gentle and circling, like a thumb between rabbit ears. Then, I tried to ask her.

'Muma. Papa. Where did they go?'

All she could say was, 'We don't talk of them any more.'

'Are they with God?'

And if she had said yes, what then? What would I have become?

She blew out the candles and out went the warmth in her, her knee leaving its contact with mine. She sent me to my room with instructions to memorise the illustrations on the first page of the

Great Book, to copy the shape of letters I was too young to understand. Instead of answers, she gave me stories. That was how she boxed me up and sealed my mouth until all those questions had nicked my insides with tiny, invisible scars. That was why, against the wall she built, I stopped asking questions about my parents, where they were and why my face had been burnt in a fire. Instead, all those unanswered wonderings swelled into a curiosity, a part of me I struggled to contain.

I see my grandmother in flashes now. She comes to me in the dark, when the cold, the hunger, and the insomnia take over. The white cord of her plaited hair down the centre of her back, her bones pushing through thin skin. The sound of her closing the Great Book between her hands and the quiet she commanded afterwards, like the earth needed to resettle. Her smell in a room, slightly sour and wet, animal, like goat milk left in a cup. This was the house where she made me. A soft thing, moulded, made stiff and fragile by the fears she embedded. At night, in the dark, her stories of the women in the water transformed every shadow, every noise. A gull's midnight cry was a Seawoman's calling; the tide hitting the rocks was them summoning the sea to do its worst, to scare us into surrender. *Keep them from your door.* There was nothing to listen to but the sea, the roar of the waves a beast outside, keeping me awake. I could picture the Seawomen in every detail, their circling, shimmering bodies, plotting, cavorting, dancing with the darkness. Some nights, if the sea sounded close, I wept, convinced that one morning I would wake and find I'd been abandoned by God and my feet turned into a tail.

No matter the weather, she woke me at dawn, and when she was still able to, we walked the island's tilt. I could not complain or refuse. I knew what Father Lambert had written about the dangers of idle minds and idle bodies. Walking the island gave us a chance to appreciate our separate existence, the prospect of Salvation we'd been given. It would take the whole day to walk the full way around, but my grandmother could never manage further than the land where the market was held, every first Tuesday of the month, without a rest. Our island was not steep with mountains or crowded with trees; it was not flat, but uneven. Parts of it stood high above the sea, a staggering drop from the cliff's edge, but at what I thought of as the bottom of the island, the south, the land sloped gradually into a bank of rocks until you could reach the tide. At a higher point, we could see all the way down to the harbour in the south, but if we were in the south, looking up, the scattered croft houses looked bunched together by Lambert's Hill, slumped as though they were slipping towards the cliff edge, rolling on the lumpen hills of grass and rock.

On these walks I was the opposite of my grandmother – small and fast, my hair dark and unruly in the wind. We were waved at by crofters, by the wives hurrying to bring in their washing before the gales. They looked from me to her and said in hushed voices what a blessed miracle it was that I'd made it out alive. *How is she? It's a shame with her face.* I had given up on the childish bonnet and battled the gales to pull my hair around my face instead. My grandmother would talk about God, how her strength came from the guiding words of Father Jessop.

When we passed the crofters, they eyed me but asked my grandmother about the weather instead. She had a gift for forecasts.

They'd look skyward with her. 'What's coming for us tomorrow?'

And she would lick the entire palm of her hand and raise it into the breeze, crumpling her fingers into a ball.

'Cold. Hail coming.'

'And the cattle, can we risk leaving them outdoors, you think?'

'Inside until midday you'll be good. Then see.'

The men wanted to hear about the winds that would dry their stackyard and the fishermen's wives wanted to know if their men would get home before the sky came rushing down in wet you couldn't see through. My grandmother could smell a storm three days before it arrived, and on an island like ours, everyone planned their lives by it.

'Men who work the sea know how dangerous it can be. Out there on the water so close to *them.*'

The fishermen were attuned to the signs of bad luck, like we all learnt to be, sensitive to the feeling of something wrong on the horizon. For them it was blood skies and setting off on Friday mornings. For others it was fever, rotting crops, headaches. These were God's warnings. The Seawomen were close, plotting. Someone's sin was beckoning them nearer.

'It's all part of their plan. To overturn boats and see men slip and struggle,' my grandmother said. 'They'd be glad if there were no men at all. They want the whole world to be like them.'

Sarl liked showing off her gift, collecting coins for her forecasts. Women with gifts had worth. There were women who knew how to crush the right herbs to heal a pounding head or a mixed-up stomach. Women who could suck a splinter from a foot. Women who knew there was a baby brewing just by touching. Women who said they could tell if you were going to marry a dark-haired man or a fair man just by the way stones landed when you threw them. All of these were gifts from God, nothing like the meddling tricks that came from the sea. I didn't know what my gift would be, or if I'd ever have one.

But even my grandmother, with all her foresight, could not predict what would happen the summer when I was four years old, and the storms began.

In the years after the fire, what the crofters called 'the miracle' of my being spared the fate of my parents, more fishermen came to our door to ask my grandmother for the forecast, to pray for them. Skies could change by the hour, men arriving in their wet caps and sodden waders, their faces blistered from the salt wind, all wanting to hear good news. They wanted my grandmother to send a prayer their way. Herring was all the Otherlands wanted. The way our island made its living. Fresh food straight from the belly of the sea. It was rare to the Otherlanders. Precious. Exotic. Not like it was for us, abundant on our doorsteps. They were desperate for it. Father Jessop told us about the so-called food they relied on in the Otherlands because they'd ruined their own seas. Food pumped with chemicals and hormones, processed and mechanical, meat cultivated in jars, nutrients produced in laboratories. Nothing grew in the Otherlands; the land was too toxic, he told us. I'd never been more grateful for our soil, our plates of root vegetables. It was hard to imagine a land so destroyed, even though there was no question of its truth – we knew he'd seen it first-hand, visiting to report back on the horrors he'd witnessed. His descriptions were so vivid it was like I'd seen it myself. The earth they lived on was not like ours. It was rotten, flooded, infested. All the warnings they'd ignored from God.

We never walked to the harbour. We never went that close to the water. There were times when we were walking that my focus would slip, my attention drawn away from the things I knew – the grass and the sheep, the fences and kittiwakes – and instead directed towards the sea. On a clear day I knew it was possible to see a haze of distant islands, but none of us looked for them. It was better to pretend our island sat alone. They were a wound on our pure, separate existence. Anything outside the island God had given us was an abomination. But there was something about the sea, the constant motion, the changes in colour, the way it surrounded us, that made it impossible to ignore.

Once, before that terrible summer, when I hadn't even realised I'd been staring, unmoving, at the water, my grandmother grabbed hold of my arm.

'You listen. You listen to this. You never look at the sea! It's head down, blur your eyes if you have to. Hand over them, like this.' She put her own hand up, shielding her eyes. 'Never!'

'It's a bad place.'

'More than bad. Evil. You don't look, you never look. You get sick. Evil gets in. You'll see things. Hear whispers. Mad things. Do things. All bad. Terrible things. You will betray God. Then God will shun you. You want God to turn His back on you, damn you? Damn us all.'

'No.' I thought I might cry, but in those early years I taught myself how to stop it by biting the inside of my cheek. Crying in front of her never made things better.

'You don't look at the sea, you don't think of the sea and you never go near it. Want to know what happens? When you were a baby. No. Before that. Long before. Sometime. A woman, she looked out at the sea and those Seawomen, and they called to her. You know what they said? They said, "In the night, when everyone's sleeping, you go to your neighbour's house and you curse it. You curse that house." And she did. She babbled and she shook. Her eyes all criss-cross. The message getting through. The next morning, the cows lay dead in the field, but worse, the baby, stone cold in its little cot. Blue lips and horrible dead eyes. All because she looked at the sea and shunned God from her soul. The Seawomen had what they wanted, another one on their side.'

My grandmother took hold of my shoulders and gripped hard, making sure I had my back to the water.

'God sees you looking out there and He thinks you are dissatisfied with the world He gave you, the life He created. You're like the people of the old world. That's what ruined them. You look out there and they will see it. They will make you one of them. They see your weakness, the lack of God in your heart, and know they have you.'

She dotted her finger from my temple to inside my ear, then back to the soft part of my head where it felt as fragile as an eggshell. 'You'll let them in here. Once the sea gets in, the Seawomen always follow. Always do.'

I knew a little about the old world and how it had come to ruin. How Father Lambert John inspired a following and heard a calling to start a new world. God in his ear. A fresh beginning on a remote isle. Far north. A thin skin between our world and the Lord's.

I knew the stone-walled cottages had existed long before. They were from the old world, and Father Jessop John lived in a building that still had a sign saying 'Observatory'. His family slept in a place where once they used to catalogue species of birds on box-like machines. I had never seen a machine. Machines did not exist on the island. They were the first thing Father Lambert John told his followers they had to sacrifice if they ever wanted Salvation. It was not called Eden's Isle then, but something else. When it was not holy. It was a remote, quiet place, for sheep, a few families, visitors. It had a harbour, a port, a ferry for the guests and a place to stay, a landing strip for aircraft, a shop full of woollen clothes – or so Father Lambert's journals said. They had a generator – an old version of the one we use now. Wind turbines. The remnants of the old world lived on like ghosts we knew little about. The useful stayed, the corrupting destroyed.

In June, the weather turned. Wetter than I'd ever seen it. The storms were brutal, sounding as if the sea was fighting itself. You could hear it from indoors, the sea hurling boulders, beating down into the coves. There were times when it felt as if the whole island had moved, the pulse of thunder rattling under our feet, spinning cups off the table. Roof tiles lost, sheep drowned. You couldn't even stand outside. I was wide awake, rigid, too scared to sleep. The sea was wild. Was it calling to someone? Or answering? What if I had heard something? What then? I hid under the bed, blocking my ears, in case it was me they wanted, prayed to God until my grandmother heard me from the next room and her heavy feet paced in from the landing. It would pass, she said, it always did. But there were hours of the night, in the midst of a war with the sea that we'd already lost, when not even prayer could save us.

It was affecting the fishermen. There were days and days when they were unable to leave the harbour for herring, and my grandmother's forecasts were only bringing more bad news. After church one sodden Sunday, dreading another week of grounded boats, she sought out Father Jessop.

'Is there reason to be worried, Father? About what's to come?'

He looked at her, then me, the both of us still wet through from walking to the church in the rain. He was dry, wearing pristine robes, his skin as smooth as candle wax. He was young then, early thirties, vivid blue eyes and hair the colour of sunlight through a window. He wasn't like the rest of the men on this island: wind-savaged and exhausted.

'The storms are troubling. But with the right action . . . Could you find it in you to visit the harbour? To say a prayer? Those men already have so much belief in your readings of the weather, I'm sure coming from you it would ease their fears.'

I saw her swallow. 'Father, the harbour. It's . . .'

'Take the little one with you,' Father Jessop said, making me jolt as the surprise weight of his hand petted the top of my head. 'It'll pose a good test for you both. Nerve. Faith. Keeping your eyes down and the Lord in your thoughts. Let's see her young devotion isn't half-hearted, shall we?'

The next day we did as he instructed. Next to me, my

grandmother's mouth was woolly with prayer, gulping down breaths like drink to still her nerves. Only Father Jessop could persuade her this close to the water. She never even visited the harbourmaster, Barrett; he was her cousin by marriage and oldest friend, but he lived overlooking the boats. She did not eat before we left; she was deathly quiet apart from her words to God. The walk was downhill to the harbour along rough paths that needed concentration in wind so fierce. It was hard to imagine the shape of the island when I'd only seen pieces of it, but I thought of it like a scab I once had on my knee, oozy and uneven, with raggedy edges. The harbour was near the old lighthouse, where black rocks tumbled out into the sea, scattered by a giant's hand. I drank everything in, all of it unseen before by me. There were a few fishermen's huts circling the harbour and a bell in the centre, which was to be rung in an emergency, but mostly it was boats and nets and lobster pots. There was also a station hut for the Keepers. They guarded in shifts, checking each boat, each fisherman, before he left and when he returned. Two of them watched over the harbour during the busiest times of the day; at night, under lock and metal fences and with boat use prohibited, there was only one Keeper on guard.

The nearer we got, the more I thrummed with a different feeling. One of adventure. I'd never been allowed this close to the water before.

It was Anderson we saw first, Barrett's younger brother, wading out into the water, one hand welded onto his cap to keep it from being pulled into the sea by the gales and the other on a rope, attempting to heave his yole out from the mud. He shouted at some of the other men to help and three men piled on, fighting to free it from the mud's sucker in the rain. I could taste the wind on my tongue, the salt rawing my insides. The vastness of the sea overwhelmed me, and Father Jessop's words about keeping my eyes down and the Lord in my heart seemed impossible.

A Keeper approached us with a stride that made my pulse dizzy. I caught a glimpse of the water. Briefly. The frothing grey sheets of it. I shot my attention to my feet.

'Turn around,' my grandmother said to me before he was close enough to hear. 'I don't want you looking out there.'

I did as she said, guilt throbbing in my chest. I had looked. I was too curious not to.

'This is no place for women,' the Keeper said.

'We were sent by Father Jessop. To pray. The men need hope.' There was an authority in the way she spoke that seemed to override the nerves she had as we walked there.

'Right,' he said. 'Well, keep her away from the edge. She's too young to be here.'

'She has the Lord with her.' She pulled the chain of my cross pendant to show him, choking me.

'Sarl!' Our heads turned towards the sharp call of her name. It was Barrett, emerging from one of the huts where the men made desperate attempts to repair their storm-wrecked vessels before broaching the water for another futile try.

Hearing anger in his voice, the Keeper stepped away and back to the boats, and I shrank against my grandmother's side. I always hated when Barrett came to visit us. She told warm-eyed stories about growing up with him, how he'd once saved her life, but he frightened me. His smell, potent with wrack, his face covered in white thickets of hair. His solitary eye, his missing hand. I had imagined a hundred stories about how he lost both, and all of them slopped in my stomach like spoiled soup. Like he'd grown from the sea himself.

'You shouldn't be down here. And – Lord! – not with the girl! What will people think if they see her down here?' When he was closer, Barrett's voice was less harsh, but it was still deep and growling, enough to make me shudder.

'The men, they need faith,' my grandmother said.

'The men need the storms to pass. Which they will. In time.'

'Father Jessop sent us.'

He said nothing for a moment. 'Sarl, please just go home. Take Esta away from this place. There'll be talk.'

'The men haven't made it out the harbour for days. The whole island is talking about it.'

'And they'll be out there in the morning for another try.'

'Only to turn back home again.'

'The storm will pass. Conditions will be fair enough by dawn.'

'You've not been on the water in years; what would you know about conditions?'

I peeked at him through squinted eyes. He bristled. I remembered a few months before, around the time of the festival, hearing the two of them argue over something that happened years back. I was hidden upstairs, away from it, but afterwards I heard their voices change, the sound of them coming together. I imagined her putting her arms around him, but I'd never seen her do that before, not even to me. I'd seen other people hold each other, skin smoothing skin. It looked nice and I practised alone, arms wrapped around my body, closing my eyes and pretending.

'I know the water better than any of these men. I can't – I won't – have you hanging around here.'

It was then, noticing the raised voices, that his brother Anderson came over, interrupted, clucking his tongue against his teeth. 'This is a woman's doing, no question. We never get storms like this in the summertime,' he said.

Barrett seethed. 'Stay out of it.'

At my side, I felt my grandmother stiffen. She turned to Anderson, ignoring Barrett. 'Have you seen any other signs?'

'Ain't the storms proof enough?' Anderson hesitated. 'Why? You seen anyone? Heard anything?'

'If I had, I'd have gone straight to Father Jessop myself.'

I could see the men who were standing around the harbour and tightening the ropes and chains to secure their boats looking over at us. It was only the gutter women who came down this close to the water, and they were specially chosen. Women who had proved their resilience against the influence of the water by giving birth to three or more children. They could withstand being this close, they were hardy against the whispers, the temptations. What would they think about us here – me?

'Enough of this. Take her home,' Barrett said, firmer.

'We'll take your prayers,' Anderson said. 'Anything to know God's on our side.'

My grandmother smiled, reaching out to clutch his hands. I winced at how wet he was, how strongly he smelt of another place.

'Start the prayer for us, Esta,' she said, shutting her eyes like she often did to gather her spirits.

Barrett walked away, his anger boiled into silence. His sharp moods only made me more fearful of him, relieved that he'd left, relieved to start the prayer.

'Dear Lord . . .'

On the walk home, my involvement in the giving of the prayer buoyed my mood. We had been close to the water and we had survived. I had glanced at the sea and nothing bad had seized hold of me. But I thought about Barrett and what he had said about us being down there, me especially, and what people might say if they didn't know our reasons for being there. I wanted to know more about him. I knew some questions were out of bounds – questions about his missing hand, his absent eye. But if he knew the water so well, why wasn't he out on the boats fishing? What had they argued over before and why had he sounded so sad around the time of the festival, the time we all enjoyed most? I asked.

'Think. It's obvious,' she said.

'His hand.'

'There was an accident.'

The thought made me sick and I wished I hadn't asked.

'A man with one hand and one eye alone in a boat? He would drown. No question.'

'And that's why he's sad.'

I tried to say it less like a question but a conclusion I'd reached myself. I didn't want to push it by asking too much. It didn't matter that I was a curious child. It was as though my grandmother had a daily limit; at any moment she could raise her fingers to her temple and press on the blue-lined skin, ignoring anything else I might say. Her headaches. She said they were as loud as the sea storms.

'The harbour is all he has left now. No children, and his wife gone . . . If the fishermen fail, he fails.'

'What happened . . .'

My voice trailed away. Something stopped us in our tracks. I never got to ask her more about the accident, about Barrett's wife.

Our ears were filled by the toll of the church bell, a clanging so loud and sharp the whole island could hear it. Everywhere we looked, croft to croft, men and women were running towards the sound.

Two

My grandmother grabbed my hand and we ran uphill against the rain. I felt the strain on my knees, not knowing why we were running, but knowing we needed to follow the others. The church was white-harled and glowed on brighter days like a singular tooth in the grass. When we reached the church grounds there were so many islanders pushing and shouldering that the wire fence on the pathway, the one erected to prevent the sheep nuzzling at the door, was beginning to collapse. Through the trample, I could hear snatches of panic. In the wet, everything slipped and slid. I held onto my grandmother's waist. Some of the women already had red faces from crying, and as we waited for the doors to be opened, the rain lashed even harder, seeping in between our layers of clothes.

The door of the church was unlocked by a Keeper, and the crowd flooded in. The church wasn't built for us; it was built in the time before, when fewer people lived on the island, so it was too small to take all of us at once. That meant a rush, pushing and shoving, a desperation just to get through the doors.

Every available space was crammed with pews, but most people were standing, too shaken to sit. I wanted to ask my grandmother what was happening, but I could see her head snatching from left to right, trying to piece together the news from the rumour.

Something had washed up on the beach in the storm.

Father Jessop arrived, flanked by two of his sons, both Ministers, wearing their dark shirts, marching in through the double doors shortly after my grandmother and I had found a space at the front of the nave. She'd used me as a spade, and steered us through the airless crowd.

A sense of relief drifted through the room when Father Jessop appeared at the altar. I could feel my heartbeat slow, the tension easing. In his arms he carried a wooden box I'd never seen before.

He hushed us like children, all with a softness in his features. 'I need everyone to stay relaxed and very quiet,' he said. 'We're here with God's protection. There is no need to panic.'

A woman beside me sobbed, open-mouthed and wet, into her husband's chest.

'I need to prepare you for what you are all about to see,' Father Jessop said to the room. He held the box out in front of him. It was ornate, carved. His words conveyed a warning, but the box suggested majesty, buried treasure. I was hot, not knowing what to do with my damp hands.

'What I have here is a reminder of the constant threat we must endure. Proof that we are not doing enough. Proof that God is being forgotten, that sin is being fostered among us.'

There was a shift in the room, a muttering torpor. The word *threat* sank in my stomach.

'It was found among the red weed of the strand line by one of our Messengers. I want you all to remember that it is not here by mistake or accident. It was left behind as a warning.' Father Jessop's fingers ran across the front of the box. 'We need to ask ourselves serious questions.' He paused, and the room creaked with the mass of bodies. 'Ask yourself – have you been listening to God? Trusting Him, following Him? Or have you been betraying His word? This here, in this box, has the answer. It is a sign.'

There was the click of a lock, and Father Jessop hesitated before he opened the lid. The air in the room tightened, and even he looked like he had to steel himself. It took me years to see this moment for what it was, his every movement measured, orchestrated. It took me years to understand why it was such a performance. He had a solemn look on his face, handling the box with reluctance, like a healthy man approaching the sick. We watched on, thoughts ticking over as he pulled back the lid and reached inside. He grasped at something, not with a fist, but pinching it between his fingers, and lifted it into the air. It unfolded, wider than his hands, longer than his forearm. It looked like fish skin, but devoid of shine, grey and translucent in the centre, curling and crisp at the yellow edges where the salt water had dried it. Scales, perfect and symmetrical, arcs of colour where they caught the light. It was too large to be a shedding from any fish I knew.

The crowd seemed to step back at the same time, the sight spurring gasps, mouth by mouth, like a shift of daylight rolling over the crofts. Cries and questions and murmuring everywhere. *Is it? What? What? What? How? Why?* He held the room. It was hot, pounding. Bodies pushing, drawn breaths, crying.

'What is it?'

But all my grandmother could do was shake her head..

'This here is the skin from a Seawoman's tail,' Father Jessop said. 'It's a warning to us that they're near. Watching. They're waiting. And they will return.'

A worry bloomed in me, so sudden, so vivid, I felt the ground sway under my feet. No longer just a story, no longer just an unseen fear. Real. Shimmering. Threat.

One woman threw herself at the Father, falling to her knees, the impact making him stumble, and a Keeper stepped in to carry her off to the side. I was paralysed watching the terror ripple from one body to the next.

Father Jessop adjusted his robes. His jaw had the hardness of a fist. He spoke with a volume for all of us to hear, but there was no anger in it.

'Get a hold of yourself, woman! Don't make us ask ourselves what you are and what you've done!'

The room was stunned into shaky breaths. We looked at the woman, dragged away from him by her elbows. Was it her who'd brought them back into our waters? The feeling in the room was the same. A burning need to be rid of her. While everyone watched her, I looked at Father Jessop, his eyes as black as night. Everything smooth knocked out of him. The change in his posture made my chest tight.

My grandmother pressed down on me until I could feel handprints of pain.

'What do we do?' I asked her, pleading, lips fat with a sob I knew I had to hold in.

'Believe in Him. Trust,' she said. I could feel her rocking on her feet as if in prayer. 'We've done wrong. We haven't done enough.'

I looked back up at Father Jessop, the same routine we always had when there was fear and panic – we turned to him. I didn't know it then, but he had us all where he wanted, trembling, on our knees, willing to do whatever it took.

'It should be clear now to all of us that the storms we've experienced these past weeks were no ordinary change in the weather,' he continued, each word ringing in the arches above the low burble of fear. 'We must be vigilant. There are women right here in this very room with answers.'

Like everyone else, I looked around, searching for clues.

'If the storms were not proof enough, then perhaps sight of this will convince you. There's evil here, giving them out there power. It is hidden, lurking. In your neighbour, your mother, your daughter. Somehow, here in this very room there is a servant of the Seawomen, and if we don't find her, if we don't fix her, they will come to our shores and they will damn us; they will take the good in our souls and destroy them.'

We had to stop it from happening. He told us to look for signs, to watch, to be wary, to report. Even those we loved. Even if we had only the slightest suspicion. There was no other way to prevent our destruction unless we were watchful. He told us to keep records of any lapses in behaviour, any godless speech, any shaking and tremors, and take any notes to the Observatory and post them into a Suspicions Box. My skull was thumping with instruction, rules reshaping. Threat everywhere. Heads around the room swung back and forth again, eyes lingered, and some women looked, then looked again at another woman just so they weren't seen staring at the ground, panicked and ashamed. A woman on the far side of the church caught my eye and wouldn't look away. I was the one to break first, and instead found solace in the images in the stained-glass windows. God, He was the way I could keep myself safe. I knew there was no other way.

In the weeks that followed, Father Jessop promised he would make the island safer than ever. We stood at the patrol port watching as a new ferry was deployed to guard our borders. There were three of them in total by then. Huge ferries imported from the Otherlands, their metal hulls digging great clefts through the water and casting beams of light across the surface. They circled the island, giving the coastline a haze of gold. The Seawomen could still bewitch us, mind and body, if we loosened our faith, but these ferries, he told us, were a deterrent to any of them daring to swim into our waters.

Cheers roared up when the new ferry came into view.

'Are we safer now?' I had to shout over the noise of the ferries' engines, their blasting horns and piercing lights.

'Safest place in the world. That's why we're here.'

Every house containing a woman was searched, room by room. The Eldermothers' chapel was busier, but even in the street, between the crofts, conversations were short and functional. One wrong word and your name could land in the Suspicions Box. Rumours circulated. Grudges were investigated. Women who confessed slept in the chapel chambers were stripped and cleansed until God had granted forgiveness. Others were taken from their houses by Ministers holding lists of accusations and slept in rooms they called 'cells' in the old lighthouse. What exactly happened in these cells we could only guess, but if a woman repented, complied and gave the right answers, she could be redeemed. Some women were made to stay with the Eldermothers at the chapel until their souls were clean; some confessed their indiscretions in church. Some were taken straight to Father Jessop. One by one they returned, forgiven, absolved. The rest of us relieved, ever watchful.

The storms had eased to a clattering wind, so the fishermen took to the waters again, believing the worst had passed. They were wrong. A string of quiet days followed before the news of a shipwreck came to shore. The wreck was another sign that a curse was taking hold. The Seawomen were trying to scare us into submission. I never wanted to leave the house again. Even walking to church or to the chapel, my chest was tight. I couldn't breathe at the thought of catching a glimpse of the Seawomen, at the thought of having my name slipped into the Suspicions Box.

The shipwreck was all I dreamt about. I didn't even know what would happen to a woman if she was found to be bewitched by the Seawomen. I wouldn't find out for another four years, until a woman was Untethered right before my eyes. But we were told often enough about what the sea did to a body to be able to picture it, and after the wreck, I couldn't think of anything else.

My grandmother noticed my preoccupation with the shipwreck, the death of it stagnant in the living room where we sat. I was on the floor, on a rug as pale as a patch of damp. She was seated in her usual velvet chair, turned away from the window. I was finding it difficult to play, my wooden dolls sticking to the folds in my hands, and the chitter from their painted-on mouths always returning to the violence of the sea. I shunted their dumpy bodies towards a box my grandmother had given me to use as their church, their only place of Salvation.

My grandmother lit her smoking pipe and spoke to me for the first time in hours.

'Shipwrecks only take men who don't have faith in God,' she said, studying me. 'Don't pity them.'

The dolls were confused about where they should go, what they should pray for. I moved them to the church and back, church and back, with nowhere else to go. Three men had died. Two had families, sons a little older than me. I had cried for them, prayed for the dead men. Everything I did seemed to be the wrong thing. I nodded at my grandmother to show I understood her, her face blurring from the glare of the window behind her, and the dolls marched silently around the perimeter of the rug, their own island.

'Your grandfather drowned at sea,' she said, blowing smoke into the room.

One of the figures, a man with a straight painted mouth and a cloth hat, rolled out of my hand, under a chair, and hit a table leg. My grandmother looked at it, then me, giving me a look that said I shouldn't grub around the floor to collect it – I shouldn't have dropped it in the first place.

'Left one morning on a boat. Seven others. Five of them came back,' she said, her statements punctuated with drags on her pipe. 'Twenty-two when he died. I was six months pregnant with your mother. He came from a funny little family. All short, tubby girls apart from him. I think that's what made him wrong in the head. All those girls. You can't trust a woman who gives birth to so many girls. Like she's building an army. It's unnatural.'

It was surprising how much she revealed when I hadn't asked a question first. She talked about him in a detached way, as if he was another of her tales, not a man she'd made a child with. No loss, no tragedy, but deserved.

'There was always black in his soul. He was a daydreamer. Blasphemer. Always doubting the decisions God made. It took me too long to see it. It was why the sea took him. It was where he belonged.'

The thought of my grandfather having the darkness in his head made me sick. Fishermen were protected from that, weren't they? The sea getting into their heads? I'd seen it for myself, young new fishermen struggling to stand still in front of Father Jessop, their faces pink with nerves as he blessed them, their boats. You had to be a man of faith to be a fisherman. Without that, they were asking to end up at the bottom of the sea. Father Jessop had to trust them enough to know they'd bring no harm back to shore with them. Any man leaving the island by boat, be it fisherman, supply puffer or patrol, had to be blessed – vessel too. Wasn't my grandfather protected? Was he that wicked that the sea took him anyway? And what about the others who had died in shipwrecks?

My grandmother must have seen my doubt, so she leant forward in her chair, stretching out towards me so far it looked like the seat might topple.

'God can't protect you from your own soul, not if you've already turned your back on Him. Like your grandfather did.' She stared me down. 'He didn't pray enough. Like you.'

Then it was my own body I saw flailing, weed reaching for me, stitching me to the seabed. I looked at one of the dolls in my hand, a woman, a red mouth.

'What about my mother? Was she like Grandfather?'

What I really wanted to ask was: is it in me? Is my fate already written?

Her hands came up and cradled her downward-pointing head, and I knew I was in trouble.

'Enough! Questions, questions, all the time. Pestering me. A pest! That's what you are. My head! Lord, the tests you send my way.'

I watched on as she rocked. I knew what I was supposed to do in times like this. As quietly as I could manage, I shut my dolls away inside their church and took them up to my room. Opened the Great Book with a rush of familiar relief. Those stories were a comfort. They stopped me thinking of my grandfather and the other drowning men, gave me hope that God resided in me. That I'd be saved. Reading them helped block out the feeling that deep within me, built into the very bones of who I was, there was something wrong, something I needed to fight against.

Three

When the weather turned brighter, the sky carrying streaks of blue, my grandmother managed to coax me out of the house. The sunshine was God's doing, His sign that things were changing, danger abating. She was a little way ahead of me on the path, my caution still tying me to the house. She got talking to a man tending to his henhouse, and out of the corner of my eye I saw something to the left of the path, nestled in the grass. It dazzled in the sunlight. I edged closer while she was distracted, seeing a perfect, unbroken shell. How had it got there? And how had it managed to arrive without a single crack? I knew I shouldn't have gone near it, but it compelled me, calling me in a way I'd never felt before. It was the kind of beautiful thing I wanted to keep all to myself, use to adorn my plain bedroom. Checking I wasn't being watched, I bent down to pick it up and ran my finger along its edges. I should have put it back, but something wouldn't let me. We never walked on the beaches or in the cove along the coast from her house, so the closest I'd seen to a complete shell was shards among the shingle, images from school. Never the real thing. I turned the shell over and slotted my finger into the inside. It was as warm as skin.

'What are you holding?'

My hand closed around the shell and I tucked my arm to my back. Had my grandmother been watching me? If I dropped it, she'd hear the noise of it hitting the ground, and I had nowhere to hide it.

'It's nothing. Just a stone.'

'Let me see.'

'Nothing.'

'Open your hand.'

She snatched up my wrist, prising my fingers apart.

I was tearful, shrinking. 'It was just there in the grass. I didn't know what it was . . .'

'Lies! Look what you're turning into!'

She pulled me forward with such force, my hand closed reflexively around the shell.

'Drop it!'

Such was the venom in those two words that I let go, the shell cracking on the path.

'Now crush it. Let me see you. Prove to me. The Lord. Destroy it.'

I couldn't move. Without a moment's hesitation, she raised her boot and stamped over and over, obliterating the shell until it was lost to the dirt path.

'If you ever . . .'

'I won't! I won't.' I let out a sob that hurt, knowing she would not be able to look at me again until I did something to prove I was sorry.

On the Sunday, my body was leaden as my grandmother took me to church. Her coldness made me heavier. As we arrived, I felt a small shift of hope that the church, with its hymns and prayers, would drown out the dark. She told me that the service was a special one, one where young girls like me would be invited to take part. Maybe afterwards, she said, I would understand the danger of what I had done. Before we even had a chance to take a seat, Father Jessop stood in front of us.

'It's good to have you here today,' he said. It was a smile that made my stomach flutter. I liked being near to him, to God. He looked at my grandmother and his smile widened. In church, my grandmother's face took on a warmer colour, her mouth serene at the edges. It was one of the few places she seemed to settle.

'You look well, Sarl,' he said.

'I am, Father. Thank you for noticing.'

His fingers flexed and I felt them on my collar, dry and cool. But he was wrong about my grandmother; despite her smile, she didn't look well. Her eyes had the pink tinge of sleepless nights, her skin sallow. She had always been faithful to God and afraid of the sea, but the sighting of the Seawoman's skin had pushed her over the edge, and at home she had started fasting, locking herself away in her room more and more. Keeping herself away from me.

'It would be good to pay you a visit next week. I'm sure there's more I can do to help your ailments,' he said.

'Father, you've done so much already. We owe you our thanks, the island is—'

'The work never stops,' he said, with a slight bow of his head.

'Yes, yes. Perhaps if you come to visit, we can pray together.'

'Like old times.' His smile made his eyes disappear into his face as he leant down to speak to me. 'Has your grandmother told you that when I was a boy, she used to come and look after me? She used to sing and tell me all sorts of magical stories. But it was the praying I enjoyed the most. The two of us together baring our souls, speaking with God. Your grandmother is closer to God than many here. She is truly a special woman.'

I knew the story, but I looked at Father Jessop attentively, pretending I didn't. His mother had been a good friend of my grandmother's. Grandmother had rocked his crib and sung him songs to get him to sleep, songs about women waiting on their fishermen to return, songs about the island. As a baby he had never fussed or wailed, was never sick. He had walked and talked before most were even crawling. My grandmother gazed at him like she had given birth to him. Like she wished she had.

She took to her pew and Father Jessop led me by the hand. My face flushed with the attention he bestowed.

'This way, sweetheart.'

We were a row of five girls at the front of the church, facing the congregation. There was another girl my age at the front, but she didn't join in. She was Father Jessop's youngest child and his only daughter, Mull. In time she became my friend, my only friend, but at the time I envied her, sitting there without everyone's eyes on her. She had a delicate mouth and smiling blue eyes like her father. I wanted to look at her and make her see that I was like her, admiring her father, one of God's children, but I was too shy, too bruised by all that had happened.

We were each given a mirror and we held them out, just our hairlines reflected, afraid to look fully at ourselves. I had the urge to mist mine with my breath and draw silver lines through the white.

Standing up there felt like the edge of a cliff. I could see the adults watching, enraptured, controlled by Father Jessop's every word. No one glanced away. In that moment it was impossible to imagine that anyone would – or could – ever speak up against his methods.

I copied the others, still and silent, dressed in my best clothes, long sleeves, long skirt, high-necked blouse. One by one Father Jessop asked us to look into our mirror.

'Have a good look,' he said. 'Tell us, out loud, what makes you beautiful. Why are you special?'

I hated looking at my face. The scarring was raised and pink, the size of a palm, spread across one cheek. Fires burn fast, it could have been worse, but I saw the mark and saw ugliness, felt pain I couldn't remember.

One of the girls, Crescent, the daughter of the baker, spoke first. Father Jessop loomed behind her. 'My nose is small and pretty,' she said, loud and clear like he'd told her to.

There was a quiet in the church that sounded like death. Not one face in the congregation smiled, not one of them looked like they agreed. Years later, when I was an adult, I watched this same test play out in church with another group of young girls. Knowing what was to come, I sat at the back, pinching my skin to stop myself crying. If I'd said something, what then?

The next girl was also older than me but in my class at school. Seren. Her father was a Minister, with a stern face and thick fair eyebrows. She was the same: light hair, milky face, but prettier than all of us. She had her chin pointed upwards, her cheeks dotted with freckles and colour.

'Vanity is a sin,' she said. Her words rang out with confidence. Father Jessop had been standing motionless, elbows clasped by his hands, but now he was open-armed, presenting Seren as the perfect example to us all. The congregation responded with what felt like a collective breath, a shuffling of limbs under their clothes.

When it came to my turn, and the next two girls, we followed Seren's example, burying all thoughts of our reflection. At the start of the line, Crescent trembled.

'Turn your mirrors to the floor,' Father Jessop said, and we followed.

I was sweaty-handed, scared to look Crescent's way. I could hear her uneven breaths trying to keep the tears in. Father Jessop crouched by her side.

'What upsets you?' he said.

She could not speak.

'Is it because the sin came so easily to you? You did not think, you just let the words out freely?'

She nodded, stray hair sticking to the wet of her cheeks. 'I didn't mean to.'

Father Jessop addressed the congregation again. 'It's never too early to learn.'

Then he turned to us girls and I saw the room blur. I was hot, conscious that I might have gone red like Crescent.

'Girls, do you see what path Crescent stepped forth on today? Do you see how she has wronged?'

I was exposed, like his words were aimed at me. I did not want to be the reason for the storms, for men drowning out at sea, for other worse ruins. I did not want the Seawomen to come. I knew it would be the End of Days. That was what everyone called it.

'Today, Crescent calls herself beautiful. Tomorrow, she has urges, temptations tapping away at her. Do you see how it starts? It's a disease. It might be something small, a lie, a desire to steal or cheat, but this spreads from one pretty head to the next, and before long it is a path that has no way back. Not even God can save you. Any of you.'

He crouched to Crescent's side again and held her mirror so she could see her own reflection. I saw her wince and avoided looking at her again. I looked for Mull, instead, but her face was turned to the floor, lips bitten red, studying her shined shoes.

The hairs on the back of my neck rose like someone had whispered across them.

'Where do these urges of sin and wickedness come from?' Father Jessop asked. He projected his voice as if he was asking the room, but the question was aimed at us.

There was a hot beat of uncertainty, then beside me, Seren raised her hand.

'The sea.'

We all knew she was correct.

Father Jessop smiled. It was wide and full of teeth and then it was gone.

'And where exactly? Who do we find in the sea? Who takes power from your sin and encourages it? Who waits for the day they can rise against us?'

We were all thinking of the same image. Silver eyes and tails, slick and fast in the deep. Messengers of darkness.

'The Seawomen.'

The eyes of the congregation turned to me. I'd spoken. Blood rushed to my cheeks. In the pews, my grandmother was nodding, finally proud of me.

'I can sense what you're thinking, girls. God is telling me right this minute what thoughts are rushing around your little heads. You're thinking: "I'm a good girl. I pray twice a day, I listen to God. I go to church. I would never become a servant of the Seawomen. I would never let them take hold of me."'

I was convinced by him. God really did know our every thought.

'Wrong. Whatever you think, whatever you do, their darkness is waiting to take hold of you. It was a woman who caused the end of paradise. It was women of the old world who turned good men to sin. It was women who refused God and rejected motherhood and turned the world upside down. This paradise here relies on you. One wrong step and all this is gone. The Seawomen were born in darkness, a mutation of everything wrong in this world, female creatures who rejected God and found a way to shun men. They crave your sin. They feed on it. They want you to turn your back on God and use you to help destroy this island. Listen to temptation and you condemn us all. You, your mothers, your fathers. All of us, damned to the abyss.'

His voice climbed and climbed until his bellows reached the highest pitch of the church roof, and with every word, I shrank.

'Esta.'

My name cut through the room like the toll of the bell in the harbour on a frosty morning. I reacted, frozen and slow, as if I had never heard my name before.

'Come with me, please.'

When I turned to look, Father Jessop had his arm around Crescent, his fingers playing with the ends of her buttery hair. He had taken her to the font. Behind them there was a ledge at the back of the church upon which were four deep jugs. Father Jessop looked towards them.

'Esta, I'd like you to fill the font with water from those jugs. Do this with the utmost care.'

The jugs were as heavy to carry as I imagined a small child to be, and I had to hold their weight against my entire body so as not to spill a drop.

'Good girl.' His approval felt like the sun. He beckoned the other girls to join us, and we gathered in a semicircle around the font. I remember the glisten of fear, damp above Crescent's top lip.

'Crescent here made a grave mistake today by letting the darkness sway her, didn't you, sweetheart?'

She nodded. Her face reminded me of a wild rabbit I'd seen once, eyes startled, picked to death by seabirds.

He straightened. 'The important thing is that we learn from our mistakes, that we see the consequences of falling into weakness. Only through repentance can the Lord forgive us.'

Father Jessop urged Crescent forward until she was peering into the font I'd filled. He placed his hand on the back of her head, and before I even had a chance to question what was happening, he had pushed it into the water. She was frozen at first and the water sloshed like a bath. Any minute I expected him to release her, but he held her down even when her body began to struggle and thrash. He was still, except for a flicker of a muscle in his cheek. Like the slick of a herring caught in a net. The water bubbled, moaned with her efforts to escape.

At last he pulled her free from the water by her hair and left her gasping and dripping. She sobbed, and he leant down to whisper something into her ear, making her quiet almost instantly. From where I was, I saw a flash of his teeth, a thinness to his lips.

He dried his hands and placed one on the centre of the open Great Book.

'Lord, thank you for showing Crescent the right path. We're

grateful for your mercy today, your protection.' Then to her, 'You've earned your forgiveness from God, Crescent.'

He turned back to the rest of us girls.

'Remember this when you hear the whispers of the Seawomen, luring you towards sin. Pulling you towards what you know is wrong. When your mind strays from God, remember the way dear Crescent struggled and choked. Today God spared her and taught her a lesson, but follow them towards darkness and you, my girls, will not be so fortunate.'

Crescent was a different girl after that sermon, almost mute. No one gave her a towel or a blanket, no one came rushing forward to console her. She was marked. Spared only by God's forgiveness. Her deviance, her mistake, was so slight, and yet she would never escape it, never stop people from looking at her in a certain way. She didn't come to school the next few days; she had caught a fever, which we all knew was another sign of her sin. When she returned, girls and boys alike avoided her, making noises when she got close, inspecting our bodies for rashes and boils, marks on our palms. She might have cursed us. What lurked in her might corrupt us all. There were boys who saw a way to exploit her new weakness, tormenting her, jumping out from behind doorways, chasing her into hiding. She scared easily after that. It only took one mention of the Seawomen (a rumour, a glimpse, a nursery rhyme, a dead herring slipped under the collar of her dress) and she would burst into tears. She began to carry the Great Book with her everywhere, to hardly speak if it wasn't quotes from the scriptures. But it wasn't just her; none of us was the same after that sermon. None of us could forget.

Four

We held our breath waiting, though no one wanted to say it out loud, for news of a sighting. A glimpse of a tail, a naked woman with silken hair rising from the sea. We were waiting for a whole army to come for us. There was gossip and panic from school to church to the market. Everything glimpsed became our biggest fear. A seal pup, the fin of a minke whale, a wet-headed walrus. But never a woman. Not yet. As each day passed without another sign of darkness, without a woman suspected and found barren, and the weather improved, Father Jessop convinced us it was our increased obedience in our faith that was keeping us safe and the Seawomen at bay. We sat on the edge of our pews as he spoke.

'Proof,' he said, the word ringing as tall as the steeple. 'Proof is what we ask God for, what we look for. Signs that our faith is working, signs that we are doing the righteous thing. Tell me, raise your hand, tell me the proof you've seen of faith in action, the retreating of darkness from our shores.'

We looked around and hands shot upwards.

A fisherman's wife reported larger hauls of herring. That was agreed by hums from other wives.

'Plentiful seas! Yes! God is rewarding our loyalty with food for our plates. What else?'

A crofter stood. Crops thriving, healthy calves. We applauded each response, each sign that our efforts were working. Father Jessop opened his arms, head tilted back, thanking the Lord with a rapture that awed us all. Then finally, proof none of us could deny, he asked five women to stand, all of them round-cheeked and their bellies huge. Two of them had had their names in the Suspicions Box, but this proved their innocence undoubtedly. Pregnancies – that was God's sign above all.

43

'New life!' he cried, gasping, overwhelmed. 'Pure bodies, strong hearts! The island thrives and we will not surrender to the dark!'

I felt tears in my eyes. Relief and joy. The din of cheers. Even my grandmother clapped with everyone. It was working.

But Father Jessop reminded us we couldn't leave it there. One wrong step and we knew they'd come again. The crops would be ruined, the children sick, locusts climbing the walls, motheryears passing without a flicker of life. Our Salvation hung by a thread.

The following years passed without curse, without a sighting of anything in the water, though the dread seemed to linger over all of us like a fog. Paranoia caged us, obedient in fear. I was seven now, my energy expanding as my grandmother's was depleting. The equinox festival was weeks away, a bright spot of jubilation as it always was, to shake the harshness of winter from our bones as we danced and ate and lit bonfires long into the night. We called it the Festival of the Land, celebrating what was ours, treasuring God's watchful eye. It was my favourite night of the year.

As preparations took place, my grandmother complained of tiredness. In recent months she'd struggled even to walk to church without leaning against me on the final incline, and she made me do the hardest work in the allotment. She stood elbow-deep at the sink, supper on the stove, and began berating herself, muttering about something she had forgotten. I watched her move around the room, agitated, filling a crate with freshly pulled vegetables and writing a note.

'You'll have to go,' she said. 'Wrap up warm and take this with you.'

It was growing dark outside and I never left the house alone at night. 'Where?'

'Take this to Barrett. It's not good for him to be hungry and alone today.'

'What's today?'

'Just hurry, will you!'

'To the harbour? On my own?'

She considered it for a moment, knuckles on her hips, staring into the supper pot. 'It'll be a test. If you make it to the harbour and back without any trouble, then you'll know you have the Lord's favour.'

'I can't.' I hesitated. 'I don't want to.'

'Out.'

'What if someone reports me? Thinks I'm bad?'

'You tell them I sent you to make a delivery.'

She gave me a cold, hard stare, then marched across the kitchen and opened the back door, a swirl of cold frosting inside. My feet were glued to the floor.

'Go. Go on with you!'

My head fell, the crate too heavy for me and already pulling on the muscles in my shoulders. I was sure I'd drop everything on the way, helplessly watching as it rolled over the cliff edge and disappeared forever. On my way out, she stopped me and hung her own cross pendant around my neck, so now I had another, double protection against the water. I'm certain, looking back on this night, that she used this as a test herself, wanting to know whether she had done enough to stop history repeating itself. Or would she need to be stricter with me, stem the parts of me she hadn't managed with my mother? As she closed the door behind me, I did everything I could not to cry, biting the inside of my mouth until the flesh tasted of pink blood.

The wind was an animal that night, every howl spooking me to walk faster. I whispered prayers as I got closer to the harbour, anything to mask the calling of the sea. I hadn't been anywhere near the harbour since the day the Seawoman's shedding was found, and the thought of returning after everything that had happened felt like an insurmountable challenge. It wasn't far to walk, but the light in the sky was diminishing and I had forgotten to take a torch with me. As the boats came into view, I realised it was not the harbour that was my biggest fear, but the thought of being alone with Barrett. It's difficult to remember how he seemed to me then, how it was to be so afraid of him. This hulking, sullen man, full of secrets. My grandmother said she didn't want him to be alone. I was supposed to be his company, but I'd spent my childhood hiding from him. What would I have to say to this sea-stinking man with a permanent scowl? Him, in the dark, with no words and a single eye staring? How was my grandmother so certain he wasn't from the sea himself?

Waiting at the door, I went over and over it until he appeared, a slice of his weather-warped face pressed into the doorway gap. The surprise of seeing me leaked into his features, both of us silent. I didn't even want him to speak; I wanted him to accept the gift and close the door on me so I had an excuse to leave.

He looked me over, then behind me, searching for my grand-mother. 'What are you doing here?' he said, like you would to a doll blown there in the wind.

'I have this,' I said, looking at the crate rather than him as I lifted it towards him.

'What for?'

'For you.'

He kept staring, then shifted, chest puffing out, backing up to widen the door. His invitation inside was a nod. I followed him in, still carrying the crate, trying not to look at his good hand, which was twitching and held behind his back.

'Shut the door behind you!'

I jumped. He was already deep inside the house, shouting back to me as he walked away. I shut the door, leaning against it, both me and it trembling.

His house smelt like the outside did, of fish, of weed, of brine. But it was too dark to see anything but the glow from the kitchen, so I followed it, elbows in, crate hugged to my chest. I could hear him clattering and my mind raced ahead of me. The only other light came from the living room; my eyes were drawn to it, a room where a fire roared a tempting orange. There was a chair, angled away from the fireplace and pointed towards the open doorway. On the chair a dress was draped, red, rich and smooth. I paused, unable to stop myself looking at its colour, the length of it spread on the chair as if a woman had been sitting there until her body had suddenly vanished.

Barrett made more noise in the kitchen and I hurried on through the dark, low-ceilinged hallway, spine locked at the thought of him catching me snooping. I realised with relief that the noise was him making tea for me.

'I put honey in it,' he placed the cup on the wooden table.

'Thank you.' Now there was no way I could go straight home. The cup was steaming.

'Honey used to do the trick when you were wee. But you're too young to remember that, eh?'

I blinked, embarrassed. I was too young to remember him ever looking after me, even though my grandmother told me he had. I lifted the crate of vegetables onto the table, noticing a glass filled an inch with brown liquid. He saw my eyes pass over the glass and snatched it from the table, pouring the drink down the sink and rinsing it with water. When he placed it down again, he did it slowly, with the care of a mother putting her infant in a cot. His attention darted into the hallway, where from the front of the house we could both see the glow from the harbour lights. He went out into the hall, following the sound of footsteps outside: a pacing Keeper trying to stay warm and awake.

When Barrett came back into the room, it was like he'd forgotten why he'd left it in the first place. He looked a little startled, as he sat at the table, smoothing the bushy edges of his beard with his shaking hand. My grandmother was always complaining that he was late and forgetful.

'Thank you for this,' he said, gesturing to the crate, his voice thick, like he had a stone under his tongue.

'We dug them up today. Well, I did,' I said, concentrating on the steady line of words. I could talk about the garden and not look at him properly, not pay attention to the room, which looked like a mirror of the harbour, filled with nets and oars and broken boat parts, slicks of sand sludge on the floor. He'd brought the sea with him, inside his home. If men were a risk, if the Eldermothers had inspected the houses of men who lived alone like him, he'd have failed their scrutiny. But the sea didn't influence men like it did women. We were much more dangerous.

'I'm sure you're a big help.'

I didn't know what to say. I stared at my tea, wishing it was cool enough to drink. He pulled out a chair beside him and patted the seat for me to sit.

'She's not expecting you back straight away, is she?'

I shook my head and sat down.

'It's nice to see you.' He hesitated, putting his hand on the table near me, like he wanted to touch my arm but was too afraid to. 'I'm surprised she sent you on your own.'

'She's very tired. Weak in the legs. But she said she didn't want you to be hungry and on your own. Not today.'

'Ah,' he said, a strange and soft sound coming out of him. He looked away. Once at the table, I saw what I'd missed before: next to the glass was a slip of paper and a pencil, a partially sketched drawing of a woman with plaited hair, looking serious and half turned away. I thought of the dress in the living room. The lines of the sketch were soft and feathery. I couldn't imagine a man like him, or any man, drawing something that looked so tender.

Barrett picked up the paper. 'She remembered,' he smiled sadly.

My grandmother said that Barrett used to visit us a lot when I first moved in with her; helped her with the garden, made the shelf in my room, made me a little pulley pram on wheels from an old box and junk the puffers brought back. But I couldn't remember any of that either.

'The more years that pass, the harder . . .' He spoke to himself, fumbling with the sketch, the paper fluttering like a wing in his shaking left hand.

'You're good at drawing.'

He smiled again, but it vanished when he looked back at the picture. 'Not any more. I've almost forgotten what she looked like.'

He showed me the grey drawing. Sadness roiled in his voice until he cleared his throat.

'Ten years ago. To the day.'

'She's pretty.'

'It doesn't do her justice.' He crumpled the paper and my heart leapt.

'Who is she?' I put my hand on his arm to stop him destroying her, even though I could guess who she was.

'My wife. Mae. This is how she wore her hair when we got married.'

'I like it.'

'Yes, so do I.'

'How old? When you got married?' It was different with him; asking questions was allowed. It stopped the tears swimming to the surface of his eye.

'Oh, young. But we were in love.' He opened up the drawing, smoothing its edges. 'We met at a dance. One of her sister's friends had just had a baby. It was one of those nights when the whole island was out celebrating. Life was good.'

The words came out of him like I wasn't even there, like it had been so long since he'd spoken about Mae and he didn't know how to hold it in.

'I'd never danced before. Two left feet. But the next day I turned up at her father's croft with flowers and we talked for hours, even when the rain started coming down. She wasn't scared away. We fed the cattle and we laughed . . .'

I wanted to tell him, my tiny hand on his moth-eaten jumper, that I understood what it was like when someone you loved was gone. We sat in the half-dark together, with only his tearful breaths between us. Barrett broke the tension, and unloaded the items from the crate.

'Forget all that, forget it.' He accidentally tore the kale in his hand, then with no real sense of purpose began shredding it, pinning it to the table with his stump, as if he was trying to rip it into nothing.

My heart hammered, but I tried to still him. His hand was scarred and cut, rough from years on the water. The kale was just scraps now. He stopped.

'You don't need my sad stories.'

'I like stories. Grandmother tells me them all the time.'

'Well, no happy ending in these ones. Mae . . .'

'What happened to her?'

'She got sick. We were trying for a baby and then she got sick. Really sick. But I left her alone, in bed asleep, and I went out on the water. Because a storm had just passed and I thought I had to get back to it, I had to do my part. She looked so frail, but I thought, I'll only be a few hours and then I'll be back home to look after her. I went to your grandmother and she told me the weather would hold . . . I had to fish. I had to make a living. And Mae, she told me to go. You see,

49

she was a fearless woman. Not every woman would be happy living by the harbour, but she had no doubts; no bad luck had ever touched us. We had a good life. A good life. No reason to worry. But when I got back, the house was so quiet, and when I went upstairs, I was too late. I should never have . . . She was gone.' His eye was wet when he looked at me.

'I'm so sorry,' I said.

He left the kale alone and turned his hand over so mine sat in it for a moment.

'How old are you now?' he asked.

'Seven.'

The answer seemed to make him sadder, and I didn't know what to say to make it better.

'You don't have any children?' I asked.

The question surprised him, but a smile rippled under his beard. 'You're a curious little thing, aren't you? Be careful.' He squeezed my hand. 'No, I don't have any. Mae was given her motheryear late, long after we married. Years went by. They thought because I was always out at sea and she lived here, so close to the water, that it might take her longer, that she wasn't ready. She was quite pale, thin. Not very strong, not strong enough to give the baby a fighting chance. So the Eldermothers waited, and they waited, but by the time she was granted it, she was too sick to . . .' He moved the drawing of her between us so we could both see.

'Did she draw too?'

I stayed still, listening to his tales of the past, of Mae, drinking my sweetened tea and another afterwards. His stories spilled on and on until he was telling me about what it was like to be a fisherman, life on the boats. He told me the names of the boat parts, never hesitating to answer my questions, and I absorbed it all. Only later, as the boat words came back to me, did the guilt set in. I was jittery at the thought of this new language; that no matter how easily he had told me, I wasn't meant to know it. I reasoned: who else did he have to tell? No wife, no son. Only me. I felt sorry for him, so I listened, but if my grandmother found out, she'd march me to the Eldermothers herself. It was like the shell all over again; I couldn't help it. His words passed over my stomach like a low foam. They were keys, opening the door of a different room, a world I hadn't known before. A door I wouldn't be able to shut. As long as I kept it secret, as long as I kept praying to God, everything would be all right.

I stayed until it was fully dark outside. Barrett gave me a torch and said he'd walk me home.

'I didn't mean to shout at you before. You can come again, any time,' he said. Something had shifted between us.

It would have been better for him – for me – if he'd pushed me away, denied my curiosity, spoken to me under the weight of rules and doctrine that everyone else did. But he couldn't. He shut out everything and everyone else but me. And who's to say that if he had, it would have changed what happened?

He walked me home. By his side, I didn't even notice the sound of the waves, the boats knocking together.

Five

Almost two years after I sat in Barrett's kitchen, the forbidden language of boats and water like a new current in my bloodstream, everything changed. It started in the middle of a winter's night when I woke to my grandmother screaming. I ran to her bedroom, night clothes sticking to my body's damp, and found her kneeling on the floor, tears flowing down her face. She didn't notice me, not even the sound of me running to her, not the door as I opened it.

'Grandmother?'

Her head snatched around, her silver hair slick with oil. Her eyes were puckered, white and sucked of moisture, as though she had been crying until there was nothing left.

'Something's wrong,' she said.

I was not brave enough to comfort her, still reeling from the sound of her screams. I was afraid of it starting again. She stared at the wall. I could see shadowy marks across her back where her nightgown had turned translucent from the wet fear of her body. Through it I could see the notches of her curved spine like a sideways fence, pushing against the fabric.

'On the island. Something is wrong on the island. I can feel it.'

'Did you have a nightmare?' I thought of the times I had woken up in a cold sweat and not dared to tell her about the dreams I had in case those too would make her think there was something wrong with me.

'They're here again. I know it.'

I didn't need to ask who.

'No, no.'

'Go and get the Book! Now!'

I ran back to my room for it, hearing her mutter: *It's happening again, it's happening again.*

She didn't let me go back to bed that night, even though I could feel the tug of sleep through my prayers, the words on the page lulling me. At first light she made me wash and dress, then she stood in the open doorway of the cottage, expecting to hear the church bell toll. She was shaking, sweating, reading every ailment as another sign of curse.

Our answer came in the hours that followed, hours that dragged with her insistence that we fast, to clear our minds of anything that would disrupt our prayers. Father Jessop sent Messengers round to each house, informing us that there had been a fever in the north of the island, children hot and shaking. We were to be watchful.

'Signs,' my grandmother said, looking at me to confirm her worst fears.

And there were more. In the days that followed, a young married woman roused suspicion in her husband by talking in her sleep. Rumours spread from croft house to croft house that she'd also foamed at the mouth, that he'd found her cold and distant. At school, stories started that she'd been caught standing on a cliff edge, staring out to sea. My grandmother, still sleepless and weak from worry, asked around at the market for any more news. I couldn't follow it. It sounded as if they were speaking another language.

'We've had our thoughts about her for some time,' one of the women said. They were neighbours and had no doubt that the rumours were true.

'Who is she?'

'Lark's wife.'

'Her? What's wrong with her?'

'Eleven months of her motheryear down.'

'And nothing? No baby?'

The woman widened her eyes. 'And now this. It's her, isn't it? Got to be. She's the reason.'

A fortnight later, we watched her body float face down in the sea. She was gone, and with her so was the influence of the Seawomen. There were cheers. I knew my grandmother would sleep soundly that night. The first of my life. Now I knew what happened when the accusations stacked up, when a motheryear passed, when a woman could not prove she was righteous, when repentance wasn't enough. It was so much worse than Crescent at the font.

The memory of that day is a part of me now, tough like hardened skin. You never forget your first. You hope and pray it will be the last you ever see. You already know. Deep down. It'll happen again and you will have to watch. The screaming, the waiting, watching her body tied down, the boat rocking and shunting, capsizing. Drowning. The point where you can see with your own eyes what it means to be a woman.

I was wrong; instead of a return to normal, after the Untethering my grandmother's moods got worse. We continued to fast; I was allowed to eat meagre bowls of soup and oatmeal before sunrise, then and only then. Whenever her paranoia struck, we went to the Eldermothers. At the chapel, I gritted my teeth under the cold buckets of water tipped over my head, the way their bony hands dug into my skull. If they lingered over me, I panicked about what they might read in my soul. *She is not like her mother*, my grandmother told them over and over. *She's not. She's not.* At home, she hid away, clinging to the Great Book, refusing to let either of us bathe in case the water cast our thoughts to the sea. The windows were shut, curtains drawn, and as the weeks wore on, my world got smaller and smaller.

School was my one reprieve. I hadn't dared to visit Barrett at the harbour, despite his offer. Before the Untethering, before everything had started going wrong, I took him things from our garden on the odd occasion, digging up turnips and cabbages before they were ready, just as an excuse to go and see him. To sit in the kitchen when it was getting dark and drink honeyed tea. To talk about things that weren't the Great Book, or how grateful we were for the John family making the island our home. But there were still things we *didn't* talk about. I didn't share my private disappointment that school taught me about the old world, but never the Otherlands or further. I didn't tell him that I wanted to hear about what life was like in those places. But back then, I wasn't sure I could admit it to anyone, not even myself.

One afternoon, having not seen my grandmother for days, I found the courage to knock, instead of leaving goat's milk and boiled eggs outside her door. There was no answer. I inhaled, my tiny, hungry frame trying to expand, and turned the door handle. She was in bed, face hollowed, lips the colour of a bruise. I rushed over, relieved when I saw her fragile chest still rising and falling. She almost sank into the bedclothes, shivering, though when I felt her, her head was scorching, her skin the same paleness as the blankets.

I tried to lift a glass of water to her parched lips, but it ran from the creases of her mouth.

'I'll get the doctor,' I said, trying to keep my voice gentle and reassuring, even though inside I wanted to run.

Her eyes widened with alarm and she grabbed at me. 'No! No. He interferes with God's plan.' She could hardly get the words out, rasping for breath, long, confused pauses.

I started sobbing, helpless at the fevered state of her, worried about what it meant. I couldn't look after her alone. I left the house, leaving doors swung open in my haste, thrusting my weight against the strength of the wind. The weather hadn't calmed, even after Lark's wife had gone – another reason for my grandmother to worry.

The harbour bore the worst of the storm. As I approached, I struggled to stay on my feet. It was late afternoon and loud, the boats returning with their last haul of the day. I tried not to look, to just focus on my breathing, but the noise and activity was too chaotic to shut out completely. I could see one of the young fishermen unloading a dripping net of thick silver bodies, then spreading it in front of the gutter shed. I'd never seen the fishermen at work up close like this before. There was shouting back and forth between him and a man named Franklin. I knew of Franklin because whenever I'd come across him on the island or seen him at the festival, he'd been aggressive and often drunk. One day he would become my father-in-law. At the shouting, I scuttled to the house, knocking and waiting at the door, desperately hoping Barrett was at home and not teaching the young deckhands in one of the huts. After a few slow minutes, he appeared in the doorway. He grabbed his coat from the peg before I had even finished explaining what was wrong.

The doctor came to the cottage at Barrett's insistence, even though I tried to object. He told us that my grandmother had an infection, that the fasting and exhaustion had only made it worse. Barrett started pacing the room, angry that she wasn't looking after herself. I'd never seen him riled like that, and even though she'd been doing this for God, for the island, I couldn't find anything to say to defend her.

'She'll improve. She's malnourished and weak. She needs good iron-rich foods, plenty of fluid and rest.' The doctor wrote a list of instructions for the nurse when she arrived. It was an optimistic diagnosis, which even then, knowing how frail my grandmother was, seemed unbelievable.

'She fasted for the Lord. To receive His guidance,' I tried to make him understand.

'Honourable it was too. And now she needs to eat, sleep and look after her God-given body,' the doctor said, laying his hand on my back. 'Those are the things the Lord needs her to do.'

'What was she thinking?' Barrett said, still pacing.

'I'll pray for her,' I said.

'Good. We all will,' the doctor said; then, to Barrett, 'And the girl will stay with you.'

Barrett stopped, looking sheepishly at me. 'She can't stay here?'

'Only if you want to see her in the same state as Sarl. She already looks very thin. I wouldn't like to leave her here alone.'

I tried to keep my face still, devoid of expectation.

'I guess she'll have to.'

'That's settled, then.'

I froze in my seat, unable to meet Barrett's gaze. I couldn't bear the thought of living so close to the water.

'How long do you expect this to last?' Barrett asked.

'A few weeks, give or take.' The doctor directed his words more to me, attaching a smile to his mouth like trying to fit a shoe the wrong size. He raised his voice to something attempting to be cheerful. 'Don't you worry, young lady, she'll be quite well again. The nurse will see to that. Back to normal under God's good care!'

Barrett followed the doctor out into the hallway, out of my earshot, but when they spoke, I heard everything.

'Maybe I'm not the right person for the job. My work . . . my house . . . it's not right for a young thing like her to be around. What will people say?'

'I shouldn't think it'll be too much of a challenge. I've got two of my own. Girls, I find, they're best treated like animals. You feed them, keep them warm, set boundaries. As long as she prays daily, she won't bring much trouble. It's a few weeks; what harm can it do?'

'If that's the case . . .'

'There's always the Eldermothers . . .'

'I won't send her there.'

I worried they would.

Barrett came back into the kitchen and held my gaze. 'What do you think, Esta? Do you think you'd be all right to come and stay with me?'

I nodded, reaching out at his kindness.

Barrett waited downstairs while I gathered some things: a single bag of clothes, the Great Book and a cloth doll. By the time I was ready to leave, the nurse had arrived and was standing in the hallway. Her name was Norah, and she was tall and wiry, not how I expected a nurse to look.

She smiled at me, cautiously, with her hand on the banister, ready to go upstairs and look after my grandmother. 'Do you want to go and say goodbye to her before you go?'

I heard her up there, babbling and confused in her delirium, the odd shout that made me jump. I could hear her calling my mother's name. *Maddow. Maddow. Maddow.* Norah looked away. My grandmother was *her* concern now, and any feverish thing she did or said was Norah's to endure. I shook my head. I didn't want to go up there. I followed Barrett out of the cottage and down towards the harbour, my new home until she was better.

'You make yourself at home,' Barrett said when we arrived. He began loading logs into the fireplace to warm up the room.

I remember the moment I stepped into that house with my bag – with the knowledge I would be staying there, more conscious of the water than ever – because after that, nothing would ever be the same again. The large windows revealed so much of the sea, I saw my arms reaching out to steady myself every time I walked past one of them. My stomach gave the same slop-slop as the water, my feet concentrating on balance. Looking was unavoidable. The noise of the harbour below was constant, like a pulse. When a storm was building, like it was on that first afternoon, the spit pattered endlessly against the side of the cottage and outside the door. Barrett commented on it like it didn't even matter to him, while I sat on the floor, my back to the windows, nervous and twitchy. The room seemed to echo the thrash of the rain.

'You're safe here,' Barrett said when he noticed me trying to hide from the sight of the harbour below. He looked longingly towards the windows. He couldn't sail alone any more, couldn't even take a boat out to catch his own supper. It was far too dangerous in his condition. 'Well, the seals will love it out there today.'

'Seals?'

'Oh yes, they love it when the rain's as heavy as this. We'll probably get some washed up along the cove on a day like today.'

That was almost enough to make me want to look, but I was still my grandmother's child, still rooted to the floor, trying to block out my fear with scripture. Barrett couldn't possibly know the dangers of being a girl, and now that I'd seen what happened to women who had been influenced by the water, I had every right to be scared.

But after that first restless night, the presence of the harbour fell away into the background. Soon, the things I liked best about staying with Barrett won out over the things that made me uneasy. The comfort of the spare bed, the pillows that kept me snug, the drink of goat milk he gave me before bed, mixed with honey.

'I put in an extra spoonful,' he winked. I hadn't ever tasted anything that comforting.

There was no fasting either, no restrictions on when or what I could eat. He didn't even ask me if I was hungry; just handed me slices of thick buttered bread, curds and bowls of stew, pickles and fried herring. After school, the afternoons were not how they had been with my grandmother either. Not shut away, hours of prayer and reading from the Great Book. One afternoon he saw my fatigue at turning another page and said:

'Why don't you put that away for a while. I've got something for you to do instead.'

I was reluctant at first, dedicated to repentance as I was, trying to keep my grandmother happy even though she was out of reach, but then he presented his drawing pencils to me, and my heart leapt. In recent months, in the height of her paranoia, my grandmother had said frivolous activities like drawing were a waste of time and a distraction from prayer, but here Barrett was, offering me the chance, permission granted.

'I'm not very good,' I said.

'Won't know until you try.'

'But what should I draw?'

He shrugged. 'Whatever you like.'

I looked for objects in the house to draw until I ran out of things that interested me and tried to copy one of his sketches. A seal. It needed improvement, more character in its face.

'Here,' Barrett said. 'Let me help you. I'll describe him and you put it down.'

He described the seals and their fur in such detail that I could touch them.

'You know,' he said, starting and then hesitating when I began a new picture. 'Your mother could draw. Maybe you get it from her.'

My pencil stilled on the page. I knew so little about her that anything, even something as small as this, felt like discovering treasure; like the time I found a clean yellow feather from a firecrest on the way to school and kept it hidden from my grandmother, from everyone, in case it was taken from me. I looked up at Barrett, hoping he would tell me more, but he was quiet again, like my grandmother got when her tongue was wet with drink.

'What did she like drawing?'

'It all came from up here,' he tapped two fingers against his temple. 'Her imagination. She used to walk around with paper to draw on. Sometimes when the sun was out, I'd see her outside the cottage scribbling away.'

I tried to picture her, sitting on a grass bank outside my grand-mother's house, but I could conjure nothing but the pencils in my own hand. My frustration was building again, giving way to old curiosities. But Barrett had already turned away.

'You keep at it,' he said hesitantly, pulling on his coat. 'I'm needed in the harbour. I'll be back in an hour or so.'

I drew and drew, lost in concentration. I thought the more I focused on improving my sketches, the closer I would get to my mother. I forgot all about the Great Book and the prayers I was supposed to say before bedtime. And when Barrett came back, appraising my efforts, there was none of my grandmother's screaming or claims that she'd seen scales and shadows in the water, no stories designed to scare. It was a relief to be away from that house. Barrett was no longer the dark, mumbling figure who turned up at our cottage reeking of the sea, the man with too many secrets. I could even see a slight slant to his mouth beneath his beard, like he actually enjoyed having me around. That I wasn't a chore, or a burden, but company, wholesome. Wanted.

Six

Like the doctor had said, a few weeks on, my grandmother was well enough for me to go home. Barrett came with me to make sure she had improved. As we approached the house, we saw the nurse rushing out the door. She had her head bowed and didn't look well herself, drawn inward; not the tall woman I'd seen enter my grandmother's house weeks before.

'How is she?' Barrett asked.

'Better. She's out of bed, she's managing to eat. I'm sorry to leave like this, but I have to get back to my family.'

'Thank you for looking after her.'

Norah nodded and hurried away. Was my grandmother the cause of her red eyes, her quick escape? Did she talk to Norah in the same way she talked to me when her headaches were flaring? Or worse – had she accused Norah of being bewitched, a Seawoman in waiting?

My grandmother was downstairs when we arrived, supported by a cane. The house felt cold and I missed the swell of heat from Barrett's fireplace. There was no great reunion when she saw me, no arms around each other, no shared sentiments about having missed each other. Barrett briefly left us alone to make tea, but even then she looked me over, expecting to find something obviously wrong.

The two of them sat talking for a while as Barrett checked on how she was feeling. She shooed me out the way, but I pressed my ear against the door to listen. She asked if I'd behaved, if I'd studied and prayed, cleaned up after myself. But her concern about me didn't last. She was soon drifting back into talk about the old days, of growing up together.

'If anything happens, I want you to look after her.'

'Don't give me that kind of talk.'

'You and Mae never got the chance. It's only right. But I don't

63

want you to go soft on her. That's when the trouble starts. I know it. I see it. It's in her bones.'

'She's just a girl, Sarl.'

'That's why I worry.'

Outside the door, my hands, on my knees, stuck to my dress. Was she right? I was back under the spell of that house, her rules returning to me like muscle memory, guilt rising thick and fast, fear filling the spaces in between. She put me back to work again in the garden as soon as Barrett was out the door, but there was an absence inside me. I missed the smell of rust and brine in the harbour, the chorus of gulls in the morning. I missed the grind, the men's voices and jeers of success. I missed hearing about the weight of the hauls brought back, the gutter women's songs drifting in through the window. I missed Barrett and his easy company. Rather than slip back into the rules and conventions of my grandmother's order, I resented it.

The way things were could not last. Something would break – and it didn't take long.

Spring came a month later, and the island was abuzz with excitement for the Festival of the Land. In school, the celebrations were all anyone could talk about. What food we would eat, what clothes we would wear, what this year's effigy would look like, who would dance with who. We celebrated many things – births, marriages, pregnancies and motheryears – but the Festival of the Land was when the island really came alive. It was a chance to remember Father Lambert and his followers building our ancestors a new beginning on Eden's Isle; to celebrate what he had done for us, the Salvation we were ensured by his work. Everyone from the young children to the Keepers came together. Even the ferrymen from the patrol boats were given permission to come ashore, leaving their illuminated patrols static out at sea. As excitement for the festival built, we were reminded that God would be watching. There was no need to fear the Seawomen on a night like this, because the equinox marked the anniversary of Father Lambert driving them away from our waters – and on this special night, they wouldn't dare come back.

School finished early for the afternoon, with preparations under way: banners and streamers made from old sails, a bonfire built, market stalls arranged. I was walking home when an urge to be close to the water grabbed hold of me and wouldn't let go. I can only describe it now as something wild, innate. It was unstoppable. Everyone on the island was busy; my one and only chance.

But this one opportunity had a flaw – I wasn't alone. I had made a new friend. Mull, Father Jessop's only daughter. To show my desire in front of her was one of the most dangerous things I could have done, but I'd never felt an urge like it. One afternoon, when I was staying with Barrett, I'd asked him to draw me a full map of the island, everything he remembered from seeing it on his boat, so I could finally picture every edge my grandmother hadn't let me explore. He'd done it happily, pointing out sea caves, stretches of water where he'd seen a porpoise and then an arc of coastline, past the repaired sea wall. A sheltered, hidden slither of land he called a cove. I knew that was where I wanted to go.

Mull was a few inches taller and rounder than me. But she wasn't ten yet, and at that age, it seemed important to count the differences. She had a dimple in her chin, like someone had pushed their thumb into her before she was fully baked. It had been her suggestion to walk together; with her father and brothers busy, her mother helping to prepare the feast, she was in no hurry to go back home. It was the first day we'd ever spent any real time alone together, though I'd watched her, silently, across the classroom, twinning her movements as if I could obtain a sister. She always seemed out of reach. Father Jessop's daughter: far too important to be a friend of mine.

When we reached a fork in the road, she should have headed further south to the old Observatory, but instead she paused.

'Can you stay out to play?'

I nodded almost too quickly. 'My grandmother's already at the churchyard helping to decorate. She won't mind.'

Grandmother wasn't there; she was in our garden, digging produce for the festival market, but I couldn't go home now. I had to go to the cove. Even if it meant persuading Mull there too.

So we played – chasing and cartwheels and running from make-believe storms. I edged us nearer and nearer to the cove. I heard Mull laugh for the first time, so loud and throaty it toppled her. We weren't sisters, but we were alike. In her, I saw the glimmers of difference. She wasn't the girl I'd seen in class, or with her family in church. Shedding that cold, unreadable layer. It wasn't until later that day, until shy words had grown out of our play by the old lighthouse, that she asked about my face. Her hair was pulled back and I wanted to touch it. It looked like kelp, the type that fizzed across the land, withering in brown scruffs. She didn't wear it down, wasn't told to let half of it hang, covering one side of her face, like I was. It surprised me how self-conscious and timid she was for the daughter of the man who spoke to God. She wasn't like her older brothers either, who commanded respect with their towering stature and Ministry shirts. Because of who she was, I'd have told her anything she asked.

'What's wrong with it?' she said, touching her own cheek with delicate fingers.

'A fire,' I said. 'When I was a baby.'

'Oh. Why?' she asked. 'How did it happen?'

As soon as she asked, I realised I didn't know.

It was the first time anyone had asked me outright about the fire. It seemed the others had been told not to, or had been too afraid to ask.

'Does it hurt?'

'It did before. A lot.'

She looked at my face, head tilted to the side, assessing what she could from the way it was hidden by my hair.

'Where are your mum and dad?' she asked.

'Gone,' I gave her the only answer I had.

'Gone where?' Her whole face screwed up, starting at her nose, an expression that told me she didn't believe me. 'You mean, from the island?'

'I don't know.'

'No one goes from the island,' she said, with a confidence that was all her father.

'But what about the stories?' I felt uncertain even asking. There were tales of those who'd attempted it. Cursed, doomed folk who didn't believe in God and did not appreciate the chance of Salvation the island gave them. I tried again, to see if she'd remember having heard the rumours from years and years ago. 'The fisherman and his wife? Taking her sister and child?'

I'd heard many versions of the tale. It was the ones that ended in the most horrifying ways that I found most convincing. Sometimes there were no men in the story at all, just women taking boats and rowing by themselves. One version told of a woman who left her crying children behind. But they all ended the same way. God punished them for forsaking the life they'd been blessed with.

Mull shook her head. 'No one would leave!'

Perhaps she was right. If leaving meant drowning, who would even try it? I was plucking at the grass at the side of my leg, picking away at my doubts. She was bound to know more than me.

I swallowed. 'What if . . .' A false start. She stared at me, waiting for the rest. 'What if they wanted to leave and go somewhere else?'

'But where?'

'The Otherlands?'

Her eyes widened, her whole body leaning towards me, then she broke out into a laugh. 'The Otherlands!'

Heat prickled in my face.

'Do you know what it's like there? The people are *monsters*,' she said. 'The way they look, the way they walk and talk. It's all wrong, Esta.' She covered her face in horror at the thought. 'No one would want to go there. When Daddy comes back from visiting, he tells us all these terrible stories.'

I nodded fervently at her to show I agreed, I understood. Father Jessop went to the Otherlands a few times a year to report back to us about what it was like, to warn us, to remind us. 'It's a bad place.'

'We're so lucky. I wouldn't ever, ever want to be there and be like them.'

I didn't want Mull to lose interest in me, or think I was strange for talking about the Otherlands and saying my parents were 'gone' when I meant dead. My hopes for a friend, for an adventure, were dissipating before my eyes. I'd learnt, watching the interactions of other girls in school, that friendships were built through exchanges. Secrets. Gifts. Trading skills, like braiding hair, and teaching each other how

67

to weave daisy stalks together to make a chain. I didn't have any friends. I didn't think I had anything to trade until that moment she covered her face. I stuck out my hand.

'I'll show you all of it,' I said, nerves and excitement bubbling as one. I had a plan. 'But it has to be somewhere secret where no one else can see.'

'There's no one here.'

'Someone might be watching. I know where we can go.'

All through our play, it had been itching at me, that need to test the boundaries, to know if the water twisted us into evil like the sermons said. In her, I saw what I wanted: hope. I wanted her to be like I was, wanting what I wanted. And if I could persuade her to follow me, then maybe I wouldn't be so alone.

I led her to the south cove, remembering the way from Barrett's map. It was risky, stupid. She could have run screaming, she could have told her father straight away, reported me to the Ministers. But regardless of who she was and any doubts she had, she followed, desperate to see the secrets of my burnt face, to be the only one allowed to look up close. Perhaps she was used to following, obeying, drowned out by a house full of important men. Or perhaps, like me, she just wanted a friend.

When I was sure we were alone, I peeled back the sheets of my hair and showed her what she wanted to see, the full damage to my face. She looked with interest, not disgust. I tucked my hair back behind my ears, exposing my cheek, still pink and raw. In response, Mull showed me a thin white strike of lightning on her shin. A fall from a long time ago. One of her brothers, so disgusted that his mother, the wife of the man who spoke for God, had broken her string of sons by giving birth to a daughter that he pushed Mull down the stairs.

It wasn't long before the guilt caught up with Mull about where we were, what rules we were breaking. She was righteous in a way that made my stomach drop.

'We shouldn't be here,' she said, shivering as she looked around the cove.

I was distracted, pretending I hadn't heard her. I spied a perfect, unbroken whelk shell, the tip of it buried in the sand, the colour of an egg. Without my grandmother there to stop me, I freed it, knowing I wouldn't be forced to crush this one.

'We're not allowed here.' She took my hand, pulling. 'Come on. We need to go back.'

The whelk shell fell from my grip but didn't even crack.

'Wait a minute,' I said, my feet rooted, head tipped up to the air. I was desperate to have something important to say, to be more interesting than just a girl with scars, the orphan who had no other friends. To escape my grandmother's shackles. So acute was my fear of us separating, of Mull going home to the Observatory and me going back to solitude, that I opened my mouth with a lie.

'Did you hear that? In the water.'

Her head whipped around.

I pointed to some far-off place in the grey. 'Out there. I heard something.'

'What was it?' Her face had the colour of sickness and her eyes skittered everywhere.

I gripped her hand, feeling her pulling away, ready to run. 'A seal? Maybe it's hurt. You didn't hear it?'

'No. What if it's something bad?'

I dropped her hand and took a step towards the water's edge. When I looked back at Mull, she was frozen, her mouth pinched. Her head shaking.

'I want to go home. I don't like it here,' she whined. 'We can tell someone in the harbour and they can look for it.'

'It'll be too late by then. We have to look now.'

'It might not be a seal.' She blinked several times, clearing the murk of fear in her eyes, watching me roll up the bottom of my dress.

'But what if it is?'

'Please, Esta . . .'

'It's all right,' I told her. 'I've got this.' I showed her my pendant, pulling it from under the neck of my dress and kissing it. My large silver cross. 'God will keep me safe.'

'But the Seawomen!'

'They can't get you if you've got God on your side.'

'No, Esta . . .'

Her voice wobbled, but I was running with the lie, the confidence that her attention gave me.

'You shouldn't,' she said. 'I can't see anything! Esta, we should go.'

'We can't. The seal needs us.'

'You can't go in the water!' She couldn't bear to watch me.

I turned around, took her by the arms, made her look me in the eye. 'One minute. Just to check the seal.'

In a quieter voice, she said, 'I can't even see it.'

My hunger overcame fear. I was too close to change my mind, to make up a new lie. I took off my boots and socks, hiked up my skirt. Mull only watched as I thrummed.

'I'll pray for you. Ask God to help the seal,' she said, reaching some sort of acceptance. I'd taken charge. All she could do was watch and pray.

In that moment, in touching distance of the sea, nothing else mattered. I would be the first girl ever on the island to wade into the water. I heard Mull behind me, muttering to God. I put one foot in first, into the dark sand underneath, and let my toes grip. It was instant, too cold to be real. The shock of it leapt from bone to bone until I held my tongue between my teeth to stop the chatter. The sea pulled at me, numbing my skin until it didn't feel like mine. I had to keep quiet, keep going. I didn't want Mull to leave. I didn't want her to realise I was lying.

I called out for the make-believe seal, clicked my tongue. I put in my second foot and edged forward, feeling the next wave and the next, combing me further from the shore. My fingers, my wrists, wet. I wished I had the security of a boat to hold onto, ropes to keep me steady. The rocks were too far away to cling to now. As I waded further, I forgot all about the land, about God and the trouble I'd get into. I wanted more of the sea. It was a strange feeling of weightlessness. Soon I was treading water, a phrase I knew only from Barrett. Then my foot slipped underneath me, stealing my balance.

Panic set in. The darkness wanted me. The pull of the Seawomen. I was flooded with a sudden and searing conviction that all those stories I'd been told by Father Jessop and my grandmother, all those warnings, had been true all along.

Mull shouted out and her terror matched mine. I'd been looking at the horizon, but the shouting made me notice, made me look down to see myself submerged, how far out I'd been pulled. I bleated, looking back at her, back to the land, pushing handfuls of water away as if trying to unbury myself, but the opposite happened. Mull rushed to the edge, and waded in behind me, pulling on my clothes, trying to drag me back to shore. The cove was too secluded, the islanders too busy – there was no one around to even notice what we'd done. That was my plan all along, but this was the danger. We were both in the water then, both of us scared and frozen, unable to swim, all sense of why I'd done it, why I'd wanted it, lost.

How we made it back to land is a mystery, elbows and knees planted, shivering. Nothing but fear and survival. The shock left me struggling to breathe, as if something cold and heavy had sat on my chest. Mull's focus was still out to sea.

'Dear Lord . . . dear Lord . . .'

I have such a strong memory of her crying, saying it over and over again, but getting no further in her prayer because her sobs were too large to contain. I was helpless and guilty, arms down by my sides, wishing I could comfort her.

Instead, in solidarity, I managed to mutter a familiar prayer, the words clashing in a chatter of teeth. We held hands, everything shaking. Mull's eyes were streaming, her face wan. She just kept pointing out to sea, her mouth flaring, tongue quivering.

'I saw it,' she said.

'Saw what?'

'What you saw. In the water. I've just seen it.'

I managed to stand up, clicking frozen kneecaps into place, searching across the water.

'There's nothing there,' I told her.

'I saw it. Just now. A creature!'

'No, you didn't.'

'It wasn't a seal! It had a face. A real face.'

Her crying grew louder, her breathing more erratic. 'There's something in the water!'

I made her look again, turning her around to face it fully. To stare at the depths of our fear. I'd made it up. She was cold and delusional.

'There's nothing,' I said. 'Just the sun on the water. It's all silvery there. Look.'

'There was something. You saw it!'

'I must have been wrong. I didn't see anything when I was in the water.'

'But you said!'

'You must have imagined it. The shock.'

'You said!'

'I thought . . .'

'Nothing?' She stared harder and then crumpled into my side. The whole of her shook. 'I want to go home.'

I held her, stroking the back of her hair as if I was years older than her, feeling loathsome. I wanted to go home too. She found reassurance in my comfort, her tears shrinking to snuffles against my neck, and I let her hold onto my cross in her cold fist.

'You should wipe your eyes again,' I was conscious of how red and blotchy she was.

She showed her face. 'Better now?'

'You can't say anything.'

'But—'

'We'll both be in so much trouble.'

'What if it was bad?'

'We have to pretend that everything is normal.'

'Lying?'

'No, we just won't say.'

She sniffed, absorbing my advice. 'We were playing.'

'We didn't go to the cove. We shouldn't even mention that place.'

'We sat in the grass.'

We had our story. It didn't matter what the truth was, because we agreed we'd never go back there, we'd never go near the water again. We left the cove, warming each other and practising our excuses. We had the festival to get ready for. By the time we were back at my cottage, Mull was smoothed into being ordinary, determined to pretend a whole different afternoon had happened between us. Neither of us wanted to ever think about it again, let alone admit to what we had done. We were friends then, bound by this secret. I trusted her.

'It probably was a seal, wasn't it? They're exactly that silver colour,' she said, still jumpy even though we'd both managed to stand in the wind enough to make our faces look normal.

I hardly heard her. My head was still in the water. I could still taste the salt.

'Definitely,' I said.

'Seals are nice.'

The shiver had reached my bones. I can't remember what we did or said next as we parted ways. I can't even remember the festival that night. The memory of the cove overrides everything else.

I lingered outside the cottage for a long time after Mull left to get my head straight. Real, not real, real, imagined.

I'd lied to her again. I *had* seen it. Silvery. Not sunlight. Not a seal. A face, a real face. A glimpse above the surface. Scales. Gills. A body disappearing under the water, swimming away. Not a Seawoman, but a boy.

WIFE

Without the armour of God, she will be enticed by her own desire. Forbid her fall. For only the clean and faithful will be sanctified. Let her be modest, controlled, grow with her ear turned toward man, her mouth quiet in duty. From a dignified woman, blood will come and wives will be made. In her blood is life, and in the life is her promise to God.

FLESH 51:84–87

Seven

Before I turned fifteen, on Saturday mornings I volunteered to help clean the church. There were five of us, all with cloths, wiping down the pews and the front of the Great Book, on our hands and knees scrubbing at the stone floor. Me, Mull, Crescent, and twins Abeth and Phasie. The twins were the fastest of all of us, working in synchronised rhythm. 'Slapdash', Crescent called it after they'd left, missing the corners where grime and mud from outdoor shoes congealed. But Crescent had reason for wanting to impress with her efforts. No one had forgotten that she'd been the one to be made an example of.

The twins were the only ones of our group not to stay for choir, to linger among the pews and talk about the girls older than us who were preparing to marry. They only talked to each other, under their breath, in their own secret code. I was envious. Mull and I were friends, but we weren't like sisters. All the secrets we shared between us went unspoken. Like that day in the cove. It was as though I'd invented it. After the festival, Mull was absent from school for a while, sick, but when she returned, she denied it had anything to do with what we'd done. She promised me she hadn't said a word about the water.

What I'd done, what I'd seen, had convinced me of my need to atone. The friendship we had that day felt like the friendship of two different people. No longer stories and chasing and invention, pretend adventures in magical worlds. Our friendship centred around our faith. Saturdays cleaning, choir. We talked about school, about the Great Book, the good men on its pages, the women we aspired to be. We imagined what it might have been like to arrive on Eden's Isle with Father Lambert in that exciting time of rebirth, a community coming together to live as God intended.

There were moments, when the two of us were alone, walking

home from our Saturday cleaning, when I considered bringing up that time in the cove. I longed to confess what I'd really seen, but the more I thought back to that afternoon, the more it felt impossible. My cold and sea-addled mind playing tricks on me. This was what we'd been warned about. I pleaded with God to be forgiven, but I had to show Him too; I had to embrace the life my grandmother had always wanted for me.

My body was changing, breasts pushing through my tunic. I woke one morning to find a slug of brownish red on the bedsheet, and waves of shame. It had been all the things the Eldermothers had prepared us for – a nagging discomfort low in our bellies that flared into something bloated, sometimes sharp – and yet when it came, it did not have the sense of a blessing, that God had granted me woman-hood, but a sense of a clock ticking. The sands of my childhood rush-ing through my fingers.

My grandmother caught me, after that first blood, running cold water over my stained sheets.

'So, it finally came,' she said from the doorway, as if she suspected it might not ever happen.

I was frightened by the changes in my body. What it meant, the expectations that came with it.

As soon as my blood came, I was required to visit the Eldermothers every day. There were new lessons I needed to learn, new protections given to preserve and strengthen me. I shuddered through the cold of a cleansing now everyday and afterwards unquestioningly, drank down a cup of cloudy, bitter-tasting liquid we were given. This, we were told, in our moment of transformation, was the height of our vulner-ability and we were to be watchful of new warning signs – changes in mood, weight, lust, exhaustion. Surrendering to these was to lose sight of our purpose, as good as giving ourselves to the sea. Now I was a woman in body, I saw how much more there was to be afraid of and how near that danger felt.

I began to notice children more, the way they would pull on their mothers' hands; the soft waddling arms and legs of infants as they struggled to find balance; women with growing bumps, making them heavy and causing them to complain of nausea. I could see my years ahead so clearly, like they had already happened. And with my changing body, I felt all eyes on me. I remembered as a child, after the Untethering, asking my grandmother why women had to have babies; why that meant the difference between living and being sent to sea. She looked at me with thunder in her eyes, grabbing hold of my arm so tightly I felt the sting of tears.

'You want us to die out and them to take over? That's what you want? The whole world like them? Godless, disgusting?'

Once my blood had arrived, any choice I imagined for my future was gone.

Newly conscious of the attention my body might bring, I started arriving late to school. I'd seen it happen to other girls with growing curves. Some of the older boys, a group of around five of them, the ones with ambitions to be Ministers, started practising at playing powerful and tormenting the girls. They knew all too well how acutely we felt the responsibility of the island's safety now, how every rumour of the darkness spreading was a burden we carried.

They targeted girls who arrived early, quiet girls too shy to say anything as they crowded round.

'Ugh! Smells like fish,' they said, sniffing around then collapsing into laughter as their target held her tears inside, her friends edging away.

I'd seen one of the boys, Doran, smear some of his father's limpet bait across a girl's back for another 'trick'. His younger brother, Ingram, who'd become trapped within the circle of jeering, was scarlet-cheeked, eyes wide.

'Doran,' he said in warning. 'Dad'll go mad if he finds out.' I thought he might move to pull his brother back by his jacket, but he didn't, and his words died under the roar of laughter.

When seaweed was found in the hood of a girl's coat, it was obvious that the same boys were behind it. But still she attracted whispers, suspicion, and spent a night in the chapel chambers being cleansed. These boys modelled themselves in Father Jessop's image – a weight to their walk, stiff, straight shoulders, marching legs, the Great Book held under their arms. Ministers before they'd even received the uniform.

But before long, tricks and games at school weren't enough to satisfy them.

It was a wet day, and we were led outside for an hour's exercise around the field that surrounded the school, all of us together. Exercising in the rain was uncomfortable; our long dresses stuck to us like a second skin. I had no energy, no motivation, but Father Lambert's words were quoted back to us. Exercise was good for the soul. The mutated bodies of the slovenly Otherlanders were described to us in graphic detail as a deterrent for our laziness. The sessions were as much a part of our day as lessons from the Great Book and hearing about the history of the island. Our future roles required us to be fit and strong, be it for the demands of child-rearing, or physical labour in the crofts or the harbour.

The usual laps of exercise were to the stone wall and back. Crescent passed me, smiling as she went.

'You know it passes quicker if you run!' She poked out her tongue.

I puffed air into my cheeks in response, watching her plough on ahead. I hardly took walks with my grandmother any more; she was too tired, too weak to make it any further than the Sunday service. I opted to stay indoors or visit the church, threw myself into tireless chores, rejecting offers to visit Barrett or go anywhere close to the sea. I had avoided the harbour for years. Slowly but surely I was wringing any curiosity for the water out of my system.

I concentrated on my feet on the ground, not wanting to make a fool of myself by tripping, but when I stopped to catch my breath, I saw a group of older boys catching up to Crescent, crowding in behind. The changes in her body already remarked upon in church by Father Jessop. I remembered the pink in her cheeks, in mine, when he drew attention to her, saying, 'What a good sign to see our young girls budding into women.' I knew what he meant. She already had ample breasts, child-bearing hips.

The way the boys moved across the grass shoved anyone else out of the way. Crescent turned her head back, seeing them swarm around her. I watched as she tried to speed up, tried to sidestep them and take another path, but she was surrounded. I looked towards Mull, who was also watching Crescent's movements. She gave me a faint smile. Did she not have the same stomach flip that I had? It was clear that this was becoming a chase, a pursuit that we were all observers to, and yet none of us tried to catch up with her. Neither did any of the boys outside of the pursuing five; no attempt to rescue her from their attentions. Part of me was just relieved they hadn't joined in, hadn't been hungry for the same thrill the others sought. I saw Doran's brother had stayed back again, his sweat-dark hair falling into his eyes.

The group jostled each other, laughing and making comments we couldn't hear. I had ground to a halt as I searched for a teacher. One of the boys leered close enough to stroke Crescent's hair, and it came loose from its neat tie. The boys circled in, cormorants double her size. There were too many of them for me to see what they were doing, but I imagined them touching her, testing her, and the hairs on the back of my neck rose.

A few unbearable seconds passed before we heard the handbell ring, the teacher standing under the school's shelter oblivious to what had passed. My heart pounded in relief as the boys dispersed, sprinting back inside and leaving Crescent trailing behind. I tried to stay back and catch her eye in some kind of apologetic solidarity, but her gaze remained averted for the rest of the afternoon, her bright pink skin cooling as we returned to lessons. All those years after I had helped fill the font, complicit in her head being held underwater, I had not shaken the guilt.

The rest of the day I was distracted by the sounds of the schoolroom, the scrape of a chair, a laugh from upstairs. When I heard a male voice, it took hold of me, top and tail. I wondered what they might do to her the next time we were outside. The light diminished from the window; it was almost time to go home, and I had sudden images of them following her when she was alone. My knuckles were white around the edge of the desk.

I watched on the sidelines as they taunted Crescent across the next three days. I watched them touch her breasts and laugh, saying, 'How else do you expect us to find a wife?' Other boys looked on like they were taking lessons.

All the teachers were women, and like us, they were afraid of what might be reported, where the blame would fall. It was expected of those boys. They were exerting their authority; playing at being men. Their hunger was only natural, it said so in our doctrine. But reading it from the Great Book and witnessing it for myself was a different matter.

When Crescent missed a day of school, I was almost grateful she'd been spared. But when she returned, she didn't even try to run during our exercise session. As I caught up with her, hoping that with two of us the group would stay away, I saw she was crying.

'What's happened?' I asked; then quieter, 'What have they done?'

I reached for her hand, but she held it away.

'You shouldn't be around me,' she said, and ran off, distancing herself from everyone, not saying a word.

Later in the day, I heard her name whispered behind hands, and in the hallway a word I'd never heard before. *Whore*. The intent of it landed like it had been meant for me, for all of us. I caught snatches of rumour, but it was Mull who was the first to tell me what had happened, grimacing and choosing her words carefully. It was a Saturday before we began cleaning, and Crescent was nowhere to be seen.

'You haven't heard? She's been putting her mouth ... on the private parts of the older boys.' Her voice was so quiet I thought I imagined it.

Whore. Dirty slut.

'Who has?'

Her eyes widened. 'Crescent.'

'No.' All heat drained out of me and what remained felt like grief.

'It's true. These boys want to be Ministers; they wouldn't lie about something like this.'

'Who was it? Which boy?' I asked, stomach turning.

Mull took my arm, leaning right into my ear. She was tearful. 'It was all of them. She did it to all of them.'

'She wouldn't. You saw how they were with her.'

'She's already confessed.'

I pictured Father Jessop's hand on the back of Crescent's head, her whole body thrashing. What would happen to her now? As the days passed, I grew sick at the thought of what the boys had done, knowing that whatever confession Crescent had given, it couldn't be the truth. She stopped coming to school, and taken to live with the Eldermothers. Her father had sent her there, worried that her reputation would tarnish business at his bakery. For the boys, Crescent was history; the thrill of the chase had stopped. They needed a new target.

Spring came, and a full blister of a moon appeared on the deep blue sky. Another year's festival arrived, and with it a shift of excitement. But for me, the idea of a big party didn't sit comfortably. Crescent was back in class, but she sat alone, her reputation shattered. Her father had even started giving his bread away. After her confession, word spread that she'd admitted everything to Father Jessop, confirming the boys' version of events. She'd been possessed by unnatural lusts, but we were assured that whatever influence the Seawomen had had over her had been cleansed from her. Those demons were gone.

In a moment of vulnerability, I had confided in Mull my reluctance towards the festival.

'It doesn't feel right to sing and dance and have a good time, not after all that bad luck.'

'That's exactly why we should be celebrating! To show them the power of God, our strength.'

And she was right in some ways; the familiar sight of the festival in full flow did lift my mood. It centred around a market in the churchyard. Sellers with baskets of handmade goods, everything from soaps and oils to pies and hats. Tents of food. Collective prayer. Puppet shows for children. Pipe players whistled familiar tunes, newborn babies were cooed over. It was bustling when I arrived with my grandmother. She'd been too tired to dig that year and sell her own offerings, so had a basket of blankets for sale instead of muddied root vegetables. We walked past the maypole, the bonfire, where the young boys chased, losing themselves between the legs of the adults. They screamed without being told to be quiet or slow down. The festival always unleashed a release like that. My grandmother and I took in big smoky breaths. As I looked around, I began to feel grateful again, the joy in our saved community.

Through the fog of bonfire smoke came wafts of food and drink, sweet dumplings and turnip pottage, ale and damson wine. Musicians and storytellers, dancers gathering crowds, all eager to be reminded of how Eden's Isle began. Alongside the drifting folk songs, my grandmother led me towards a fish stall manned by Franklin and his three sons. At the front of the stand, Franklin took orders and collected money, while Doran stirred soup and his brothers divided their time descaling and loading fried fish into bowls of paying customers. I kept my head down, thinking of Crescent. Thinking of the glee on Doran's face when she had stopped coming to school.

There was a clatter, a bowl dropped.

'Ingram!' Franklin shouted. I jumped out of my skin, looking up. 'Clean it up, you clumsy bastard!'

Ingram scrambled, mumbling his apology, as Doran and his older brother, Weir, laughed, their elbows knocking together.

I turned away, focused on a dance happening behind us. A man and woman taking on the roles of sailor and Seawoman, him mesmerised by the lines of her body, the ways she was woman and the ways she was not. He put his mouth to her breast, his hand on the slip of costume scales, her would-be tail. There was a frisson of feeling in my body between my legs, at the sight of the contact. I tried to do what we were told: to resist and ignore. But I could not stop watching the dance, engrossed by the familiar tale, the way it would end in the sailor's victory, the power of God. Ahead of us in the queue were three patrol ferrymen, glad of a night off. With the ferries anchored out at sea, their glow hovered in the water, warning the Seawomen to stay away.

'Peace be to the land,' my grandmother greeted Franklin when we arrived at the front of the queue.

'And to you,' he said. 'What'll it be?'

I silently begged my grandmother to ask for anything but soup, but she clung to the same traditions year after year.

'Two soups, Doran. Quickly,' Franklin relayed her request.

I saw Doran look up, flushed, his moustache limp under his nose like a fish. He caught me staring and smirked.

After we ate, finding somewhere to sit among the noise and heat, and the push of drunken bodies, the band jolted to life playing a tune that seemed to merry everyone to a louder volume. Fishermen sang shanties that boasted of fish they'd caught, Seawomen they'd slaughtered. They banged pots with sticks, pans with spoons. The bigger the noise, the more we weren't afraid. I spotted Mull in the crowd, and my grandmother, too tired to move, told me to go and enjoy myself.

Seeing me, Mull grabbed my hand, pulling me from stall to stall, collecting food and treats as we went. Curd fried in butter, potato pies, blackcurrant jam on hot cakes. The glee on her face shook the tension from my shoulders. I wanted to borrow it, if only temporarily.

We were walking the stalls, Mull wanting to watch one of the ritualistic games childless women played for luck, when she spotted Father Jessop.

'Daddy!' She threw her arms around him. Behind him the drumming simmered and the crowds bowed their heads in respect, excited to be celebrating alongside him. This was just the beginning. Later there would be his speech and service, an array of women and their good deeds celebrated, where they were honoured and protected. Later he would come to one of the favourite moments of the night, when announcements of marriage were made, young men and woman standing by the bonfire and matched together with God's blessing.

'Peace to the island, Father,' I said.

'And to you, Esta. Are you enjoying the festivities?'

'Very much.'

He smiled, giving Mull's cheek a stroke. He breathed in, chest expanding, and took a glance around us. 'God's blessing really resonates on a night like tonight, doesn't it? If our ancestors were here to see this now! Life as He intended, thriving! How fortunate we are to be here.'

With the light from the fire, it was as if God was shining on him too that night. His smile, the moonlight glittering his hair. Later, in the churchyard, he would kiss the foreheads of young girls, bestowing them with luck.

When Father Jessop left to greet other islanders, Mull and I became separated. Perhaps I lingered too long at the jewellery tent; perhaps she had seen someone else she knew and skipped off to celebrate with them, and I'd been too distracted to see where she'd gone. I looked for her, stretching up onto my toes, trying to find a higher vantage point, dodging the spills of carrot liquor and drunken jeering. I looked for that flash of golden-brown hair, but there was no sign.

I was close to giving up, wanting to return to my grandmother and find a place near the front of the service, eager to feel God again, the promise of the night's ultimate protection. I needed Father Jessop's reassurance more than ever. But then my heart stopped in my chest. Doran and his friends, gathered a few feet away, conspiring, scouting the crowd. They had drinks in their hands, snarling, laughing between themselves. My insides hollowed. I had to get away. I thought how easy it was to lose someone at the festival, the chaos and noise – so much could slip through the cracks on a night when everyone's focus was on having a good time.

'Esta! Hey – Esta, is it?' They shouted for me.

I shrank, turned on my heel, ducked to push through the throng.

'Hey . . . wait for us!'

I tried to keep my head down, to focus on a way out, my feet stumbling on the uneven cobble where wild grass sprouted. I knew, even though I didn't – couldn't – look behind me, that they were following me. On a night like the festival, with everyone gathered on the church land, there was no place to run to, no croft house with a buttery glow from its windows, no door I could knock on. I could have hid myself deeper in the crowds, but they'd still be close behind. No one would help me, any noise I made, any fear I had would be lost, mistaken for jubilation.

I kept moving but I had no real plan. If I got home, when my grandmother returned I'd tell her I'd felt unwell and left early. But I wasn't thinking of excuses then, I wasn't thinking at all. Just moving. Nobody noticing. None of them sensing anything in the way I pushed through them. The words running through my mind. *Whore. Dirty slut.*

One older man shouted after me, noticing my escape from the festival, not seeing the boys following me.

'Oi, girl – where you headed?'

I looked back, stretching a dry smile. 'Peace be to the land.'

'An' you,' he called. I didn't take another look to see if he shrugged and turned away, back to his drink, back to his celebration.

I could see them, feel them. The snickering, the low voices attempting to hush themselves, crept across my neck. I snuck a look behind as I got further from the festival gathering and saw them, the same boys who'd harassed Crescent.

I quickened my pace, trying to keep my steps looking brisk and natural to hide the need I had to run. There was no hiding from them, there was no detour that could confuse them and let me sneak away. They smelt blood. They were behind me, thudding on the path, closing the gap between us.

Eight

I ran. Along overgrown banks of gorse, down the flanks of wild grass where the ground was pitted and treacherous with rabbit holes and rocks. I caught a glimpse of Doran behind me; it felt like he was being deliberately slower than he could be. Was it a test to see how far I was prepared to run? To anyone watching, we were kids playing. They were laughing, roaring and purple with it. No one would have seen me and worried. Not on the night of the festival.

I spotted the abandoned lighthouse in the distance, locked up with nowhere to hide, and I climbed down the cliff, into the cove, towards the dark tumble of rocks and stacks, boots slippery and hands bleeding, knees scraping the rough edges of stone. I was surprised how much of my surroundings I could see, the moon and patrol lights giving me hope that I could get away. Even with a lifetime of warnings about the water, the danger within us, that was nothing like the fear of the boys getting closer.

My destination didn't stop them like I'd hoped it would. I was closer to the water than anyone would have wanted to go. But where else to hide? I could hear their shouts, rasping in the cold, as I looked for somewhere to conceal myself. The moonlight made my skin metallic. A brief fantasy came to me, sharp as a pinprick, of the boys scared stiff at the image of me. To them I would have looked like a Seawoman. For a moment, my body empty of breath, I was delirious and empowered by the thought. The hunger I felt for watching them suffer caught me off guard, and I tried immediately to suppress it, deny it as a light-headed passing. I blamed the thought on being too close to the sea, its bewitching proximity.

I tried to focus on what adults said about the older boys, how we should humour their spirits. Chasing was in their nature. Of course they were interested in us, our bodies – we were to be their future wives, mothers of their children. I knew that a desire for sex, for power, prowled within them.

But I'd seen what they'd done to Crescent and I didn't want it.

I could hear them, saw the points of their shadows peer over the cliff edge, shouting so I would hear it.

'Maybe she drowned!'

'With any luck!'

'Or her friends took her back where she belongs!'

More laughter came, vicious and cawing. I pressed my spine against the cold firm of the cliff walls, praying to God that they would leave me and He would save me. I needed Him more than ever.

Above me, it went quiet. I imagined them thinking I'd tried to hide in the nooks of the old lighthouse, going there but finding nothing. I should have known better.

I saw them: five dark insects grappling down the cliff steps towards me.

'There she is! Esta!'

It was Doran who called my name, extending the sound like I was a stray animal that needed rescuing from a wire fence. He twisted the tone, saying it again so it sounded playful, teasing, like I was in on the game.

'Estaaa!'

They had me penned in, all taller, all stronger than I was. I backed away, my boots sinking into softened wet sand. There was no way out, nowhere to climb, nowhere to run to where they wouldn't catch me first. The wind was circling the cove, tendrils of my hair whipping into my eyes, making it hard to see. They laughed when I stumbled, but when I corrected my stance, it only made me step faster. Towards nothing but sea. Wide and dark and clawing.

'What are you doing all the way down here, Esta?' one of the other boys cooed. He was more muscular than Doran, had a head as round as an egg.

'On festival night too!'

'We only wanted to say hello,' Doran said, white breath spurting out of his grin.

'Yeah, just to celebrate with you.'

Their bodies blocked out the light of the moon. I took a step further back, the tide tonguing the heel of my boots. As they moved, my body's reflex was to take another step away from them. Now the water lapped as far up as my ankles, and the chill jolted through my chest. One of the five nudged the boy next to him, pointing downwards. I was in the water, shins wet. It was their turn to take a step back. They breathed out a sharp noise of surprise.

Doran, however, didn't show any of the hesitation that the rest of the group wore. His teeth were bared. The battle became about the two of us alone, and the rest of the boys disappeared from my vision. I looked straight into his eyes and took another step back, and another, not stopping until the water was pushing and pulling around my thighs. I wanted him to see I wasn't going to stop. This was for Crescent, for me, for the next girl they might try it with.

Doran lurched forward, his features squinting with focus. He wanted to chase me deeper, until the water rose above my neck. One of the other boys took his arm and wrenched him back. I saw the expression on his spooked face. He looked like he could see the future – what I was, what would become of me.

'Doran! Come back now!'

'Leave her!'

The others in the group had widened the distance, but Doran was unmoving, glaring at me from the water's edge. I spread my arms and waded further out, a backwards walk of pretend steadiness. I watched the shore, the dark ridge of island, watched as the boys became smaller. Two of them, one on each side of Doran, tried to pull him away. But he was transfixed, hungry for the end. My heart thrashed in the cold terror of the waves against my chest, the ground loose under my feet, but I kept on, watching as one by one the boys ran, scrambling to climb back up the cliffs. The words they left in the air stayed with me.

What is she?!

Doran was the last to relent, the most stubborn of the group, taking one final look at me, the water, what I was, what I was doing, looking like he was about to vomit. I watched him kick up the stones under his feet.

He fled. Finally I was alone.

It had been years since that first time in the water. I had forgotten how cold, how fast, how deep. That first time, there'd been the safety of daylight, and Mull to rescue me from the sea's grip. Now, there was nothing left but the pull of the water, begging at my feet. Tiptoed and unsteady, I tried to find resistance, to push down and use stones as my anchor.

My chest felt tight and my prayers too weak. My arms flailed against the direction of the pull, trying to find something to steer me back to land, but the ice of it rooted around my spine, numbing me powerless, scooping me backwards instead, into the drag of the tide. I was losing the fight. Fulmars overhead swooped and dived, laughing at my struggle. But as they disappeared into my periphery, a flash of wing and flight, my thoughts rolled into something darker, my stomach convulsing, convinced that soon, surely, something worse would come for me, my helpless body drifting further into the pit of darkness. I looked behind me, at the glow of the patrols. No one was there to save me.

I gasped for air, holding onto it like it might be my last. I didn't know how to coordinate my limbs, how to float. All I was doing was making it worse, frothing up the tide with my kicking and pushing, taking fistfuls of salt water as though that would pull me right.

Then something changed. It felt at first as if I was being coiled, wrapped in wide ribbons of weed, but then I knew it was different, warm. Hands. There were hands around my waist. I was too delirious to fight, starved of comprehension. I saw movement in front of me, my brain catching a flash of silver and believing God had sent the moon to save me. The moon with hands would save me. I wanted to kiss it in thanks. But as my mind became clearer in a rush of relief, I saw a body, a man's body, muscular and naked, fast and writhing. Not the moon, but a man. I was pulled against him, solid, slick and firm, those same hands tighter around my waist and one of my legs hooked. This was a body that knew the water; this was someone who could swim. A man from another place. As he held me, fighting against my struggle, I knew this was it. The darkness had come for me. I slumped, expecting to be dragged to the bottom of the sea. Resigned, I clung, sea-urchin suckered against this body, hands finding skin and scales. This was my fate, the slow twisting of my body against his underwater.

But then, everything cold and wet and fast and not down but upwards we went, together, suspended in time until the pressure of the surface broke, head and shoulders and mouth finally finding air.

This was not the story I knew. This was where it all began to fall apart.

I was still clinging to him, to a body I couldn't make sense of, to a situation that didn't fit. To the thing that had saved me from drowning. All I could focus on was trying to stay alive. The air that found my lungs was patchy and spluttered, coughing salt water and bile into the sea below.

'Steady. Breathe,' I heard a voice say, different to the voices I knew; something musical, like a jangle of wind through an open window, the low brush of a calm tide on the shore.

I was confused, could have invented his instruction, but I followed it anyway, remembering how to feel, remembering the up and down of my chest, the in and out of breath without the fear of taking in water. I was so focused on breathing that I didn't have space in my thoughts to wonder who he was, why he had saved me. We were moving again. This time my cradled body moved with him, with the rhythm of the water, not against it, free, not a prisoner of the sea's control. We weren't moving deeper into the sea's grip, but out of it, where the tide was calmer, back to land. But still uncertain, still delirious, I kept my eyes closed as if it was some fragile dream that could be broken and I'd be back there in the cold and the dark again, drowning.

I kept my eyes shut until we'd moved out of the water, until I felt the solid mass of sand and stone under my feet, collapsing exhausted onto it, my dress clinging to me like the wet pelt of an animal. Everything was stinging and bleary, my eyes raw with salt. When I opened them finally, he was a dark shadow against the night. Nameless then, but when I think of that first glimpse now, his name rides through my body. Like waking from death. A gasping heartbeat.

I was grounded, away from the sea, his hands still around my waist from lifting me out, but my clothes and skin were so wet all I could do was shiver, feeling as hard and exposed as a sea-spat pebble. I concentrated on trying to breathe again, feeling delusional and sick.

When I was brave enough to look at him, he came to me in pieces, ethereal and confusing as a dream. In the light, both of us were moon-skinned and grey, but he had a sheen to him. I'd never seen a man's body before, but I'd heard girls talk. I knew he had what other men did. I looked quickly away from the parts of him only a wife should see, heat rushing to my face. I looked at him, stalling, creeping, like entering a lightless room. He was a man. But he wasn't. He had skin, and scales. There were gills on his neck, fluttering.

And his face. His face. So close to human. I pushed at the stones to scramble backwards.

'No! Get away from me!'

His eyes widened, head tilting and revealing more of his angular face in the light. I gripped the largest stone I could reach.

'Back! Get back!'

The sea roared behind him. His hair was pale and slick to his head, a confused curve to his mouth, which was as full and delicate as a woman's. He looked about my age and I wondered what those eyes of his had seen. I shunted backwards to try and get away from him.

'I'm not going to hurt you!' he said, hands raised.

'Monster!' I gasped, breath erratic, teeth clenched. I swung at him. I was nowhere near touching him. He gripped my wrist, shook the stone from my hand. I was winded by shock. I opened my mouth to scream, not thinking of the consequences, not thinking about what could happen if I was found alone with a creature like him. He put his webbed hand across my mouth. I tried to gnash my teeth, bite him, but he held firm.

'Stop! Stop! Quiet!' he said, hushing me. 'There's someone up there!' He was looking up at the cliffs. His face was so near I could smell the whole ocean on him. He was terrified.

He loosened his grip. I looked around wildly for somewhere to hide. Time seemed to split in two. Half of me was running, screaming from the creature and back up the cliff. The other was spinning, alive, barely recovered, water reverberating in my head, looking at this strange half-man, questions stacking up behind my teeth and fearing the boys who'd tried to drown me. The creature's expression was so human in his raw fear, something in my gut kicked in, instinctive that it united us. If they came back and found us like this, we'd both be dead. They were moving fast. I heard them getting louder, shouts blending and indecipherable.

'She'll be drowned by now.'

'Not if she's one of them.'

'We've got this in case!'

'A harpoon! Do you even know how to use it?'

'We'll be surrounded!'

'We can take them all out with this.'

'Someone needs to go back to the festival and tell the Keepers. The Ministers. Anyone!'

'I'm going to see for myself,' Doran said. His voice rose unmistakably over the others.

'We'll never be Ministers if Father Jessop finds out.'

'Hey, Doran, slow down!'

This wasn't happening to me. It couldn't be. I was paralysed, listening to them get closer. The voices grew louder as they shouted at each other, three of them deciding to check if I'd drowned, and if I hadn't, to finish the job before anything worse happened.

'Who are they?' my rescuer asked, eyes darting up to the noise, moving his hand away from my mouth but still hovering close.

I was frozen in an endless cycle of an impossible choice – the gang or the sea. Them or him. I felt like a child, wanting the sand to swallow me, for someone else to make the decision. I expected the stranger to dive back into the water, disappearing like a trick of light. Was he thinking the same thoughts I was? The boys charging forward with rocks and harpoons. He didn't move, looking between me and the sea. I imagined us torn apart, slaughtered, our bodies hung on hooks in the churchyard for all to see. Him a monster, me the same in their eyes.

'They're coming for you,' he said, realisation dawning as he took in the sight of my shaking body. He held out his eely hand, the same hand that had rescued me, an imploring look on his face. 'There's no time,' he said. 'There are caves, along the coast. We can hide.'

I looked down at his hand, then up at the approaching mob.

'What are you?'

'Come with me or wait for them. It's your choice.'

Nine

I took the creature's hand, gripped it, cool and wet. I looked left and right, then out to sea. Nowhere else to go.

'We'll have to swim, it's the quickest way,' he said. 'I'll take you.' He pulled me to my feet.

'Where?' I asked, urgent. I struggled, swaying into him, caught at the waist. I wasn't ready yet. It was too late to do anything else.

'They're coming!'

'Just hold your breath.'

The stranger pulled me against him, holding me in the same way as he had done before, and back we went to the mercy of the sea. The icy water chopped straight into me, and I closed my eyes again, surrendering into our escape. The pull of the tide and the pull of him dragging me through the water, the unbearable cold that made it seem like I'd never be warm again. My thoughts fled my body as if I was about to die.

He took me to the caves, edging round the rough shape of the island's crag, both of us hidden in shadow. They were partially filled with water, and once we were inside and he placed me down, I had to climb up to a ledge to escape it. Even there, the water was up to my legs, the pull strong around my knees. Before long, these caves would fill.

The deeper we went, the darker, more endless and hopeless it felt. Anxiety gnawed at my chest, convinced it was a mistake to be there, that I should have left the stranger and run. Yet I couldn't bear the thought of the alternative. I was trapped there with him and I had no choice, no control over what happened next.

I felt him move away, and my ears swilled with blood, relief that he wasn't taking me somewhere deep and dark to slit my throat. But then a voice in my head: *he still might.*

'We'll hide out here until they're gone,' he said, almost answering my doubts. He was regaining his breath like I was.

I leant my back against the cave wall, gripping onto the ledge. The cave was so dark it was like being blind. I turned my cheek against the rock face, whimpering, echoing in a wet and desperate loop. The water could rise in here and then what? I couldn't even see my way out.

'Who are they?' he said through the dark. 'I saw them chase you into the water.'

I couldn't answer, and I sensed him somewhere close, like there was a pulse of him trying to reach out and touch me.

'Don't – don't come any closer.'

He had held me, taken me to safety, but I couldn't stand the thought of being near him, not knowing what he was, how long he'd been in the water, watching. He had to be from the dark sea; there was no other explanation for him.

There was light coming through the opening of the cave. I turned my face towards it, looking across the water to the cove. From here, I'd be able to see the boys if they came close, carrying their weapons. What if they could see me, smell me? And what if they caught me with *him*?

He moved toward the opening, the bulk of his body blocking out the light.

'No!' I called, then quieter, 'Don't!' I thought of those boys' eyes and what they might do.

He moved away from the entrance, back into the dark. Outside, the shouting continued, the noise putting a block between me and him, the questions circling my head.

There was a jagged bank of rocks leading from the cove towards our hiding spot. It would take nerve, careful balance and a slow pace, but was that enough to stop them? They gave instructions to each other, dividing up, looking for me in the water.

'Who are you?' I asked the creature, my voice low and nervy. I couldn't push it. I could only guess what he was capable of.

I braced myself for his answer, to have my fears rise all over again. The question was feeble, not even close to asking everything I wanted to know, barely exposing how overwhelmed I was by the unknown.

'Cal,' he said, his gentle voice revealing a secret. 'My name's Cal.'

A name. It made him real, it made him almost a person. Not just a monstrous creature that I had endless questions about, but a man too, with thoughts and a history and secrets like me. When he spoke in the blackness of the cave, he was a disembodied voice, a shape in the dark.

I didn't want to tell him my name, in case the exchange made our worlds closer, so I dug again, for more answers. 'Where are you from?'

'The water,' he said.

'Where?'

'All over. Anywhere I choose.'

'Esta!' they called from outside, my name becoming a chorus of demands.

'Esta!'

'Estaaa!'

'Did they hurt you?' Cal asked, close and quiet. In his voice was something else, a twinge of worry. The risk for him was just as great.

'I'm fine.' The words came out like two hands pushing him away.

The voices outside the cave seemed to be getting nearer, loud and drunk. Some of their shouts were slurred, but it was always Doran I heard the clearest; his words alone had a way of getting through.

'I'm not leaving here until we find her!' He'd made it across the rocks. He was near the cave, voice echoing. The others had moved away and were searching another part of the beach.

I exhaled, resting my head, staring into nothingness above.

'Esta!' Doran called my name again, ever closer.

I felt a movement in the dark space, Cal pushing past me. I reached out to stop him this time, fingers grabbing, and there was contact, skin to scales, my hand on his shoulder, the force of my fear against his fury, his courage.

The light in the entrance of the cave dimmed. I could smell him. Doran was there, risking the water up to his thighs, striding into the dark. Cal eased us back.

'Esta . . . I know you're in here.' Doran's call echoed as he plundered deeper into the darkness. A chill ran up my spine. I heard him move through the water, speaking to himself in frustration at not having found me. 'Fucking Seawoman! Maybe she did drown.'

He made his way back to the rocks.

Cal and I stayed, breath ratcheting, neither of us moving until we were sure he was completely gone. We played our own game of dead silence, held firm against the cave walls, begging the boys to leave. The time felt endless, both of us saying nothing, his nervous breath rushing across the back of my neck. I held my arms around my body for warmth, wanting all of this to go away.

'Are they gone?' He sounded as scared as I was.

'I don't want to look.'

He was quiet for a moment. 'Did you hear them? What they said?'

'Yes.'

'Why were they chasing you?

I couldn't let myself answer.

'Your heart's racing,' he said.

I could feel it, thumping against my chest. I put my hand there to dampen the sound.

'That's how I heard you before, through the water.' He paused to explain. 'I can hear things you can't. It's a sensitivity. It's how I know if there's any danger in the water. Predators. Boats. Fishermen.'

My head fogged with questions again. What else could he hear? My thoughts? The way my whole body trembled?

'You could hear me underwater?'

'I heard you drowning,' he said, and I shuddered. This was what Father Jessop meant when he talked about the way humanity had changed, mutated into something ugly, against God.

'But why you were there in the first place?' I asked.

He hushed me again as a splashing noise sounded from outside.

We listened to the dripping roof, the resettling sounds of our breath, paying attention to every noise. When Doran had stepped into the cave, what I'd felt was primal fear, sharper than when I started to think about who Cal was.

I looked out towards the entrance of the cave. They were still out there on the peninsula of rocks, waiting. What if they stayed all night?

What then? Could I wait it out in the cave, water rising, trapped with this creature? Did I have a choice?

'I need to get out of here,' I said. 'The water, it's . . . If they don't leave and it rises any higher . . .'

'There must be somewhere else we can hide,' he said.

'If we leave the cave, they'll see us straight away.'

I felt him move away.

'What are you doing?'

'Seeing if there's another way out. A passage, another cave, somewhere the rock has eroded.'

As he searched, moving around the walls of the cave, our bodies came into accidental contact again. I felt light-headed, like the sickness of standing up too fast.

I could only hear and imagine him. I thought of him away from our island. How many caves had he explored? How many times had he needed somewhere to hide? When he rose from the water with a splash, the boys' voices outside felt distant, and I found the courage to speak again.

'You've been here before. To our island.'

He didn't give me an answer. All I had was the drumbeat of my own flailing courage.

I tried again. 'I saw you. Years ago. I know I did.' The silvery sheen, the boy's face. An impossible sight. We'd seen each other, our eyes had met, and it had scared me away from ever wanting to go near the water again.

He said nothing; there was just the sound of him moving, hunting for a way out.

I had to get him to listen. 'Cal!' The shock of his name on my tongue spread through me like claws. It was like having power to finally use it.

'Once before,' he said, finally.

My stomach twisted. 'Why?'

'If it hadn't been for you drowning, I'd never have come so close to a place like this!'

My heart lost its rein. 'Are you . . . ?'

'Am I what?'

I was a child, blankets pulled up over my chin, toes curled, nightmares outside the window, frothing in the sea beyond, sleepless at the thought of them coming to get me.

'Going to hurt me?'

I couldn't see him, but I had the feeling he was standing still, watching me. 'I had the chance, didn't I? To drown you. To eat you. Or whatever it is you think I might do.'

I put my hands over my face, fingers pressing against my eyelids to stop myself crying.

'They chased you into the sea, knowing you'd drown,' he said.

'I had to run where I knew they wouldn't follow. They thought they had me trapped, that I wouldn't dare go in the water. Because as soon as a girl goes near—'

Distracted, I lost my grip on the uneven ledge, slipping into the water below. My arms flailed, my scream lost to the sea's clutches, my head disappearing underwater.

I struggled to the surface again, reaching out for him. Coughing.

I felt his hand first, groping for mine, then it was his arms lifting me up.

'What if they heard me?'

'They're gone. I checked,' he said; then, more reassuring, something I felt in my chest, 'They're gone.'

My breath was shaky against him, his body strangely warm. His hands shifted around my waist and I thought how easy it would be for him to drown me like he was something from our stories.

'Are there . . . others, like you? Men with gills and . . .' I tightened at the thought. I could see the scene unfolding, our men and theirs. Sharp blades and hungry mouths. But the men I pictured hunting him wore faces like Doran and the others, faces I never wanted to see again.

'Somewhere, maybe,' he said. It sounded weary, lonely. He hesitated, face turned towards the cave entrance. 'Do you think it's a trap?'

'I don't know,' I said, wishing it wasn't a possibility.

'What are they like?'

'Cruel.'

'Are all your men here like this?'

I wanted to deny it, but all I could picture was the way everyone had turned against Crescent, even her own family.

I could feel Cal considering me. Through the dark I tried to look at him again. There were no hard lines between where the man of him began and the creature ended, skin and scales and gills blended as if they had always been made to form a body together. Like that was the natural way of things. He was no trick, no costume.

'I'm going to have to help you swim out of the cave,' he said, peering through the narrow entrance.

I could see where he was looking, the water too high for us to clamber our way back to the peninsula.

'I'll go first,' he said. 'But take my hand and I'll pull you through.'

'You can't let go. I don't know what to do.'

'I've never met a girl from an island who can't swim.'

My head spun with the prospect of it. The thought was frightening. Exhilarating. If I'd known how, I could've escaped Doran without a second thought. Cal had seen so much. Other islands, other women. Women in the water, girls who could swim, who knew how to manipulate their bodies to make it easy. I was the abnormality to him.

He turned me to face him. I could make out his eyes in the light. We were level.

'Take a deep breath, stretch your lungs as far as you can. And when you're under, kick your legs, keep your toes pointed down. Trust me. Just do what I've told you and you'll be fine.'

He moved me towards the jagged entrance, so I had something to hold onto. I clung on. I wanted to be out of the cave, where the white moon was making everything glow. I watched him go under, then turn back around in the entrance to find my hand.

'Ready?'

I wasn't, but I took his hand and breathed in as deeply as I could, just as he'd told me. It was only seconds underwater, but it was different this time. I kicked like he'd said, brittle at first, then fluid, gliding. I had my eyes closed, so all the sensation was confined to a motion, smooth, fast and dizzying, until the surface ripped and I was back in the air again. It had all happened so fast. Eyes wide open and I felt a rush, my head pointed to the stars, catching my breath.

I rested my hands on Cal's shoulders, drinking him in: his strangeness, the iridescence of his skin in the moonlight. The euphoria of swimming to safety made everything strange, beautiful. His gills, so delicate, shifting like eyelids. He wore a coin pendant around his neck and it disappeared under the surface. The water rippled out around us as we stopped, and I trusted it enough to look at the sea, at him. I was surprised that I didn't feel any desperation to be back on land. Cal was watching me carefully, saying nothing. I swallowed, trying to find the words. He seemed to sense that I needed a moment suspended, away from the island where the boys had hunted.

We climbed over the rocks and I was first to the land, so I reached out to help him, my hand rough and gritty around his. I saw a look of surprise cross his face. Both of us were on edge, keeping watch over the headland, jumpy at every noise. I expected him to disappear as soon as I was back on land, but as I wrung salt water from my skirt and hair, he lingered. I saw his eyes take in my scarring. I tried to look at him when I didn't think he would notice, as if just by looking I could solve the questions plaguing me. The unease in my chest fighting something else. Being on land again, the island's power beneath my feet. It was a reminder of who I was, why I was there. The life God had set out for all of us.

'You should go now, in case anyone sees you,' I said.

He didn't move; he was thinking of something else. 'You said you'd seen me before?' It came out like a question.

'A long time ago.'

'I remember it,' he said, then softer, 'You.'

On land, it was different, seeing him out of place. Something wrong and unnatural. My deep-set fears caught up with me. I was uneasy that he remembered me, the haunting of my past sins.

'You can't stay here,' I said.

'Before. You were in the water when you saw me. A little girl in the water.' His words took me back there, made me twist with discomfort.

'I need to go.'

'Weren't you?'

I pulled the heavy wet of my dress away from my body. The weight of it was a reminder of everything I'd done wrong. Everything I'd have to scrub from my skin when I got home. 'No, I—'

'Strange place for a girl who can't swim.'

'I was only there by mistake.'

'You looked right at me. I remember your face.'

I stood still, the breeze picking up and my skin stiffening with the cold. Mull and I had been in this exact spot, rubbing ourselves warm, tears streaming in the shock. I'd told her there was nothing out there. And after a time I'd been sure that I'd invented it. The sea's trick. But here he was, standing in front of me, the thing I'd been so afraid of.

'I was curious. That was all it was.'

'Of what?'

'It doesn't matter.'

'Tell me?' He was gently prising me open.

'The water,' I said, wiping the guilty tears before they had a chance to fall. 'I wanted to be in the water. I wanted to swim, to be a part of it. To go somewhere else.'

'You talk about it like it's the worst crime in the world.'

'It is. Here.'

'Why?'

'The water is where the darkness lies.'

'You mean . . . the Devil?'

'The Seawomen.' I looked at him, breathless in my admission of my forbidden desires, but he was still. 'I thought if I was just in the water for a moment, I'd be okay, that nothing bad would happen. Scratch the itch and it would be over. But then I saw something.'

'Me. Your worst fears coming true.' His words were stiff, angry.

The light made both of us blue. I wanted him gone, but I wanted him to tell me all the things I didn't know.

'Run away, then. Like you did before.' He was looking across to the dapple of lights from the patrol ferries. On another night they would have been out there, warning him from getting too close.

'You don't understand.'

'I do. Different worlds. Different monsters.'

I was silent, uncertain of what to say. He had saved me, and yet I couldn't shake the fear of who he was and what he might do to our Salvation by being here.

'Those boys,' he said. 'Will they leave you alone?'

I was surprised by his question. 'I hope so.'

I couldn't bear the thought. Would they fear me or report me? Double their efforts to make me give in to them? It wouldn't take long to collect accusations if they wanted to see me like Crescent.

'And if they come after you again?' He turned back round to face me.

I didn't have an answer; just gave him a sad shrug. He looked between me and the vast expanse of sea. I was sodden. It would be hard for him to understand, to believe I was the same girl who'd spent a lifetime looking away from the cliff edge, praying to keep the water out of my thoughts.

'Are you still afraid?' he said, gesturing to the water.

It seemed like a ridiculous question when I had almost drowned, but knowing how to move through it left me feeling dizzy, powerful. I didn't know if I should be afraid of myself.

'Of the Seawomen?' he added.

I paused. 'Have you . . . do you know them? Have you ever seen them?'

He took a step nearer, and held out one of his hands so it caught the gleam of the moon, the thin webbing looking like misted glass. I watched him inhale, stretching muscle, the scales changing colour in the shifting tension. Above the ribs he was smooth, like sea-worn glass. But so human. A collarbone and a chest, sinews of muscle under his shoulders. I wanted to focus on that.

'What do you think I am?'

It was inevitable, but I wanted so hard to be wrong.

'Your mother . . .' I said, a confirmation rather than a question. I felt sick to ask it.

'She's been gone a long time. Years. But sometimes it feels like I've always been on my own.'

The emptiness he talked about knocked inside me too, but I shook myself. If she was one of *them*, I should have been glad to hear she was gone, one less monster in the world.

'But she was . . . ?'

He nodded.

My eyes were on him, trying to make sense of it. We would have known, we would have been warned if creatures like him existed. Men. There would have been stories and sightings. Pictures of these half-creatures. A bigger threat to God's image of man.

He held his hand closer, encouraging me, showing me proof that he was real. I stretched out my hand in the space between us, touching the membrane between his fingers. It was warm and fragile, smooth as the shells I had coveted. He didn't move, didn't jerk away. We moved cautiously, a form of dance. My hand hovered and I barely breathed when he took my wrist, giving me permission to touch his body, the transformation around his middle, where man met sea. I'd never touched anyone in that way before.

'You can work it out,' he said. 'What do you think happens when a man from the land lies with a Seawoman?'

I pulled my hand away. His touch was poison.

'The Seawomen bewitch men. Drown them,' I said.

'That's just a story.'

The images I had then were of bodies slick and slipping. In the tides, in rock pools and against stacks. I had known desire. I had known what it felt like to want the forbidden. I had felt the same about the water. In his words the two were together intertwined, the water rising, hands sliding. Sex was for marriage, was a sacred act. The water was the opposite, and still they came together in my mind. The thought of it held me tight. The curiosity of desire was shameful, immoral, and yet the seed of the thought was wild and spreading with heat. Everything I thought I knew was collapsing around me. I took a step backwards, hot in the face as if he had slapped me.

'My father lives here. He's one of your kind,' he said. 'I came here to find him.'

Ten

I stared at the black swirl of sea, the life draining away from me. Not one of us, not our men.

'Look at me.'

I was repulsed, pulling away. 'You can't be.'

'You knew it from the moment you met me. Why else would I be here?'

'To hurt us. Watch us. Corrupt us.'

'I didn't hurt you.'

I backed away from him, tripping on stone, arms out to fend him off.

He kept following, kept talking. 'He's here. My father. He had one of your boats. Your way of speaking.' Then, with a bite to his voice, 'Your primitive understanding of humanity.'

'No.' It was all I could say.

He got closer and I pulled back. He'd catch me if I tried to run towards the cliff steps – and what if he continued to follow me?

'His boat capsized. My mother saved him when he was stranded.'

'It's lies. She told you a story, that's all. A children's story.'

'What do you know? You've never seen past your own coastline.'

'I know a man from here would never . . .'

'Then explain this, explain me.'

I couldn't.

His voice quietened. 'You've been living here, away from it all. The world as your men tell it has moved on. We don't all look and think like you.'

Could I imagine, even for a second, that what he said was true? One of God's men betraying us all to lie with a Seawoman and never admitting to his crime? Living on our island, sullying our chances of Salvation? But there was no other explanation for Cal that made sense.

'You could be any man's.'

He unfastened the thread around his neck and held the pendant out, the coin swinging, towards me.

'Take it,' he said. 'It was my father's. It's all I have left of him. The only thing she had, apart from me.'

'What does this prove? You could have stolen it from a wreck.'

'He gave it to my mother before he left.'

I had nothing of my mother apart from a pair of earrings that had been saved from the rubble. I knew his look. I knew what it was like to have just one thing linking to the past, doing little to fill that emptiness.

'Take it!'

I held it in my palm, as light as dust, ran my thumb over the front. A worn outline of a face I knew too well. Dinah's face. On the back was the letter A, scratched into the surface. The kind of pendant that was sold at festivals.

'A for Aria. He did that so it could belong to her.'

Our eyes met. Stayed. My thumb warm on the surface of the coin. I wanted to throw it back at him, accuse him of snatching it from the neck of a corpse, but I could see what it meant to him, the way he held it out to me like it carried his whole life.

'Do you know his name?'

'She wouldn't tell me. She said it was better if I didn't know, if I never came looking for him. She didn't want me to come here.'

I bristled, swallowing down thoughts of his mother, what she was. 'She was right. You should never have come.'

I pushed the pendant back into his hand and sidestepped him to get away. The cold of the sea had reached my blood, leaving me shivering, whimpering. I wanted rid of him and everything he'd told me, everything he'd made me become.

He had no problem catching up with me on the cliff steps. He took my arm, pulling me back. If what he said was true, it meant everything else was a lie.

I wrenched myself free from his grip. There was no use screaming for help.

'Go!' I spoke through gritted teeth.

'I want to know him,' Cal said. He sounded desperate.

'You will drive God from this place.'

'I won't hurt you or anyone else.'

'You being here will destroy us. It'll ruin me. You've no idea!'

I slipped, foot coming away from its purchase in my hurry to get away. I fell, grazing my hands and knees, tearing my dress and bumping my head all at once. I pushed his hand away.

'You're bleeding,' he said. The pain struck me in an instant. I eased back down to level ground, perching on a step, and touched where my head stung. There was blood on my fingers.

'See,' I said, swallowing, trying not to dissolve into more tears. 'Bad things are happening already. You did this!'

'I didn't touch you.'

'You didn't have to. You bring curses with you.'

Now we were out in the full moonlight, there was no question of how different we were. The adrenaline of the water, the darkness, must've tricked me. Any trust I'd had, any curiosity I'd felt was wrong.

'I'm not here for revenge,' he said, answering the question I hadn't asked. 'I need to understand him, how I came to be. With my mother gone . . . I'm half a person. I'm no one. And he must be a different kind of man to have been with her, different to what they say of the men on this island.'

'Who says? What do they say about us?'

We were on holy land, living out God's wishes, preserving God's image. What could he think about us that was perverse?

'When you saw me the first time, I was a boy. Thirteen, just after my mother died. She always made me promise I'd never go looking for him. She was fearless, but when she spoke of this place, she was afraid. She told me the people of this island wouldn't understand what I was; that if they caught me in the water I'd be skinned alive. She said what this place wanted was their idea of purity, humanity as it used to be, to hold back the changes of the rest of the world. She wasn't sure my father would be any different.'

I looked away briefly, struck by the same thought. What kind of man here would welcome a son like Cal?

'But I didn't listen. That missing part of me was too strong a pull, no matter what she said. I remembered what she'd told me, about how well guarded the island was. Patrol boats and knives and nets. Men who would sooner hang me from hooks than listen to who I was. Men who'd look at me like I was some sort of disease.' He paused. 'Am I wrong?'

I shook my head.

'She knew what the island was. Its history and how it had started, how fear had been stoked in their people. But then she told me about when she met my father. That he'd come on a night where the island was busy celebrating – the equinox, the anniversary of driving the Seawomen away; the same festival every year. Music, dancing. She told me what my father had told her. That he'd taken a boat and left. The people were distracted, their guard was lowered.'

'That's why you came tonight. The patrols . . . You knew you could slip through unnoticed.'

'It wasn't much of a plan. I just wanted to know him.'

I watched the wind shift over the water, the rolls of the waves growing. It hadn't felt that rough to be in it, it hadn't felt that far away.

I looked at him again, the way his mouth had softened to something serious and pleading.

'And does he know?' I asked, aware that a man would rather die.

'No. He left her before she even knew she was carrying me.'

I felt the chill, the cuffing of the wind, and had the shiver of my grandmother's damp breath in my ear's whorl. A bedtime story about a cruel-hearted mother who left her children and climbed into a boat, bewitched by the spirits she heard from the water. Mull dismissing each and every one of these tales. No one leaves. Why would they? How could they?

I put my hands on the cliff steps, rising to leave.

'You must have an idea of who he could be. Can't you see something of him in me? Something familiar?'

His words held me back. Could I? Was there a glimpse of recognition hidden there, under everything that made him so different?

'You can't be. You just can't.'

'Please, help me. Like I helped you.'

I was silent, frozen on the steps, feeling him growing frustrated. I screwed my eyes shut, desperate for this all to go away, to return to how things were. He took a pace nearer, bridging the gap between us.

'All this talk of the darkness and the Seawomen and what they do to you. But those men up there . . . the ones who chased you into the water. They're not the good men, the men of God you pretend they are. The way you live here, severed from the rest of the world. It's wrong.'

I looked at him, my voice shaky. 'We're protected.'

'By who? Men like them?'

We were standing close. He smelt so strongly of the world forbidden to me that I couldn't stop the way it clenched my stomach. The smell of the sea was a constant, but it was different on him, sour, physical, cleansing. I could feel it drifting up through me, making me sway, linger, as if I was in the water again, uncertain, convinced I would sink but unable to resist its pull.

'I need your help,' he said. 'It's my only chance.'

Could I lie, promising him I'd help, only to lead the Keepers straight to him?

'I can't.'

'Please.'

'If I was seen with you . . . If anyone found out . . .'

'Then a year from now, right here . . .' He was making plans in front of my eyes.

'A year . . . it won't change anything.'

'If they hurt you. If you can see who I am,' he said, one last plea. 'Meet me here. If you change your mind.'

Our eyes met. There was a rush of noise and lights behind us, interrupting, coursing up into the sky. A bang, a fizz that rippled across the back of my neck. Fireworks. The night was nearly over. The mauve lights jewelled over Cal's skin. One look at him against the festival celebration and my fear of curse came flooding back. I was a woman now. Weak. Vulnerable. Easily ruined. What would he do to the island? To me? Empty wombs and empty cots for years and years, storms and misfortune, disease and misery. He would wreck it all.

This time, I didn't wait. Clambering up the last of the steps, grappling over the headland, I ran all the way home, full with the fear of God.

Eleven

I lay awake for hours. I had scrubbed and scrubbed, using soap and oils, and yet I could still smell the brine on my skin. Him. The sour reek of the water. Hear the cry of gulls chasing light across the sky. I gave up on sleep and got on my knees, but as much as I pleaded with God, the sea had sunk through to my bones. My mouth dried up with prayer, one running straight into another, and my skin held the imprints of the floorboards, the lines and knots, all in commitment of my repentance. I longed for the marks to be permanent, proof. *Lord God, please have mercy.* I can hear those words now, urgent but hollow. My prayer had to compete against all that I had done. Swimming, the trust I'd placed in this half-creature, the curiosity, the enduring sensation of his unnatural skin on my fingertips, the cool gleam of his flesh. I begged and begged for forgiveness, desperate that it might be enough to save me.

The next day I woke from broken sleep, weak behind the eyes, the previous night feeling like a strange and vivid dream. But I couldn't escape the truth. I had not dreamt Cal. I could not dismiss him, what I had done. Frantic sobbing prayers were not enough. I was feverish, an ache that bloated my body. I could not lift my limbs or turn my head. The room taunted me with its light like a scalding band of metal across my temples. This was my punishment.

I dozed again, delirious, dreaming of bare flesh and salt water, two fish bodies convulsing in the rhythm of the sea, swimming further and further towards somewhere else, somewhere unseen. An upturned fishing boat, a mouth, hands, gills. Now I can see it with sense: I had gone to bed the night of Cal still frozen, hair wet, shaken, refusing to commit to rest until I believed God had heard me. I'd passed out. I'd mistreated my body like my grandmother had hers. That was what had made me ill. But I did not believe that then. It was impossible not to absorb the guilt, to blame Cal. To blame myself. God was punishing me and He had every right to. The sickness was another curse. The warning sign of something worse on the horizon.

A scuttle of birds landed on the roof and I jumped from my skin, the bedsheets wet with sweat. As I lay sick, suffering in my guilt, the house was deathly quiet. I wondered about my grandmother. Had she gone looking for me at the festival? Would she bombard me with accusations? I shut my eyes, trying to think about how I might explain myself, and then I heard her outside my door, struck by a coughing fit, unable to catch her breath. Her old habits of fasting and sleep deprivation had returned in recent months. It was all for God, food and rest replaced with prayer, but she was ill again. Exhausted and frail. There was nothing I could do to stop her; I could only watch her grow sicker and sicker.

She came to my room and saw the state of me, feeling my forehead with the back of her hand. The contact of her bones under thin skin made me clamour for her in a desperate way, like trying to hold onto a rush of falling sand. *Stay*, I wanted to say, but my mouth was too dry, my intentions too timid. I wanted her and her faith to make me right again, good. Without her I was done for.

She let me sleep, but the next day she had questions for me.

Why are you sick?

What have you done?

Who have you been near? What girl has done this to you?

How have you betrayed the Lord?

There was talk at the festival about an outbreak of fever in the east of the island, a suggestion of curse, she said. My stomach clamped. She told me more, that three sheep had died, a child had started sleep-walking. Whoever she was, this female culprit, this cause of sickness, my grandmother wanted her found and punished.

I was silent, but I wanted to scream, beg. *I* was to blame. *I* was the one leading the island to ruin. The confession rotted inside me. This was the path I'd chosen now, irreversible.

'What's this?' she said, her fingernail scratching the line of scabbed blood at my temple.

'I fell on the way home from the festival.' I felt my heart thunder with the lie.

'Clumsiness is weakness,' she said. She stripped back the covers on my bed, cold rushing in against my clammy skin. 'Up you get. You fight this sickness. The Lord disapproves of such laziness.'

I looked down at my heavy, pathetic body. The water had done this. It would take all my energy just to sit.

She clapped in my face, breathless afterwards. 'You get up or I send for Eldermothers. Too much darkness here already. Not in my house. Get up.'

I thought of the Eldermothers' white presence in the room, the way they spoke sending chills down my body. The thought of them standing over me, pulling and twisting me into shapes, gave me the propulsion I needed to sit up and swing my legs out of bed. I'd have done anything to rid myself of darkness, but if they came, they'd expose what I'd done. They'd see it in me with one look.

She clicked her fingers at me. 'Knees,' she said. 'Pray.'

I did as she asked, even though the room was spinning.

'Nothing passing your lips today. You must be empty to receive his wisdom.'

The hunger would feel like punishment, but I willed her familiar methods to work. Something had to fix me. And if that was what it took for the bad luck to disappear, I'd do it.

'I'll find out why you're sick,' she said, my hands together, head bowed. 'I know you're lying. Eyes give you away.'

So I became her. Fasting, not sleeping, burying myself under the words of the Great Book, crowding out my thoughts with prayer. I promised myself it would work, and as the fever lifted, I chose to believe it was a sign. Days later, I returned to school. I looked gaunt, but my grandmother would not have rumours spread about me, so before I left, she pinched and rubbed at my cheeks.

'If they ask, you tell them you ate spoiled meat.'

I didn't question whether this lie was a forgivable one; I was too churned up with the thought of coming face to face with Doran and his friends again. I thought I knew fear, I thought I understood what kept me awake at night. But being surrounded by that pack of boys again was a greater terror than coming face to face with Cal, the man who was meant to be a monster.

When they finally laid eyes on me, they looked at me like I had silver skin and wet scales. Like I had risen from the dead. Something within me changed when I realised: there was a power in it I hadn't expected. I looked straight at them, head held high.

In class, Seren brushed past me. 'We thought you were with the Eldermothers.'

'I was at home, sick. Bad food.'

'Just something we heard.' She shrugged as she returned to her seat.

But as the day went on, there were no whispers behind my back, and no one turned away like they had done with Crescent. They *hadn't* told anyone. I tried to think what the boys must have done that night. Did they wait for news that I had disappeared? No church bell rang, nothing from the Messengers. No sightings of Seawomen emerged. The last place they'd seen me was the water. I'd disappeared, then reappeared without any explanation. What must they have thought? I'd defied them. Defied God. I could have drowned. I could have returned with an army of Seawomen on my side, spreading curse like frost, acre across acre. But here I was at school as though the night had never happened.

I was naïve to think that because the group of boys had been silent, dumbfounded by my return, I'd escape further torment. One afternoon, the last of my class to leave, I was cornered, trapped behind a closed door, Doran's breath against the back of my neck. He had my arm twisted and pushed me against the wall so that my head smacked against the framed painting of Father Lambert. The room was cold and smelt of the peat outside.

I struggled to free myself from his grip, before making myself slack. He slammed his hand on the wall, close enough to my face to make me wince and pay attention.

He pushed his face against mine, his words coming through his teeth with spit. 'How did you do it?'

'I got out. Back to land.'

'You were in the water, like one of *them*. We can all fucking see it. What you are.' He tapped at the side of my head with a ragged nail, then ran his fingers across my scarring. 'Bad luck's in your blood.'

In the centre of my throat, something seized.

'No one burns alive unless they deserve it.'

'God saved me.'

'Yeah, *you*. But what about your mother and father? I wonder—'

'Don't talk about them.'

'You'll end up the same.'

When he finally freed me, the release made the tears rush out. He grinned at the sight.

'You left me to drown.'

'You went into the water all by yourself.'

'You chased me! And then you ran.'

'We left it to God.'

I raised my head to meet his eyes. 'But I'm still here. He answered.'

He shook his head. 'You'll be found out. And you'll get what's coming.'

I felt a shiver at my nape. It wouldn't be long until he was made a Minister and granted unquestionable power. I thought of his father, Franklin, the sweat and herring reek of him, the combative way he spoke to his wife in church, the bruises we would see on her at the chapel. Doran was just the same. He walked out, leaving me alone, finally able to hold my wrist where he'd gripped me. Against his word, I was nothing. He'd made it clear he wouldn't stop. He'd bide his time if he had to. If Doran had his way, I'd be thrown into a yole before I even had the chance to prove my innocence and carry a child. If he was never going to let me out of his sight, then I had to be more careful.

When I was cleaning the font, or sweeping between the pews, or when we were waiting for the puffer to arrive with supplies from the Otherlands, I ran through every bleak thought of what might happen to me. It began to consume me, pushing between my promises to God. There was no space for redemption when the fear was so animal. It followed the same pattern as my nightmares: my body bound to an upturned boat, and no matter how much I fought, I could not save myself. Doran and the rest did nothing more to intimidate me, but it left me on edge, nervous of being alone. I walked home from school with Mull, but I wondered how long before they would use my friendship with her against me, spreading lies that would make her keep her distance. I had no reason to believe Doran wouldn't uphold his threats, not after Crescent.

I carried on helping in church, attending chapel, lighting candles, but whatever promises I made, whatever prayer, I never once spoke about Cal, how I'd felt, what I'd done. I was always holding back, hiding. No prayer ever emerged with the full conviction of my heart. How could it? It wasn't like before, after Mull and I had been in the water. This time it was impossible to confine him to imagination and pour everything I had into repentance. That would never be enough. The idea of him, this impossible man, living out there in the water, left me with too many unanswered questions to pretend I had none. I couldn't carry on as if nothing had changed, not when I knew he was planning to return.

In the summer, I watched on as Doran's ambitions came true. A Minister. A whole ceremony in church that spoke of honour and respect and command. The sight of him in his uniform made me want to launch myself into the sea. My grandmother had started using an imported contraption – a seat with wheels that I could push – to get to church. She couldn't walk further than to the bathroom without help, and as her health deteriorated, again she latched on to signs that a woman on the island was to blame. Doran becoming a Minister gave her hope of protection, that the more men we had to root out evil, the better she would feel. I could not sit and listen to her when all I wanted to do was scream. I went where I knew I would not have to talk of fear and curse and protection.

Barrett answered the door in a stained shirt. I had not been back to the harbour house since I was a child, but there was no surprise in his face, only warmth.

'Hungry?' he asked, the door wedged open against his hip and the smell of cooking enticing me in.

When we were sitting at the table, eating herring milts on thick cuts of bread, he asked, 'No school?'

I frowned. 'No, we finished weeks ago.' When the summer came, instead of school, we were expected to help out on the island where we were needed – with the animals, the arable land.

He nodded, as if he'd known all along, and cut me another hunk of bread. 'You're getting skinny again.'

'Grandmother doesn't cook much any more. It tires her out. But I don't mind.'

'She sleeping now?'

'I saw her upstairs to bed before I left. She sleeps a lot.'

'She had the doctor round? The herbalist?'

'Just the Father.'

Barrett filled his mouth with strips of torn bread, and I stared at the hard line of his hunched shoulders. He knew what I did, that she was making herself sick again and there was nothing either of us could do to stop it. I looked around the sun-brightened kitchen, the light exposing the room's crowding, the junk and paperwork, the collection of broken reels and frayed ropes. It was worse than the last time I'd seen it.

'You can always come here,' he said, using his finger to clear the gummy bread from under his lip.

I was about to agree, aching for his company, when there was a banging at the back door, the door that led straight to the harbour. Barrett excused himself and shuffled out, and I pulled back my chair to spy into the hallway. I heard the raised voice of one of the fishermen.

'They've been waiting an hour. You said you were coming. Where you been?'

'I got caught up with something. I'm coming, I'm coming.'

Barrett returned with his coat over his arm, cap in hand. 'New lads. Need teaching. Take your time. I'll be back later.'

'Did you forget?'

He shook his head. 'They're impatient, that's all.'

He left, and I pictured him heading down towards the huts, to the young lads learning to be fishermen. He had told me about the types he trained: the cocky ones who thought they knew everything but came back to land so sick they cried for their mothers; the nervy boys who learnt quickly that the only way to get out of any bother was to row, row and row again. Sometimes they were as young as fifteen; just wanted to be their fathers, skin salt-cracked and weed rashes spreading from their wrists to their elbows. All of them dizzied by nerves and adventure.

I finished lunch, washing up his plate and mine, putting the rest of the bread in its tin. The state of the kitchen played on my mind. I could feel my grandmother taking shape inside my body. Barrett had lived so long without a wife keeping his house tidy, he could use my help. But it wasn't all goodwill. Cleaning up for him gave me a legitimate excuse to uncover, to move, to snoop. I had a reason to go upstairs, into the attic, where the past was hidden away. It was a room I knew existed, its lone window looking out over the harbour like a glassy eye, but one that was sealed off from the rest of the house. Even when I'd stayed, I'd never seen Barrett go up there, I'd never seen the hatch door opened. Everything about it had the calling of a secret.

I went up there, up the ladder, a torch wedged under my chin and a box of outdated paperwork, concerning boat leases and listings of vessels beyond repair, hooked under my arm and hugged to my chest. There was no real intent that afternoon. But like anything kept out of sight, I was too weak to resist.

The attic was a shrine. Boxes and furniture from years ago. I couldn't believe he'd kept so much. I envied its survival when my own past was ash. Before Barrett, this house had belonged to his father, and his grandfather before that. On and on. Each one of them had taken the role of harbourmaster, each keeping records, teaching, repairing yoles, tracking the weather. The history of the island's fishing industry was contained in those four walls. My grandmother used to say the island never would have survived without Barrett and his family. It was in their blood. There was so much of Mae in the attic too. I could almost smell her, a dull, sweet smell cutting through the old sea-washed house. There were boxes of clothes, her books, her needlework, a vanity dresser. My heart stopped at the sight of a crib, one side of it smashed, like broken ribs. I wanted to get out of there quickly, guilt and scattered dust making my lungs feel tight. I was disturbing a burial ground. I made space for the box, deciding I wouldn't come back, I wouldn't tidy anything more. But in my rearranging and shifting, trying not to damage anything, there was one box, coated in thick and salty furs, that kept getting in my way, kept drawing my attention. A box that if I'd left it alone could have stopped me before it was too late.

I left the hatch open and took the box to the kitchen, into daylight, so I could see its contents properly. Inside were books, so covered in dust I had to open a window and shake them to make the covers legible. They were diaries, the name *E. Philips* on the front. I found myself taking apart the contents of the box, item by item, revealing years' worth of journals, along with sketches and maps, quilting the table with the sheets. Maps of the entire island, every cove, every rock bank, bay, beach and arch, even the stacks and skerries out to sea. As I turned the pages of one notebook, I saw more maps, named islands and seas, islets and archipelagos, large land masses that didn't even look like islands. Words that meant nothing to me. *Hollandstoun. Sumburgh. Foula. Atlantic.* Question marks were littered next to these names, some crossed out, some rewritten clearer with a new understanding.

The scale of the unknown had me enraptured until I was sitting in the half-dark. My understanding of the world was shrinking. I was back in the water with Cal, dumbfounded at the possibility of being only a speck, of a world vaster and more different than I could comprehend. So much I'd never see. I'd known before, but that day I finally understood what it meant that the perimeter of the island was the limit of my life. And still, even with the maps and the books, the observations and ponderings, I hadn't found a mention of men like Cal, that anyone but me knew he existed.

'Esta.' My name on a breath. How long had Barrett been in the room? The maps and notebooks spread across the table; he eyed the papers like they were blood.

I hastily pushed myself up. He approached, a shaking hand taking one of the pages. Compass points. A name of a place I'd never heard of. He dropped that, scrapped around for another. Rough hand, rough paper.

'What are these?' All the age drained from his voice. He sounded like a child, a wobble of fear underneath it.

I realised, when the noise blurted out loud, that I was sobbing.

'I don't know.'

He picked again at them, shuffling one after another in his hand.

'I'm sorry. I didn't mean . . .'

'Where did you get them?'

'Upstairs. In the attic. I wanted to help. Tidy up.'

'Upstairs? Here?' He looked around the room like he didn't recognise it, white in the face.

He picked up a journal and found the label revealing the owner, the cartographer behind these maps.

'Egan. My great-uncle.' He raised his hand to cover his face, one of the papers sticking to his sweating palm and flapping when he lifted it.

'I'm so sorry. I was only . . .' I was breathless, tears falling silently. 'Until I looked through it, I had no idea.' I was waiting for the moment his rage would explode, when he would haul me to the Eldermothers, show my grandmother exactly what kind of girl I was. Instead, he was shaking almost as much as I was. He began gathering the pages, piling them back into the box.

'Don't just stand there. Help me!'

I jumped from my skin, clumsily lurching forward to sweep the papers into a pile, to pack them away again.

'You should never have touched this stuff!'

I nodded with fierce agreement, unable to stop the tears. Bad luck. Bad luck. Bad luck. He lifted the box under his arm and carried it to the living room, where the fire roared. He was surely going to report me. What then? Would I have to live in the chapel with the Eldermothers, cleansed until I couldn't feel my skin? Stand in church, bowed in front of Father Jessop, and confess everything I'd done? How then could I stop everything coming out with it – Cal, the water? How could I ever escape the punishment that was surely coming for me? I could feel it building up inside me, wanting to purge, to tell Barrett everything so the forgiveness could come in one flood. No more secrets, no more hiding. That was the only way I'd ever stand a chance of Salvation.

I heard him mutter, a desperate questioning to a room with no answers. 'Why here? Why this house? This whole time, when . . .'

I saw him linger over the papers, the breadth of the world on the flat pages.

'When your mother was . . .' He looked at me and shook his head, as if deciding against continuing.

'My mother?' I took a step nearer, holding my breath.

He looked back at the papers and stumbled around for the right words. 'Some time before she died, she asked me what it was like to be on the water. Whether I knew what was out there. Other places, life beyond the borders.'

I thought I knew what he was trying to say. That I had her flaw. Curious in a way that made it dangerous, that made me doomed. Perhaps if she hadn't been curious . . . Perhaps if I wasn't . . .

Her fate would end up being mine. That's what I thought he was trying to tell me.

'I told her, what does it matter? What matters is here. Your home, your family. I should have told her not to ask.' The papers shook so much in his hand I thought he would drop them. 'It's better not to know, it's . . .'

And then, one by one, he crumpled each sheet and fed it to the flames. My heart leapt and I couldn't explain it. The words that had been foreign to me, the place names I'd tried to remember, burnt into ash. In the months that followed, I closed my eyes at night and tried to remember fragments. I would try and piece them together, murmur and memorise the names of places that were slipping away from me, just to keep them alive. This outside world, these missing edges, places I would never know. Places I wasn't even sure were real. But in that room, all I could do was sob.

After the fire had taken every last page and licked against the notebooks of Egan's innermost thoughts until they were charred and curled, Barrett sat heavily by the fire. It was only when he took his hand away that I saw he'd been crying. I'd been standing by the hearth, numbly watching the flames take hold. The maps had gone from my hands to the fire in a matter of minutes. I hadn't said a word. Didn't know what to say. I did the only thing I knew to do. I took the Great Book from the shelf.

'What are you doing?'

I opened my eyes. Barrett looked angry. His tears disappeared into the troughs of his wrinkled face.

'Asking for forgiveness.'

He tore the Great Book from my hands. I had a wild, fleeting thought that he might throw that into the fire too. Only a monster would dare burn God's words.

'Do you have any idea what would have happened if anyone else had caught you with those maps? And in my house! They were in my house too!'

I tried apologising again, but he raised his hand to shut me down.

'If Father Jessop heard about this . . .'

'Please. Please don't tell him.'

Silence dropped like a stone in the room. 'Tell him?'

'I'll pray. I'll go to the Eldermothers, I'll do anything.' The despair in the speed of my words was close to making me sick. I could see my future falling away like sediment. I hadn't done enough to rid Cal from my thoughts, but if this was my last chance to earn forgiveness, I'd work twice as hard.

'If that man ever found out, it would be the death of us both!' Barrett's voice trembled, his words disappearing under the fire's crackle. 'He's done enough.'

His murmured words smarted. I'd never heard anyone talk about Father Jessop in such a way, never with spite. It was only ever women under the influence of the Seawomen who spat his name, doubted his word. He acted under God's guidance. What he did was always for the good of us all, always just. Barrett was right, though. I knew how it would look. If Father Jessop had caught us with the maps and journals, we'd have been traitors, sinners, enemies of the island, conspiring to escape. But we didn't deserve to be punished.

His expression was difficult to read. He sat unmoving, and I was uneasy in a way I had never been before.

'No one can ever know about this,' he said. 'You forget everything you saw on those pages. They never existed. You hear?'

'A secret?'

He poked at the fire, ensuring everything was destroyed. 'Anyone who says they don't have secrets is a liar.'

I took to a chair, hugging my knees against my chest. I didn't have the words any more. I was carrying too many secrets to speak. Neither of us uttered another word until the fire had died to a flicker. Barrett abandoned the poker and leant against the fireplace, head against his arm.

'All your work, Egan,' he said, speaking to the ash. 'All your work.'

I heard something else in his voice, separate from fear. Was it remorse? Regret? The more I really saw his reaction, the more I began to realise it wasn't the sight of the maps themselves that had scared him, the thought of the outside world encroaching on our sacred island, but the fear of discovery. And what might happen if we were caught.

Twelve

I turned sixteen and another spring arrived. The island thrummed in anticipation of the festival, with greater fanfare than the year before. The bonfire was built bigger, more players had joined the band, food and drink were prepared in abundance. But as the preparations took shape, Cal's return gnawed away at me. The festival and him were intertwined now, inescapable. What had once been a time of ascending joy and excitement competed with a ferocity of guilt, fear. Finding the maps had only made it worse.

For the first time, my grandmother was too ill to attend the festival, and in the days leading up to it, I was almost grateful to be busy nursing her, changing her damp sheets, hearing her rattling breaths as she slept. I stayed by her bedside and read her the scriptures she demanded, but as the days passed and the festival edged closer, I couldn't ignore it any longer. All I could think about was him.

By then my grandmother lived entirely in the upstairs of the cottage, unable to tackle the stairs, the curtains drawn to keep the sea away. She made me report to her any rumour of misfortune, any time a woman looked pale in church or lined up to speak to the Eldermothers in private. She asked me to tell her about the weather, the health of the livestock in the crofts, and each time I relayed the state of the island, her fears deepened. She latched onto the smallest thing in my reporting, convinced of the darkness spreading.

I absorbed her paranoia, keeping check on my reflection for signs of something wrong. Markings on my body, silver in my irises. I was sleepless looking after her, but still I prodded at the circles under my eyes, found threads of my hair left behind on my pillow. These weren't signs, but with her in my head, I read them as though they could be. Signs of my God-given body rejecting me. And yet these signs were insignificant compared to the weight of what I'd done. I kept questioning. Where was the curse, the consequence of every sin I had committed? I lived out each day in perpetual terror that it was only a matter of time before God showed them who I really was. But a year had passed since I was with Cal in the water, and no curse had touched me.

On the night of the festival, my grandmother refused the doctor again and turned her head away from the soup I'd made. There was nothing left of her body but bones, but still she fasted. Her conviction that curse was behind her sickness hadn't faltered. If God hadn't cured her, she was certain she wasn't working hard enough.

She had a fever, the blankets tucked around her tiny frame as she struggled to hold the Great Book. I stood by the window, looking out at the darkening sky, the bright moon taking me back a year. Where was he now? Waiting for me? Wondering if I had changed my mind?

'*Return to me. Promise me with all your heart, your body. Weep, pray, bare your soul. Feed not on bread, but on His guidance.*'

I listened to my grandmother read aloud. Words that had once been reassuring, grounding, washed over me. What if she was right? If I resisted temptation, if I truly shut out Cal and everything beyond, then maybe she'd be well again. Maybe God was punishing me through her. Maybe my presence in the house had only made her worse. My efforts so far had been weak, half-hearted, but perhaps this was my chance to reject temptation once and for all. If I didn't go to the cove, he'd give up and never come back. I could forget everything. I could earn my Salvation.

'*. . . if she ignores what is right, it is sin. But you who love Him and obey His voice, you will inherit the kingdom.*'

'I'm not going to go to the festival tonight,' I said, breaking the tranquillity of her prayer. 'I'll stay home with you.'

'Don't insult me! What will people say? You! No, you go, you honour God tonight. You honour this island.'

Her anger weakened her, setting off a chain of coughs from her chest. I tried to offer her water, but she turned her head away, going back to the scripture.

'Do you really think those words alone will make you well?'

Were they enough? Enough to save me?

With shallow, struggling breaths, she closed the Great Book on her lap. 'And if I stop? What do you want for us? For them to come and take over? The darkness to spread and spread?' She looked at me. 'Maybe it's too late.'

My tongue clicked in my dry throat. 'What do you mean?'

'You know. You're like her.'

My racing heart already understood.

'Maddow. I see her. In you.'

Somehow she had the energy for such viciousness. I threw myself towards her, wanting to pull off the covers and rip her away from comfort. I snatched the Great Book from her hands.

'How would I know who I am? You never tell me anything about her!' I loomed over her, shaking with anger.

She started coughing again, deep and clattering, as though she was comprised of broken parts. I stood back, watching it ride through her, too furious to help.

The fit ended and she closed her eyes to conserve energy, to speak, every word laboured. 'She doesn't belong in this house. She never did.'

'Your own daughter!'

'Her father's daughter. Nothing of me in her.'

I thought of my grandfather, the images she'd planted, his writhing body, skin mottled with lichen, at the bottom of the sea. The way she spoke about him like he was nothing but rot.

'She was still my mother and you've kept her from me.'

'She gave birth. Her duty. She was no mother.'

I threw the Great Book to the floor and the thump struck horror across her face.

'See! Lord help me!'

'Why won't you tell me?'

'You're too much of her already! You know any more and—'

'What? I'll be cursed like her? I've already lost a family! I burnt!'

'You were saved!'

'And she deserved to die?'

She sucked in another breath and the coughing began again, wheezing that shook her whole frame. I could not look at her, could not pity her. All I felt was rage. I left the house without even saying goodbye. I wore my mother's earrings, and with them a feeling that she would have left the house like this once, hating Sarl, resenting her. Hoping there might be a better life out there away from the island. I had watched Barrett burn the maps, but that curiosity, that longing hadn't been destroyed; if anything, it was stronger than ever before. Cal was the only one who might have answers. My head was a storm of my mother. My grandmother. Cal. Resentment. Frustration. The horizon. Indecipherable memorised words. *Hollandstoun. Sumburgh. Foula. Atlantic.* What might my life have been if my mother was still alive? If I'd known freedom.

I made my decision. Back then, I thought it was impulsive, born of anger, heightened emotion, but I know better now. The thought of seeing Cal again was deeper than a fleeting choice; it was a current under the surface of my skin. Had been since I knew he existed. Had been since he promised to return. My promises to God were only surface. I didn't want to go back to ignorance. I couldn't. Now that I knew that life beyond our borders didn't match the stories I'd been told, I couldn't settle without seeing him again. Faith could not quell what he had ignited.

I needed to show my face at the festival first, ensure I was seen, that I wouldn't be followed, then I would go to Cal. As the festival unfolded around me in laughter and smoke and fire, I was hit by the reality of what I was agreeing to, the danger of seeing him again. I would have to look for his face in the men from the harbour; I would have to believe that a man sworn to God had committed the ultimate sin without consequence.

I made sure I had spoken to girls I knew, Mull, Seren and the rest. I'd been seen by Father Jessop, conscious of every minute, jostled between men and their drink, children laughing and screaming, when I saw Doran. This year he was no longer helping at his father's stall. He was wearing his uniform, hands held behind his straightened back, attention focused on the words of another Minister at his side as they watched a group of pretty unmarried women dancing around the maypole. The sight of him. I was in the water again, helpless, salt-choking. I saw the yole, the oars beating me down. I wanted to show him my defiance, proof that I was enjoying myself, but I didn't have the nerve. I wouldn't give him the opportunity to chase me again. I slipped away, leaving as the islanders congregated for stew and stories, oblivious to the way my heart raced. It was only the sheep who saw me.

I took a torch with me, blunting the light against the palm of my hand, and pulled on a knitted hat from inside my coat, hoping that if I was spotted, no one would believe I was a girl. What kind of girl would be out at night, away from the celebrations? I asked myself the same question.

I passed the old lighthouse, and at every noise I imagined footsteps. The likeness to the previous year made me shiver. I carried on, down the cliff into the cove, edging towards the waterline, though this time because I wanted to. I looked up, the stars like scratches of silver in the dark. I felt so far away from anything. When the waves rolled closer, they folded into sighing curls on the sand. It didn't scare me to be so close this time. I knew I should have turned back. But what was there to go home for? Already my chest felt tight with thoughts of the future.

I waited. Hopeful, desperate, lost. Minutes passing slower and slower. I tucked myself into the shadows of the cove, hugging myself warm, not daring to think he might break his promise. I lost all sense of how much time had passed, convinced any minute that the fireworks would tear into the sky and I'd be forced to return home.

Out in the water, the moonlight caught a silver shape. A fulmar, alone and insomnia-plagued. But it wasn't as fast as a bird. I looked again. Cal's body rose out of the water. I wanted to call out to him, yet still a part of me wanted to run. But I was rooted, watching him swim towards the land, until he was close enough to wade to shore, the water rippling out around him. I let my eyes roam over the strangeness of him. The moon was so clear that his skin gleamed in the silver of the sky, the light reflecting on the coin around his neck. If I wanted to hear about the world beyond, if I wanted to know if Egan's maps were true, then it couldn't be like before; I couldn't refuse to believe what I saw with my own eyes.

I stepped out from the dark, removing my hat so he could see who

I was, my falling hair lashing in the wind. He jolted at the sight of me, then stood still, so we were just staring at each other, uncertain. I stayed where I was, his shadow casting over my skin. I didn't shrink back, but I prickled with the same ingrained fear.

'You came,' he said, then looked behind me. 'Did you come alone?'

I nodded, my hands creeping around my body for warmth, for protection.

'You didn't tell anyone?'

'No one.'

He seemed to take in my words slowly, his attention focused on studying the cove, the imposing rock faces. He didn't understand what would happen to me if I'd told anyone, how they'd accuse me of bringing him here. My life was just as much at risk as his.

'You changed your mind?' he said.

I shut my eyes. The truth hard to unbury. 'You were right before. I don't know anything about the world. All I have are stories.'

When I opened my eyes again, he was by my side, so that we were both facing the spread of water, further than I could ever imagine being. Out there was the soft haze of lights from the anchored patrol boats. They were motionless, like ghosts tethered to the perimeter. I thought of them suddenly sparking to life, hunting him down. I knew about the patrol men harpooning seals and whales by mistake, bringing their grey bodies to land and selling them off for meat. In church, Father Jessop would describe the patrols as diligent; their dedication to protection meant lapses in judgement were unavoidable. Even if that meant seeing the sad eyes of the seals gazing back at us in the market, making me look away. Tonight the ferries were empty of men. I didn't like to think of our island with its guard down, but if it hadn't been, Cal wouldn't have been in our waters and my life would have ended, my drowned body loomed over by those like Doran.

When the quiet between us became uncomfortable, I spoke again. 'I should've . . . I meant to say thank you. For saving me. Not just run away.'

'Anyone would have done what I did.'

'Not anyone.'

Behind us stood the headland where a year ago we'd heard the taunts and appetite for violence. It clung to the air. 'Have they hurt you again?'

'No. Not yet. But we have to be careful. You can't come here any other time, it's too dangerous.'

I looked at Cal and he seemed to have the same understanding as I did. Some threats never disappear.

'Your father . . .' I glanced at his pendant. This was the reason I was meant to have returned, to help him. In the moonlight, his face was so clear. If I'd looked harder on that first meeting, if I'd wanted to, maybe I'd have seen enough in his bones, in his expression, to trust his word about who he was and why he couldn't stay away.

'I almost didn't come back tonight.'

'What?'

I couldn't bear to think about how I would have felt if he hadn't come back.

'How you reacted . . . What kind of welcome would he give me? It's hopeless, isn't it? What chance do I have?'

'You still came.'

'I managed to stay away before. For years. But there's something scratching away at me, always calling me back. It must be him, the part of me that's his blood. Island blood. There's too much I don't know.'

My thoughts turned to my mother, the maps, the weight of the things I would never know the answers to.

'Where do you go?' I asked, hesitating when he looked attentive at my question. 'I mean, where were you before you came back here?'

He nodded west.

'An island?' I asked, pushing towards what I wanted to know. My mind was empty space. I couldn't picture a thing.

'There aren't many islands this far north,' he said. 'There used to be. I think. Centuries ago. But not since the waters rose.'

'I've heard of that. Floods.' I stopped, looking sheepishly down to the ground, remembering what Father Lambert had written, what we were told to remember. Floods and natural disasters, those were the start of it, God's punishment for the corruption of His world. That was when things started changing, when God helped to take us away from it, to protect what was good. I couldn't tell Cal that, couldn't explain what we believed.

'You live underwater?'

'Some of the time. My body can't withstand it for too long.'

I looked at him for an explanation, and he put his hand over his chest, which was scratched and pitted with scars.

'My lungs weren't made for it.'

Too human, I thought, darkening. God didn't make us for the water.

'It was different when my mother was alive. Now I move around. When you look like I do, people have their own ideas of where I should be.'

I had so much to ask him. I wanted to know what he had seen, where he'd been and what he'd done. How much of what Egan had written was true. I wanted to hear about another life, one that wasn't as small as mine, but I knew so little I didn't know where to begin.

He leant forward, and I watched him root around in the silt for something and come up with a pebble. He held it flat in his palm, the stone black and smooth, then he exhaled and threw it as far out into the waves as he could. I held my breath, watching it skip-skip-plop into the water. He searched for more stones. I was transfixed. I'd thrown stones on land to see how far they'd go, stones to knock over tins, but nothing like this. A pebble could never skim the ground like it did the water. I watched him resume his game, seeing our lives, our pasts diverge before my eyes. Cal made the forbidden look easy, fun.

He threw another pebble to ride the arc of a wave. I waited for him to carry on speaking, conscious that if all I had were questions, he'd tire of me like everyone else did.

'I tend to stay this far north, on the sunken lands. There isn't much life there; most people fled to higher ground. But the ones who stayed are used to the water. They find their own way to live. Houseboats. Or build their houses on platforms above the water. Life like that won't last forever, but they're like your kind – can't let go of the way things were.'

Once, I'd have felt sick to imagine people living like that, but listening to him talk, I wanted to know more. How could they stand it?

'You don't find many places that welcome outsiders. People stick to their own kind, their own business. But there they tolerate me.' There was a seep of vulnerability as his eyes met mine. 'Once I was on my own, the endlessness of the world started to feel empty.'

'I don't know how to help you,' I said, growing warm with guilt. 'I don't know how to find him.'

He gave me a solemn nod and lashed another stone into the tide. 'What man would admit to it?'

I was crushed by the sadness I recognised in his voice.

'My mother, she's dead too. I never knew her.'

'How long have you been without her?'

The sky drew my eyes upward. 'Forever.'

He mirrored my gaze. I wanted to be swallowed by its vastness. Once, I'd thought she might be up there, keeping watch. Salvation. My grandmother's words had banished those thoughts.

We stared upwards, both of us silent and thoughtful.

'You know, in some places, "Esta" means "from the stars".'

I flinched. My name meant my world should have been endless. It felt mocking. Hurt curled inside me and the sky seemed to pull away.

'Maybe it means something different here . . .' he said.

'I didn't think it meant anything. I never thought . . .' I said it more to myself than him. Had she wanted that for me? The stars, the open space? Or had she chosen it because a name was as far as I'd ever reach, my parameters restricted to a word I'd always carry with me?

Above us, the night was taunting and bright.

'I always look at them,' he said. 'On a clear night, you can navigate anywhere by those stars.'

Sometimes they too had felt like the edge of the sea. Too vast, too far away. I blinked, clearing my tears.

'How?'

He stood behind me, and his hands, feather-light and cautious, found my shoulders and turned me to face north, so that our eyes met the same patch of night. 'The star you're looking at. The brightest one. Polaris. The whole sky turns on that star.'

'North.'

'That's right.'

'Polaris,' I said, my mouth finding a new shape.

'Polaris.'

He took his fingertips away from my shoulders and I turned my head to check he was still there behind me. With him here, I wanted to know everything. I pointed. 'And those?'

'Together they're called Cassiopeia.'

We separated, turned back towards the waterline. I wanted to ask him the names of the places I'd memorised, but I worried about them coming out garbled. I worried about him telling me they were inventions. A part of me was too afraid that they might be.

I picked up a stone from the shore and returned to his side. 'Show me.'

'Like this.' He demonstrated how best to throw it, how to flick my wrist so that the pebble skimmed the water at an even rate. My first try was a failure, and the next, the stone sinking without so much as a spring.

'Try again,' he handed me another. 'Aim further out.'

I concentrated, moving my wrist like he had shown me, and that time shot it a little further.

'Relax your hand when you let go.'

'It's harder than you make it look.'

We kept it up. My turn, his turn. I watched him carefully, listened to his advice, each time a little exhilaration when my stone managed to skip further than before. His encouragement was getting warmer, pushing me to want to be better. When his next throw failed and mine triumphed, the burst of achievement was briefly cheering. I could almost believe this was normal. I crouched to the lick of the tide and took a handful of stones. I raised my arm to throw them into the sea's mercy, but Cal's webbed fingers grazed against my forearm.

'Wait,' he said.

He studied the fist of stones, his hand still on my skin. I couldn't get used to how he felt.

'Open your hand.'

My fingers uncurled slowly as though I was holding splinters of glass.

'You see there? It's a clam shell. It'll shatter if you throw it. You should hold onto it. That kind of pattern, those lines that meet and splay – you see – it's rare. It can give you luck.'

'Luck?'

I let everything but the shell fall through my fingers. The pebbles and stones, the scraps of weed. The clam shell was patterned in rings, dark and white, the bulbous shape of a mushroom head.

'Beautiful, isn't it?'

I looked at its uniform design, the way it shone in the cast of moonlight. It took my mind to far-off places, to the unknown and unseen.

Cal rooted around in the shallows for a larger shell and emerged with an abalone, its pearled insides as smooth as his skin.

'This one's special,' he said.

I looked down at it, powerless.

'If you put it to your ear . . . some say it's the sound of the sea. It's just air, circling back, but try. Listen. Close your eyes.'

He held his hands underneath mine, supporting the shell, encouraging my hand upwards. Permission. I cupped it to my ear and the sound closed in around it. I heard wind, and tides, an echo of a much bigger, distant world. It lifted me off my feet.

'The whole sea,' I said.

I was lulled as everything around me became distant. My fingers froze around the shell. I thought of shards. My grandmother's boot. It was as though I had inhaled the sea, a dark hypnotism, and welcomed it into my body. I pulled the shell away from my ear, holding it hot in my palm.

'What's wrong?' Cal asked.

I started to pull away, but he held my wrist. 'Don't. Not yet.'

'I can't find him, Cal. I wouldn't even know where to begin.'

I looked at his fingers against my skin, and then he put his hand over mine, the two of us cradling the same beautiful shell.

'You came back here to help me.'

'I thought I understood how the world worked,' I said. 'But none of this makes sense.' I took a sharp breath. 'I found maps. Lists of places. Hollandstoun. Sumburgh. Foula. Atlantic.'

His face was impassive.

'Are they real?'

'Where did you find maps?'

'Have you heard of those places?'

'They're old names.'

'But they exist?'

'Atlantic used to be the name for a stretch of sea.'

'Where?

'West. Far from here.'

'And the rest?'

He turned his face away, looking northwards, out past the patrols. 'Foula.'

'You've been there? It's close?'

'On a clear day . . .'

Through my skin was a chattering, collective voices all saying the same: *Otherlands, Otherlands.*

I dropped my hand away, leaving the shell to crack on the stones. I pushed past Cal, to the thin strip of sand that transformed to shingle, to rocks. I removed my coat, bundling it onto the sand, a frustrated whip of it into the wind, and steadied myself before climbing out onto the rocks.

'What are you doing?' he cried.

I couldn't explain it; a need had taken hold. A need to breathe, a need to be further away. A need to *know*. This brae was as far as I'd ever get. I could only look out towards the horizon. I kept going and going, the rocks slippery under my boots, bent over at the waist for balance. Cal took to the water, swimming alongside. I'd thought I wanted to hear about the world beyond the island, but hearing about it only took it further away. It would have been easier to hear that Egan had made it up, that I was no closer to knowing anything about the wider world, but now I knew and could do nothing about it. I had come back for selfish reasons, not to help Cal, but now I didn't know what I wanted, only that I couldn't stand still, I couldn't keep to the island's perimeter any more.

'I could teach you,' he said. The offer burst out of him like he'd been wanting to say it for some time.

'What?'

'To swim.'

'I can't.'

'You did it before, when we were in the cave.'

'I had no choice then. This is different.'

'You wanted to. That's why you ended up here. I could teach you how.'

'No, I can't.'

'What are you so afraid of?'

My head was full of the water, of stories. I thought of the illustrations in our books, the sightings, the boastful drunken stories from the fishermen, the scaled skin that was washed up on our beaches. I thought of my grandmother's tales, of Crescent's head forced underwater by Father Jessop because she'd been vain, just like the Seawomen. But Cal had been further, seen more. He knew the names of places, words that had never even been spoken on this island.

'Tell me about them,' I said, looking straight at him. A familiar chill rooted through my spine. 'The Seawomen. I want to hear it from you.'

'Why?'

'I've only ever seen a glimpse. Heard stories.'

'They haven't been near this island in centuries. Nowhere near. Not since your people took it as their own. How can you have seen a glimpse?'

'They've been in our waters. That's why we have patrols.'

'You think the patrols are keeping them away?'

'They've tried to come here, to ruin us. I've seen a tail. Skin, shed skin.'

He looked bemused. 'Shed skin?'

'They left it behind as a warning that they were coming for us, encouraged by our sin.'

He looked out towards the water, what I'd said playing over his features. 'Shed their skin? What do you think they are – serpents?' He almost laughed.

'I saw it.'

'They'd never come back here. Never.'

'But they're close, waiting.' I heard the quiver in my voice, almost a question.

'No. Not after what your people did to them.'

'The sightings. The dark sea.'

'It wasn't them.'

I wanted to get back on land, away from the water, return to the comfort of what was solid, what I knew. I concentrated on my feet, memories crumbling under his words. If it wasn't their scaled skin, what was it? Why was it held aloft in the church for all of us to see? And if the Seawomen weren't lurking, combing the sin out of our darkest places, then why the storms, the misfortune, the fever?

Cal followed me. 'The Seawomen. They're not who you think. They're gentle, peaceful.'

I sat on the rock so we were face to face.

'How can they be when they can get inside our heads? Can make us do terrible things and have terrible thoughts? Thrive on our sin?'

'How do you know that's true if you've never seen them?'

I backed off at the flare in his voice, thinking of the women I knew who had been taken away to the chapel, who'd had the Seawomen cleansed from their soul. Women who'd admitted in front of the whole congregation that they'd been weak and malleable. Lark's wife, drowned, taken by the Seawomen, childless, a sign impossible to deny.

'I know what they do to us.'

'You've no idea!' Cal cried. 'Your people came here and they saw a species in the water they didn't trust, thought was outside God.'

'They *are* outside God!'

'Your people used them, they made them the enemy. You, you shut yourselves away from the rest of the world! You're the ones who don't belong in this world any more! You and your beliefs. The Seawomen, what have they done? You use them as someone to blame. Anything that doesn't fit with the world you wanted to make.'

'They come from darkness, they carry darkness. The Seawomen are—'

'Part of them lives in me.' He took a step nearer, hand to his chest. 'I've seen the world. I know what it's like out there.'

'You don't know what they really are.'

'What would they want with your island? People like yours. Following some twisted version of God. Pretend good and evil.'

'We have to protect ourselves.'

'The darkness doesn't live in them, Esta. It's *here*. The way they make you think, the way they keep you here, afraid of anything outside of your tiny world, terrified of anything different.'

I fell silent, his words stinging. Any denials and refusals that came to mind were weak. Cal stood there, unravelling everything I knew, everything I held onto. He'd seen the world and I'd seen nothing, knew nothing. Doubt iced through me. I shook my head, hands over my ears, trying to rid myself of the conflicting voices.

Cal's touch was gentle on my cheeks. 'It's all right.'

I slumped, my hands fell away. His eyes were dark and kind, stirring in my stomach a rolling, unsettled tilt. I'd blamed the water for everything, torn myself apart, suppressed feelings until there was nothing left. The water hadn't harmed me, no curse had come for me like they said. What was true? What was to fear?

'You don't have to be afraid any more,' he said.

I was conscious of each point of skin where we touched, our faces so close there was no difference between my breath and his. This close I saw nothing monstrous, nothing deceitful. I placed my hands either side of his face, its strange angles softened in his concern. I had no understanding of my world any more. I wanted a part of his. What he knew, what he'd seen. Him.

I made a small noise of hesitation, my face turning in the direction of the water, all that was forbidden. I felt myself move to unbutton my dress, to run headlong into the waves, to launch myself as far as one of the stones we threw. But then a bell rang out from the harbour. A clanging that sounded far across the island. Reality. We looked up. Cal must have seen my face fall. This was not a bell of festival celebration, but a sign that something was wrong.

'Go. Now!' I got to my feet. 'As far and as fast as you can!'

'Is someone coming?'

'I don't know. Something's wrong.'

He gripped my hands. Gathering ourselves, stalling whatever might come.

'Then go,' he said. 'Run!'

'Next year.' It was me this time, words bleeding together in a promise. 'Tell me you'll come back?'

And with a look of agreement, he was gone, back into the water.

Thirteen

I didn't make it as far as the festival, to where I was last seen, to the glowing embers of the bonfire. I was out of breath, doubled over from running uphill, desperately hoping the wet hem of my dress wouldn't be noticed. It was Mull who saw me first, caught me by the elbows. There was a young man with her, tall and stocky. I tried to recall his name, but Mull kept shaking me. I could only see her mouth moving, her face grave and unreadable.

'Give her this,' the man said, and it came to me who he was. Aden, one of the older boys from school. A hog farmer's son. What was he doing by Mull's side?

I watched Mull consider the flask he'd given her as he explained nervously, 'For the shock. Mam swears by it. Sip it.'

Before I knew what was happening, as I was still staring at Aden's beetroot face, Mull was pushing the flask against my lips, and a burning caught me in my throat.

'Where have you been?'

'I heard the bell . . .'

'Your grandmother! Barrett found her passed out at home. He went to check on her. He was the one to sound for help.'

I wasn't making sense of what she was trying to tell me, too distracted by the pair of them. Aden put a soothing hand on Mull's arm. I could only watch dumbly as this intimacy played out between them, wondering where it had come from, when it had started. Had I really been so fixated trying to repent, to push down my feelings, that I'd missed what was happening between them?

'The doctor's with her now,' Aden added.

'At home?' I was already running, tripping over my feet.

Mull caught my arm, pulling me back. 'Where were you?'

'I have to go and see her.'

145

'Esta!' she called, a rise of annoyance in her tone. 'Your dress . . .'

I ran without answering her. When I reached the cottage, the door was open, and in the dim hallway, the doctor was in a quiet, serious conversation with Barrett. They both looked my way when I clattered in.

'Where is she?' I had already put one foot on the stairs.

'She's very sick,' the doctor said, his voice inflected with a warning. 'It's more serious this time. She's feverish and I'm afraid isn't coherent at the moment.'

'I found her on the floor. Collapsed. I think she might've choked,' Barrett said.

I pushed away the voice in my head that told me I was to blame for this. 'I want to see her.'

'Tread carefully,' the doctor said.

When I reached her room, it stood cold. The bedcovers had drowned her, her emaciated grey form disappearing in the blankets. My heart sank. Was I too late? I dropped to my knees at the side of the bed, touching her gnarled hand. She was clammy, a fire under the damp sheen of skin. I tried to uncurl her stiff fingers to let her know I was there, and at last, she grunted, moaned, her head falling to the side, eyes opening to acknowledge me.

Her last words to me all but disappeared when I saw the state of her. She tried to sit up, but was too weak to move.

'Shush,' I said, easing her back to the pillows.

It took her a long while to form the word, her mouth clenching and pinching, but at last it came out, clear into the room.

'Maddow!' She squeezed my hand. 'Maddow.'

I tried to rub some softness back into her bony arm, swallowing thickly before I spoke. 'I'm her daughter. Maddow's daughter. Esta.'

I combed the sweat-wet hair from her face with my fingers, cooing over her like a child. My heart broke at the state she was in, the suffering, her confusion. 'It's my fault,' I said. 'I'm to blame.'

'The house,' she said. More nonsense sounds and words that didn't fit together to make a complete sentence. *Sorry* and *father* and *no* and *baby* and *back there* and *tonight*.

The room fell silent as I cried over her ramblings, thinking repeating the words might help her explain.

'Maddow. Maddow.'

My grandmother reached up to paw my face, to find the parts of me that were her daughter. Her features contorted and a groan of deep, animal pain began in her throat and cracked in her mouth.

'What hurts? What can I give you?'

'Maddow, I'm sorry. Sorry.'

'No, no. She's gone,' I said, trying to comfort her with my hand on her cheek. An echo of her words from so long ago. But my words came with a tenderness, the words I wanted her to hear. 'Maddow's gone now, but she's at peace. She loved you.'

She thrashed under my touch, moaning again, her breathing laboured. I tried to hush her, but she only grew angrier.

'He said . . . I thought . . . He!'

She dug her nails into my arm. Her skin was on fire.

'The . . . the right thing.'

I could only make out half her words, helplessly watching her face screw up tight in pain, tears leaking. In all our years of living together, I'd never seen her shed a tear.

'Maddow,' she said again.

This time I complied, taking her bony hand in both of mine, knowing I might never get to hear her say my mother's name again. I had lived in hope that one day she might tell me more about her, or share the truth about what had happened when our house burnt down, but I knew then, when the doctor stepped back into the room to give her something strong to help her go quietly, painlessly, that I'd never hear it. She wouldn't make it through the night.

'I'm here,' I said. 'I'm here.'

I opened the Great Book, which was still in the same place I'd thrown it. Had she tried to reach it and fallen? I found a passage I knew she found comfort in, and began reading until her eyes shut and I heard a creak outside. I turned to see Barrett in the doorway.

'There's nothing you could have done,' he said, and I saw him take an uneasy look at the book on my lap. 'There's no one to blame.'

'I should've done more.'

'She's been ill for a long time. Guilt won't change things.'

'Forgiveness might.'

He put his hand on my shoulder and said my name. 'There's nothing to forgive.'

My head bowed. I couldn't bear to look at either of them.

In the bed, my grandmother stirred, and Barrett stood over the other side, opposite me. His body creaked as he knelt. She reached for him, but it was only her finger that moved.

'You remember,' she said to him. 'What you promised.'

His eyes flicked over me and then back to her, and he ran his finger along the inside of his collar. 'Sarl . . .'

'You'll look after the baby.'

'She's a woman now,' he said, uneasily, and I coloured, realising he meant me. He looked at the wet of my dress.

'Mae,' my grandmother said, and Barrett's mouth sank at the mention of his wife. 'Like she would.'

Barrett and I were bound by his promise, her dying wishes. Him afraid of the responsibility, and me afraid of myself, of my world without her.

The doctor arrived back an hour after she'd left us, Norah again by his side. He showed no surprise at my grandmother's death when he entered the room, touching her forehead like he might take her temperature and then, when he confirmed it, placing coins on her eyelids. Her mouth was slightly parted and I'd left her that way, but with one swift movement of his hands, one under her jaw and the other on the top of her head, he sealed her up. I couldn't pretend she was sleeping any longer. As we'd heard her slipping away, breath shortening, I had felt her hand stiffen. If I was responsible, could I bring her back? Nothing worked. My silent prayers went unanswered. Too far for redemption.

When Father Jessop arrived, Barrett had distanced himself from the bed, not saying a word. Father Jessop kissed my grandmother's forehead, then mine.

'Such a loss,' he said. My hand went to my face so he wouldn't see the next rush of tears.

His gaze swept over the bed. 'The island is unsettled tonight. I can feel it.' His hand on my forearm jolted me. 'Esta, can I speak with you alone?'

I rose from the chair, my thoughts and soul elsewhere. As we left the room, me trailing Father Jessop, I caught a glimpse of Mull's face, looking away from me like there was something interesting in the weave of the rug. He closed the door behind us, and I was suddenly conscious of my being unwashed and unkempt; convinced I still smelt of the sea.

He took one of my hands. 'I'm so sorry for your loss. This island will be poorer without her presence. We all will.' He paused. 'It is such a shock, so unexpected to lose one of God's own so suddenly.'

My mouth dried, became papery. 'She hadn't been well for a long time, Father.'

'Yet you left her on her own to come to the festival,' he said. 'And she was well enough then? Sitting, walking?'

'I left her in bed. She was upright, talking, reading from the Great Book . . .'

'And a few hours later . . .'

I lowered my head, watching the way his fingers circled my wrist.

His voice changed. 'And how was the festival?'

'It was . . .'

'A peculiar thing. Mull said you disappeared. She tried looking for you.'

I tried contorting my face into confusion or surprise, ready to bleat out an explanation for my disappearance, but all I was doing was shifting my features, giving him no answers.

'Did you leave the festival and go somewhere else?'

'I was . . .'

'Where were you?'

There was a shuffle of noise in the next room and the door opened, the doctor appearing and gesturing to Father Jessop for a moment in private. I took a step back, letting the doctor take my place, saved. Father Jessop might have been interrupted, but his suspicions wouldn't go away. The doctor held the door for me and indicated that I should go back inside.

Norah immediately put her arm around me as I entered. I held onto her, softening into her floral scent of motherliness. They had pulled a sheet over my grandmother's face, placed a wooden cross on her chest. Norah put her mouth to my ear and told me everything would be all right. I'm not sure she believed it, but it was what I needed to hear.

Father Jessop returned and beckoned Mull impatiently.

'There's darkness in this house. Esta, a week with the Eldermothers,' he said. 'Then we can be certain.'

My stomach plummeted, the air taken out of the room. The doctor cleared his throat. Beside me, Norah stiffened.

'The girl needs comfort, somewhere she knows thick.'

Father Jessop's face was pinched at the mouth, a red flash in his cheeks which he quickly controlled. 'What she needs is to be cleansed before anything further befalls us.'

The room was thick with tension. I could hardly breathe.

'She's a child. Her grandmother has just died and you're going to send her to sleep alone in the chapel?'

The doctor shifted on his feet. 'I think she has a point, Father. Sarl's been sickly for years. If anything, the girl's done a good job of looking after her for this long.'

'You'd do well to remember who she comes from,' Father Jessop said. A vein in his neck became a ridge, pulsing.

The doctor's voice was calm, persuasive. 'And Sarl raised her well. Only a child of God would nurse and tend, fast and pray like she has, all in the name of her grandmother's health. If there's darkness at work, Father, it's not in her.'

I was too afraid to move. All eyes were on the Father. His word had always been final. He knew Barrett had been entrusted with my care, but he spoke directly to me, nothing soft left in him.

'Don't let your grandmother's efforts to keep the dark from your door be for nothing.' He left, Mull by his side. Only later did I wonder how much she had confessed to him.

Fourteen

In those first days of living with Barrett, I carried my guilt like a second, thicker skin. All day and all night the percussion of the sea was a reminder of what was so close and what I couldn't reach. But with every moment of longing came the thunder of irrational thought, the certainty that my betrayal killed my grandmother. Barrett brought back to the house with him the sound of gulls and the ripe smell of bladderwrack. My stomach tightened even before the door swung open. The thought of the smell alone was enough to make me picture her dead in her bed. The sea knew what I was, pulling at me at every opportunity.

Barrett and I hardly spoke. This new arrangement, with all that had happened and all the grief I carried, was nothing like last time. I asked him about his day out of politeness, my way of greeting, but he seemed warier of talking about the water. Had he started to see me the same way my grandmother had, the way everyone else had started to – a harbinger of bad luck? Perhaps, like I had, he had fixated on Father Jessop's warnings about my future. There was a time when I might have told him about Cal. I imagined a reaction – confusion turning to curiosity, asking me to take him to the edge of the cove and wait for this strange man of the sea. But then, a slow, stern glance before reporting me to the Ministry, watching me get locked away. I remembered the maps, how desperate he was to keep suspicion from his door; how reluctant to have a girl with a family blighted by tragedy in a house that overlooked the water. I couldn't tell him my secret. I was already too much of a burden, a bad omen.

One night over supper, he seemed too distracted to eat.

'You, here, they're going to be watching us both.'

'I won't be any trouble.'

'It doesn't stop people talking. About you. About me.'

'I should go to the Eldermothers.'

'You be safe. Careful. That's all I want. They don't need any reason to come here.'

The more time passed with my grandmother gone, the more I made my own choices. When Barrett was out of the house and I was sure I wouldn't be caught, I found a vantage point on the first floor, pressed between the wall and the window, body masked in part by the long, heavy curtains. From there I watched the boats coming and going, hungrily learning the way the men worked, the untying of the mooring ropes from their complicated knots, the launching, the way they jumped into the hull without the boat so much as rocking.

I studied them until I could imagine the physicality of them, even when I closed my eyes. I saw the nets spread out in front of the gutter women, a proud display of the men's daily efforts. I saw them return, crofters often coming to help, grappling on the stones to reach the ropes to help heave the yoles out of the rough. In mornings, when dawn broke like an egg in the sky, I would lie and listen to the pranging and heaving of the boats being loaded below. I imagined myself in cap and galoshes, feet finding balance in the rock of the hull. I imagined setting off, following the gulls as they dipped and dived, returning in a boat browned in algae.

I watched the Keepers too, the way they scrutinised each boat before launch, pacing up and down the harbour, asking after men who weren't present, inspecting the haul. And all the time I wondered, was there a way to leave this island? What about Cal's father? I looked at each of the fishermen's faces, struggling to memorise their features from above, where most were obscured by woollen hats pulled down over their eyes. I ran through conversations I might have, deals I could make. I didn't have money or the desirable curves of a woman. I didn't have anything in me to persuade them. It was impossible. I had nowhere to go and no way of getting there. Life beyond the borders seemed nothing more than fantasy.

Every day the door clattered and Barrett began work in the harbour below, I would tell myself tomorrow, *tomorrow* I would find a way to ask him, to hint. Ask him if he'd ever known of someone leaving, ask him how to row against a tide. But there was no way. Instead I woke in a cold sweat, dreaming of Cal's body appearing in one of the nets, his limbs tangled with weed, and with the windows open to the harbour, I would stiffen at any talk – even joking – of men spotting something in the water. I became someone who jumped each time the bell sounded, convinced that the next time it rang, it would be because of him.

One day, when Barrett was down in the harbour repairing boats, I took myself back to the old house. It still smelt of her. Old milk, warm skin, bruised vegetables. I edged around the ice-cold rooms. I climbed the stairs and stared at her bed, trying to reshape our last real conversations, trying to string together the meaningless words she'd needed to set free. My head pounded with regrets, things I should have said to her, answers I should have pushed for.

I stayed there and watched the hours pass, the house uttering its familiar noises, the leak of wind in a draught. It was the kind of eye-watering wind that made you feel that if you submitted, it would carry you away. Eventually, when I was starting to feel stiff and cold, I took items from her drawers and arranged them on the bedcovers like treasure. Scraps of paper, a pendant, vials from the herbalist, a sewing kit inside a tin case. There was so little of her left, no keepsakes, no trinkets that told me anything about her that I didn't already know. At the back of the drawers I found knitted clothes, a wooden rattle, tiny baby teeth in a drawstring bag, an embroidered 'M' on the front for Maddow. There was nothing in the house to prove my mother had ever lived beyond infancy.

My heart jumped at a noise outside. I crept back downstairs and saw someone approaching the door. It was Norah. I hid, back to the wall, with the pulse of a thief. I listened to her leave, but as the sound of her quietened, regret caught up with me and I chased after her, feet thudding on the path. When she turned, I saw a gathering of flowers in her hand, tied by twine.

'I've been thinking about you,' she said, handing them to me. I had never been given flowers before, and I couldn't find a way to hold them without the heads crumpling, without the petals threatening to tear.

I watched Norah, now skittish, she seemed different to the woman who had stood by my side and spoken firmly to Father Jessop.

'I wanted to see how you were, but I didn't want to disturb you down at the harbour. I thought I would leave these,' she said, indicating the flowers. 'I didn't mean to speak for you the other night. Only, if you were my daughter, the Eldermothers' chapel is the last place I'd want you to spend your days.'

'Thank you.'

'It's no place to grieve. My niece spent time there and . . .' She trailed off.

'I came here to—'

'You don't have to explain,' she insisted. Her eyes were wet and it reminded me of when she had been at the house before, how she'd left my grandmother's sickbed the first time.

'You might not remember . . . when you nursed my grandmother, years back,' I began, looking up at the old house.

'Yes?'

'Did she make any sense? Did she talk or mutter in her sleep? I remember . . . she called me by my mother's name, and near the end, it happened again.'

'Oh.' The sound was almost a stopper in Norah's mouth. She struggled to swallow.

'You don't remember. That's all right.'

'She was drifting in and out of consciousness for a long time. And if she said things . . .'

'Did you stay with her? Talk to her?'

'Yes?'

'Do you remember anything of what she said? Only . . .' I took in a deep breath to compose myself. 'Only I know nothing about my mother, and I think she was trying to tell me something, at the end.'

'It's difficult to remember. It was a long time ago,' she gave a short, nervous laugh. 'She wasn't making much sense. At the end, it was like her thoughts were spilling . . . She could have been dreaming. Delirious.'

Norah was a tall woman, but in that moment she looked shorter than I was. Her blabbering had stopped. 'You really look like her, you know,' she said. 'Your mother. Around the mouth, the chin maybe.'

The wind howled between us. There was a slight give behind my knees. Here was someone who'd known her, who might talk.

She blew upwards into her eyes to stop herself crying. 'I shouldn't have—'

'Did you . . .' I stopped myself. 'I've heard things about her. People whisper. But now, I don't think I'll ever get to know who she was.'

Norah cut me off. 'I didn't really . . . Your face . . . It's familiar, that's all.'

'But you know something? No one wants to speak about the dead . . .'

'Sorry.' Her expression was blank, shielded. She pulled her coat tighter and glanced upwards. 'It's about to rain. I'd better . . .' Avoiding my gaze, 'Take care of yourself, won't you?'

I could do nothing but watch her hurry out of sight.

I still woke in the mornings expecting to hear her cough from the next room. Instead, I would hear the coarse shouts of the fishermen in the harbour below *Away! Away!* as the dawn spread across my pillow. I curled into a ball and willed for sleep again, to dream of being in another world.

When the funeral finally took place, the churchyard was full. Some two hundred followers stood around the pyre. This was a sign, Father Jessop said, of Sarl's standing and respect on the island. The sight of him made me uneasy. When he looked at me, it was as though he was peeling back my skin.

'Today we gather in sadness to send Sarl on her way,' he addressed us. The ceremony had opened in the usual way we remembered the gracious dead. Flowers scattered on her sheet-covered body, men bringing peat to add to the fire. Coins pressed into his hand. He told us that giving money to the church was a way of showing how much worth we placed in God. Sombre hymns were sung and the sound cocooned me, all of us in unison. I could understand why my grand-mother found peace in it. It made me feel closer to her, to those promises I had once made.

'Sarl was a woman of unflinching faith. She had the ultimate trust in God, even in the face of tragedy and loss, even when she endured hard sacrifices. We pray for her eternal peace, as her journey to Salvation begins.'

Barrett was restless beside me. He was saying goodbye to another loved one.

Once the final prayers were said and the flames lit underneath her by the Keepers, we watched the fire take hold, the smoke rising to the heavens. Afterwards, Father Jessop would scatter her dust in the sacred earth.

When the ceremony was over, I gave solemn thanks to the islanders who offered me their prayers, who shared with me their fond memories of her, and gradually the crowd dispersed, a few remaining to pay their respects at the pyre. Mull emerged, standing alongside the hog farmer's son again. I hadn't seen her until she approached and when our eyes met, I tensed. She leant up to whisper in Aden's ear, and he sloped away, giving me an attempt at a sympathetic nod.

She came to put her arms around me, and I let her. I had been away from school, away from everyone. Seeing her was a raw reminder of that night.

'I'm so sorry,' she said, her voice so gentle I could not help but soften. Was she sorry for more than my grandmother's death? I didn't know; I still don't. My eyes rested on the nape of her father's neck, the square line of his shoulders. He wasn't a man she could easily lie to.

'If you want to talk, or take a walk to distract yourself, I'm here,' she said, smoothing the hair at the back of my head. 'I'm sorry I haven't come to see you.'

'It's fine. I wasn't in the mood for company.'

She turned her mouth nearer to my ear. 'I've been staying at the chapel.'

I pulled away, saw then her sallow skin, her tired eyes. 'Why?'

'Father.' Aden lingered close by.

'You're together?'

She played with her sleeves, nodding. 'Only for a while.'

'You never said.'

'I would have told you before anyone else, Esta, I just didn't want my brothers to find out. Or Father.'

'He sent you to the Eldermothers for keeping it secret?'

'He caught us together and he worried I'd . . .' she lowered her voice, 'sullied myself.'

'You wouldn't.'

'No! I could never. And Father knows that now, but when he found out, he was furious, said he wanted better for me than a farmer's son. That's why he sent me to the chapel, to repent, to earn his forgiveness and seek guidance from God.' She recited the lessons drummed into us. 'I was wrong to lie and cavort around with Aden with no thought of how it looked. I know that now. If Father had forbidden me from seeing Aden, it would have been all my fault.'

'He hasn't?'

She let a smile edge out. 'God showed him that Aden is a good man, a faithful one. He's one of seven boys – can you believe it? So when we reach age, we have his permission.'

'To marry?'

She smiled before guilt dropped her expression. 'It feels wrong to talk about it now.'

'No, I'm pleased for you.'

She pulled away slightly; my head a haze from the pyre fumes and the drain of emotions. Her world had not shifted, had not flattened like mine. The secrets she kept meant nothing in the end. Her joy felt so far from my own mood that I could barely summon words from a deep tangle.

'You must be so happy,' I said.

'I know it was God's decision, but if He had chosen anyone else for me . . . And you will be happy too, when the time comes.' She spoke too insistently.

Father Jessop approached, interrupting us, a single tear running down his cheek as he embraced me.

'Oh Esta,' his voice breaking up.

He smelt different, almost devoid of scent. In my life I hadn't thought much about my father. I hadn't needed to. It had only ever been my mother I missed. There wasn't a place for another man in my life, with both God and Father Jessop demanding enough. In his arms, I was frozen at first, unsure how to hold myself around him, afraid my body would betray me. But he held tight, my breathing steadied by his, by his arms around me.

'She's at peace now,' he said as we separated. Hearing it from him was so final. He gave me a cloth to wipe my eyes, keeping his arm around my middle.

'I can't believe she's gone.'

His hand cupped my face. 'She was like a mother to me too. I know how you must feel. But you're never alone, sweetheart. You're a child of God. Don't forget that.'

I tried to nod.

'*Have* you forgotten that?' he asked.

Heat flooded to my face, and being conscious of it made it worse. 'No, Father.'

'Have you let God's words slip from your heart? Because if you have, you can come to me and we can help. Sarl worked so hard to keep you on the right path.'

I swallowed, afraid that the tears pushing at me would give away my guilt.

'You're strong enough to withstand the temptations? Even living in the harbour? Does he encourage your faith?'

'We pray together.' My voice wobbled, and even I wasn't convinced. 'It's what she wanted for me, to live with Barrett. He's a kind man.'

In all my years of going to church with my grandmother, I'd hardly seen Barrett attend, and when I asked him about it, he said he had too much keeping him busy in the harbour. Most of the fishermen were the same, working on Sundays. Barrett preferred to pray in private, he said. But since his worry that we'd be scrutinised, he had attended every weekday service by my side, praying and singing hymns like we both meant every word. Father Jessop had seemed surprised to see him there, listening to stories of good deeds and rules, God's power and punishment. He performed devotion, but I didn't understand until years later how much he struggled to sit there, burning in his own secret rage. He went to church for me. He suffered to protect me, to prove I was safe under his care.

'Perhaps that's what he's always needed, a good woman to steer him back into righteousness,' Father Jessop said, looking Barrett's way.

He was silent then, studying me. His thumb swept over my scarred cheek and I had a strange feeling in my stomach.

'*The spirit is willing,*' he said. '*But the flesh . . .*'

He leant in to kiss me before he left. I was alone again. He knew what I'd done, what I was. It wouldn't be long until everyone did.

Fifteen

In the late summer, when the sun was bright and held onto a vague warmth, Mull and I walked to the chapel, necks arched, looking at the sky. In the grass was a confetti of mottled pink flowers, and by the cliff edge, the busy shuffling of puffins. Above us we watched the turn of the sky, each cloud morphing and separating until it crawled out of sight.

She pointed up at the shapes. 'Rabbit.'

'Loaf of bread.'

'Angry crofter.'

'And his mangy old dog.'

Together we laughed. I looked back across the island, along the path we'd taken, passing white houses gleaming in the rare sunshine, washing lines blowing in the breeze. The sheep were still grazing, scattered as far as the eye could see, basking in the heat of the sun. Like them, we relished the warmth, the long days and vast pink skies when the sun finally sank. It was the sort of day when I tried to keep my eyes firmly from the horizon. The sky was so clear there would have been the haze of the Otherlands if we'd looked. *Foula*. I shivered. But of course I didn't look. I knew better than that.

I took in lungfuls of sunshine air and felt myself split in two. Outwardly I was the same girl as ever, the solid weight of the Great Book carried against my chest, saying grace before meals, praying before bed, keeping my eyes away from the slick of blue sea, but inside I was a whirl of bruising, conflicting fears and thrills. Life on the island felt easy in the everyday, but underneath it all, I knew there was more out there. But then I'd be sitting on the church pews, heavy, guilty, God-fearing, sea-fearing all over again.

Mull pulled on my arm and both of us were squinting back at the clouds. She gave a soft inhale of delight.

'Look, it's a baby,' she said. I saw her hand sweep her stomach.

'It's a bug. One of those black, big-bellied things with the horrible little legs.'

I expected her to laugh, but the air was empty. She stopped in her tracks. In the distance, we could see other girls our age and older standing outside the chapel, waiting for the Eldermothers.

'You always have to ruin anything nice I see, Esta.'

'What else do I ruin?'

She didn't answer, but quickened her pace towards the chapel. I could see Seren in the distance, her friends beside her, all of them with their hair cut to the same length. Mull had asked me if I thought it would suit her, and despite the hollowed-out sensation, I'd told her yes, and watched her reappear like another copy of Seren. I *had* seen the baby in the clouds, but I didn't want to say it. Babies were all anyone our age could talk of now.

'Have you heard the news?' Mull asked as we approached.

That kind of question always made my stomach lurch, but she carried on before I had the chance to speak.

'Seren is getting married next month!'

'What? To who?'

'Doran, of course! It had to be a Minister, didn't it? I couldn't imagine her marrying anyone less. Her father saw to that.'

Doran. Even his name made me want to run, but Mull was already ahead, shrieking into the crowd of girls with excitement, joy for this happy occasion, clutching Seren's hands. A wedding meant the whole island gathered, a feast, music and garlands of flowers. I was one step behind, feeling the ticking clock, unable to suppress the anxiety.

We stepped inside the chapel, the air smoky with sage. After we were cleansed, our bodies wet and pimpled with cold, we arranged ourselves in a circle. We were instructed to purge our dark thoughts, confess dreams and temptations, quiet moments in the middle of the night where we'd been lured to touch between our legs, and with enough remorse, would be forgiven. The Eldermothers felt our bodies with their skeletal hands, reading our souls, finding the married girls among us who they deemed ready for their mother-years, ready to submit to their holy duty. Those ready would no longer attend the daily ritual because their time had come. The rest of us who drank were jealous they'd reached this momentous stage. Today, three girls knelt in the middle of us, each of them already partway through her motheryear, each of them yet to conceive. Father Jessop said that women on Eden's Isle all descended from healthy, righteous people. Infertility and deformity were not in our blood; only a lack of faith and a disturbance from the Seawomen could ever disrupt the natural blessing of life. I looked at these women, performing the visualisation rituals the Eldermothers gave them, trying not to picture them in a boat, on their backs, carried out to sea.

In the final months of school, lessons for girls were centred around domestic tasks, skills our teachers told us Otherlands women shunned. This was where the downfall of society began, letting men or machines complete women's roles. We were taught to cook family meals, grow vegetables, bake, clean, sew, knit and nurse. Everything that would make the island thrive, make us competent wives and mothers. We pored over Seren's copy of *Notes to Wives*, a pamphlet written by Father Lambert, based on his marriage to Dinah, and when our teacher was out of sight, some of the girls, who had heard straight from newly-wed Seren, would exchange everything they knew about the marital act, making it sound unclean and painful. I sat, knees squeezed together, lips clamped, keeping those low, fluttering feelings I'd had at night, between dreams, a secret. Pleasure was meant to be of no importance to us, only duty.

In the autumn, during harvest, when school had finished for girls my age, who were marrying or taking on bigger roles within their households, I found work in the largest arable croft, helping to grow vegetables that would then be sold from the shop. The work was physical, brutal on the coldest, wettest days. I welcomed the way my body thrummed with hurt when the day was done. I was grateful too for my mind to be taken away from the harbour, the press of the future. Every month that passed, every blood that came, I couldn't stop thinking about the child I would need to grow to earn my place. I hadn't even thought about the man who would be chosen for me.

In my darkest days, I reasoned that there was no way of stopping time, just like there was no way of having a different future.

Lower Farrow was the croft where I worked alongside two other women in the allotment. The house that overlooked us, as we made space for the seedlings with our knuckles, was dark-roofed, two chimneys and white stone-flecked walls that glared bright into my eyes whenever the sun was out. One of the women who worked in the garden with me was around my age, and the other much older, a grandchild on the way. All the other workers called her Nanna, because her hair had lost all its colour at the age of twenty. She liked to talk. Not just about the crops or the weather, but about personal affairs, which always left me wary of how to respond. She had stories and gossip about each member of her sprawling family, from her aunt's escaped hens to the second cousin who'd lost a quarter of his teeth during a fight in the alehouse over a bet.

In my first months of working there, I talked little, answering Nanna only when she spoke to me directly, but mostly letting her and Lyne chat between themselves. I had no family stories, no husband. I was even timid about telling them I lived overlooking the harbour. Most days they arrived for work before I did and were deep in the topic of Lyne's 'sweetheart', as Nanna called him. Cowan was his name. He worked on the patrol ferries, the revelation of which made the skin along my collar warm. He was one of our gatekeepers. I felt resentment for a man I didn't even know.

'Did you pick, or was he chosen? I can't remember,' Nanna asked Lyne, grunting as she heaved a layer of soil onto the freshly planted kale seeds. We occupied the same area of the plot, close enough that we didn't need to shout, but distant enough that there were times I could keep my head down and fade out Nanna's stories about her sisters' marriages.

'Chosen,' Lyne said, using her forearm to wipe her nose, which was streaming in the cold. She tired easily and was soft in the mouth where Nanna was hard. 'Not that it mattered. As soon as I saw him, I felt like I'd picked him myself.'

She was nineteen, due to be married in the summer. Cowan had been chosen for her because he had just one sickly younger brother and a mother too damaged internally to carry another child. His bloodline was a risk, weak, his mother under scrutiny. Lyne came from a fertile family, five siblings, the youngest of whom was conceived when her mother was forty-three.

'I look forward to the wedding,' Nanna said, and then looked to me like I should agree. I could only smile, nodding in detached agreement.

'And then you'll be busy with the babbies.'

Lyne's face rounded and she patted down the earth like she was tucking in a blanket. 'I'm itching,' she said. 'There's twins on my father's side.'

'Hey, wouldn't that be something! The island hasn't had twins in a while.'

'My mother gave me this when Cowan and I first met. For luck.' Lyne wiped her muddy hands on her overalls and then from the neck of her shirt pulled free a pendant. From where I knelt, I could just make out the shape of a woman carved into the wood. Dinah. It was the same as the statue of her in the chapel, the one that some women kissed for luck when they were trying to conceive. God's ideal of a wife and mother, of a woman. Looking at the pendant, I thought of Cal's.

'Let me see. Oh, would you look. It's perfect. Hey, Esta, isn't that perfect? What a perfect gift from your mother, Lyne.'

'Perfect,' I repeated, with nothing else to say.

Lyne ran her thumb across the face, then tucked the pendant away. I could see her focus drawn to my scars. 'It was your mother . . . wasn't it?' she said to me. 'How old were you when she died?'

'I . . .' I clammed up, looked at Nanna as if she might save me, but she had her head up, watching, listening for my answer. 'Three. I think. Around then.'

I half expected Nanna to change the subject, or for Lyne to ask if the adjacent plot needed raking, but instead Nanna began.

'The thing I always wonder is this . . .' she put down her trowel and wiped her hands on her dungarees. 'Always thought she must have started that fire herself. Fires don't just happen on their own, you know.'

'We shouldn't—' Lyne said, hurriedly, but Nanna hadn't finished.

'It wouldn't surprise me. You know what was going round about her.' Nanna gave me a knowing look. 'And another thing – something I heard at the time, don't hold me to it – only one body was found. Too burnt to see who it was, but they said there were three of them died in that house. Three. So what happened to the other two? Course, you were only a babbie, you wouldn't know, but you, Lyne – do you remember it? What was her name? We never saw her again.'

Lyne shook her head, not knowing whether to look at Nanna or at me with pity.

'She was the sister to the nurse. The tall, dark one. Norah.'

I was frozen with this new information. Norah's sister?

'Are you sure Lyne, you were only wee yourself.'

'We shouldn't speak of the dead while the crops are growing. It's bad luck,' Lyne said, shutting Nanna up.

I said nothing the rest of the day, but inside I picked at the scab. There was such coldness in Nanna's voice that I couldn't ask her any more about my mother. I would hear a version I didn't like, one I wanted to defend against. There wasn't a single person on the island who didn't know the story of how my parents had died, but none of them had been there, none of them had answers. At another time in my life I'd hear of the aftermath, the way the blackened husk was left standing for a few days, still smoking. Some avoided it, found the sight of it unbearable. But for others it was the opposite, flocking to see the remains, lingering in morbid curiosity, swapping rumours. How many bodies? How long did it burn? What about the baby inside – how was I rescued? How did it start? The place was eventually demolished, and no new house was built on the ground where my mother, my father and another woman died. I was the only living thing left to show it had ever happened.

In the afternoon, we were needed indoors for pickling, and our fingers would wrinkle with vinegar. Being inside didn't change the atmosphere, but Nanna had fallen into a new topic, giving Lyne her best advice for conceiving a child.

'Diet,' she said. 'People forget about that, but it's the simple things. Milk, lots of it. Honey and garlic, in a paste, before every meal. And sleep too. That's important. But I tell you what does work. Sharing a bed with a pregnant woman – course, you don't want to touch the bump, no, that'll do no good to either of you. It's something about the smell, the heat.'

She carried on. Full moons. Burning sage. All of it Lyne took with a serious nod, her eyes travelling left to right as though her brain was keeping notes. Nanna's advice rotted in my ears. I still hadn't been able to shake free from what she'd said about the fire. If she was right, then I knew who I had to speak to.

After the next Sunday service, girls crowded around Seren, marvelling at her body, her belly. Three months on from her wedding, she was already pregnant, showing a slight bump when she pulled her dress tight. A week after her wedding, she'd been granted her motheryear by the Eldermothers, and we'd all attended the ceremony, listening as she was declared healthy, physically and spiritually. It helped too that she and Doran came from good families, with a history of strong, fertile men. Seren was jubilant to be granted her motheryear so soon after her wedding, and when it was announced, she kept reminding us how rare and honourable it was, as if we didn't already know. As though our whole girlhood hadn't been spent watching women get married and wait and wait for their motheryear. Some wives waited years until they were deemed ready, their faces graver and graver until the Eldermothers finally looked them up and down, pinching their flesh and telling them their time had come. Those like Seren, whose wedding day and motheryear ceremony happened side by side, were the holiest, the purest of us all.

In the church, I pulled away from Seren and the attention the girls our age lavished on her, spotting Norah at the back, dealing with her youngest's tantrum.

'Let me help you,' I said, stepping in to lift the little one out of her seat. Lily, the squawking girl in my arms, was darker than her sister, and louder. The elder girl, Fia, with her paler, rosy complexion, held onto Norah's hand, blinking up at me as if to ask who I was.

With a signal of my head, I indicated we should go outside. When we were out of the confines of the church, I suggested I help her home with the two children, especially with Lily quiet in my arms, mesmerised – or frightened – by my scarring. On the walk there we made general chit-chat: the weather, the puffins, her children, my new living situation, everything a veil over the subject I really wanted to talk about. The children helped with this; they were a good distraction, especially Fia, who sang on the way.

Norah's house was in the north, up by the turbines, but not as far as Lambert's Hill, which I was thankful for. The walk was uphill and tiring at the best of times, but with Lily in my arms, it was more of a battle.

'Do you know what the hill was called before they named it after Lambert?' Norah asked.

I was so awed by the thought of new, secret knowledge.

'Me neither,' she said with a sigh. 'I see it every day and it plays on my mind. What this island used to be. How little we know.'

My skin grew warm. This kind of talk wasn't normal, and yet because she had started it, I wouldn't be the one to close the door. I thought of what Cal had told me about the old names for the Otherlands. Lambert must have come here and wanted to erase history, wipe all traces of the old world from the island, including its names.

'And the island itself?' I asked. 'Do you think it had a different name?'

She gave me a look. 'I don't think it was always Eden. Do you?'

A line had been crossed. Inside me, adrenaline skipped at the thought of someone else on the edges like me. An ally. When we arrived at her door, she thanked me for helping with the girls and ushered them inside.

I looked hopefully through the doorway. 'Can I come in?'

She held onto the door protectively. 'Why?'

Nerves fattened in my throat, but I managed to get the words out. 'I think there's something you're not telling me. About my mother. And your sister. Please.'

Norah became still; even her eyes didn't move. She stared straight past me. 'What do you know about my sister?'

'There's a woman where I work, at Lower Farrow, who said there were three people in the house that night. The night of the fire.'

'. . . Give me a minute to clear up, then you can come in.'

When she let me in, there were an inordinate number of chairs in the room, as though there had been a group prayer, but some of them had been scooted back, abandoned.

'I shouldn't have forced my way in uninvited.'

'It's only mess,' she said, offering me a seat.

There was a noise above us, the ceiling slackening under footsteps. 'Full house. My girls, my cousin Olsen and his wife, their three.' Norah's husband had died of blood poisoning not long after Lily was born, and we all left flowers by her door.

'You must be, what, seventeen now?' she said, after returning from the kitchen with two nettle teas. I wondered if she used the tea-making to gather her thoughts. 'And you haven't been given a husband yet?'

I shook my head.

She folded her legs underneath her on the couch. 'I hope you get one of the good ones.'

'If I'm lucky.'

'You'll make the best of it when the time comes.' There was some-thing unguarded about her in her own house, the way she sat and spoke, that drew me in.

'Before, you said I look like my mother?' I turned my face away as soon as the words left me, the question too vulnerable.

'A little.' She paused. 'It's under the surface, more of a spirit. Your hair is very different, though.'

I smiled, enthralled to hear there was such an obvious difference between us. It made me feel closer to her.

'I loved your mother's hair,' she said after a while. I treasured every word. 'She had this dark, dark hair cut to just under her chin. My mother made me wear mine in a plait, and I was so jealous.' Norah's smile was almost breathless. Her hair was a violet black. She shook her hand through it. 'Years of tying it up made so much of it fall out.'

I leant in, expecting her to tell me more, expecting my mother to come to life, but instead, 'It must have been hard growing up without her.'

'It's harder not having her here now. I like hearing about her.'

'What do you think she'd tell you?'

'I used to think she might have the right words, but now I'm not so sure. People mention her in passing. They say things.'

'Your grandmother never . . . ?'

'When she was sick, I think she was dreaming or trying to tell me about her, but . . .' I locked eyes with Norah. 'You never mentioned your sister before.'

There was a flinch in Norah's face, and she stood up. My fingers dug into the edge of the seat cushion, waiting for her to tell me to leave, but she walked to a drawer and pulled out a square of white, a handkerchief. There was an 'R' embroidered in red.

'Rose,' she said, holding the handkerchief out towards me. 'She was older than me. Beautiful, funny. Of course, she didn't see herself like that. She used to spend so much time with the Eldermothers. I used to think she wanted to join the chapel, but it wasn't that. I think she hoped they might help her . . . that they might change her. She couldn't see that she was perfect as she was. It took her years to finally see herself, without this show of regret and guilt they'd given her. She realised in the end, but it wasn't me who convinced her . . .'

Her words drifted and then she scrunched her body as if trying to reclaim it.

'Your mother did that,' she said, as I ran my thumb over the stitches. 'I couldn't tell you before. I couldn't talk about it. But Rose and your mother were close. They used to spend all their time together. Your mother, she was clever and quite serious, tall – much taller than you are – and she could sing. Really sing. She and Rose used to make up these ridiculous songs.'

As Norah spoke, my head was a swirl. I tried and tried to picture Maddow, then Maddow and Rose. But there was no shape or detail to them. The thought of them laughing and singing was magical. In an instant, my mother was more alive than she'd ever been.

'Why didn't you say before? About Rose? The fire . . . she was there too, wasn't she?'

'I didn't think it would help. I—' She interrupted herself. 'Rose has been gone a very long time. Sometimes it's easier not to remember. To let her go.'

Above us, there was another creak in the ceiling. I felt unwelcome and I made my excuses to leave, and she thanked me for my special way with Lily. At the door, she stopped me, touching my arm.

'What I've told you, about Rose,' she said. 'You won't tell anyone I said that, will you? People talk enough.'

'I won't say anything.' She might've been holding back, but Norah wasn't going to tell me more if she couldn't trust me.

'We're not supposed to miss women like that, not when they're gone. Not when they're . . .' Her voice trailed off. I tried to follow her meaning, watched as she forced a smile. 'But we do, don't we? How can we not?'

Thinking back on that time, I understand why all thoughts of the fire, of my mother and Rose disappeared so quickly. I remembered Norah's words about letting go. I had lived with my mother's absence and the questions about her life for so long, and what good had it done me? I knew I didn't want her legacy. Rumour and reputation. I could not live and die on the island like my mother had, dogged by stories of tragedy and bad omens. I could not die and be remembered as deserving it. How could I pursue this futile task of finding reason in her death when all around me I was told the only way to save myself was to be the opposite of her? I heard it from Barrett, to keep the past buried, and now I'd heard it from Norah too. But the festival was soon, Cal a beacon in the distance. I couldn't bear to stay away from him, no matter the risk.

Sixteen

One night as I neared home, walking downhill towards the harbour, dusk close behind, I saw smoke coming from the chimney. Something was wrong. Barrett was never home that early, and it was my job to light the fire. The nearer I got, the tighter the knot in my stomach. All bravery leaked out of my boots when I opened the unlocked back door, hearing voices inside. I was tired and my clothes were dirty, scuffed at the knees, soil under my nails and smeared across my face. I heard a voice. Doran was in the house.

I pressed my ear to the door.

'What time are you expecting her?' Another voice joined Doran's. It was Father Jessop. His placid tone didn't put me at ease like it did in church. It was the opposite, a roiling fear.

'No woman should be out of the house for hours without reason. It's this sort of lack of boundary that worries me.'

'She works. She's a hard worker.'

I could feel the pressure of the room, even standing in the hallway, so I made my arrival known, re-shutting the door with a bang, wanting to rescue Barrett from their questions.

All the men in the room stood when I entered. Barrett was the slowest, and my attention lingered on him, the way his hand curled protectively around his stump. He looked tired, winded. Father Jessop came forward to embrace me. He rubbed his thumb over the cross I wore, resting on my chest. The contact was intimate, lingering. He put his arm around my shoulders.

'What's wrong?' I asked.

'Do women always think the worst?' Father Jessop asked, giving a stale laugh. I expected Doran to join in, a mirthless tug of noise, but his face was all contempt. Father Jessop indicated to the others to sit, and led me by the hands to sit too.

'Remind me how long you've been a woman?'

I folded my hands in my lap. Tried to remain calm.

'Since I was fourteen. I'm seventeen now.'

Father Jessop was quiet in thought before moving on to pleasantries: choir, visits to the chapel, my work, reminding me not to use too much of my energy on the land, but to look after my body too.

'The festival,' he said, in a booming way that shattered the still unease in the room. It took all my effort not to react, as though he knew it was on my mind. 'A few weeks from now . . . It's going to be a special one. I need you there by my side on the night. I don't want Mull to have to go searching for you again.'

'What's special about it?'

He placed a finger to his lips. 'I wouldn't want to spoil the surprise.'

When the festival came, I could hardly speak. I had dressed, then found myself unable to leave the room, no air, pain from my chest spreading outwards until my fingertips tingled. I pushed the weight of my body against the wall and hoped it would seal me in. There was a knock on the door, Barrett's gruff voice.

'It's time to go.'

I stood in front of him. It took all my effort not to cry. I was angry with him too, inexplicably, as though he should have been able to persuade Father Jessop to change his mind.

When we arrived, I did not have the stomach for food or drink or dancing. The bonfire smoke made my head hurt; the sight of the dancers, their familiar seductive trance, made my insides roll. I couldn't even feign interest in the stalls, could barely raise a smile for those I knew. The celebrations glided past me in a dream. Even Barrett could see the way I stumbled, stared into space, leaning in to talk to me over the music.

'You have to try,' he said; then, more kindly, 'Don't let them see you like this.'

The night was racing away from me. I pictured Cal in the cove, waiting, assuming I'd changed my mind or something worse had happened. I didn't like to think about the latter, that he might dare to come looking for me. I checked my grandmother's old wristwatch repeatedly, and watched as Father Jessop joined in the revelries, passing from group to group, deliberately dragging out my torture.

Two hours passed before he was leading me towards the bonfire, beside Mull and Phasie. Crowds gathered, the music silenced and Father Jessop rang his ancestor's golden bell. His smile was lopsided. I stood there beside the two other girls with their nervous giggles, feeling like bait on a hook. Mull pressed her hand into mine. I was numb, but it wasn't the first time I'd had to put on an act, so I smiled, looking at her, holding myself rigid against the collapse of all hope.

'Welcome to you all on this most glorious night!' Father Jessop began. 'We thank every man who has delivered fish in his nets this year, brought food to our tables, every woman who has resisted evil and presented a child of God to our island. We have seen healthy children grow before our eyes, formed in His righteous image. We have seen fertile land and plentiful seas. We have seen the continuation of the values the Lord wishes his creations to uphold. Another year of glory. We celebrate this night not just for ourselves, but for the generations to follow. For the preservation of our people and the pathway to Salvation.

'This island was built with care. Men and women coming together as God intended, to fulfil the needs of Salvation, to keep our home thriving. Tonight, as we look around us, we see in each other's faces God's work living true, living as we ought to. Tonight we must look forward as well as back to preserve this sacred place we have built.'

There were ruffles of excitement as he spoke. This was the part they looked forward to. It was the part I'd once loved too.

'Marriage has a greater purpose than affinity. We don't make the mistakes of the old world. We marry for duty, not love, to fulfil God's wishes. And with that in mind . . .'

I was not in my body as it stepped forward, as I was presented, a ram for sale.

'. . . tonight we carry out God's plan.'

I fell away with every word. Father Jessop called out the names of three men, but I didn't hear them. I was barely able to focus when a man stood in front of me, could only take him in in fragments. Tall, all elbows and shoulder blades, his auburn hair unkempt and falling into his eyes yet flat on top, like he'd been wed to a fisherman's hat, the one I could see balled in his right hand. He had a ruddy complexion, lips thin and dry. But his nerves, head slightly lowered in front of me, gave him an endearing quality. His eyes too, slightly small for his face, but lined with long lashes, were handsome. If I was any other girl I might have been grateful to be given a man with his looks. Except he wasn't just any man. The dark, the shock had helped conceal him, but now I could see. The man chosen for me was Ingram, Doran's younger brother. A look of him around the jaw, the planes of his forehead. I wanted to run.

'These unions are made for an optimistic future,' Father Jessop said, extending his arms out to us. 'And it gives me great pleasure that my daughter is among the brides tonight. These are righteous men from good stock, and their strength will compensate for any weakness, any indiscretions we might see in these brides. These men are strong in mind and faith and each will keep his wife in check and away from the dark temptations that crowd her, so long as she obeys him.'

There was nodding and grunts of contentment in the crowd. If I stayed still enough, I'd be invisible, an unattractive, miserable prospect. Ingram could refuse. Men had a say. But judging by his meek smile, it was a decision from above and he had as little choice as I did. It was already decided.

'We'll leave these lovebirds to talk awhile,' Father Jessop laughed. 'The rest of us – drink, be merry, give thanks. Next week they'll be married and we will celebrate again!'

The cheers flared in my ears. A week. That was all I had before another shackle came down. A woman's life belonging entirely to her husband, moving into his family's home. I would belong to that same house soon. Seren would become my sister-in-law, Doran my brother. As soon as I married Ingram, I would sleep in the room next door to the man who had left me to drown, for the rest of my life.

I couldn't let it happen. As the gathered refilled their cups to toast to the future, I saw Aden take Mull's hands, swinging her arms with excitement; I saw Phasie take a step closer to Wynn, visibly triumphant that she would marry before her sister Abeth. And then Ingram and I were alone. His hands twisted with indecision. I couldn't stand the thought of them on me, but soon I'd have no choice. I pushed mine deep into the pockets of my coat. He nodded at me, a greeting without saying a thing. He seemed to hold the words in his mouth for a long time, false starts of flustered noise.

'You live by the harbour now?' he asked, rocking forward on his feet, a tangle of awkwardness. I noticed he had the same thin, hard line of a mouth that Doran had, but there was less animation in him, like the thought of marrying me had exhausted him.

My eyes moved upwards, my answer obvious but silent.

'I'm training. For the fishing boats. Like my old man.'

'I know.'

'You're friends with the John girl? Mull,' he asked.

At the mention of Mull, I tried to look at her sidelong, a cry for help, one she was oblivious to. She was the happiest I'd ever seen her, smiling up at Aden like he'd shown her the stars.

Ingram was looking at her too. 'That's her,' he said with a nod. 'Seren's friend too.'

'I'm not a friend of Seren's,' I said, not wanting him to expect me to be anything like his brother's wife.

'Suppose I haven't seen you together.' He looked down, licked at his mouth, feet folding inward. Was he thinking about her then, this gust of pure womanhood who had swept into their house and carried out all the duties expected of her like she was honoured to do so?

'Do you want a walk, around the stalls or . . . The girls wearing the crowns are about to . . .' His voice barely lifted above the crackling bonfire. 'I know it's strange like this.'

'It's late,' I said, his apologetic nature almost making me feel cruel, but I was thinking about the cove and how long it would take me to escape there.

'Some time until the fireworks still. We could watch them together. If . . .'

'I'm tired.'

'Right then.'

My words had dented him, and I was almost sorry for that.

'Another day.'

'If you like.' He gave a sort of shrug. 'We should get to know each other. I could show you the house.'

I looked at him blankly.

'You . . . you like music?' He pulled and folded the hat in his hands and felt the tug of the band starting up again.

'I don't want to dance.'

'Right then,' he said again. Our attention was caught by Mull and Aden, moving towards the musicians. We did not have that. We couldn't.

'S'pose you're not hungry either?'

I confirmed his assumption, and he laughed nervously before it turned into a grimace. 'You always enjoy yourself at the festival like this?'

'It's never been like this.'

He conceded. 'You're right.' He scuffed at the ground in his tattered work boots, and I thought of my new duty, to clean them, to wash his clothes and bathe his hands when they were cut and infected, ruined by salt water. 'We should . . . try and make the best of it.'

The smoke was getting to me. I felt a hysteria building. I wanted to laugh. He was waiting for me to speak to fill the distance. I kept my mouth shut.

'It's God's plan and He knows better than all of us. We just follow what's right,' nodding to himself like he was trying to convince me as well as himself. He glanced at my scars then away again.

I stared at him, the haze of the fire. I didn't see the handsomeness; it was just the empty face of my inevitable future.

'It's all boys in my family,' he said as a point of pride. All boys? Another son would make everything all right. 'Lots of kids too. Might be a bit crowded for a while until we get the house sorted. There's three of us brothers, then Seren and Vayle. You now as well, the kids . . .'

'Ask your brother how he feels about this match,' I said. 'He must have known you'd be given me.'

'Doran? He hasn't—'

'You must know what he thinks of me.'

He pulled at the hat in his hands.

'You learn how to live with him.'

I wouldn't learn to live like that.

'This isn't down to him. We're obeying God,' Ingram said.

He stepped forward and I didn't back away. He could have been a worse man. They could have forced me to marry a bully, a drunk, a widower three times my age. I tried to think of the positives I could muster. Father Jessop could have picked a man as punishment, a man who'd keep me docile with his fists. Instead he'd chosen a boy, barely a man, gentle, God-fearing. Not like his brother.

But from the corner of my eye, I saw one of the dancers, dressed up as a Seawoman, and the water came back to me. The salt, the weed, Cal, the thought of freedom. I ached.

Ingram held out his hand like he was going to shake mine. Like we were men concluding a bait deal. This hand that in time was meant to become as familiar as my own.

'I need time,' I said, my own hands staying where they were, tucked away. 'I need to think.'

'All right.' He put his fisherman's hat back on, pulled it down until it reached his eyebrows. 'We'll see each other soon? It was nice to see you, Esta.'

When he had left, returning to his father's stall, I could finally breathe. Mull and Phasie had left to spend time with their promised, too giddy, too distracted to remember me. I was conscious of the time, how little of the night was left. Barrett came into view. He carried a bag with him, opened it up to show the contents.

'Got you this,' he said. It was my favourite, blackberry bannocks.

'Maybe later.'

We faced the bonfire. The heat and the smoke made me want to hide in sleep.

'He's a good lad. Hard worker. Patient. I never have any trouble with him.'

I knew that was the closest he could come to saying that everything would be all right. What did it matter when we could do nothing to change the outcome? Ingram was to be my husband whether he was a good man or not.

'We could look at what Cunningham's got for sale. I could do with a new table.'

'Barrett, I can't—'

He didn't suggest anything else. The festival marked a whole year since my grandmother had died, yet around us it was like nothing on the island had changed the way I had.

'I keep expecting to look up and see her haggling at one of the stalls,' he said, echoed my thoughts.

I was silent, cold, my body turning away from his sympathy. 'I'd rather be on my own tonight.'

'Right you are. I'll keep these for you at home, then.' The bag of bannock rounds rustled in his hand.

I watched him leave. Soon I would take my chance. Following behind clusters of families, hiding among the noise, edging closer and closer to an escape, until the band struck up and the dancing and whooping began again and finally I could slip away.

I ran until every bone hurt, adrenaline my only fuel. Blisters breeding blisters, ribs that felt bruised. I was sure when I finally staggered to the cliff that the cove would be empty, that I'd lose everything in a single night.

I gathered up my skirt, tearing down the uneven cutaways in the cliff side, desperation squeezing at me. Sand, shingle, rocks, I ran straight towards the sea, breathless, deafened by my own heartbeat, wet running from eyes and nose. I could not call for him, so I stood, water up to my shins, my body screaming the name I couldn't say. I bowed, looked right into the water. Wondering, would it be so bad to drown tonight? To end it, to feel something? To have control.

A hand touched me. I jumped. Made of nothing but ice and fear. But I knew that weight, knew that hand, wanted to fold into relief. Cal, the moonlight striped through his wet hair. He was older, more handsome, too real to be one of my dreams.

'I almost thought you weren't coming,' he said.

I didn't let him say another word, throwing my arms around him, his sea-cold meeting the heat of my tired, panting body. He didn't flinch, but softened, surprised, his hand touching the back of my neck. I couldn't hear anything over the shock of my pulse. Not even the sea.

'What is it? What's happened?' he asked.

I said nothing, refusing to pollute the time I had left with him. I breathed him in, and stared out at the black waves. Fixated. Then I stripped myself of my coat, my boots, began pulling my arms from my dress.

'Esta?' He'd had the same concern a year ago, but I was scared then; now I had nothing to lose.

'You said you'd teach me.'

'Now? Right now?'

I bit down hard inside my cheek, thinking about how quickly the night was disappearing.

Cal could only watch, drawing back as I left my clothes on the stones, removing everything, even my underslip, until I was as naked as him. Our moonlit bodies stood in contrast side by side. He looked at me, unmoving, my chest rising and falling. I wanted him to touch me, to hold me, but I walked instead across the rocks towards the waterline. I could feel his eyes on my body, but my focus was the dark cape of water. Nothing would stop me. Bare footprints landed in wet sand. It had been so long, but the cold was familiar. I launched myself forward, striding further and further until the water was pulling me off the ground.

Cal called out for me to wait. I kept moving. Thicker and faster the waves came, darker and colder. My heart taking frozen gulps.

He swam in front of me, our skin so close to touching. The water glided around him without resistance, whereas it took every effort for me to keep steady.

'You need to slow down,' he said. 'Your body has to adjust to the cold.'

I ignored him, pushing forward, blood freezing over.

'Easy! You'll hurt yourself.'

The water pressed us closer, enough for him to feel every crackle of my pulse. My body felt as slick as his. My hand met his hip, my thigh brushing his. He wasn't holding me, carrying me, but our bodies moved as one. We were floating. Surrounded. Submerged. An echo of before. He reminded me how it went, a hand on my chest.

'Breathe.'

He smiled, but I couldn't.

'You've changed,' he said.

I inhaled sharply to dull the chatter of my teeth. 'Taller.'

That smile again, sending a buzz straight to my gut. 'It's more than that.' He touched my chin, his face turning serious, tilting me towards him. 'Tell me what's wrong.'

'Just teach me,' I said, toeing the water to move further out. I didn't want my life on the island to exist. My body bobbed uneasily, one leg kicking, the other stuck still. I clutched hold of him, one hand on the centre of his chest, his patchwork of scarring.

We talked then only in instructions. He made me hold my breath until my lungs were stretched at the seams. He placed one hand below my ribcage and told me to breathe deeper, release in short, incomplete bursts. He was so patient and I felt stupid.

We started where the water was shallow. His hands loosened to let me lead, like learning to walk again. My body tried to glide. Under my feet I felt the sharp edges of shells and bird bones but I managed not to lose my footing. I slid over obstacles, weightless, flowing; the deeper I went, the greater the pull. Thoughts lapsed, the cold clamped around my chest and the gulp of air I found was tight and dusty. I flailed and splashed, hyperventilating until I managed to right myself.

His hand disappeared under the surface, and then I felt it flat against my ribs. 'The colder you get, the tighter it will feel.'

His fingers were so close to my heart. Blood pounded in my ears.

'Lie back,' he said, lowering me into the water.

Above us, the starred night spun, as the water hit my spine, the back of my neck, until finally the cold needled into the crown of my head. It took me like I weighed nothing, and even though my body screamed danger, I remembered what he had said: to relax, to breathe, letting me mimic the actions of swimming without any fear.

The water seemed to grow more powerful the further we went from the island. He taught me how to hold my neck, arc my arms in the water, but I forgot his instructions, my arms splashing down, frothing the surface, until my eyes were bleary with salt water. He steadied me, but I was eager to swim alone again, stubborn determination pushing away all his caution. He murmured words of encouragement and I ate them up, freedom exploding in my veins.

I came to a stop and looked across the water. What would it be like to relinquish complete control? Where would I get to, if anywhere at all? There was no place for me out there. A world beyond my understanding. A world I could never reach. I put my hands on his arms, a part of him so arrestingly human. His ridges of muscle could have been from pulling ropes and hauling crates in the harbour. For a moment I let myself imagine a different life for us, but I couldn't get the picture to fit.

'Just for a while,' he said, 'forget about that place.'

I looked away, blinking through my tears and the onslaught of defeat. How could I forget? I was about to become a wife, more bound to the island than ever before. Cal could see my grief, but he didn't ask me any more questions. He held me close, stroking the wet splay of my hair.

'I should go back,' I told him, shivering.

'You've only just arrived.'

'I'm sorry.'

'So this is it? Until next year?'

The water seemed suddenly still. 'I'm getting married.'

I hated the way his expression changed. 'When?'

'Next week.'

'A week.'

'I don't have a choice.'

'Is he a good man?'

I didn't have an answer.

There was a flicker of something on his face I couldn't read. If I told him that I wanted to leave, that I wanted a different life, would he find a way? He had already shattered my idea of the impossible. If he couldn't save me, then who could?

I touched his face, eager to commit him to memory. 'I always knew the day was going to come that I'd have to . . . do my duty. That's what my life was always going to be. No swimming, no sea, no islands. No world beyond. No you.'

'You shouldn't be there. You're not like the rest of them.'

'There's nowhere else.'

His face was still, grave. We were so close that my breath matched his rhythm. He kissed the edge of my scar. Again, above my lips, along my jaw. I pressed my mouth to his. Slippery, salty-sour. I was conscious of my body in a way I had never been, a thrum of need, a power that scared me.

'Are you saying goodbye?' he murmured.

'I don't want to.'

'Then don't. We'll keep meeting. Even if it can only be this night.'

I allowed myself the dream that it was just the two of us, free to do whatever we wanted. Sometimes I do it now, cold and alone, in the dark. I pretend he's there; I pretend we have a chance.

'Lie for me,' I said. 'Pretend it can be you and me like this some-where else in the world, somewhere that will have us both. Where they won't look at me with you and . . .'

'Esta . . .' His face crumpled.

The tips of our noses touching. 'Make it up,' I said, kissing him again. 'So that at least when I'm dreaming, I'll have somewhere else to be.'

MOTHER

Then, only in cleanliness, comes her reward. It is done. A child in His image. Watch the mother nourish the son. Watch her teach him to please his father and obey the word of God. But above all, keep your eye trained to her, the mother, so that she may restore the earth, for that is her calling. On and on, until her fruit runs dry.

DUTIES 62:52–53

Seventeen

Ingram and I married a week after the festival. A week after I'd swam. The ceremony took place on a mild afternoon. Inside me was a storm. I wore a garland of flowers, arranged by one of the young girls volunteering at the church. She'd bitten her lips pink and her eyes were wide with anticipatory hunger for the step into womanhood I was about to make. I had felt that once. As I bent to receive my garland, I wanted to whisper *run* in her ear. But I was exhausted. Ingram was plain-faced and serious speaking his vows, his clammy hands holding mine as he made his promises. I knew he meant them, even if inwardly he was as unhappy as I was. He'd combed his hair, smelt of perfumed soap. We kissed to cheers. It was done. The earth falling away. My whole life flattened to a single word. Wife.

When the feast had been demolished, I sat on a stool, the night of celebration racing around me, and Mull saddled up beside me in her dress, giddy on dancing and breathless joy, asking me what was wrong. I told her it was happiness keeping me subdued. The pressure of being centre of attention.

'It's a happy occasion!' she said. 'The start of the rest of our lives.'

'Doesn't it worry you? The thought of being a wife, a mother?'

I watched Ingram, the man I couldn't bear to think of as my husband, given drink after drink by his brothers, jeered on, the runt of the family married to a woman like me. Earlier, I had heard his brothers jibe about the wedding night and I'd pretended not to hear. Mull looked over to where my attention was focused.

'He hasn't hurt you, has he?'

'He's not that kind of man.'

A few days before the wedding, when my head was full of dreams of swimming, the way Cal had touched me, Ingram had appeared at the door of Barrett's house with a loaf of bread his mother had made.

I hid and watched him wait for an answer that never came. He left it on the doorstep.

Aden was in our eyeline, chasing some of the children, pulling faces, pretending to be a bear. He was large enough for it, making them run and scream. We laughed at his antics. I was happy for Mull and resented her in almost equal measure. There weren't many girls on the island who got to choose the man they wanted.

'Has his mother warmed to you yet?' I asked, looking at the barrel-shaped woman nearby.

Mull sighed. 'I don't think anyone would be good enough for her son.'

'But you're a John.'

'It's the John sons that matter,' she said. She leant against me. 'I'm so glad we got to share today. Aren't you?'

I nodded. There was truth in it. Out of anyone, I was glad it was Mull. But there was a level of openness I couldn't risk, not when she'd been the one to notice my disappearance on the night my grandmother died, not when she'd seen me wade out into the water. I couldn't have her dwell on what made me different.

'I'm nervous,' I said. 'For tonight. To be his wife.'

She hugged me tight, nudging her mouth to my ear. 'Tonight will be fine. Seren told me it gets better with time.'

I felt no desire for my 'husband', but pleasure was not part of our duty, neither was want.

Mull stuck out her hand. 'Come on, dance with me.'

I took to my feet, held her hands, let the dizzying spins career my thoughts away. I wanted to dance right out of my body. When it was just the two of us, nothing else seemed to exist. But when the music stopped and our hearts returned to their usual rhythm, she excused herself to see her new husband. I stood alone, watching their intimacy, and it couldn't have been more obvious how different our lives were.

In those first few months of marriage, in the house we shared with his siblings, I remember two things as clear as if they happened yesterday. Ingram's cold, chapped hands, my head turned towards the window; and long nights awake, the baby crying in the next room. Doran and Seren's new baby, an ugly thing with too much hair. He cried like no other. In the daytime when he bawled, I could feel Ingram watching me, waiting for me to react. If my grandmother had been alive, she would have told me that a baby so new, so close to God, could sense there was something evil in the house. I'd have known who she meant. Ingram cooed over the boy, slotting his finger into baby Morley's fist. I could feel the longing clinging to him like sea mist. I only held the child when he was thrust into my arms, and struggled to find the platitudes expected of me. Hiding my grimace when Weir elbowed his youngest brother to say, 'You'll be next, Gram.' It came out of his mouth just like it did Doran's, less of a brotherly tease and more like a competitive challenge. But unlike Seren's joy of having her motheryear granted as soon as she was married, mine hadn't been.

The Eldermothers kept reminding me it was good to be in a house with children. The noise, the smell, the presence of fertile women would all help encourage visualisations, to picture our infant in our arms, all the ways we could show God we were ready. I had visited them, encouraged by Seren, who had volunteered to attend with me, reminding me that we were sisters now.

'You're not ready yet,' the Eldermother said, her words stinging. Seren had stood there, scrutinising me in the same way. The fear inside me was heavy, at having to go home and admit to Ingram, or worse, the whole family. But in me also a relief bloomed. If I could hold out, then perhaps I could see Cal again, and together, this time, we would find a way out.

The Eldermother pressed the heel of her hand across my lower belly.

'You know what is wrong,' she said. 'You feel it already. A black mark.'

I expected her to say more, to see through my skin and speak it aloud in front of Seren – my grandmother always told me it was impossible to hide anything from the Eldermothers – but she said nothing of my secret life.

Afterwards, though, Seren wouldn't engage me. I wanted to

speak to her before we reached the house, to persuade her not to say anything until I had the chance, but that wasn't what stopped her.

'What did she mean, a "black mark"?' she asked me.

'I don't know.'

'There are young children in the house.'

'You can't think that I—'

'I'm a mother now and I have to be cautious of these things.'

'I'd never harm a child.'

'Not intentionally.'

'Not at all.'

'You should speak to Ingram. Be honest with him.'

'There's nothing to say.'

'Do you think it was living with the old man? The boat man?' she asked.

'Barrett? What can he have done?'

'Well, you living so close to the water like that. Or was it your mother?'

'What about her?'

Seren gave a half-shrug.

'I didn't even know her,' I said.

'You don't have to *know* her. You're part of her.'

'It'll be my time when I'm ready.'

'And when will that be?'

I assured her I was trying.

After that, she started making me separate, fortifying meals, dropping suggestions into conversation about how I should pray, what passages to read, hinting in front of Ingram, making mealtimes unbearable.

One night, as Morley screamed the house down in the early hours, the sound getting under my jaw, it took everything I had not to get out of bed and leave that house. Walk in the dark, shake off the noise, the tension. Escape. Ingram stirred beside me.

'You awake?' he asked, his cold foot touching my shin, which I quickly drew away. 'Seren thinks the baby's ill.'

'He's a baby, they cry all the time.'

He sat up in bed, watching me in the dark. 'She's worried about him.'

'She needn't be. There isn't a woman on this island as faithful as her.'

'Perhaps it's something else,' he said.

I saw a shadow of a bird move across the ceiling.

'Have you heard something?' he asked.

'No.'

He readjusted the blankets, patting them flatter. 'You're meant to tell me everything.'

'If I'd heard something, I'd tell you. Besides, Seren knows far more people than me. She would hear it first.'

The mattress underneath us slackened and firmed as he moved into a more comfortable position to talk.

'What do you want to know?'

'Anything. About your day, about your thoughts.'

'There's nothing worth saying.'

He sighed. 'It's been months, Esta, and you treat me like I'm a stranger. Like you've forgotten how to speak!'

'I'm used to being on my own, talking to no one.'

'Well, things are different now,' he said.

'I liked how it was.'

'I want us to be like man and wife.'

'We share a bed,' I said petulantly.

'It would be nice to have the rest of a marriage.'

'We can't be like Doran and Seren.'

'I know that.'

'I told you that from the start.'

'Esta . . .'

I bolted up, swung out my legs and sat on the edge of the bed. Knuckles into the mattress, head bowed, gathering strength.

'I went to the Eldermothers. With Seren. To ask them about my motheryear.'

'I know.'

My head snapped round, and I glared at him through the dark. 'Go on then.'

'Seren told me that the Eldermothers said you're not ready yet.' He spoke in a measured way, like I had become someone who needed tiptoeing around. He chose his next words carefully. 'They said that there's a darkness in you.'

'That's not what they said. She's twisted it.'

'Don't take your moods out on her. She was trying to help. She was worried about you.'

'She interferes.'

He laid a hand on my back. I was too drained to shake him off.

'I'm doing everything right. They told me I have to wait.'

'So what did they mean, about a black mark?'

Morley's crying had weakened, and I felt the lure of sleep clawing at me.

'I'm tired.'

His hand fell away from my back. I heard a sighing shuffle, but I stayed where I was, eyes half lidded. We had been married for more than a hundred days and I had felt every single one, forever playing a part. I felt the bed move again, shaking me out of my trance. Ingram pressed his damp forehead on the nape of my neck, putting his arms around my middle. He didn't like to sleep on an argument. He didn't want his parents' marriage. He'd confided in me that he bore the brunt of their volatility. Showed me *his* scars.

'We don't have to talk,' he said. 'You're right. God will bless us when it's time. If it takes you longer, then . . . so be it.'

I put my hands over his. Most husbands would have gone to Father Jessop by now, but he hadn't. We held each other. There was something deep and enduring within me that craved physical contact, that him touching me filled. But it was impossible not to let my mind wander. His head moved, and his mouth came to the crook of my neck. His breath was too hot and stale, his skin too dry, but if I tried hard enough, I could picture Cal. I had hoped our wedding night might be all it took. We had kept the light on, regretting it when it exposed our bodies in the sickly light. Tonight we kept our eyes closed. I felt him harden. Both of us imagining somewhere else, another room, another bed, another body.

* * *

Months went by like this, and when my eighteenth birthday arrived, I had been married almost ten months, still without a motheryear ceremony, and no miracle child conceived. A failure.

The festival was two months away, and even Ingram had commented on a lift in my mood. Every passing day was a step closer to being able to breathe again. I hoped to spend my birthday with Barrett, but Seren had insisted on preparing a meal, the table piled with food. It was Doran who led the prayers before we ate, standing at the head of the table.

'Lord, we thank you for this meal, for our clear nights and calm seas, and for your watchful presence among us. For protecting us, for guiding our women onto the righteous path. Bless this table and those who sit around it, bless the children, those growing and those yet to form. And finally, Esta . . .' he raised his cup towards me, giving me a glance that rippled down my spine, 'may the Lord look after you especially on this blessed day.'

The others joined in offering their well wishes. Doran had never said a word about what had happened between us in the past. He and Seren had treated me like a stranger when I moved in, but I always felt it in the air between us, like a threat he could use at any time.

'All right then, let's eat,' he said, taking his seat.

There was a shift of laughter and chairs withdrawn to stand and serve. Seren placed a plate loaded with dark meat and greens in front of me. There was no reprieve from her routine, the way I was singled out among the women.

'Still no joy?' she said softly, though the table was small enough that everyone could hear.

I caught Vayle's pitying look. The men began talking among themselves. I could only hear snatches of conversation over Seren and Vayle discussing the food preparation, but certain words snagged my skin above the noise. Fences. Nets. Fortress. It was enough to make my throat close, the food turning to ash.

'Not long now,' Doran said, and I realised I'd drifted in and out, overcome with heat and sickness.

Beside him, Weir nodded, and I looked at Ingram, trying to catch up to the pace of their conversation.

'How soon?' he asked.

The table hushed. Doran drew attention with a scrape of his chair. 'A year, maybe a bit longer.'

'What is this?' I asked, surprised to hear my own voice out loud, the first words I'd spoken since the meal started. The room seemed to shrink, eyes looking between me and Doran.

'It's only in the planning stages for now,' he said, pausing to drink. He pushed his plate out of the way, preparing himself. He didn't speak directly to me; his words took shape between all of us. 'A new way to keep us safe. We're going to build fences, a whole barrier around our waters. Twenty foot above and deep as we can get. Nothing's getting in or out, apart from the boats.'

'There's been noise in the harbour of something being seen in the south,' Ingram said. I immediately thought of Cal, risking coming back before the festival, though I'd warned him not to.

'It'll be nothing. Fishermen and their bollocks,' Doran said, interrupting his brother. 'These fences have been years in the making.' It sounded like he was echoing Father Jessop.

'It seems like a good idea,' Weir said, as the rest of the table agreed Ingram red-faced from Doran shutting him down.

'Now, can we move on from this awful talk of the dark sea?' Seren asked. 'It is Esta's birthday!'

Doran's moustache swallowed up under his nostrils as he grinned. 'But it's good news! I'm sure Esta will be glad to hear it.'

I smiled weakly, my head spinning with images of our horizon lost to great sheets of fencing. No way out, no escape. Nothing getting in or out. The relief and chatter bubbled up in the room, buoyed by a sense of victory and protection, but it was as much as I could do to keep my food down.

'Who caught these?' Doran asked, pointing to a plate of salted herring. His voice had the boisterous edge of too much drink. He pointed at Ingram. 'Was it you?'

Ingram nodded, fist against his lips, trying to swallow to give his comeback.

'Your bait can't be up to much if this is all you brought home! Dad brings back three times as much.'

Weir said nothing, but his gums glistened.

'Same bait as Dad.'

'Difference is, Dad knows what he's doing.'

'Doran . . .' Seren knew the routine: Ingram's meek habit of letting his brothers say whatever they pleased. She locked eyes with him across the table. 'It's plenty, thank you, Gram.'

The drink flowed and I barely touched my plate. Weir was suddenly on his feet.

'Quiet,' he said. 'Time for some happier news.'

I wished I could disappear that very moment.

Vayle looked up at him, leaning on her elbow, her hand concealing a grin. 'Sit down, stupid,' she said. They had a matching laugh between them like a secret code, their expressions mirrored. Everyone paused and watched on as Weir straightened, propped up by Vayle. His thumb drew shapes along her collarbone. As I watched this small act of tenderness, I could imagine what Ingram was thinking. That they'd been like us once, thrown together as strangers, and they made it look easy, familiar and tender in a way we'd never be.

'What's this?' Seren said, her voice a light squeal like she'd already guessed.

I knew before it was even said. It stuck like dry bread in the roof of my mouth. Everything held still, waiting for the inevitable.

'The Lord has blessed us again,' Weir said. 'Vayle's pregnant.'

Chairs fell away in celebration. Forks dropped, hands opened to hold and hug and smooth over her stomach, which wasn't even showing. Seren began crying, but I sat unmoving. All of it hit me at once, spreading like water in lungs, until I wasn't at the table any more, I was somewhere else, watching the celebration from above.

Ingram. The weight of our childlessness was obvious in the room. He was overly loud in his congratulations. He put his arms around Vayle and then Seren, a hand on the small of her back. They parted, eyes brimming with tears, embarrassed almost for their open show of emotion. I had to get out. Too many thoughts of the barriers, of the way those in the room thought of me as a useless hollow of a woman. Ingram and Seren returned to their seats, happily touching cups. No one looked at me; no one wanted to.

* * *

In the month before the festival, Seren recruited me to help her clear out some space in the house to prepare for Vayle's new arrival, and dutifully I carried old furniture out of one of the upstairs rooms.

'Where will it go?' I asked, expecting her to suggest we use it for firewood or donate it to another family. She led me around the back of the house, down a short, overgrown path to a shed that in all my months of living with them I hadn't known was there.

'What's this?' I asked, stopping a little behind her on the path.

'An outhouse,' she said, a wrinkle between her eyebrows. 'Just full of the boys' old junk.'

As she unlocked it and daylight poured into the gloom of the shed, the mothy smell of rust and wood peppered my nose. When my eyes adjusted, they were drawn to the little things. Old tools, hooks and hammers, boxes of childhood items. Shelf upon shelf of untouched remnants of the past. And at the centre of it all, an upturned yole on a workbench. Rough and unfinished, with planks missing. But there it was, a boat, no chains or locks, no Keeper guarding its coming or going. I shifted closer, hungry to lay my hands on the wooden slats, struck by visions of me dragging it to water. But Seren beside me was a reminder of my limits, the rules.

'Whose is this?' I asked.

I hoped Seren interpreted the quiver in my voice as fear.

'Ingram's,' she said. 'Franklin gave it to him, said it was useless and unseaworthy. I think Gram's been trying to prove him wrong. Fix it up, make it as good as new. He'll manage it, I'm sure.'

She hesitated approaching the boat, but then smoothed her hand against the hull. She had the confidence to do that; she'd already proved herself.

'I think . . .' she said, pausing as she considered whether to carry on. 'Well, his hope is to pass it down to his son . . . Hasn't he mentioned it to you?'

It didn't matter that she acted like I knew nothing about my husband. Here was a boat, here was a chance.

When the festival came, I had a flicker of an idea. Under my dress, I pulled on a pair of Ingram's torn waders that I'd found forgotten in the bottom of a trunk. Just the thought of them against my body was thrilling. I dressed with Cal in my head, imagining his reaction when I told him about my plan for the boat in the shed. It had to be now.

'We're leaving to help Dad set up the stall,' Ingram said, calling into the room before he settled in the doorway. 'Are you coming?'

'One minute,' I said, pressing my hands against my chest to try and calm down.

'You look nice.' He seemed nervous, lingering, unsure of whether to follow up on the compliment. 'Has it really been a year since you and I . . . since we were matched?'

Our eyes met in the mirror. He had not felt every hour like I had. I broke away from his gaze and concentrated on checking my reflection, hoping there was no obvious sign of my rebellion. I needed to be normal. Invisible.

'All set. Shall we go?'

I couldn't eat or drink a thing. I tried to burn away some of my energy with Mull, dancing around the maypole with the twists of dyed ropes in the traditional weaves and plaits we'd learnt as girls. Mull was talkative that night, itchy and alive. She was in the same position as me, without news of her motheryear, but there was something knowing in her smile as we spoke about the year to come.

We crossed our ropes together in time to the music and she squeezed me. 'It'll be soon for us, I can feel it!'

I wanted to stop, to hold her close and tell her everything, but I had no choice but to keep it all inside, treasuring our short moment of contentment, lost in the music and hoping she would at least remember me as I was, and not listen to the stories that would be spun. I wanted to free her from the island too, but she was happy, her smiles were real. She couldn't know the truth.

Mull returned to Aden, telling me she'd see me later, and I walked the length of the stalls, noticing every minute that passed. I tried to look for Barrett, knowing I'd feel calmer in his company, but there was no sign of him anywhere. Even if I couldn't say goodbye, I wanted the chance to tell him what he meant to me. I had gone to his house the day before and found him staring into space, the front door unlocked. My arrival had made him jump out of his skin.

'Are you not working today?' I'd asked, handing him a box of radishes from Lower Farrow.

'It's Friday,' he said, looking at the box as if he was unsure what to do with it.

I laughed the kind of involuntary, nervous laugh that just slips out. 'It's not. It's Tuesday.'

He approached the kitchen table, where his log books were spread open. There was a grid of days, names, dates and times, a few shaky pencil marks of things crossed out. He jabbed at the page with his finger.

'Friday.'

I looked too, a nervous feeling in my stomach. He was pointing to a date last week.

'Here,' I said, moving his hand to the correct day. 'Here's today.'

He stared down, head tucked to his chest. 'Tuesday? Is it?'

I didn't want to ask; I didn't want the guilt of knowing and leaving him behind, but I had no choice but to ask. 'Are you not feeling well?'

He took heavily to one of the chairs and rubbed his hand across his face, then looked again to his log books like they were a stranger's. He'd always had a slightly confused way about him, struggled to remember all the names of the lads in the harbour, but other aspects of his work life he could retell in such acute detail that the rest just became his way – a kind of hazy vagueness, an ability to ramble on and lose his track of thought. I had to block out that low kicking sensation, a need to abandon everything and look after him.

'You're tired,' I said. 'That's all.' I'd come with the radishes as an excuse, hoping to put my arms around him and give him a sign that my time on the island was ending, so that when I was gone he would remember my last visit and cling to that. Standing behind him, out of sight, I wept.

'I'll let you get some rest,' I told him, and left.

I hated the thought that I wouldn't have one final moment with him. I visited all his usual festival haunts. I thought about the recent months when I'd seen him. So distant and distracted. It must've been difficult for him when I'd moved out, but there was something else fogging his mind. He insisted he was just getting older. I'd mentioned it briefly to Ingram after a visit, and he told me how Barrett was working less and less in the harbour, and that when he did, his teaching disintegrated into tangents and confusions.

As I embedded myself into the throng of the festival, my attention floated in and out of conversations as I passed.

'. . . she didn't look well at the chapel.'

'No, what else have you heard? There are new lambs at Hythe Fields. They haven't been affected, have they?'

'You know Sterling? She's only got three months left. There's always been something about her I've never trusted.'

I pushed through, and saw Seren and Ingram in deep conversation away from Franklin's stand, in the shadow of another stall, hidden by the noise and bustle around them. I backed off, not wanting them to see me, but they didn't care about anything around them. They were leaning in, Seren's head pointed down, one hand touching the back of her neck. He was talking, she was smiling, shifting her hand from her neck to brush loose hair out of her eyes. For a second, his fingertips touched her wrist and she lifted her face to him. Their closeness made me blush.

How had it passed me by before then?

The first few dinners we'd shared, I'd shrunk, watching Seren and Doran, Seren and Weir, and Seren and my husband talk with ease. I feared I'd never know him. Not in the same way. I remembered my first meal in that house, a new wife, unable to touch any of the feast they had prepared. For entertainment Doran had told an exaggerated story of his younger brother's attraction to Seren when he was a boy. He had howled and the rest of the table had laughed along. It was a cruel way of belittling Ingram, embarrassing him and me. Seren had grown uncharacteristically self-conscious, fingers at her pink collarbone, helping herself to more food as a distraction, and Ingram had reached for the brandy to occupy the strange shape of his mouth. They had laughed, but it barely touched their faces.

As I stood there watching their intimacy, it was a relief to say goodbye to them, to that house. All of it washed over me. It didn't matter any more. I'd be free.

I turned my back on them. My thoughts were already racing ahead. The cove. Cal. I couldn't let myself linger on the details. If I made it away now, they would realise too late. I could feel the freedom already. Until. Mull. It was the top of her head I noticed first, the way it was adorned with silver. A crown, charms tinkling from it as she tilted her face in a lopsided grin. My stomach knotted. In her hands was another crown, for me.

'Are you ready?' she asked, a little too loudly.

Behind us I heard Seren gasp with delight, leaving Ingram behind as she approached, brought over by Mull's declaration. My hopes of invisibility were falling away by the second. Seren had never worn the crown, she had never taken part. She hadn't needed these silly island games of luck. She was pregnant before any of us had blinked. When she didn't see my mood mirror hers, her eyes widened with shock.

'Don't tell me you've forgotten?' she said, her incredulity almost a squeal. 'She has! She's forgotten.'

'I didn't realise it would be now. It's already late.' I'd miss my chance.

'It's tradition!' Mull said.

The tale was, Dinah had worn a crown like this every festival. To retain the crown at the end of the game imbued the wearer with her fortune, her prospects of fertility. Before I could make my excuses, bile rising, Mull placed the crown on my head and dragged me forward. My neck felt as if it would buckle under the weight as we walked, and all I could hear was the jangle-jangle of the charms, the sound that was meant to drive the Seawomen away.

A crowd had gathered to watch, most of them men, penning in a patch of scrubland, joy in their voices. One of Mull's brothers presided over the game, arranging us into a circle. Childless married women, all of us without our motheryear, all of us hungry for a change in luck, all of us wearing crowns. I knew the rules. I'd seen the game play out before, walked by as the roars and the cheers reached a crescendo, covered my ears as the clamour from the crowd made the earth shake. The game was simple. In the centre of the circle was a doll of a Seawoman, made of sacks, stuffed with cloth scraps, sand and seaweed.

Her face had been embroidered with horrifying features. Mull's brother, Keller, held it aloft. We had to destroy it.

'Tonight's winner is the last woman standing. You rip the head off this doll and keep your crown on, victory is yours. Understand?'

The nerves of our collective had an energy that made my fingers tingle. Winning didn't guarantee a motheryear – only the Eldermothers had that decisive power – but it showed a readiness, a propensity for luck. Another test to pass. To retain the symbol of Dinah's crown meant destiny. To breed boys. End the Seawomen. Preserve the island. Reach Salvation. To fail, to hesitate or stumble, that was as much an indicator of what we were as victory was. I saw the crowd thicken and shift. I saw Doran come to the front, eyes fixed on me. A smile.

A whistle. Fingers and tongue. Who moved first? Teeth and claws. Blood. A thump. Bruise. Bone. Slip. Pull. Hair between my fingers. An elbow. A boot. Spit. Dirt. Bite. Limbs too fast and I was at the centre of it. No air, no direction. A flail, a push, a grab. Sight of the tattered doll, thrown out of reach. My heart went with it. My chance. My luck. I shoved. I fell. The crown still there, still heavy. Doran's face. Ingram. Blood on the sheets. An empty cot. Knots at my wrist. The sway of a yole. The Eldermothers saying *not yet, not now, not ever.* Bad luck. My mother. Grandmother. No fortune. Not enough faith. I pushed up. A growl. Fight. Centre of my chest. Possessed by something feral, uncontrollable. Now. Or never. A woman at my side, falling down. Crack. Crown skittering away. Heads butting. My shoulder barging into a woman's back. Watching her trip. Another down. Two came away bleeding. The Seawoman high in the air, tail, guts spilling. Cheers. Clamouring for more. Mull slipped, crown lost. Three left. A wrestle. Scratch. My hair yanked back, neck lolling. I lunged. The doll captured in my hands, feet firm. I used my teeth. Two hands. Ripped the head clean off, tossed the body into the spectators. Braying. Hungry. Satisfied. I tasted blood. Touched my scalp, cheek. Blood. Black. Faces in front of me swaying, coming into focus. I'd won.

Beaten by exhaustion, I dropped to my knees, seeing for the first time this facsimile of a Seawoman in my hands. I was shaking. Around me the women left in my wake, cut lips, clothes ripped, weariness giving way to amused defeat. They helped each other up, lamenting their lost crowns. I dropped the doll's head, looking down at my hands. A body I didn't recognise. An unfamiliar rasp of breath. The discarded severed head. What had I become?

I didn't have a chance to think. Keller announced me as the winner. The crowd swarmed to congratulate me; women touched my fortune-filled crown. I was floating. Numb. Euphoric. Broken. They chanted my name. At every step was recognition, someone wanting to buy me a drink, wanting to see me up close, the woman who had destroyed a symbol of *them* with her teeth.

They did not see how it had destroyed me too.

The night wore on and I was trapped. I was too late. I couldn't go. The fireworks burst across the sky and died. All my hope with them. All my plans for nothing. Cal would think I'd given up, that this was the end.

I was chained to Ingram's family. Was this how it was always going to be now, for every festival? The sounds of their celebration making me smaller and smaller.

Ingram was drunk and happy, dropping straight into a deep sleep as soon as we got back, but I didn't, couldn't. I left the house – not caring if I was caught, not caring if Doran was awake, listening – and made straight to the cove. Sat and shivered, face pressed into my knees, the tide coming closer and closer. But no tears would bring Cal back.

As I was about to leave, resigned to the emptiness ahead, I noticed a single pale shell upturned on top of a dry rock, balanced deliberately, and something glinting in the belly of it. It was an abalone shell, the same as he had held up to my ear to let me hear the world that existed beyond my reach, and when I moved closer, inside was Cal's pendant, left behind for me. A message. Hope. A promise of return. I fastened it around my neck, the cool of it warming instantly against my skin.

Another year. What if it was too late by then?

Eighteen

The cliffs were crowded with warblers the morning of my motheryear ceremony, the sky an odd, sickly gloom of orange. I could see my breath, the one sure sign I was still alive. It had been three months since the festival, since I'd tied Cal's pendant around my neck. The day had finally come. The countdown was about to begin. Had my victory at the festival been enough to convince them I was now worthy of a child? Had my 'black mark' really disappeared? Mull had been granted her motheryear at the same time, and I couldn't dismiss the feeling that she'd convinced them of my worthiness.

The chapel was lit with candles, and my hair dripped onto the clean white tunic I'd been given. The other women of the island lined the nave, hands clasped, humming joyfully as we were led to the chancel. One by one these women were invited to the front to give me and Mull their prayers and advice, for mothers to stroke our stomachs, for newborn children to be proffered for us to hold. We were ready to be mothers ourselves now, God had decided. Here was our year to prove our worth. Inside, a part of me died, but I wore a face of stone. Only Norah drew anything from me.

'It will happen,' she said, before moving away and another woman was in her place.

Don't dust under the bed. That disturbs the spirit of the unborn.

Lie with your husband during a full moon.

Kiss Dinah's statue seven times.

Keep your front door unlocked and make sure nothing blocks it.

Women approached me to hand over their children. As I stared down into these innocent, unknowing faces, I could only see futures without choice. I wanted to set them free somehow, to pull them to my chest and whisper about the world out there. I couldn't look at Mull. I wanted to suck the happiness out of her. But I did the only thing I could. Comply, say my thanks at each blessing, make my promises to God.

'You will feel a change now,' the Eldermothers said at last. 'God is ready to bless your wombs with the fruits of life. Feel Him inside you, the energy within.'

Mull smiled at me, her fingers splayed on her lower stomach.

'I can feel it,' she said, looking at me in wonder. 'A tingling.'

I felt nothing.

Later that night, Ingram came home from a day catching herring, the smell of brine through his hair and hands. For a moment, he was too much of a reminder of what I wanted. Something stirred. I responded to his kiss in a way I hadn't before. When I withdrew, he was as surprised as I was.

He touched my stomach. And just like that, all my desire fell away. Reduced to a job that needed to be done.

Weeks folded together hopelessly. Every day seemed a futile trance until the night. To lay there. I don't remember any of these nights, except an exchange of fluid, bodies moving into place. A burning sensation after I emptied my bladder. A trip to the herbalist. Two months went by without success, with more pitying looks from Seren, a grimace from Ingram at the sight of my blood.

'Will this ever work?' he asked one night when the room was hot with our slowing breaths.

It has to, he wanted me to say.

Instead I put my hand on his thigh, to kiss him and prove I was willing, I wanted it, I was doing everything I could. But his cock curled away as he rolled onto his side and shut down any further attempt to try. We lay there in shame.

Neither of us is really here, I said to him, but only in my head.

His affection for Seren filled every room, pushed me out. He had a different smile for her, a different way of speaking. With her he shared all his little jokes about his day, while with me it was functional: the weight of his haul, how much he sold, what was for supper, the sex.

As we lay in bed, outside the threat of a storm circled the island like a predator. The rain matched the tension in my body. The seams of the sky would split and then the questions would start: who was to blame for this? There was no child yet, no proof of my faith, and more bad luck for our family. Here was the evidence and accusation stacking against me.

My fingers found their way to Cal's pendant. The last fragile symbol of hope. When Ingram had seen it for the first time, treasured against my naked skin, I had pulled away from letting him touch it.

'It was my mother's,' I said, and watched a look of concern pass across his brow.

'Why would she have had a fisherman's charm?' he asked. 'Will it really bring you the luck you need?'

'It's mine now, and I'm wearing it.'

'You can have mine,' he said.

'I want hers.'

I held onto it and thought about the spin of the world, a beach I could explore unrestricted, a sea with tides I could learn and swim through. I would come and go, sail a boat, row from horizon to horizon under the stars. I thought about Cal showing me the way, unlocking my freedom, following me not from duty, but with desire, free will.

I lay there and let the rhythm of the rain wash over me. My skin itched with a craving for touch. Cal's absence had grown a hunger in me. The pressure of his hands on my hips, pulling me into the water, making me weightless. I wanted that again. A lifetime of it. The power, that searing cold, body to body.

Weeks later, Vayle and Weir's son, Irwin, was born, and it was decided, in a family meeting that I sat on the edges of, that it was best for the household if I gave up working at Lower Farrow entirely to help Seren and Vayle with the cooking, chores and childcare. Weir, the eldest of the brothers, was the unspoken head of the household, and gave me no choice in the change of situation.

'Lower Farrow puts food on our table,' I said.

He raised his palm. There was no discussion to be had here. It was decided. 'You can tend our garden. Grow whatever you can. That will be enough for us.'

And so my opportunity to escape the household confinement, to have independence away from Seren, Vayle and their young boys, had diminished to nothing. Even my visits to Barrett were scrutinised. I had gone to see him every week, even though in recent months he was irritable and didn't seem to want company, but when I mentioned him once over supper, Seren asked, 'Do you really think it's wise to be visiting the harbour so often to see him? It's your motheryear.'

My throat burnt, a scolded child.

'He's family,' I said.

'We're your family. And it worries me that it might affect your chances,' she said.

'Visiting Barrett won't stop me having a child.'

'Maybe not. But we are told to avoid going near the water.'

'We live on an island.'

'We'll talk about it,' Ingram said, shattering the momentum I felt. I wanted to leave the table, cause a scene, start an argument, but everything I did could be used against me. There was no fight left in me any more.

One morning after chapel, I lingered to make sure Seren and Vayle left before me. I told them I was waiting to speak to the Eldermothers in private, and they seemed satisfied. I had made eye contact with Norah during the service, a pleading attempt to get her to meet me afterwards, and it seemed to work.

We made small talk until we were far enough away from the chapel.

'No luck yet?' she said as we walked.

I faltered at her directness, but there was something about her that made being open feel easier. It was not like the way other women spoke; she cared.

'I've tried everything. I even buried a small knitted doll. That's what one woman at my ceremony suggested. Knit it and stuff it with bay leaves and bury it in sheltered ground. Something to do with letting the land read my desires.'

'And that didn't work?' she said, her lips pulled to the side in a wry smile when I looked at her.

I gave an embarrassed laugh. 'It sounds ridiculous to say it out loud.'

'People say all sorts,' she said. 'You have to wonder whether they even believe it themselves.'

'That's how I've started feeling, though. Ridiculous.'

'You're desperate, and that stress won't help.'

'It's not like I haven't been trying. I have. I pray, cleanse. I'm doing everything the family want. Keep faith, they all say. Pray and have patience. But time's running out. It's like I can see it happening . . . at the jetty, and there's nothing I can do about it.'

'You can't end up like that,' she said. 'You can't.'

Her voice changed and we came to a stop on the path. She took my hands. Her anger buzzed through. We were always told that women were soft, women were gentle.

'I'm worried my time will run out,' I said.

'Do you know how many times I've seen it? Women who've done nothing and had their whole lives ruined by the words of a man?'

I looked at her, my surprise obvious, but she carried on.

'Crescent – you remember her?'

How could I forget?

'Then you must have heard the stories. What those boys said she was. She came to me in tears. Sick. Wanted to know if what she'd done would make her ill.'

'I know what they did. They forced her.'

'And where are they now? Ministers. Rule-makers,' she said. 'And Crescent? She'll be lucky if she ends up the second wife of a man who beats her, with the reputation she has. And it'll happen again, and again.'

The power in her expression, in the conviction of her words, made me feel like I was falling. If they only knew a woman's true strength.

'No Untethering,' she says. 'It can't happen. Not after everything. Not after your mother . . .'

'There's no way to save me. If I don't have a child . . .'

'Maybe you won't have to,' she said, eyes ablaze. 'I'm trying,' her voice a harsh whisper, her grip tight, 'to find a way out.'

I could only just hear her through the sound of ringing in my head.

'To leave,' she said. 'Leave the island.'

Nineteen

We hadn't seen the bloated sky, the way the drizzle had turned to a heavy downpour, glooming down, thick and fast.

'There's a storm coming,' I said. My grandmother would have known about it days ago; her head would have thrummed with the smell. She would have warned Barrett when she saw him pass our cottage, told him to prepare for the worst, no boat trips, no hauls. She always said storms were an omen. Standing there with Norah, I could almost believe that we were the reason for it.

Norah pulled up the hood of her coat and I saw what I hadn't seen before. A slight change to her clothes, a gathering. She looked down, seeing what I was, hand passing over her stomach. Her husband was long dead, and she was pregnant.

'You see why I have to leave?' she said.

'And go where?'

'Anywhere. I'm not afraid any more.'

My eyes glanced at her body. 'Whose is it?'

'Not here.' We were having to shout at each other through the rain. 'Give me time. I'll tell you everything.'

'I haven't got time! And neither have you.'

'You have months,' she said. 'So have I. And that's what we need. Just give me time to sort things. Come to me in a month. Tell no one. I don't want anyone to see us together.'

The storm came and kept us inside for days. House thrown sideways, roof damaged. No chapel, no church, no fishing. All of us trapped inside together, watching each other. Ingram found confined life unbearable. His brothers' children upstairs were headache-inducing. Outside, sandbag walls were built as tall as men, and livestock was moved indoors. We heard about the rest of the island through the

Messenger boys who were out through it all, telling us that Father Jessop had ordered prayer and good faith to see us through. When I prayed, all I could think of was Norah and how desperate I was to see her, to ask her about the plans.

The household lived on cured meat, food from jars, corners of cheese, handfuls of seeds, and vegetables I managed to salvage from the allotment before it flooded. I was soaking, my feet slipping on the sliding ground, the soil giving way to trenches of water. Ingram had to pull me away.

'It's too late! Leave it,' he shouted through the rain. He didn't know I couldn't bear to leave the only thing I'd cultivated, my only worth in this house.

Later, when I was warm and dry, sitting by the fire, mourning the wasteland of the garden, the barren soil, Seren smirked at my hopeless attempt at sewing. She and Vayle had cajoled me into making baby clothes, trying to convince me that it showed God I was committed.

'There's something happening here, I can feel it.' She sat beside me, picked up the quilt she was making.

'We always have bad weather,' I said. 'This is nothing new.' I spiked my finger with the needle until the skin broke in a satisfying bead of blood.

'God doesn't give us weather like this without reason.'

I drove the needle into a second finger and pressed them together, put them up to my mouth to taste metal. I couldn't leave the room without making a scene, so I sat there grinding over my resentments, foreseeing the way this storm would be twisted and analysed and pinned to an innocent woman.

The sky spat and roared, and as Vayle and Seren sat, imprisoned in their terror, their paranoia led them to ask questions about the women of the island. We'd boarded the windows upstairs so as not to scare the children. I remembered the storms of my childhood: my grandmother watching, dreading what to come.

'They strike the houses of all the girls who have nasty thoughts,' she would say, smacking her hands together right next to my ear to mimic the sky's cry. 'You! If you're not careful.'

I would count every strike, praying and praying, thanking God every time it stayed away from our roof.

This storm felt personal. It was worse when Seren caught me with another bloodied bedsheet. Outside, the sea coughed up fronds of weed and I had dreams of my name called on the wind, Cal washing up on the beaches. Then I dreamt again, this time of Cal above me, the give of us together, slick and full, uncertain where his scales ended and my skin began. I wanted him so much I was sure the lightning would hit the house.

Days into the storm, Seren cornered me in the kitchen as we tried to scrape together something of a supper. One of the neighbouring farms had slaughtered a work horse and was sharing out the meat and bones.

'There's definitely something amiss. Did you see anything before the storm? Have you heard something?' she asked.

'About what?'

'Groups of women,' she said, drying her hands on a cloth, putting pause to what we were making. 'Talking, plotting. You know what I mean. I've heard about women trying to pass messages to the Otherlands.'

I tried not to think of Norah. 'Why would they do that?'

'To ruin this island. It's the spirit of the Seawomen behind all of it.' She looked at me like she couldn't believe she had to explain it.

I went to speak, turning back to the stove, but she hadn't finished.

'Ingram said you hadn't mentioned anything to him,' she said.

'That's because I haven't seen anything.'

'You know it's your duty to tell him. Like I tell Doran. Even about friends of mine. Any suspicions I might have.'

I twisted my hands into my apron, eyeing the knife in front of me. Every thought I had turned to violence, being trapped in that shrinking house. 'I know that,' I said.

'It only takes one woman, one sin. It spreads. It could even spread into this house.' She paused, choosing her words carefully. 'It could even be why you haven't managed . . . How many months has it been now?'

'Four.'

'Almost five,' she said.

211

'I know.'

'Now the storms. And the rest.'

'What else?'

'Crofts are flooded. One of the farmers told Doran that their calves were dragged over the cliffs in a mudslide. Then there's disease, sheep gnawing at the fence posts, moulting their wool.' She moved towards the cupboards and opened one. 'And don't you think our food is rotting away faster than normal?'

Ingram came in from the outside, bringing with him a howling gust, his clothes dripping everywhere.

'Oh Gram! You look exhausted.'

He'd been back at the harbour again, trying to set out, but none of them made it far. I stayed where I was, stirring the broth that would barely stretch between us, as Seren rushed over to dry him.

'It's a disaster out there! A fucking . . . ! If this goes on any longer, we're ruined.'

I jumped at his raised voice. He looked like a different man, absorbing the rage of others in the harbour. It hulked under his skin.

'Come and warm up by the fire,' Seren said, steering him away.

His eyes met mine, just for a second. 'People are starting to talk.'

Later that night, he sat slumped on the bed. After ranting about the failed trip, the weather, whatever woman was behind it, he was calmer. As we undressed, the room was fragile with the sounds of the battering storm.

'There's something . . . Seren thought it was better if I told you. She's pregnant again.'

I was holding my breath, watching him from the corner of my eye. 'That's good news. How far along is she?'

He scratched an old scar on his wrist. 'Early days, I think. Due in summer.'

I knew then, deep in my gut, that her baby was his.

We filled the emptiness of the bedroom with routine. We prayed, him studying my devotion like he was testing me. I pulled up my nightdress, watched him struggle to get hard. We'd had fruitless months of trying, his body at all angles on top of me, bulk and pressure on my chest. Every day there was hope, a chance to rise above his brothers' belittling remarks, his runt reputation. But then I would bleed again.

After we were done, my legs in the air like I'd been told, Ingram rolled to the side, and I wondered if he was already thinking of my Untethering, how he would cope with the shame of an audience seeing that he'd been given a cursed wife who had brought nothing but bad luck to his door.

I cannot remember how many days passed before the storm lifted. I was weak and listless, crawling through unsettled sensations in my sleep. I woke one morning to an empty bed, the sound of gulls returning, a splinter of light appearing under a cloud. I couldn't wait any longer.

I glazed past the shop, the bakery, where Crescent's father emptied lice-ridden flour into the street before closing up. The whispers all said the same: a woman among us was rotten. Signs were all around; she needed to be found. I headed towards Lambert Hill, passing the crofts, the flooding, the stone walls and the shed roofs that needed repair. I didn't run, I didn't keep my head down. Everyone was keeping watch for women acting strangely. I knocked at Norah's door and it felt like an age until she answered. I stood there wishing I'd brought something with me for a cover, like the Great Book, or something I was trying to sell. Even though there wasn't a soul in sight as I waited for her to answer, the hairs still rose on the back of my neck.

Her bump was still slight, and well covered by large, loose clothes. She led me through to the kitchen. Her daughters and her cousin's children were at school, Olsen and his wife working on one of the farms. When Norah wasn't needed as a nurse or midwife, she worked on one of the crofts, making butter and curds mostly, but she'd made excuses to stay at home.

'The smell of it is starting to make me feel sick,' she said, sitting at the table.

'What will you do? How long can you keep it a secret?'

'As long as I need to,' she said. 'I can make the clothes bigger. I can stay at home more. I'll just say I'm sick.'

'And won't the Eldermothers visit?' If they did, that would be the end of it.

'I hope they'd trust the word of a nurse. If not, Olsen said he will speak for me.'

'Does your family know?'

She nodded. 'We don't have any secrets, not any more.'

'And what about when it arrives?'

She smoothed her hands across the table and I had a sudden visceral memory of doing the same with the maps, of the place names I had treasured in the back of my mind. I didn't want to raise her hopes and tell her, not now there was nothing left of them.

'I'm the only midwife,' she said. 'I can find a woman who needs a child. I thought about . . .' She trailed off. 'I could get rid of it. It would be guesswork to find the right herbs, but I could do it. But I know there are women here who need this child.'

'Give away your child? What if someone found out?'

'Isn't it worth the risk? To save someone when they need it more.' She spoke shakily, her voice weighted with tears, then composed herself. 'Then I would go.'

We didn't talk for a long time. I wanted to hold the moment – the idea of fleeing – close my fist around it, scared of what a release might bring. Norah made us both tea, pouring a little brandy into the cups. We drank and it stung my throat.

'There's something else,' she said. 'Something I should have told you. Something I need to tell you now.'

She put her hands against the table, like it was the only thing holding her up. 'I need you to know that I didn't know the truth either, not for a long time. There was the version of things I knew, and then . . . and it takes a long time to see things how they really were. Things I once thought were ungodly, and now . . .'

My stomach roiled. That feeling of the truth changing was all too familiar.

'And you. I didn't know much about you. It didn't feel right. You were young, and your grandmother was all you had . . .'

'Tell me.'

She was stalling. She moved her chair in closer, her knees knocking mine. 'I never knew what the right thing was to do. Even now.'

'People talk of my mother like a ghost. All these rumours about who she was and things she might have done.'

'Your mother and Rose . . .' She stopped, started again somewhere else. 'I thought I knew what had happened, but when I came to nurse your grandmother, she started saying things . . .'

'She kept saying her name.'

'I think she wanted to confess, before the end.'

'Confess to what?'

Numbness started in my cheeks and spread, throat to chest, arms to waist. It felt stronger than the sea had.

I moved my hand closer to Norah's. 'Start from the beginning. Please.'

She hesitated. I'd never had a picture of my mother, only her name. My grandmother had wanted to name her after Dinah, to invoke her spirit, but my grandfather had fought for the name Maddow, after his mother, and that, my grandmother said, was her first mistake. She was more of him than anyone else.

'I told you they were close. Maddow was all Rose could talk about, the only person she wanted to spend any time with. Our parents didn't mind it at first. Rose was the perfect daughter. She had all the fear and conviction in the Lord that they could want. And they knew your grandmother had raised Maddow to be just as strict in her faith. They had no worries about their friendship. Why would they?

'Our mother used to joke that they were more like sisters than Rose and me, but when they turned sixteen, the joke started to wear thin. They were more interested in each other's company than going to the chapel. There were even rumours that they'd been seen beach-combing and fishing from the cliffs using stolen lines. So my father told Rose she needed to look for a husband, and if she didn't find one, he'd have Father Jessop arrange it. She was beautiful – your mother too. Maddow was tall and pale, stark and sharp in her features, but my sister was more of a picture-book beauty. Some said she even had the look of Dinah about her – large oval eyes, long wavy hair and a figure that would have got her lots of marriage offers if she'd tried. I remember being jealous of that. Her being the elder, getting all this attention and showing no interest. Being in love, being married was all I wanted, but Rose ignored every boy who liked her.

'Then your mother cut her hair off, right to her chin, and things changed. By all accounts, your grandmother screamed like someone had died.'

'God's glory,' I said, repeating what she had said to me when she brushed mine.

'Sarl thought no man would marry Maddow looking like that. She thought it was a sign. She made her stay with the Eldermothers. When my parents heard, they tried to stop Rose from seeing her. They told her the Seawomen had hooked Maddow. They spooked her. Told her all the horror stories they could remember, reminded her of an Untethering she'd watched a few years before and said that if she stayed with Maddow, she too would end up drowned. They told her Maddow would rot her from the womb outwards and they made her write down everything that would prove Maddow was one of *them*. They must have made her lie or written the accusations themselves. I heard them scream at her that Maddow would be the death of us all. I'm ashamed to say it now, but a part of me was glad. I was jealous. Though really, when I think about it, all I wanted was the freedom they had. With each other.

'After Maddow was released, they packed Rose off to the chapel too. It was like she died. They made her stay there for a year, only two visits home. I couldn't understand it. No one had ever stayed that long before. When she came home, she was a different person. Gaunt, lifeless, her mouth filled with the Eldermothers' words; all she talked about was honouring God and Father Lambert's mission. It frightened me to see her whole spirit taken like this. The real Rose, the girl I had loved and hated and who had spent her days by Maddow's side, she was gone. I remember telling my mother that it was like Rose had been possessed, not by the Seawomen, but by the Eldermothers. She beat me for that, and marched me for cleansing. Made them scrub my mouth too.

'When Rose was allowed home, it was the day of Maddow's wedding, and we all went, even Rose. Father Jessop had arranged it on purpose. He'd worked out what they were . . . At night, I could hear her sobbing. But the Eldermothers could only take so much of the real Rose away. The core of her still felt the same.'

'What are you saying?'

Norah walked over to a desk, pulling free a deep drawer. She took out a book, and from inside that, a folded sheet of paper with hand-writing preserved on it.

'I managed to hide this. And keep it. After she . . .'

She slipped it across the table to me, and I skimmed the words, my heart racing, making it almost impossible to decipher them until I focused.

I have tried so hard. I have leant on God night after night, but it's you I see. You I want. Nothing can stop these feelings, not even God. I know in my heart what we feel isn't wrong. It is too physical, too innate to be anything but love.

Norah wiped her eyes. 'I know what you must think. Against God.' Her voice quietened. 'An abominable thing . . . that's what I thought too.'

I looked at the words again. I knew how it felt. I understood the fight. To love against reason, against God. These were my mother's words, and yet they were mine.

'You see . . .' her voice cracked, 'you see why I couldn't tell you everything. But if you'd seen them . . .'

'For years?' I asked. 'They were in love and they had to bury it.'

'Yes, before even they knew what they were feeling. But they weren't under any illusions; they knew they had no choice but to lie, get married and have children.'

'They wanted to delay the inevitable,' I said. There was no place on the island for their love. For them.

'It wasn't long after that when your mother fell pregnant with you, and Father Jessop found a man to marry Rose.'

'How did Rose take it?' I asked, thinking about my wedding to Ingram, the way it had felt like a mourning.

'She starved herself, made herself sick, all in the hope she wouldn't have to go through with it. It was a relief when you were born healthy. My parents believed there was hope for Rose too.

'When she married, it was like she was dead inside. But it didn't

217

last, because I started to recognise my sister again. My parents thought it was finally God's influence returning. Everyone thought she was happy with her husband, that he was the one making the difference.'

'Maddow.'

'She was the only one who made Rose happy.' Norah began folding her skirt in her hands, looking uneasy. 'I caught them first, but I didn't say a word. I couldn't bear for Rose, my Rose, to be taken away again, so I said nothing. Listened, followed them to where they met in secret. I thought I might be able to protect them. But I wasn't the only one who found out. Tarwell. Rose's husband. He went straight to Father Jessop. I think he was too ashamed to admit to what his wife really was. He said he'd caught her singing out to sea – "Seawomen songs". And . . . well, Rose hadn't given him a child.'

The room had its own heartbeat when Norah finished speaking, a sound of blood close in the ears.

'Father Jessop gave Rose a choice. Untethering, or . . .' She wiped her face, straightened in her chair, spoke steadily. 'Or he would . . . give her a child himself. She could pass it off as Tarwell's and repent and that would be the end of it. God would forgive her.'

'No. He . . . he wouldn't.'

'I didn't believe it either. But Rose confided in me when she thought she'd run out of time. She'd refused him; all that was left was the Untethering.'

Norah stared at a point in the distance, her breathing controlled.

'Do you know how many women have been persuaded to bear *his* child in the name of Salvation? Gentle girls, too scared to tell. But when they're young and afraid and alone with a midwife and the timings don't add up, you'd be surprised what they tell me, the secrets they beg me to keep. So many babies that come out looking like him, and no one breathes a word.'

I sat horrified as she carried on. Girls of fourteen, girls who were second wives, girls who'd miscarried.

'Why?' It seemed such a weak question after everything she'd told me.

'Because he can. It's control. Always has been. There's nothing holy about the "motheryear". It's an invention. It's when they decide. When we've proved ourselves to be the mothers they want. Not too young, not unfit. It's always the "pious" who are granted theirs first. Haven't you noticed? They stop drinking at chapel – and then a child. While the rest are tortured . . .'

'What's in the drink?' I touched my throat.

'A chemical. Something he bring back from his trips to the Otherlands. It stops conception.'

They said it was to help us, to strengthen our wombs! My head swam. What else is a lie?

'How can he preach about sins of the flesh and sanctity when all this time . . . what he's done to us . . .'

'He promised them that the children would be the purest blessings the island had ever seen. He told them he was acting under God's orders, that this was humanity in its true form. They were frightened.' Her voice began to shake, her hands gripped together. 'He said if they didn't . . .'

Her head fell and I moved to hold her.

'Fia,' she said. 'That's how I know it's true.'

Twenty

'I love her, of course I love her, but sometimes when I look at her, I see him staring back at me.'

I thought of her fair little girl, her cold stare, how different she looked from Lily.

Norah composed herself, shook off the past like it was rain.

'You need to know the rest,' she said, waiting for me to sit back down. 'About that night.'

A part of me didn't want her to say anything else. Not more suffering. I was battered with all this new information. Hearing about my mother and Rose, reading her words, had made me feel closer to her than ever before. I waited for Norah to speak, a swarm of images pressed behind my eyes, constricting my chest.

I started to sweat. I had a smoke-smeared vision of arms reaching into my cot and lifting me free.

The images were out of order. My past smashed to pieces.

'Your grandmother. I should have told you long ago. She was ill, dying even, and I shouldn't have pushed her for answers. I should have done my job and left her in peace, but she said Rose's name and kept talking about the fire and . . . I couldn't . . .'

'What did she say?' I asked, stiff with the memories of my grandmother apologising over and over, confusing me for Maddow.

Norah went to the drawer again; further letters, buried deeper.

'I should have burnt these, but I couldn't bring myself to. Maddow and Rose, they were planning to escape the island. They couldn't see each other, so they wrote coded messages back and forth. Rose asked me to take them and afterwards destroy them. She trusted me. Since she'd been released from the chapel, I clung to her. I saw what a difference Maddow made in her life.' Her mouth trembled. 'What I didn't know, not until Sarl told me, was that she found out, and told Father Jessop.'

'The fire,' I said. 'They tried to . . .'

I remembered the night my grandmother had died, her strange ramblings and apologies that had just sounded confused and meaningless.

'The fire was his idea,' Norah said finally. 'His great plan. He told your grandmother that sacrifices had to be made to stop the spread of darkness. He had Keepers set fire to the house. *He* told her it was . . . an order from God. To save the rest of the island. For the greater good.'

'I thought it was an accident this whole time . . .'

'She must have had a change of heart, because she was the one who freed you from the house. She's the reason you're alive now.'

'She knew I was there. Both my parents. And she said nothing? She knew the house would burn to the ground with all of us inside.'

I stood up, moving around the room but unable to go anywhere.

'And no one would've suspected a thing.'

'She was such a pious woman; people talked about her saving you like an act of God. A miracle,' Norah said.

'That night had nothing to do with God!'

'I can't defend her,' Norah said. There was no feeling in her voice. 'I won't. But you know how strong her convictions were. If she thought your mother had been taken by the Seawomen, there was a risk that you . . .'

'That I'd grow up the same.'

In that moment, the whole of my childhood began to make sense. The unfeeling way my grandmother spoke about my mother. The fasting and paranoia. The way she dragged me back and forth to the Eldermothers, convinced that I would turn into her worst nightmare. She saw darkness in me, saw the signs she had been told to watch for. All the while carrying this guilt. She'd been told that the fire was the righteous thing to do, and yet she saved me from it.

I didn't know what to think about her any more.

I had never questioned the origin of the fire. I only knew that it existed as a point in time, one that had altered my life but one we never spoke of. It had never seemed to matter how it had happened; only that it had taken my parents with it and left its scars.

But Norah wasn't yet unburdened.

'What else do you know?' All this talk of the fire had made Nanna's words come back to me. 'They only found one body.'

'Your father.'

'My mother? And Rose? What happened?'

She took a breath. 'I never told anyone. Not even my parents. I thought that if they found out I'd helped, I'd end up like Rose. It's why I said nothing when Father Jessop . . . If he knew the truth, he'd do worse. Because that night, I helped them. They weren't in the house at all. The fire worked as a distraction, kept the attention on the land while they made their escape.'

'You can't mean . . .'

How long had she held onto this? Shut out the noise of the island's stories to focus on the truth. I thought about what Barrett had told me, years ago, about my mother asking him questions about the outside world.

'They stole a boat. I don't know much more than that. There was only one patrol boat in those days, and the Keepers were busy with the fire. I don't know how they managed it. I don't know how far they got or where they went. I wish I knew more. I wish I could tell you more. Even now, I think, if only I knew, then there is hope for us, their map to follow. But there isn't. I don't even know if they crossed the border. I have to believe they made it. Now more than ever, now I have daughters of my own. I have to believe they went south like they planned, that they found somewhere to live, some freedom. They wouldn't give up. If anyone made it, it would have been them.'

I could only imagine the darkness of that night. The thought that it might never be dawn again. Two women alone out at sea with only the stars and their fear to guide them. But I couldn't see their success; I couldn't picture what their freedom looked like.

'You don't believe it,' she said.

'Love isn't enough.'

'If they didn't make it, what hope is there for the rest of us?'

I'd spent so much of my childhood imagining, wondering what kind of mother she would have been. Would she have been the type to give me a pet name, to sew me dresses, to plait my hair? But she'd left me. She escaped and left me behind. I hoped for one selfish second that she hadn't made it.

'All this time I thought of her life as a tragedy.'

Norah frowned. 'But it was.'

'She chose to leave without me. What kind of mother . . .'

'Perhaps she didn't know how to be a mother. Couldn't be one.'

'Or didn't want to. Was too selfish.'

'What choice did she have, Esta? Stay and watch the woman she loved drown? Die herself? Any choice to stay went up in flames with your father. She wouldn't have survived here.'

'She had me! She could have survived for me!'

'And do you think she wanted this place for you? She didn't have you because she wanted to bring a child into this world. She had a child because there was no other way. It's the same for you. For all of us. Think about it!' She was breathless with rage. 'How can it be about choice? None of us have a choice. All of us do things we don't want to do. We shut our eyes and turn our heads and pray to God; we marry and we lie under men just to live another day.' I heard her take another shaky, tearful breath. 'We turn away from watching the torment of girls we know have done nothing, because we know that if we don't, we'll be next.'

We had been sitting at that table for too long.

'Don't think for one minute it would have been an easy decision for her to make. She doesn't deserve your anger.'

I reached for the first letter Norah had shown me and held it, reading the words again in an attempt to understand.

'You had the right to know a long time ago,' Norah said. 'But things had become twisted in my head too. My parents didn't talk of Rose's death as a tragedy. I think it was a relief for them. In some ways it was easier to believe that version of events, just like it was easier to believe Father Jessop was good and the island was a sacred place. Being the only one to know the truth . . . it's too much to carry, too hard to fight against.'

'And now? What do we do now?'

Norah looked nervous. 'We have to get away.'

'There's no way. I've thought about it a hundred times.'

Her hand fell to her stomach. Almost instinctively.

'Who's the father?' I asked.

She pushed my question away. 'It's not like it was when your mother and my sister left. It's much harder now. We can't do it alone. We need help. We need someone to teach us how to row, to give us their boat.'

'Norah, who?'

She looked down uneasily. 'It'd be a risk for them too. If they're found to be helping us. They'll be made to suffer.'

'Was it one of the men from the harbour?' I pressed. My mind skimmed through their faces again. Perhaps whoever it was that agreed to help Norah was Cal's father, a man who saw the island for what it really was.

'A ferryman. He brings things from the harbour that might be useful to us. Fisherman's clothing for disguise, ropes and buoys in case there are emergencies with the boat.'

'But how can you trust him?'

Norah's eyes grew watery and pale. 'He's the one who told me about the chemical from the Otherlands.'

'And what's in it for him?'

I knew. With a sick swallow, I knew.

'I couldn't pay him. So he comes to the house once a week.'

'And the child?'

'I think he pretends not to see it.'

This was her plan? Could we really rely on a man willing to use her for sex? She hadn't even explained who else was in on the attempt to leave. And what about her children? And what of the outside world – so abnormal and wicked. Where could we go?

'We have to choose the right moment,' Norah said, trying to convince herself more than anything.

I didn't dare speak.

'If not him, then we speak to the ferrymen on the supply puffer.'

'If he betrays you, it's over. It's not going to work, Norah. We can't leave. It's impossible. If Maddow and Rose managed, *if* they really did, it then they were lucky. We've got no chance.'

Twenty-One

After everything Norah had told me, how could I watch Father Jessop in his robes, warning us of evil, and not see him holding her down? The Eldermothers, under his command, controlling our bodies not with a holy order but with chemicals. *Poison*. To not think of my mother's desperate choice, my grandmother watching the fire take hold. I worried about Norah and the baby she was carrying, hoping she wouldn't do anything that would risk their lives. Then there was my own body, still unchanged, despite coming off the chemicals but the thought of bringing a child into that house, onto that island, was just as unbearable.

On a bright winter morning, one of the Eldermothers took me to a private chamber. I was sure she would smell it on me, the reek of secrets through my skin. Seren had suggested I start attending the chapel for daily cleanses, and I had little option but to agree, wanting to appease her and stop Ingram's growing defeat, evident every night after he'd finished with me. The Eldermother filled a bucket and told me to take off my clothes. What she saw was flatness, an empty womb, a boyish chest. She chanted prayers as she washed me with icy water. When I flinched, she continued, telling me to stand still. I tried to focus on burying thoughts of Cal and Norah, my mother's escape. I tried to drown out my real self with images of newborns, of good, pure wishes, love for Father Jessop, which had once felt true and honest before it sickened me. The Eldermother made a loud thinking noise, her hands prodding around my stomach.

'Half your year gone. You must pray more. Sacrifice your time to God. I still see it. The black mark. And the Lord sees it too.'

'What does that mean?'

'You might never have a child.'

227

An unofficial sentence: my feet tied, the yole staggering over the building waves. I was no loss to her. I would end the line of broken women, my soul already corrupt before I had a chance.

When I came out of the chamber, Mull was waiting. She asked me how it had gone, and I painted on a smile, pretending they had given me hope.

'It's a beautiful day. Shall we take a walk?' she said.

We squinted against the gauzy sun, pausing to see the waxwings gathered on a wall. Then, further uphill, something held me firm, unable to move. I knew the ground, I knew what had been here before. This was the place, under my feet. Not just the site where my father had died, but the end of my family. The place my mother had left for the last time, where my grandmother had watched our home char before guilt took over. Mull was hardly aware that I'd stopped. She was talking about her mother-in-law, while I was thinking of her father's orders to set my family alight, to kill a child. All for the good of the island, like every other reason that was put forward to explain and justify unforgivable, inexcusable acts. The weight of it overtook me. I called out to stop her.

'Es, you look pale.'

The concern on her face was so genuine it hurt. How could she belong to this island? To the John family?

She eased me over to a low stone gate to rest against. 'Let's stop for a while.'

There were sheep grazing in the grounds that would have once belonged to my mother and father. We had our backs to the sea, but I could hear it beneath us, crashing over the rocks, a star shape of guillemots screeching from sky to land. I thought about telling her, taking her back in time to all those years before, when I had waded out into the water, and trying to explain to her how I felt. How the island suffocated me. Maybe, I thought, she'd had flickers of it herself, moments when she'd questioned her father or God or this place. Maybe she'd woken one day the same as I had, with a curiosity low in her gut.

'When we were girls . . .' I said, losing my nerve when the words were out loud and not just in my head. 'Do you remember?'

'Remember what?'

'That day, in the water. When I walked out into the sea?'

She looked away. 'I try not to think about it. You shouldn't either.' She paused, turning back to look at me. 'You don't think that's why you haven't . . . ?'

We, I wanted to correct her. We both were without a child. Except her betrayal wasn't anywhere near what mine had been. She'd been a reluctant bystander to my impulsive need to be in the water, my calling.

I couldn't answer her, finding it hard to look at her directly. I was conscious of a knot of pain at the base of my stomach, a hand reaching inside, twisting and nagging. My blood was going to come again, another chance gone.

'Did the Eldermothers say something else?' Mull tried again, probing. 'You've been quiet ever since we left.'

'They only told me what I already knew.'

She waited for me to continue.

'That it might never happen. That my soul is rotten.' I picked at the moss growing on the gate.

'You can't think like that! What happened long ago is the past. We repented and we moved on. We made a vow to God never to cross that line again. God forgives, Esta, He forgives. And it's okay, it's all right, because—'

'Does your father ever talk about my parents?' I asked, cutting her off.

'What about them?' she said, a little too quickly. I'd always envied Mull's trouble-free life, but the question had shaken her calm.

'Bad blood. Isn't that what people say?'

Her face was scarlet, an admission of guilt. How much had she joined in with the speculation, the blame? She was meant to be my friend, my only friend.

'If they have, I haven't heard it.' She pressed her hand against her heart. 'Whatever the Eldermothers have said, it's nothing your faith can't overcome. You're not your mother.' She tried to pull me out of my thoughts. 'Listen, whatever you're worried about, whatever damage you think you've done—'

'We've only got six months left, Mull. Time is running out, and I'm scared that . . .'

Above us, the guillemots were back. I lifted my head to watch their interruption, the way they squawked like they were arguing, landing on the rocks to confront each other.

'Esta, I'm pregnant.'

I heard her over the cawing and flapping but wished I hadn't. I wished her words had been lost to the sea. Her hand sat at the base of her stomach and I wondered how long she'd been standing like that, how long I hadn't noticed. Had she been setting out the hints for me all along, hoping I would work it out for myself rather than her having to tell me?

'Wow!' It was barely a word, hardly noise. All breath and shock at once.

'I wanted to tell you straight away, as soon as I knew, but the Eldermothers said it was better to wait until three months had passed, otherwise the stress of everyone knowing can be hard on the mind . . .'

'Three months.'

'It feels like forever, waiting to tell everyone, but it's already gone so fast. I really would have told you. If I'd been able to . . .'

'I know.'

'You were the first person I wanted to tell. Well, after Aden, obviously. And you would have been first if Seren hadn't cornered me and guessed. She said she could tell. Mother's intuition, she said.'

'Seren knows.'

'It's just such a shock . . . but I'm terrified I'll do something wrong and hurt the baby, or worse, I'll—'

'You won't.'

'You're definitely next. You've been praying so hard all the time, and you're at the chapel, and you've seen the herbalist . . . It means you have to be next. Definitely.'

'Mull, it's all right.'

She smiled and I tried to replicate it, keeping my tongue pushed down into the bottom of my mouth. I would break if I said another word.

I could see it then, the slight arch of her back, her adjusted clothes, the shine on her forehead. She smelt different too, something sweet and medicinal Seren had probably given her. I could feel her excitement, but all I could think about was that by the time her child was born, I'd be dead. Her child wouldn't even know me. Wouldn't hear my name. Would she talk about me at night, weave me safely into bedtime stories, keeping the truth of my fate a secret? Or would she want to forget me, her bewitched friend?

Eventually we managed to change the subject, to talk about Moss Farm and the family we didn't like who lived there, but in every conversation I felt the ever-present thread of life and death, the power of God in everything she said. In the end, it was me who wanted to go back, even though in the past I'd have done anything to stay out with her until it got dark and avoid the confinement of home.

She pulled me into her arms for a hug, and I locked everything inside.

As a new year began and the festival edged closer, another storm hit us, worse than the last. The first night, Ingram and his brothers were awake until the early hours trying to repair the roof, which had buckled again. We had prepared better this time, with more food in the cupboards, sandbags already up against the front door, buckets to collect water in the leaking upstairs. Seren's days were stricken with morning sickness, taking ginger in everything and barely lifting her eyes from the Great Book. It was mine and Vayle's job to keep the children occupied. They were scared enough to be fearful of sin, but not so scared that they were screaming and crying, unbearable to watch over. Hardy, Vayle's elder son, was old enough to know all the stories, regaling the younger children with the horrors of the Seawomen, gore and violence and everything else they were too young to understand. When I was tidying up after them, I found a dismembered crab under his bed and showed it to Vayle.

She shrugged. 'He likes to pull them apart. It's his way of taking revenge on the evils of the sea.'

The casual way she spoke about his violence sent shivers down my spine.

I took ginger tea to Seren, who by this mid-morning had found her stomach more settled. I sat on her bed, handing her the cup. Under her eyes were shadows of grey.

'Why am I so sick?' she asked. Her tone was accusatory. 'It was never like this with the others.' She let it linger between us. 'The storms are worsening, our roof is destroyed. It has all the signs of an act of God.'

'I could grate some ginger into supper tonight. It's only livers, but—'

'I'll make my own.'

'It's no trouble.'

'I think it would be better if you let me make my own supper, don't you?' She put her tea to one side and I took that as my cue to leave.

I finished cleaning the kitchen and mended the frayed seam of my skirt. The rain had quietened outside; it was just the wind battering the house, making the doorways whine. Vayle had persuaded the children to take naps in the afternoon. It was our only reprieve during the day. Ingram and Weir had gone to the harbour and Doran had been summoned by Father Jessop. For the first time in a while, I could slip out of the house without being missed.

I knew exactly where I wanted to go. Unsurprisingly, the door of the shed was locked, but it was an old bolt, untested. I pushed up on my toes and looked in through the window, staring hungrily at the shell of the boat. It was a project, more of it complete since the previous time I'd been up close. Each time Ingram disappeared to sand it, to shape spare wood into a plank for the hull, I'd feel a heat rise in my chest, a rigid, hidden anticipation.

Soon, I thought, *soon*, looking at the clinker like a child that was almost mine. I was picturing my hands on the oars, my feet tucked neatly inside, when I heard the padding of footsteps behind me and jumped, unable to hide the guilt as Seren stared me down.

'What are you doing?' she said.

She waited until she had a full house, an audience over supper. I'd told her that I'd just gone for a walk around the cottage to clear my head. I was prone to headaches, I said; my grandmother had them all the time. My excuse was unbelievable, but it was all I had.

'I need to raise something with you all, something that frightens me, that needs to be said.' She adopted a formal voice like she was addressing the church. Her eyes never left me. 'I've been sick. I've been up morning and night with it, as you know. At first I thought it was just the baby, but today I've been experiencing pains in my stomach. And now I know for sure that something is wrong in this house. I can feel it. We had the roof leak, Morley is sleepless, and Vayle tells me that Hardy's been complaining of nightmares. The storms have started again, but this time it's our house bearing the brunt of them.'

'Is the baby all right? Do you want me to fetch the doctor?' Weir asked, already half out of his chair. Doran stopped him. He must've known what Seren was about to say and he had a litany of my history to support her.

'It's the island.' Weir tried again. 'Father Jessop said in his last service that the storms mean there's something amiss. Won't be long. He'll be sending the Eldermothers round soon.'

'It's in this house!' Seren cried, a fist landing on the table and springing the cutlery together. 'It's her!'

All of them turned to where Seren was pointing.

'Tell them where I caught you. Tell them what you were doing. All this time you've sat at this table and slept under this roof!'

I pulled back my chair, straightening my hands in my lap. 'All right.'

'It's no wonder there's nothing growing inside her. It won't. It can't!' Seren cried.

Ingram snapped. 'Let her speak, Seren, for God's sake.'

His interjection, using the Lord's name in vain, rippled across Seren's skin. Her face hardened. He'd only ever been soft with her.

I took to my feet, all eyes still on me. 'I was outside the house. I went to get some air.'

Seren scoffed. 'She was at the shed, staring at the boat. What kind of woman does that?'

I glared at her defiantly. 'I wasn't looking at the boat. I was looking for spare wood. I wanted to make something.'

'What?' Ingram asked.

'A teether.' I swallowed. My hand moved on its own. Ingram followed it with his eyes, watching intently. It stopped on the base of my stomach. Like they all did, like I'd seen and learnt. 'I wanted to tell you tonight, in private, but Seren's given me no other choice.'

233

'You're *pregnant*?' he said.

There was a moment, straight after the lie left me, when I started to believe it. My mind drifted out of the room, away from the sudden flare of voices, enthusiasm, my transgressions dropped. I could feel this imaginary thing growing, the size of a fingernail, the size of a bean. If I concentrated hard enough and ignored Seren, I could feel the deep pink quiver on the inside, my own salted sea. The lie grew in my head, expanding with the light in Ingram's eyes, the longing in his face. For everything: the future, years added, toes wriggling, the soft mounds of knees learning to walk.

The lie changed the entire room. It was incredible how fast, how relief and celebration smoothed the edges of suspicion. Seren was the last to congratulate me, stepping back as one by one they all came forward. She was full of smiles and apologies, her eyes dull as stones as she put her arms around me. It was almost admirable how convincing she was. She was well practised; she must have hidden her love for him for years. Had she secretly hoped I would fail? I was going to give Ingram what she couldn't – a legitimate child, proof of our matrimony, proof of his worth. This child he could love openly; this child, unlike the one she was carrying, would not be a bastard he could never admit to.

'That's why I haven't been myself,' I said to Ingram, but directing my words to her. 'I didn't want to raise your hopes for nothing.'

The lie would give me time, I assured myself. The lie would protect me.

I found a flaw in my plan that night after the euphoria had lasted the whole evening. In bed I was sleepless, unable to relax, convinced somehow Ingram would be able to tell I was lying just by being up close with me. I told him common symptoms, lied about what the Eldermothers had said. His elation made it easy. But I only had so long before I'd be found out. My eyes fixed on the ceiling, my head beaten from thought to thought. What options were there? Pay Norah for her child, or give my body away to a man I hoped wouldn't talk? Ingram wouldn't sleep with me, not when he believed our obligation was done. I'd trapped myself in a lie I couldn't survive. Silently I wept.

My fingers found Cal's pendant, but the hope it had once held was faded. It had been two years since I'd last seen him, and he was starting to feel like a distant memory, a fantasy of another life.

I waited for the sound of Ingram's sleep to deepen, and then I left the bed. Doran had gone to the Ministry on official business early in the evening, but Ingram and Weir had drunk so much in celebration nothing would wake them. I pulled on a coat and boots over my nightdress and crept out of the house, seeking time to think, to breathe, the comfort of my old home with Barrett. I couldn't burden him with my lie, not when his moments of being muddled and agitated were becoming more frequent, but I missed his company, the way he made me feel less alone.

I made it to the harbour, but it was later than I'd thought and all the lights were off in Barrett's cottage. I jumped, seeing the torchlight from the Keeper on duty inspecting the boats. The last thing I needed was to be caught by them, so I hid in the shadows, the boats seeming to welcome me with their tune, the slosh-thunk of their moorings. It was bittersweet to be there again, to be so close to those vessels and know they were forbidden to me. I could smell the wood, the pungent ghosts of old hauls, the sour, damp smell of worn stern lines.

A light swept over the moorings and I froze. My time was up. I'd been caught. Those were my first thoughts, freezing as if the light had caught me in the act. But it hadn't. The light was not in the harbour, but approaching from the water. I crouched in my hiding spot between the sheds, trying to make out what was happening. Voices rose, a conversation between two gruff men growing louder as a yole appeared from the water, rowing towards the harbour. They moored, pulling a dark and heavy body from the hull of the boat, after a coordinated effort of *one, two, three*. It gave a soft thud against the jetty. It looked like a seal, only larger, slimmer. I recognised one of the voices and it took everything I had not to whimper. Doran.

'We stick to the plan. Is she still alive?' he said to his partner.

Could they see me? I braved a look. They had a torch with them and it caught a blade Doran removed from his boot. He pointed the torch at the body on the floor. I could see then what it was, the flapping of her tail as she winced away from them in pain.

The Keeper approached them. 'Fucking hell!' He made a hooting noise, half surprise, half congratulations. 'You really did it.'

Doran pushed up his sleeves. 'Said we would. Stupid whore came right up to us. You want the first go?'

'No, no. I couldn't.'

'Think about your daughter. Do it for her.'

I couldn't watch, but I heard the noise, a boot meeting the side of her body. I felt it all. Every kick.

'Oh-ho, still groaning,' the other man said.

'Go on, give her another one,' Doran said. 'Harder this time.'

'Where'd you find her?' asked the Keeper.

'Further than we thought,' Doran said.

'Past the border?'

'Bit further, but still too close for my liking.'

'So all the storms and everything? It was down to them.'

'Well, who else?'

Doran's pal laughed when the Keeper kicked again. Watching was unbearable, but I had to see it with my own eyes. He manhandled her tail, flapping it against the jetty.

'You ever wonder what fucking one of these freaks would be like?' the man asked.

'Your cock would fall off after,' Doran said. 'But be my guest.'

The Keeper laughed sheepishly. 'Tell me, though, what happened out there? Really? It'll be a story, this one. Did she come after you?'

'Not exactly.'

'But she would have done. We had to block our ears in case she tried anything, songs to make us drown, that sort of thing,' Doran said, taking control of the story. 'No, we got her before she even had the chance. Call it extermination.'

'One less Seawoman to worry about,' the Keeper said.

'Exactly,' Doran agreed. 'Let's finish it.' He leant down towards her face. 'This is for our girls. We don't want you here. We know what you do!'

I couldn't watch the rest. But I heard it. Her screams. Their glee. Minutes before, she'd been in the sea just like Cal, just like his mother. Then she'd been ripped from it, brutalised, dying on the land. I heard them laugh and joke, bickering over details of how it had happened, how many drinks they'd be given as thanks, their hero's welcome. I waited in the dark until they were gone, tears running down my face long after the sound of them had disappeared.

The next day I was too exhausted, too delirious to refuse Ingram when he said he wanted to show me something. He smoothed his hands over my stomach. 'This will ease your mind, I promise you.' I was lulled by his tenderness, wishing it could have been that way from the start. I followed him to the church, not seeing until we got closer that a post had been erected on the land. On it was a large hook, and hanging from that were the gory remains of the Seawoman's tail, severed at the hips, on display like a prize. House by house everyone came to look. Blood had stained the scales, but her tail looked nothing like the skin Father Jessop had once displayed in church. The silver sheen of her was so reminiscent of Cal's colouring that I faltered, seeing him instead, my mind frozen in horror.

Ingram put his hand on the small of my back. 'Get a good look. She can't hurt us any more.'

But I was howling, bent at the waist, vomiting on the ground. Other women must have heard my screams as fear, my sobs as relief. They spat on the ground, praying, happy tears springing free.

Later, in church, Father Jessop retold the story of the night before and Ingram comforted me, his hand circling my back, thinking of our child, our Salvation.

'Our island has been rocked by storms and accusations of women among us possessed by darkness. Plotting with the outside world to ruin this, our sacred home. The Seawomen are rising again and I sent these good men to the border to investigate. They felt a knocking on the underside of their boat before they even made it to the dark sea, and when one of them leant overboard to investigate, there she was, in *our* water. She was exactly as our stories tell – beautiful, bright eyes, long flowing hair. She held onto the boat, her bare chest heaving, eager to tell them that they were her saviours, that she'd been chased through the water by beasts with teeth. She begged and she fluttered her eyes. She was trying to seduce them, just like our stories say. She even' – Father Jessop clutched the altar for effect, to steady himself – 'kissed one of these men, and pulled him into the water, trying to drown him.

'But these brave men of ours knew our island was at stake. Something godly rose in them, and they fought her off. Courage won. Bravery won. God won. I can't express how close these men were to death. They had a lucky escape. So to honour their bravery and remember the constant threat we face, as women turn away from God, we hung the Seawoman's monstrous form outside for all to see!

'Her appearance was no accident, the storms were no coincidence. Women here in this very room are summoning the Seawomen closer, joining together and plotting against us, and by God, we will hunt them down. Today work starts to build a ring of protection around us. Years of preparation have gone into this fencing and now is the time to make our message clear: no longer will they corrupt our women, no longer will they darken our shores.'

There were cheers, applause. Ingram took to his feet, stamping as other men did. The world Father Jessop wanted for us was getting smaller, more twisted by the day. It couldn't carry on.

Twenty-Two

The night before the festival, I hunted Norah down, battering at her door. It was my last chance. Since Father Jessop's warning in church, I'd spent the last few weeks with my head down, careful, cautious. Everywhere, women were afraid to open their mouths in case they were reported as suspicious. I'd played my part, the pious pregnant woman, and I'd stayed away from Norah, praying she wouldn't get caught. But now there was no more time to play it safe.

She opened the door to me, her cheeks paler than the moon.

'No,' she said, hanging back, the door pulled so I could only see a sliver of her. 'Whatever you ask, my answer is no.'

It stung. All that bravery, all that power, gone. Above our heads I was struck by a smell of sage and a wreath, with crosses hung at the windows. I recognised what this was: an outward sign that she was with God, that she couldn't be one of the women who had been consumed by darkness.

She was tearful. 'There's no way, not now. No one will help us. They're not going to let us breathe without someone watching.'

'We can't stay here, you know we can't. You don't understand. I saw what they did. They hunted down the Seawoman themselves, they tortured her.'

'Esta, what am I supposed to do? They will be doing house inspections, tests, getting the Eldermothers to read our souls. This is all we have now.'

I reached out to her. 'I've lied. I told them I'm pregnant.'

'You can't keep up a lie like that!'

'I had to tell them something! My sister-in-law caught me. We've got a boat in our shed.'

'A boat?'

'It's battered, needs repair. But it could work. We could row it ourselves.'

'No,' she said, firmly. 'It would never work. It can't take us all.'

'We could try.'

'And drown?'

I had to say *something*. 'I can swim.'

Her eyes widened. 'Don't. Don't be stupid. We can't do this.'

'I can. Not well, not far. But if we could get past the patrols . . .'

'How can you? How do you know?'

'I can't explain, not now; you just have to trust me. I met someone. A man, from another place.'

'You're playing with death! It's too dangerous. And you stay away from him. If you're caught . . .'

'There has to be a way!'

'Yes. We keep out of sight, do what they say, be good women. Kiss your husband. Pretend. Pray, fast, everything and anything they want. I have to think of my daughters.'

'And when the Eldermothers find out about your baby?'

'They won't.' She pulled the door closer to her body, keeping her voice low. 'I could give it to you,' she said.

'No.'

'Pad your clothes, we could make it work.'

'Norah, there's no way. They'd know. We look nothing alike, and the timings won't add up.'

'You think they can tell? Even if they question it, your duty's done. You're safe. What proof do they have? Tell me, if you gave your husband a son, would he know if it wasn't his? Would he even care?' She looked away briefly. 'My husband, he never questioned Fia. He never looked at her like she wasn't his.'

'And if it fails? I can't. I can't.'

I felt a pressure in my skull, secrets pressing against the walls, air that would not reach my lungs. Inside the house, Lily called for her mother, and Norah had no choice but to shut the door on me, on hope.

I walked home against the wind, wanting to curl inside myself. I'd lost track of time. It was late, far too late for a woman to be out wandering the island, but after seeing Norah, I couldn't bear to go straight home. At least giving them the lie of my pregnancy meant I could tell them I'd felt discomfort and gone to visit the midwife. I hooked Cal's pendant out from under the neck of my dress, thumbing the only thing I had of him, his sign that he'd return. I looked up at the stars, aching. Would life have been any easier if I'd never met him? Would it have been better to live and die here still believing the lies? Or was it harder to know there was another life out there, one with freedoms, one without fear of the water?

I wasn't alone. The sight of another person out in the dark spiked my anxiety, until I recognised him. Barrett. He was hunched over, head down, hair ragged in the wind. I didn't want to scare him, so I kept my distance, calling his name as quietly as I could. He was in his own world, muttering to himself, heading back home.

I called again, and this time he looked up. He paused, then hurried on even faster.

I chased him.

'Stay away!' he said, his voice wavering like he didn't even recognise me; then a wail, a noise worse than a sob, and he stumbled, crouching on the ground, giving me the chance to get nearer to him. He looked wild, a different person. He was folded over, his arms cradling something. I stepped around him, crouching so we were at the same height. The smell was rotten. I had to put a hand to my mouth to stop myself being sick.

'It's all right, Barrett. It's okay. It's Esta. Let me help you.'

He grunted, before his eyes cleared with recognition as he saw me.

'Esta,' he said, his voice lifting, then falling as he remembered something. 'You're having a baby now. I heard.'

My brief relief at him saying my name sank again. I nodded, hating that I'd had to lie to him too. His tone sounded as flat as I felt. I was about to suggest we go back to his house for a drink, some time together, just the two of us like it used to be, but then I saw his shaking hand rising, one finger pointing at me. His coat opened a little and the smell grew stronger. His eyes were fixed below my throat, the drag of his features showing something more than shock. He was looking at Cal's pendant.

'Where did you get that?'

I didn't answer, instead pulling back his coat to reveal what was hidden.

'No!' he said, baring his teeth like an animal. 'No.'

In his arms was the Seawoman's severed tail. I recoiled from the sight. Up close, the hacked flesh, the dark, bloodied scales were even more horrifying.

'I wanted to take her back to the water,' he said, hugging his arms tight around it. He gave a loud, keening cry, stroking the scaled remains of the tail, the fin spilling out of his coat and onto the ground. This nightmare had come for us all.

I guided Barrett home, easing him out of his coat and wrapping the tail inside it. The shock had made him silent, compliant. I cleaned him at the sink, removing his putrid-smelling jumper, but still her decay lingered. I asked him to make tea, to keep him busy with familiar routine, and told him I would be back. I knew where to take the tail.

I left the house using the back door and made my way to the cove without being spotted. I laid her to rest, back into the sea where she belonged, and I cried, letting out all I felt. I was in the very place I'd seen Cal for the first time, had a glimpse of what another life looked like. I had feared it, something so different encroaching on our peace, but now I ached for this Seawoman, her beautiful severed tail, the unbearable suffering of her final moments. We were the monsters. *We* were.

When I got back to the house, Barrett was scrubbing every surface in the kitchen, shaking, bumping into the table and chairs. I tried to soothe him, pretend it was an ordinary evening, but he couldn't settle, his moods and confusion constantly switching. I left the coat in the tub upstairs. It was too large to burn, but the thought of cleaning it that night was too much to bear. I needed to get home before the family asked too many questions of me, but Barrett couldn't be left alone.

'Did you make that tea?' I asked him gently, trying to salve his terror. It had been left on the side, gone cold, so I set about making it afresh, reassuring him over and over that I would stay a while, until my words were a lullaby, keeping him calm.

There were moments when he forgot what had happened, forgot I was even in the room, the sound of me giving him involuntary jolts of surprise. I sat by him.

'I'm here,' I said.

One puzzle remained. His longing for the sea and his conflict between teaching me and keeping me protected. The way he looked at Cal's pendant. I laid it on the table in front of him. It all started with this.

'I don't know what I did. What was I doing?'

'You're not well.'

His mind was protecting him. It was the opposite to my grandmother: the sicker she was, the more spilled out of her.

'It comes and goes. One minute I'm here, in the kitchen, a lifetime in my head. Then the next minute I don't know where, or who . . .'

His eyes fell on the pendant again.

'But I gave this to her. How can you have it?'

'Who?' I pushed. 'Who did you give it to?'

He'd been repeating the same refrain since he first saw it, saying *no* over and over.

'Aria,' I said. 'Aria was her name.'

Every bit of colour, from the cold, from the light of the room, drained from his face.

'I . . .' He touched his mouth, trying to hold the words in.

'You can say it. It's just us.'

'I can't say anything! If I speak a word, they'll . . .' Agitated, he stumbled in his frustration. His hand, his eye – losing them had meant he couldn't go out on the water again. Had it been another 'accident'? He knocked over his tea, and in the wet, pushed everything else off the table. I looked at the mess, saw that it was everywhere. I could smell it too. Rotten food. He wasn't looking after himself. Did he know how to any more? Father Jessop would have seen the state of him and said it was God's punishment, to lose his mind, his memories.

'I'm looking after it for her, for Aria,' I said, trying to calm him down and fixing the pendant back around my neck.

'You know her?'

'I know she was kind, that you capsized and she looked after you.'

His face slackened. 'You know? You know what she . . .' His mind switched again. 'No! It doesn't explain . . . How did you get it?'

'I'll explain. I will. But I have to go. They don't trust me around you.'

He grabbed me, a wildness in his eyes. 'You can't tell anyone!'

'I won't. I promise I won't. I'll come back. Tomorrow night. Stay home, don't go to the festival. Okay? Stay right here and I'll tell you everything. We can talk. We can work this out together. I promise you, it'll be okay.'

'Esta,' he said, his voice a sharp cry. He held onto me so I wouldn't leave. 'I'm frightened.'

The back of Mull's cool hand pressed against my forehead. We were sitting together on the edge of my bed, her dressed, hair plaited ready to leave for the festival, me with a blanket draped across my lap, a downcast, half-lidded gaze. I'd told her and the rest of the family I wasn't feeling well.

'You don't feel any warmer than usual,' she said. 'Is it worth fetching the doctor? The midwife?'

I would have been grateful for Norah at one point, but she was doing everything she could to hide.

'I'm just exhausted,' I said.

The best lies start with some truth. The previous night had been fraught and sleepless. I'd had to explain myself to Ingram, and he was angry with me for forcing him to make excuses for my absence with his family. I gave him part of the truth – my worries about Barrett's health, how broken he seemed – and he softened. Ever since the pregnancy, he had been tender, forgiving. He talked of God, of praying for Barrett's health, and I had to swallow my real thoughts. What good did praying do when his mind was already crumbling? What prayer could fix that?

Ingram had held me, putting his hand on the rise and fall of my body. There was nothing there, no growth, no flicker of movement, but his hopes tricked him. Yet his joy wouldn't blind him forever.

'You don't seem any happier since the news of the baby,' he said. Perhaps he thought that had been the sole reason for my detachment in our marriage – disappointment, a feeling of failure. He thought this fixed things; that I should have been overjoyed, loving.

I didn't take pleasure in hurting him. Perhaps if things had been different, we could have been content. I lay there struggling to say the words I knew he wanted to hear, but they came out eventually. I could pretend, I could find happiness, but it wasn't there in that room with him; it came from an imagined future, one I wasn't even sure I could have.

'Do you think . . .' he had begun, sheepish in a way I hadn't seen before, 'if I put my head to your stomach I would hear his heartbeat?'

I lifted his hand off me. 'Not yet. It's too soon.'

I could sense his want, his need to shuffle down the bed and press his ear against me. It had been bittersweet to see the change in him after the announcement, the way his mood lifted, buoyed by the reaction from his brothers and the other fishermen in the harbour. In their eyes, he'd become a man.

'It's a new start,' he'd said, his chest puffing up. His closeness with Seren had cooled off, and their sudden distance, the thought of her unhappiness, made me spitefully pleased.

He kissed my cheek, nestled against my back.

'Did you ever lose faith in me? Did you think I was cursed?' I asked.

'No. I knew you were doing everything you could.' His answer was too quick. He'd rehearsed it.

'Seren thought I was.' I shouldn't have said it, but I couldn't stop myself.

He sighed. 'Well, it's easy for her to say.'

'I know you wish I was like her.'

'What do you mean by that?'

The dark room ticked over. I didn't answer, pretending to be asleep.

My thoughts of the previous night were interrupted by Seren entering the room, dressed ready for the festival, just like Mull. The men had already left to set up the fish stall and Vayle had gone with them, taking the children.

'I didn't hear you come in last night,' she said.

'She's unwell.' Mull tried to dampen Seren's harsh tone.

'You missed supper. Ingram didn't have a clue where you were. He was worried sick.'

'I'm sure you looked after him.'

Mull, who had awkwardly kept her attention focused on the bedcovers, spoke. 'Let's not get worked up. Stress isn't good for our babies. It's been hard enough today to see that hook empty outside the church.' Her words were choked up by her swallow, and Seren stepped closer to her. Marking her territory. 'It can't be a good thing, can it, for it to disappear like that?'

'Perhaps it was God. All His power causing the tail to wither and dissolve overnight,' Seren said.

'Who would do that, who would do such a thing?' I saw a flash of rage in Mull that reminded me of her father. 'I hope she's caught, whoever she is!'

Seren had already reported to me the chaos and devastation over the missing Seawoman's tail. Some women had prayed at the scene of the crime, while others had avoided it, spreading stories about a hooded woman taking the stolen tail to bed with her.

Seren tried to take charge. 'It's our night and we owe it to ourselves and future generations not to let anything tarnish it.'

'No, you're right, you're right.' Mull nodded quickly.

'Are you sure you won't come with us?' Seren said to me. I shook my head, giving her a meek smile that I hoped looked like I was sorry to be missing out.

'Seren, do you mind waiting for me in the hall? I'm going to get Esta comfortable.' Mull turned to me and I didn't argue. Nothing could stand in the way of my plans. She put her hand on my head again as Seren left. 'Are you feeling sick, or just tired?'

'It's the thought of all that noise, the crowds. You know how lively it gets.'

'We'll bring you back some treats. For when you're feeling up to it,' she said.

The sooner she and Seren were gone, the sooner I could leave for the cove. I wanted Cal to see me there, ready and waiting. When I was tucked up under the covers, Mull sat on the edge of the bed, smoothed the hair off my face. I looked at her and tried not to think of the word *goodbye*. She was the closest thing I had to a true friend. I loved her.

'I know I keep saying it, but I'm so happy you're pregnant,' she said. 'Our babies, they'll get to grow up together and be friends just like us.' Her hand touched my cheek, and I froze, the backs of her fingers grazing the thread of the pendant.

'I can't wait,' I lied.

'I prayed for you, as the months went on and there was no sign . . . I really hoped. When did you know?' She'd begun stroking my hair. 'Only you were so worried before, what with the trip to the chapel, and you kept talking about bad blood and consequences . . . things you'd done. You made me start to worry even more than before.'

'The pressure got to me, this house and . . . I'm not sure when I knew, it was sudden. When you told me about yours, I started noticing changes. I wasn't thinking straight before.'

'But you can relax now, God is with you. And anything you need . . . I know Seren can be intense, but she's been a great support for me.'

'I'm sure.'

'And my father, too, he was so pleased when I told him.'

I struggled to keep my face straight. 'Oh, you told him?'

'It's a blessing. It's a shame you're missing out tonight,' she said. 'But you've never liked the festival much, have you? It always made you . . . unsettled.' She smiled, like it was a casual observation. 'There's always a point in the night where I lose you. I go looking, but no one's seen you. I can't find you anywhere.'

I tried to laugh. 'I don't know where you were looking. I was probably dancing or at one of the stalls. It's always so crowded.'

She wasn't laughing at all. 'It is strange,' she said. 'That year your grandmother passed, and when I found you, your skirt was soaking. And this year, you're not going at all.'

The room felt hotter, smaller. 'I don't feel well, I told you.'

'I know,' she said, straightening out the bedcovers. 'You need rest. You've got to look after your child. We all have to. They're the most important thing. We have to keep them safe.'

'You have a nice night,' I said as she made to leave.

'You'd tell me if something was wrong – with the baby? I mean it, Esta. If something's happened.'

'I'm fine,' I said. 'The baby's fine. You'd better go, before they run out of honey bread.'

She smiled briefly and left. The time had come.

Twenty-Three

He was there, waiting for me. There was a quiet part of me that had worried he would never come back, but all those fears melted away. I wore his pendant over my clothes so it would be the first thing he saw, the coin shining in the moonlight. My heart caught in my throat. We had no words left to say, nothing that could possibly cover the two years apart. We collided in the middle, half sea, half sand, and I clung to him, mouth open in a cry and buried in his neck. I thought about the Ministers' plans to fence us apart. His arms came around me, wet and cold and strong, and I let him pull me into the water, away from the place rooted deep into me, the place that hurt me. The cold took my breath away. I was awake, thrumming, more than just surviving. The water suspended us, pushing against our entwined bodies, and I put my mouth against him and tasted the sea. His hands ran over me, making sure I was real and alive, then his kiss, open, wanting, made me yearn for a storm to carry us away.

Under the water, I slid my hands down his body. The muscle, the scales, the man, the parts of him that should have made him a monster. I dragged my fingertips over the smooth skin of his spine, rested my hands at his hips. There was a swell in my throat, a dip in my stomach. Those sensations felt like something half remembered from a dream, dormant heat rising deep within me. I ran my hand across his chest. I could look at his body without fear, with no hesitation. He was beautiful.

My forehead rested against his. I said his name like I was breathing out, like I finally knew how. There was a push-pull between us, like however we held each other, however we touched, it would never be enough.

'I didn't know if I'd ever see you again,' he said.

'Last year I couldn't get away, I couldn't . . .'

I put his hand against my chest so he wasn't just hearing my heart-beat through the water but feeling it too.

I led him to where the sea's foam made the shingle gleam, him across my lap, where the last surges of the waves rucked against us. I held him between my thighs, gasping each time a cold wave broke against us. He kissed and kissed me, open-mouthed, pulse-splitting, time-bending. God did nothing to stop us; no interruption, no storm brewed. Not even a spot of rain. I stopped being a woman of the island. I rolled up my sodden skirt, peeling it back over my thighs, revealing more and more shivered, goose-pimpled skin. His mouth met my neck and I felt my body buckle at the press of his webbed fingers slick between my legs. His mouth like the lick of the tide. It seemed instinctive somehow, something primal reaching out of us both, my neck arching, breath stolen. I reached to touch his gills, his lips, everything, and still the world didn't end; no, it expanded.

Afterwards, I wanted to stay there, my body throbbing against his, my nerves sharp, the feeling that he was still inside me, but time was fall-ing away and I'd made a promise.

'I need to take you somewhere,' I said. His pendant, still around my neck, dangled against his bare chest as we lay there. 'I've found him. Your father.'

He sat up quickly.

'Trust me?' I asked.

'All this time . . .' he said, doubt creeping into his voice. I'd made it real for him, more than just an impossible quest.

'He's sick. Losing his memories. His mind maybe.' It was the first time I'd admitted it out loud, and the sound of it made me tremble. Could I really leave Barrett behind?

'Have you told him about me?'

'Not yet.'

There'd be no going back after this. My thoughts turned to my mother. Would it have been easier never to have known? For her to have forever stayed a mystery? Perhaps my desire for a life beyond had always been her, pulling my heart across the water. But there was an anger too, that my loss was not caused by the ravages of fire, but by her choice to leave me behind, abandoning me to the same fate that destroyed her. Perhaps she'd hoped my path would be different, that I wouldn't be burdened with a wandering mind or a forbidden love. She couldn't have known that, like her, I would spend a lifetime fighting an instinctual desire to be elsewhere.

'I found out something else . . . about my mother,' I said softly. I shut my eyes, focusing on this new truth. 'She didn't die in the fire like I'd always been told. She got away.'

'She left you behind.'

I drew my knees up to my chest, rested my chin. I would never know what had gone through her head. But I knew what forbidden love felt like. It drove me in the same way it had driven her.

'You've never met anyone, never heard any stories about women who escaped this place? You've been all over. Someone must have said something.'

He was silent for too long, and I could see him searching for words. 'It doesn't mean it hasn't happened.'

'Or it means they never made it. They could have failed and died at sea.'

'Don't torture yourself.' He sat by me. 'Maybe they did make it, but they never told anyone where they came from. Maybe they lied about who they were. Maybe it was a way to protect themselves and make sure they'd never have to go back if someone came looking.' He locked eyes with me.

I had to tell him, I had to ask for his help. Without it, there would be no next year, no more sneaking away from the festival. I stood, shaking free of sand and wet stones, slid my hand around his. I wanted him to know, but I couldn't bear the dark cloud it would bring. What if it was impossible? Too far to swim, too dangerous for him to carry me, to drag me through the sea.

He looked at me from the side and stroked my damp hair from my face, his fingers gentle over my scarring.

'It's time to see him,' I said.

I gave him a coat I'd brought along in case anyone saw us from a distance. It was Ingram's, old and in need of darning.

'Your husband's?' Cal said when he saw it.

I moved to reassure him. 'It's duty. Not love.'

He took it from me after a beat of hesitation and pulled it on. The strange sight of its awkward fit made us both laugh at its absurdity. But that levity couldn't last.

Cal and I moved like shadows around the side of Barrett's house, keeping to the dark, communicating in looks and touches to avoid any noise. There was a bigger presence of Keepers at the harbour than normal, taking shifts to assemble the barbed fencing. Father Jessop had used the night of the festival as a marker, promising to give us all another reason to celebrate by starting the construction. We could hear the Keepers, the drunken roars of laughter, sharing in the merriment of the festival even though they couldn't be there with the rest. There wasn't a single light on in Barrett's house, and a part of me was grateful, thinking it might raise more suspicion if he appeared to be home in the middle of a celebration, but another part of me found the dark so eerie, I worried that he had forgotten. The door was unlocked like we'd agreed, and in the darkened hallway, I whispered to Cal to watch where he stepped. Hanging by the door were waders, and I motioned for him to put them on under Ingram's coat, in case he was spotted at a window, and for Barrett's sake. To see him fully, naked and scaled as he was, might have been too much to take at once.

When he was dressed, I felt light-headed. He looked wrong, dressed like a fisherman, wearing the clothes of men who would rather he was dead. I wanted to tear them off him. 'Wait here,' I said, my hands either side of his face, leaving him with a kiss. I vibrated with fear.

I edged through each room, my adrenaline too high to call out Barrett's name. The house was unnaturally still. What if he'd let slip to someone what he'd done all those years ago, after I'd dredged it up again? Or worse, what if someone had seen him with the tail and the Keepers had already taken him away? I reached the kitchen and held onto the back of a chair, regaining my breath, trying to still my thrashing heart, shivering in my wet dress. Spread over the table were log books, records, pages torn, some shredded, some illegible and scored through with heavy black marks. The destruction of Barrett's mind was showing itself in frustration, an attack on what he had once known and was losing.

There was a creak on the floor behind me, and I whipped around, blood beating, only to find Cal.

'You scared me.' I pressed my hand over my rabbiting heart.

He looked around the room, part awe, part fear.

I let him wander. 'I used to live here with him.'

His eyes widened, holding a cup mid-air then putting it back where he'd found it. 'You're family?'

'Mae was my grandmother's cousin.'

'How long have you known it was him?'

'Not long.' I let out a breath of my own disbelief, how it explained so much about why Barrett was the man he was.

Cal walked the perimeter of the table. I expected him to continue his curious inspection of the room, trying to glean who his father was from these items. Lights from outside cast an eeriness over Barrett's collection of hooks and nets. Cal picked up one of the chairs and swung it around, smashing anything in its path, beating it against the cupboards, the walls, the floor. I watched, heart in mouth.

There was a rage in him I hadn't seen. I raised my arms to shield my face, cowering in the doorway, pleading with him to stop. Finally, the chair fell apart in his hands and he looked at me with wild, animal eyes. The look I had feared the most.

I stepped back, pressing into the wall. 'What are you doing?'

'What else was I supposed to do to show him how I feel?'

'You said you weren't here for revenge.'

'That was years ago! Before he was real to me. Before seeing *this*!'

There was a noise upstairs and Cal's eyes darted above our heads.

I ran to block the door. 'No.'

'Esta.' He stood in front of me, his anger simmering behind his teeth.

'Let Barrett speak first. Please.' I took a breath, took his face in my hands. 'Please calm down. There are men outside, and if they hear us, we're all finished.'

'Barrett,' he repeated.

'You promised me you didn't come here to hurt him.'

'You lived with him in this house, and all this time he knew what this island was! He knew who the Seawomen really were. You should hate him too.'

There was a noise in the hallway behind us. When I turned, Barrett was there, armed with a wooden paddle, jagged and splintered, useless like the rest of his boatyard hoarding.

'What are you doing in my house?' His voice had the same snarl as his son's. We just looked like intruders to him.

I switched a light on and saw the recognition pouring into his face. He breathed my name like a sigh of relief.

'You came back,' he said, piecing together his jumbled memories. 'That's right. The festival. You said . . .'

'Come and sit down.'

'Who's he? Who's this?' The paddle had loosened in his hand when he'd seen me, but it was rigid again, fingers and knuckles white-tight. He took an uneasy step forward, noticing the state of the kitchen, then pushed me out of the way, coming face to face with Cal, swinging the oar clumsily towards him.

With little effort, Cal took the oar and snapped it, tossing the remains across the room. I stepped between them. Cal looked to have doubled in size, and with the leak of light from the hall, I could see the venom in his expression, the vicious strangeness of his sharp teeth. I shuffled Barrett towards one of the chairs, telling him to sit, with a gentle repeated instruction like one given to a child. When he was finally seated, his shoulders hunched, his solitary hand shaking under the table, I hoped Cal would see what I could. An old man, growing frail, who had already lost so much.

Cal stayed standing. The promise of that frightening rage still simmered. It took everything within me not to collapse on the floor, give up.

'So when's he going to start talking?' he demanded.

Barrett's attention became focused on the pendant, now back around Cal's neck. He pointed to it, frowning. 'That's hers,' he said. 'I didn't give it to you. I gave it to her.'

Both men were tense.

'Aria,' Cal said, snarling. 'Her name was Aria.'

'Yes . . . yes.'

'You abandoned her.'

Barrett's head snapped up, alerted again to this stranger he seemed to keep forgetting about, and then his neck softened, his head rolling back down, chin against chest. I touched his wrist.

Cal kept pushing. 'She wanted to remember you.'

The colour drained from Barrett's eyes, leaving behind just an impression of life. He didn't want this story unearthed, but by bringing Cal here I'd given him no choice.

'I didn't get the pendant from her,' I told him, speaking slowly so he would understand every word. 'Her son gave it to me.'

'Her son?'

'I brought him here to meet you. He's been waiting a long time for this. Her son. And yours.'

'My son? I don't . . .'

'He's yours.' I hadn't seen it before, but their likeness stared straight back at me.

He looked at Cal again with confusion, muttering to himself that refrain of *no* that he'd repeated when I'd caught him holding the Seawoman's tail.

'Twenty-three years ago you left this island and capsized,' Cal said.

'That's right,' Barrett replied, his voice almost lifting in excitement that memories were being repainted and given back to him. His back straightened, the shaking abated at the sound of Cal's voice.

'She saved you.'

'Aria.'

Cal flinched; her name spoken with lucidity by Barrett caught him unawares.

'She was . . .' Barrett drifted, his memories sailing away. 'How do you know this? I haven't . . . I didn't! I swear!'

'It's all right,' I said. 'Take your time.'

'You're her son?'

'And yours. I'm *your* son. I'm Cal.'

I heard the pain strangling Cal's voice, and looked at him, pleading for more patience.

'*My* son?'

'Can you remember what happened?' I asked.

'You're all her,' Barrett said, seemingly mesmerised by the gills, slightly obscured by the borrowed coat. 'And so little of me.'

Cal looked away.

'What happened that night you met Aria?' I asked.

Barrett's breathing became deep and laboured. 'I don't remember.'

'Tell us, please,' I urged, crouching beside him.

'Us?' Barrett's brow lowered. 'Us?'

'Yes,' I said, feeling my throat swell. 'He saved me, like Aria saved you.' There was a sadness in it, a pre-written tragedy of mirrored impossibility, but also a relief to admit what Cal was to me. It wasn't enough to explain it all, but Barrett nodded slowly.

'The baby?'

Cal's widening eyes travelled to my stomach.

'There is no baby.'

Barrett moaned in sad bewilderment. 'No baby? You're not . . . ?'

Tears were suddenly racing out of me.

'Why? Why then?'

'I had to lie. I had no choice. You know what they'd do.'

'No, Esta! You had time. Why!' He held his head, knuckles pressing in, and muttered skyward. To God. To Sarl.

'I didn't have time! They were suspicious of me already.'

'What are you talking about?' Cal asked.

I didn't know how to tell him. If I'd told him every horrible truth about the island and what we believed, he might've never come back.

'The thing is,' I said, trying to take deep, steadying breaths, 'the island has a rule. A belief. We have to have children, we have to keep the island going, with people like us.' He looked on, waiting. 'And if we don't manage it, if we can't give birth to a child in the year we've been given, they mark us as cursed.'

'Cursed by what?' He was exasperated. 'The Seawomen?'

'And my year is nearly over.'

'What happens when the year is up? What happens?'

'If we don't . . . They say God has turned His back. The Seawomen have our soul.' I put my hands on him, but they couldn't settle anywhere but his face. His beautiful, angular, pelagic face. 'They drown us.'

Cal reared back, the word *no* formed on his lips. He turned his rage on Barrett.

'All this time you've known the truth and you've said nothing! You've let women suffer and drown, trapped by lies! The Seawomen have no power at all! You knew, you knew all this time!'

Barrett stumbled back from Cal's advance. He whimpered. 'They told me she'd bewitched me. That I was wrong. Crazy! That's what they called me.

'Please,' I said, moving to edge him away. My words desperate and under my breath. 'Let him talk in his own time. He's losing all of it, every memory. Can't you see?'

'We have to get you out of here.'

Across the room, Barrett was muttering, trembling, reliving his suffering. My instinct was to sit beside him, to stay. I drew one of Cal's hands to my mouth and kissed it, held it against my cheek.

'You came here to listen to him explain, and that's what we'll do.'

Barrett sat at the table. I was afraid he might never speak again, but his eyes moved, following his memories like they were birds in the sky, waiting for them to land. I held my breath, waiting. Waiting. I didn't know if I had it in me to have more of the past upturned. I tried to prompt him by starting with what I knew – Mae, how sick she had become, how hard the grief had hit him. I was scared that he wouldn't find the words to carry on, but then he began, like I'd woken him, brought the past to life.

'She was sickly, always sickly, even as a girl. They decided she was too frail to be given a motheryear, so for years it was just the two of us and we were happy. We believed it would happen for us eventually. Mae was from a big family and I had my brothers. We had faith. But then she got very sick.'

I waited for the words to stumble in the dark. But when it came to Mae, the memories seemed so strong. His mind was like his house, crammed full of junk, but a few pieces remained, gleaming, rescued from a net. When he talked about Mae, she was so clear to him that for the first time in a long time, he began to look like himself.

'There was a lot of bad luck in the air in that time. We even thought about moving away from the harbour, from the curse of the water, but Mae knew where my work was, my family's legacy. She said it was where I belonged. But I watched her get weaker and weaker. The storms were up and the seas were wild, and Mae was sick, so very sick. Everything was falling apart. My father died, then my mother. I didn't know what to do. Stay with her or take to the water so we'd have something to eat. I made my choice . . . I made my choice . . .'

I knew how this story ended, but I braced myself to hear it.

'I left her at dawn. Out all day and all I had to show for it was a haul so sparse it wouldn't've fed a child. When I got home, Mae was . . . in the same place I'd left her. Ice cold. Ice cold. She was already gone and she'd been alone . . .

'After she died, I did too. All I did after that was drink and fish, drink and fish. When I came home, she was everywhere. Every room. And it was all my fault.'

Barrett's eyes moved to a different part of the room, and I thought we'd lost him again, but after a deep breath he carried on, girded by the anger of his memories.

'And that man. That *man*. He came here' – his voice trembled – 'and he held me as I wept. He told me God took her for a reason. He told me she must've done something. That her faith wasn't strong enough. He said she had turned her back on God and this was His response. To take my parents too, to take my wife. He. *He*.'

'Father Jessop,' I said, though it was barely above a whisper.

'Told me he'd find me another wife. One who wasn't cursed. One who could give me sons. He said it like Mae was nothing, like we should be glad she'd died. I saw him for what he was then. Evil. And all of his lot before him, leading right back to the start. Something snapped. I had to leave.'

I was scared to hear him continue. How had he hidden it for so long and not let it destroy him? My head spun.

'Night-time. The festival. Needed to be when all of them were . . .'

'Distracted?' I said, helping him to finish.

'The festival! How was I meant to celebrate, when . . .'

'How did you make it out of the harbour?'

He frowned, taking time to think. No fisherman had a reason to be out on the water at night, not when it wasn't safe.

'I think . . . I got them drunk . . . or I . . . I drugged them. They were already in good spirits. It didn't matter. I had to go.' He punctuated this with his fist against the table. He was that man again from his past, reckless and determined. He had nothing left. 'I didn't care where I ended up. I wasn't thinking. I wanted . . . the end. I wanted to be dead.'

The words came out of him so plainly, detached from emotion, like he was talking about someone else. I couldn't bear it.

'I wanted to drown. I wanted to drown.' He carried on saying it, over and over, until I tore away to stop myself breaking, needing to escape, and stood at the sink, breathing unsteadily. Cal took my place by the table, sitting awkwardly on the chair adjacent to Barrett to let him carry on.

Barrett continued to direct his words to me, even with my back to him. 'Your grandfather. You didn't know him, but he was the type of fisherman who always wanted to push it. Go a bit further, bored of the day-to-day. But not me. Even when I was out on the water, I always wanted to come back, back to my Mae. I always came back to her. The rules were the rules. To keep us safe. Just like he said. I believed it. And it didn't matter, because Mae and I were happy.'

I splashed my face with water from the tap, composed myself to face him. I wanted to understand what it felt like to take that impossible risk like my mother had done, even after a lifetime of being told the island was the only safe place in the world. Watching the islanders celebrate, full of revelry and joy, when just weeks before, his whole world had ended.

'You weren't scared of crossing the border?'

'I wasn't afraid any more. The worst had already happened. Mae hadn't been bewitched! She wasn't weak. She was strong and good. I didn't believe anything that came out of that man's mouth. What was left to fear?'

'You capsized,' Cal said, trying to push him back on course.

'Hit a rock. After that. Black. Sea and sky all the same. All of it cold and black and cold and . . . I was falling and I was glad. So glad. Mae was there, opening her arms . . . I woke up on an island. A different island. I thought I was dead. But Aria . . . I woke to this woman looking over me. I couldn't make sense of it. I thought she was Mae at first. Wanted it to be her. She told me to rest. That was all I wanted to hear. All I saw of her first was hair, a gentle mouth telling me everything would be all right. You don't understand! I thought I was dreaming. I thought I was dead.' He grew agitated, weeping Mae's name again, slumping to the floor.

'So she was nothing. She could have been anyone to you.' Cal stood over him. He wanted Aria to matter. He wanted her to live on in Barrett, for someone else to share his loss.

'No . . . no. She was like medicine! Medicine. She kissed me. You're a long way from home. Long way from home, she said. I told her everything and she understood. She could feel it through me. That pain. All of it pouring out.

'By the time I saw what she really was, the tail, the scales, the differences, it didn't matter. We talked. Hours and hours. She was nothing like what we'd been told. And when I explained to her our stories, all that we'd been taught about her kind, she was terrified to be near me. She told me what she knew – all these horrifying things Lambert and . . . and the rest had done to the Seawomen to scare them away. Butchers. Now I knew what Jessop was. I could see it, everything she told me, her version, the true version . . .'

His eyes implored me to believe. 'She saved me. You understand? They're not like what they tell you. They're not. If it weren't for her . . .'

Barrett talked like he was on borrowed time. This would all slip away before long. I didn't know how much more of his clarity we'd hear. I coaxed him up from the floor and, conscious of his exhaustion, ushered him towards a more comfortable chair in the living room. I plumped the cushions around him and found a blanket to lay across him.

Cal came into the room. His frustration hadn't dissipated. His mother's feelings of betrayal and regret were ever rawer in him, and

Barrett hadn't given him what he needed. 'Why did you leave her? You made her promises and then you left!'

Barrett grew agitated, 'Look at me! Look at what they did!' and before I knew what he was doing, he had pulled his shirt from his back.

'What are you—' and then I saw it, a patchwork of scars, whipped into his skin, long marks branded forever, property of the island, of Father Jessop's control. I folded against Cal, unable to look, to imagine that level of pain. Cal eased me away gently by the elbows.

Barrett had removed his eyepatch too, revealing the sunken, scarred space left behind. There had never been an accident; only punishment and torture.

'They did all this to you?' Cal asked, his voice suddenly filled with so much tenderness it broke me to imagine how different their lives might have been alongside each other.

'I'm sorry,' Barrett said. 'I'm so sorry.' For the first time, there was connection between them.

Cal hesitated, a lifetime of questions about who he was suspended in mid-air.

'He needs rest,' I said.

'Esta, it's getting late.'

Barrett's scarred body softened, easing into the chair in the first breaths of sleep, and I left the room, at a loss what to do. I knew Cal was right, time was against us, but I couldn't think. I wanted nothing more than to scream. I was drawn to my old room, its walls ringing with the smell of the sea. I had cried in that room so many times, feeling raw with my differences, wondering if I would ever belong. Cal joined me moments later, and we stood in the dark, hiding from the window that looked out onto the harbour below, the Keepers blowing on their fists to keep warm, checking the tautness of the moorings with their feet. I was wordless, pressing my grief against Cal, letting him ease the tears out of me with his hand on the back of my neck. I looked at the time on the clock on the shelf, the indigo cast of light.

'Why didn't you tell me?' he said. 'I'd heard stories, rumours, but I had no idea what they do to you here . . .'

'I used to think it was just. To protect us. And then I met you and I saw our island through your eyes.'

'We need to get away.'

'How?'

'We could swim.' I'm not sure even he believed we could.

'It's too far. I'm not strong enough.'

'I'll help you.'

'We'd be slow targets. They'd easily catch us. And where? Where would we go?' I took his face in my hands. 'Where would we be safe? What would they think of me?'

'They'd see you like I do.'

'And us? You in the water, me on the land.'

'I'd live on the land forever for you.'

'I wouldn't want you to. You'd be trapped.'

'We'd make it work.'

When I didn't answer, Cal broke away, sitting on the bed, the sheets rucking like a frozen tide. I went over and knelt in front of him, placing my hands inside the borrowed coat to feel his cool skin. I wanted him close. My head bowed, my forehead pressed to his throat, his jaw so close I could feel the workings of his mouth as he debated what to say.

'We should have gone years ago,' he said, sounding angry at himself. 'I should have saved you.'

'I couldn't have gone. I wouldn't have.'

'Even though you knew what life was like here?'

'I used to think it was the only place in the world where I was safe, where I'd get to Salvation. I thought . . . my mother was up there, waiting for me.'

'And now you know she's out there. Don't you want to be free? Don't you want to find her?'

Twenty-Four

I woke with a jolt, coiled against Cal. It was still dark outside, and the clock told me only minutes had passed. The emotion of the night had pulled me under and my heart raced as I pieced everything back together. I'd dreamt of a capsized boat sucking me beneath the water's surface, the black terror of drowning, then of a room, walls closing in, smoke and heat choking me as much as a rise of water. I hadn't dreamt about the fire for years. I sat up and Cal met me in an embrace. I leant into him, my breath shucking against his chest. The room felt suspended in time. If I kept my eyes closed, could we stay there forever, cocooned from the outside world? I pressed my mouth and nose to his chest where the echo of the sea called him back; he tasted of a salt song, the heart of a shell.

'We need to go,' he said, kissing the side of my head as if that was enough to clear my worries.

'Barrett . . .'

'You can't stay here for him,' he said.

'I need to know he'll be all right with me gone.'

We descended the stairs, careful to be quiet, but Barrett was already awake. He started when we appeared in the living room and looked down with confusion at his removed shirt. After redressing, he looked at Cal.

'Sorry, I'm no good with names. Let me get my books and see which boat was meant to be yours for the day . . .'

He glanced around, ready to stand up and start the day, but I interrupted him by crouching in front of where he sat, watching his face light up in recognition.

'You've come for breakfast,' he said, triumphantly, like he was proud that he remembered.

'Maybe later,' I said. 'It's still night-time.'

'So it is.' He looked back at Cal. 'It's him again, isn't it?'

'You were telling us about his mother. Aria.'

'Aria . . .' he said vaguely.

'You didn't stay with her,' Cal said. 'You came back here.'

'Yes.' He scrabbled around for a memory, a conversation.

'You were telling us about when you left her.'

'That's right.'

'She loved you,' Cal said. 'And you didn't love her back?'

It was there again, in Barrett's face, memories swimming to the surface, pulled out of him.

'Didn't know how. Not then.'

'You said she saved you.'

'In time, I could have. She was . . . she was . . . but it was a different world. And I was empty.' He thumped under his ribcage. 'I couldn't. I couldn't. We could have been happy, we could have.'

'You let her fall in love with you, and then you left her.'

The accusation hung heavy between them. Barrett's gaze drifted. He seemed to absorb what Cal had said like he'd given him a report on the weather.

'I couldn't let go of Mae. She knew . . . Aria knew. We talked for so long. She'd never met a man like me, one who didn't hurt her or want to put her in a cage. I knew she wanted me to stay, but . . .'

'How could you come back here, knowing what this place was?'

'Mae! I wanted her back. My memories.' His whole body seemed to shudder, fold in on itself. 'I had nothing left. She was here! Living in these walls. You don't understand!'

I stepped in, edging Cal aside, seeing Barrett's distress.

'How did you get back?'

'She fixed up my wrecked boat. Aria. Sent me on my way. And I gave her the pendant. I wanted to show her she meant something.'

Under my hands, I felt Cal tense.

'That was all she meant? A pendant?' His voice splintered, betraying his anger. Both he and Aria had treasured it, had clung to it for so long.

'I . . . didn't have anything else to give.'

'You came back here and watched women drown. Said nothing. Did nothing.'

Barrett's head jerked up. 'And what did you do? Who even are you, hmm? In my house . . . here . . . whoever you are.'

Cal looked stung at being forgotten again. He'd spent a lifetime weighed down with the absence of knowing who he was and what he came from; was he beginning to wonder if it was worth the pain?

'I'll tell you what I did!' Barrett said, animated again by fury. 'I tried to make things right! I came back, but it was a mistake. It was so lonely . . . So I drank again, and when Jessop found me, I was a mess. He didn't give me time to speak. He said if I ever breathed a word about leaving or what I'd seen, he would tell everyone Mae was a whore. He would find men to testify against her. He said he would take everything from me just by revealing what I really was. A drunk. A madman. And Mae. Mae.' He leant into his hand, sobbing. 'She wanted children. We both did. A legacy. The thought that Jessop would ruin her after she was gone, it killed me. I knew my word would mean nothing. I was a drunk, half mad and grieving. Who would believe me?'

His mouth was gummy, drooling as he sobbed. 'I'm a coward. I should have done something. Why. Why didn't I? Fight him, kill him? But Jessop, he told me he'd destroy everything left of her if that was what I wanted. I . . . I . . . After he . . . when he . . . He let me drink. To make me look even worse.'

'What they did to me. Jessop's men. My eye. My hand. He wanted to show me he was serious. That I was a prisoner.' He lifted his shirt again, and this time I had a closer look. 'He said God chooses His people with tests, and I had failed and it was time I paid for my crimes. He branded me. Told me if anyone saw it they'd know I was marked with the darkness.'

I felt suddenly sick, hot all over.

'Jessop is the darkness. Not *them*,' he said. He sat upright, life in his eyes, facing Cal. 'Is she still alive?'

Cal blinked. 'Aria?'

Barrett nodded, eager. Hopeful.

Cal's head dropped, and I watched as Barrett reached out. Tentatively at first. Cal had come for answers; he'd needed to hear that his mother's love hadn't been in vain, that Barrett hadn't used her and tossed her aside. Tears were coursing down Barrett's face. 'Let me see you, let me see you,' he said, tugging on the sleeve of Cal's borrowed coat. It rippled to the floor and Barrett drank him in, everything strange and beautiful about him.

'A son?'

'Yes.'

'My son?' His voice cracked. It wasn't a question, but a greeting.

He held onto Cal, looking at the son he'd made. There wasn't forgiveness or anything close to closure in Cal's face, but that word had to mean the world.

Could I reconcile the man in front of me – the man who'd lost his wife, his hand, his eye, his freedom – with the man who'd sat back and let it happen? Turning away as women died, all of us in Father Jessop's chains. He'd come back to the island knowing it was all a lie, and he'd lived with it. It was only Sarl who had stopped his heavy drinking and forced him to help her parent me. That, in its way, had saved him, given him a reason to stay alive. It was either live with the only life he knew, or . . . what? What had any of us done to raise our voice against the cruelties of this place?

This tortured man, his memories savaged. He would lose Mae all over again.

And still I found it hard to look at him. To know whether I would ever truly forgive him.

Cal in Ingram's coat once more spoke in gentle, guarded tones to Barrett, the three of us sitting in the kitchen trying to determine whether we could use Ingram's boat without being seen, if we had enough time to make it seaworthy.

'You two are losing your minds. An old boat like that? Where will you go?' Barrett said.

I could see the worry hardening into his face. Our plans sounded more impossible the more we talked about them. Neither of us had ever been in a boat. Let alone rowed one.

'It's suicide,' Barrett said, once I had laid it all out for him. 'You don't even know where you're going.'

'It doesn't matter, as long as we get past the border.'

'And together, you're going together?'

There was no other way.

'We just need your help with the boat,' Cal said. He was making an effort with Barrett, leaning in, considerate with the way he spoke to him.

'Repair it? Help you on your way?'

'You could . . .' I paused. 'What if you came with us?'

Barrett held onto the edge of the table, very still, and then leant towards me, held my face in his hand. He knew as well as I did that this was the end.

'I'll only slow you down,' he said.

'You know the water better than anyone.'

'You deserve a life away from this place, but I . . .' He shook his head. 'I made my choice. I'll live with it.'

Cal opened his hand on the table, the coin pendant shining on his palm. 'You should have this back,' he said.

Barrett's hand closed over Cal's. 'It belongs to you now.'

They stayed there for a moment, hands touching. I watched the clarity fade from Barrett's eyes, then without a word he got up and headed into the hall. I was left sitting in the kitchen with a lifetime of secrets. I couldn't tell him about the fire, not now.

In an instant, all of these thoughts shattered by a knock at the front door.

Barrett looked at us from the hallway. 'Shall I . . . ?'

'No!' My answer matched Cal's.

The knock sounded again, this time louder, pounding, and I edged towards Cal. I knew he had to go. He couldn't be found here like this. He grasped me and I thought I might collapse. The knocking continued, a shuddering through the house that was tearing us apart. I didn't want this to be goodbye.

'Come with me.'

It was all too real, everything closing in.

I dragged Cal through the kitchen, towards the back door.

'You need to go. Now.' I pushed at him, frustrated that he was wasting time. He'd get away faster than I ever could.

'I'll lie low,' he said. 'Until it's safe. I'll come back for you and then we'll go.'

I knew there was no such thing as safe any more. It didn't feel as though it would ever exist again. Cal was trying to hold my attention, distract me from what was happening outside.

'The caves,' he pleaded, 'the ones we hid away in, the first time.'

'Just go!' Barrett waved his arms at us. 'I'll get rid of them! Go!'

'I love you,' Cal said.

I was halfway to a smile, wanting his lips on mine again, the promise of the sea stretching ahead of us to a new life. Then the sound from the hallway exploded, the door crashing open, before the door in front of us met the same fate, the glass shattering in the kitchen. Keepers. A Minister, uniform askew from the drunken celebrating. Father Jessop, with eyes as dark as the earth, and trailing behind him, her face blotchy and red, tears streaming underneath a black eye, Mull.

The Keepers guarded both doors, surrounding us. Father Jessop's face was thunderous. Mull whimpered beside him, her arm tight in his grasp. She tried to wipe her tears, but couldn't move for the pain.

'You were right to speak out in good faith,' Father Jessop said.

Mull flinched at his touch. She couldn't look at me.

'We missed you at the festival, Esta.'

In the dim of the kitchen, I said nothing, keeping my gaze lowered from him, my mouth closed. I still had hold of Cal's hand, and I pictured us in some desperate, victorious escape, outwitting the brutish Keepers. After that? My imagination dried up with the impossible.

'And who's this?' Father Jessop took a step towards Cal. If there was a way of causing a distraction and helping him to escape, I willed it to come to me.

When Cal didn't answer, Father Jessop raised his voice. 'Who are you? Answer me!'

Mull's head snapped up with her father's voice. She was shaken, but

I couldn't read what she was thinking. As she looked at Cal, though, her expression changed. Realisation. Years catching up with her. Horror. She knew what he was. One clear and excruciating moment, before her curdling scream and then mine. Telling Cal to run.

Twenty-Five

Mull screaming. Barrett launching himself at Father Jessop's back. The Keepers using their fists to knock him off. The dead thump of his body hitting the table, the floor, blood pouring from his ear. Screaming. Mull pointing at Cal, looking at me with fear and horror. All of it locked into a matter of seconds. Cal fighting them off, being restrained by four men, ripping the clothes from his back to reveal what he was.

'Lord, protect us!' from Father Jessop.

Me biting, snarling, pushing Father Jessop away. A knife, a blade in my hand, waving it at him.

'Keep back! Or I'll slit your fucking throat!'

That threat was enough for everyone in the room to stop, their breath held in shock. Restrain me? Keep their focus on Cal? Who was the bigger threat now?

Cal. I screamed for him.

These are the things I remember.

I've lost count of the days, the hours. Has it been weeks? When the door opens and lets light leak in, it's the only clue I have. Outside I can picture a promise of an early summer, a yellow sun fighting and failing against a press of clouds, the mats of red weed bearding the rocks as the sea swell recedes, the smell of the kittiwakes' colony, sour in the breeze. But I won't see any of that. I will never hear the call of the guillemots again. I'll be gone.

The sea is quiet tonight, scuffing against the cliffs. I remember how it looked, stretching up to the sweeping black sky. I piece the stars together from memory and replay my last moments with Cal over and over. The regrets, the what-ifs. Our stolen moments, his body against mine, the sight of him emerging from the water and all its promise. I can't let myself think of what they've done to him, where they might have taken him. Does his body now hang outside the church for all to see? I imagine improbable stories of escape, keeping him alive in my imagination. Free. He's swimming far away from this place, he is safe, as beautiful in the water as he ever was. I cry for him, for us, for everything I've lost.

The night they brought me here, the Keepers held me down and shaved off my hair with a blunt knife. I wouldn't be sedated with the fumes they use for Untetherings, because the Ministers needed me conscious to answer questions. Doran was there and made me undress in front of the other Ministers, proceeding to poke and prod at me, examining every inch of me, from the soles of my feet to my inner thighs, for signs of my betrayal, my bewitching. He was the one to take a look at me and confirm I'd been lying about carrying Ingram's child. That gave the Keepers permission to use their fists, boots, anything they wanted to get answers from me. Motivated by what I'd done, what I'd lied about.

The Ministers hauled me to my feet, ordered me to walk around the cell, answering their questions about the Seawomen, Cal, who else I'd bewitched, what else I'd done, until I was dropping with exhaustion. They came at me with a barrage of accusations. If I fell, if I limped, I was beaten until I walked properly again. But still I refused to tell them anything. I asked about Barrett, only to be struck again. I tried begging, pleading with Doran for mercy, trying to reason that we were *family*. He waited until I was on my knees before he laughed in my face, laughed and laughed until the sound of it emptied me. Afterwards I lay on the floor listening to the Keepers talk carelessly about what was to be done with my hair. They would burn it. Hair belonging to a woman who had made a pact with the Seawomen would never set alight. This was one of their many tests, proof to be read aloud at my Untethering.

They cut my nails, took my blood, my urine, put cold metal instruments deep into my mouth. They came back day after day to check again, making notes, conferring in the doorway, some of the Ministers young and nervy around me, peeling back my tongue, lifting my tunic to check the base of my spine. They've found nothing. Not a mark.

Not a symbol or a scar or a tail. I think that's what they expect to find each time they come into the room. A full transformation, skin broken to scales. Something from my grandmother's bedtime stories. Undeniable proof.

There are times when Doran comes alone, like he might be the one to finally break me. I hear his revulsion as he examines me, his torch blaring white into my eyes. It's silver he looks for. My grandmother used to tell me a Seawoman's eyes were so silver you could see your reflection in them. *I'll know if you've been looking at the sea. Your eyes'll give you away. Bright as the moon. Slippery as a fish.* Sometimes, when I'm sleepless and pained and hungry, I can hear a phantom of her in the room with me, breathing heavily, satisfaction in her face that she was right about me all along. I was my mother's daughter, a bad omen, from the very start.

She sounds like Doran, till I realise it's him talking. 'We always knew, right from the start. You ran into the sea; you were one of *them*,' he says. 'That creature. That *thing*. You brought it here.'

I unnerve him by staying silent, withholding. I won't let him win.

One day, when he is about to leave me locked up for another day, I finally speak, press on the open wound of fear. I ask after his wife, whether she's given birth.

He pulls back. 'What did you say?'

I ask again, this time with a look of concern. He will read it as a threat. A warning. I see him swallow, drop backwards, the knot of his throat constricting the skin like a rabbit caught in a trap. His teeth flare outside of his lips.

'What have you done to them?'

'I was just asking how they are.'

'What have you done?'

His voice is fleshless, paper-thin. All I do now is sit back against the wall, face lowered, eyes up, hoping the veil of light gives me the look of something silver, something wrong. Prove what he's always suspected. He takes one last look at me and pulls open the door. There isn't even time for another beating. He doesn't say he hopes I suffer. Curse is all he can think about.

*　　*　　*

Days pass. I listen to the Keepers change shift outside, feasting on the mere sound of another voice. I hope to overhear things I'm not supposed to know. Sometimes they are careless. I hear them joke about tampering with my food, then finally I hear Barrett's name. That he's alive, but there's nothing left of his mind. He can barely remember his own name. The Keepers say he deserved it, and I sob, knowing that his torture at the hands of Father Jessop will never be uncovered, that everything he loved is lost for good. I try to listen for mention of Norah, her baby, but there is none. No one else has been brought here. Sometimes I imagine her gathering other women, plotting, an impossible plan coming together. An army Father Jessop won't see coming. One day. One day, something will break. The earth hums with the possibility.

I recognise his voice outside, the smooth vowel sounds from church services. It must be now. It must be today. I take to my feet before the door is opened by two Keepers. They move into the room with lamps, sent in before Father Jessop to check I'm still alive, to ensure I'm not primed ready to attack him. When the Keepers see me, one of them, the shorter of the two, gives an involuntary start and readjusts his hands around the lamp so he holds it in both, rather than one. Sometimes their fear revives me, makes me believe I am wicked, I do have power.

'She's on her feet, Father,' the other man calls through the half-open door, then to me he barks: 'Stay exactly where you are.'

It's his boots I hear before I see him, the metal cap and heel filling the room with an unpleasant clacking. He brings with him a chair, and the Keeper fastens the door behind him. There are new, deep scars on his face. This is Cal's doing; this is what happened to him after I was dragged away.

One of the Keepers speaks so Father Jessop doesn't have to.

'On your knees.'

Kneeling would have felt respectful and natural once; now I see it for what it is – submission, control. The more he bred fear, the more we had no choice but to look to him for protection. I feel his bandaged hand come down on my scalp, pretending tenderness in a way that has me shrinking in revulsion. He recites a prayer and quotes

Father Lambert and the evils he discovered, sought to end. He uses a torrent of words like *relinquish* and *vanquish* and *command*.

'It breaks my heart to see you come to this,' he says with an affected sigh. 'You had such a difficult start. All that suffering. But you were a strong child, and without the shadow of your mother, we all believed in your Salvation. We did our utmost to help you resist. Now look.' He pauses, almost laughing at the way my life has diverged from the path he wanted. 'You were even a friend of my daughter's! Imagine. I'm glad Sarl was spared seeing what you've become.'

'I know what she did. I know what you did.'

There is barely a reaction, but I see it. I do have power. 'Then you know how difficult it is to watch you fail after everything we did to protect you. To watch you cavort with the darkness, welcome it to our shores.'

'The only darkness here is you.'

The air cracks. I hear the slap before I feel it, the scorching spreading across my cheek. His chair topples away and he stands full height over my kneeling body.

He pulls at me by the collar of my tunic. 'There is no remorse! Nothing left in you to be redeemed!'

He releases me, and I hear his breathing, laboured and tense. I can see calculated thoughts in the twitch of his hands. The rules of the land, the ones his ancestor created, say he cannot drown me without a confession, but even I know he could justify my punishment without it. A list of misfortunes and sickness, women prepared to accuse me in public. But they've kept me here weeks; there must be something else they want. He lengthens the quiet, his boot tapping out the time.

'You seem to be very reticent in answering our questions, Esta. I hear starvation is an agonising way to die. What are you fighting for? It's over. We know what you are. There's not a single doubt left.'

'Then you know what to do with me.'

A vein on his neck tightens. 'I want to know where he is. What he is.'

'Where?' My heart thrashes. Cal alive, free. The thought of him escaping runs wild in my thoughts.

'If you won't tell us what you know, then you give me no choice.'

He signals for the Keepers, and without another word, an unspoken plan, they tie up my hands and bind my feet.

Terror rips through me. They don't Untether women at night. Maybe I'm too dangerous to be watched by other women, too corrupting.

As they manhandle me, taking me under the arms, Father Jessop speaks again, his sickly-sweet smell pressed in close.

'We did another test,' he says. I imagine the Eldermothers in their chapel lighting sage and mixing my fluids with grit from the earth, rubbing alcohol. He pauses, waiting for my guess. 'This time – the baby – it's real.'

My legs collapse underneath me, and I retch, twisting in the Keepers' grip. An animal cry, the thunder of blood whirring in my head. No. No. I launch myself at him, but I'm held back; the noise and teeth of a dog, yet Father Jessop's expression barely shifts.

'When the news gets out that you're carrying a monster's child, there won't be a man on this island who won't want to rip it from your stomach himself. It goes against everything we stand for, everything we've worked for. And him. They'll want his lifeless body hanging in the churchyard. As soon as he learns of your condition, he'll be back and we'll be waiting for him. We've taken the news to the Otherlands and spread it to the furthest reaches. There's only one way of saving the child, and that's to come back here, back to where he made his monster.'

I'm screaming, throwing my body against the Keepers, but they push me back to the floor and my fingers claw at the ground. If Cal has gone, if he's managed to get away, then this is the last place I want him to come back to.

'Take her to the harbour,' Father Jessop says.

Twenty-Six

They march me to the harbour. They've set a trap. The lights of the patrol ferries are off, but they're manned, waiting with nets, harpoons. As I'm led past Barrett's unlit house, my hope collapses. I want to believe Father Jessop invented the baby as an elaborate lie, the bait to get Cal back. But I can feel it already, the shadow of something growing. Instinct tells me it's a girl: caged and fighting like me. I feel the push in my body like she is growing faster than the nine months it usually takes, like she's trying to escape her own fate. How much of her is me and how much is Cal?

The Keepers manhandling me nod to the one on duty in the harbour, and he unlocks the gates. When we pass, he snarls like a dog at me, spits at my feet. As they drag me further and further past moored yoles, the creak of the jetties moaning under our feet, I'm expecting them to kick me off the edge or push me to my knees and hold my face underwater until I stop moving. There are a hundred ways I can picture the end of my life, but not one way I can imagine my escape. I can see a dark figure up ahead, hat and coat making a bulky shape. The unlucky volunteer taking me out to sea. He has his back to me, but when he stands full height, hearing the sound of the Keepers marching close, I go limp. The Keepers have to pick me up under the armpits, push me forward.

'Get in the boat,' they say.

The man on the jetty, with the ropes taut in his hands, turns to glance at me, but won't look me in the eye as I climb into his boat.

Ingram.

He says nothing as he unmoors, but I've seen his eyes. He's haunted. There's only room for three of us, and the second Keeper stays behind and watches the boat leave. I can hardly imagine what they must have been thinking when they heard the plan: that a woman with darkness in her soul would be taken out to sea to summon back the beast she had fornicated with. They must have worried that the end was nigh; they must have kissed their children wondering if they'd ever see dawn again. Do they notice the recklessness in Father Jessop now? Does it frighten them?

I dare a look at Ingram. He looks older somehow, though it's only been weeks. His face is set and lined, the deep ridges of anger I know from Franklin's face now in his. He will not escape the shame of me even when I'm gone, but there is a sadness in him too, how our lives have transpired. It stings to look at him and know I've hurt him. He was never unkind or cruel; he was as trapped as I was.

'Ingram . . .'

The Keeper gives me a warning look.

Ingram doesn't look at him or me, his focus solely on the water.

'I wanted to tell you how sorry I am.'

'I'll cut your fucking tongue out if you carry on,' the Keeper says.

The oars thump and the next wave jolts, thrashing sweat from all of us as the boat lifts and smacks down into the water.

I see Ingram's hands flex against the wood, the boat slowing as the waves grow taller, choppier. He can't concentrate on controlling the boat with the tension like this.

'Let her speak. They say she won't confess, so go on . . . I want to hear it.'

The Keeper seethes at his stolen authority.

I try to plead with my husband. 'I never meant to hurt you. This started a long time ago. Before I met you. Before I even understood it. I knew it was against God, that my feelings were dangerous and sinful, but I couldn't stop it. If I was a stronger person, if I'd fought . . . but I couldn't. You know what that's like.'

His eyes meet mine and the oars come down again. They are his fists and I am the sea.

'You were my wife.'

'You didn't love me.'

'This your confession? To blame me?' he says, stopping the boat, the water rocking us like a cradle unhinged. The Keeper holds the torch steady, shines it into my eyes, one of his hands clutching the side of the boat.

'I've nothing to confess. I wasn't possessed. Not by him, not by anyone.'

'Lying cunt,' the Keeper says.

'I fell in love. That's all.'

'He's one of *them*,' Ingram says, furrow deepening. 'How can you say you're not bewitched?'

'He's one of us.'

'What?'

'His father's here. His blood is ours,' I say.

'Liar!' Ingram says, quiet, not wanting to listen.

'That's why he came here. To find his father. He's never hurt me, never caused me any harm. He's no monster.'

I keep pushing. 'You've never seen them, have you? The Seawomen? All those years on the boats, and your father too, and nothing, not even a glimpse. So how can you know what they are?'

'Doran was almost drowned by one of them. That's what they are! That's why she was hung in the churchyard!'

'Your brother's a liar, you know it as well as I do. He went hunting, he sought her out and slaughtered her. The Seawomen aren't waiting for us out there. They're gone. Years ago. They were beaten and attacked by Lambert's men, so they fled. They're harmless. They were driven away and still they're blamed for everything. Don't you see?'

'That's enough!' Ingram trembles with rage. 'You've done all this and still you can't admit the truth. I didn't volunteer so I could see you; I did it so I could see the monster with my own two eyes and drive a knife into him.'

A heat of revenge bulks through his body. All that shame and anger twists him into a man like Doran. Underneath it all, though, I know there's good inside him. He powers on through the waves and we pass the patrol ferries, their size making me shudder.

Stay away, Cal, I think, please stay away. I long for him to sense it. I turn my head and my breath catches, seeing the full outline of the island in the distance. It looks small, insignificant.

The Keeper, made queasy by the rocking, wipes his mouth and presses on the base of his stomach.

'Start calling for him,' he says, making a circle with his mouth and blowing air out.

'What?'

'He has a name, don't he? Start shouting it.'

I look blankly from him to Ingram and back.

'We should start searching the water,' Ingram says.

'Shout for him!'

I do as he says, throat sore, as they cast their lights across the water, the beginnings of an impossible plan forming inside me.

I can't tell if it's my teeth chattering or the stutter of Ingram's boat against the water, but the cold has its own pulse now. The black sky, the black sea, there's no end to this. We've left the island behind, the cliffs and the great skerries of rock temples drifting away like they're nothing but grit. My world was a cell, but now the world is edgeless, expanding, and I can't remember how to breathe, there's so much air. The water swells. We are stirred and sloshed, and even though Ingram's hands on the oars look strong, against the sea his strokes seem timid the further out he rows.

The yole hurls and drops, falling the height of each new wave, and my stomach travels up and down with it. The Keeper, whose name I've learnt is Hoggan, skims the water with his light. There's no sign of Cal. Good. No suggestion of his body in the water, no sign he has been tricked by the patrol boats standing still, lights off.

'How much further we going?' Hoggan asks. He keeps swallowing, gripping his lips together, holding in his sickness. He shines his light in my face. 'Call for him again. Louder.'

I lock eyes with Ingram. I see the face I've tried to forget, the way the loss of our imaginary child has hollowed him out, slackened his mouth, contorted him in wet ugliness. I didn't just lie, I killed his child. That's how he sees it. It didn't matter that he didn't love me; he loved our child, he loved the idea of what being a father would make him. What he has left is nothing to him now, not when he will have to suffer the memory of me, other people's memories of me, until his life is over.

'I am sorry,' I say, trying again. 'You might not believe it, but I did want to make it work. I did try.'

'Don't,' Ingram says. 'That's not what you're here for.'

I call again for Cal. Throat splitting. I push on the side of the boat with both hands and call again. My weight makes the boat tip, rock off balance. Hoggan, double the size of me, thick in body and neck, leans in the opposite direction, trying to equalise the weight.

'She's trying to sink us! Fuck!' In his shouting, he drops his torch overboard, cursing and looking helplessly over the side. Water slops in at our feet. 'Look what you made me do, stupid bitch.'

'Maybe it's better to be in the dark,' Ingram says, pausing one oar to switch off his own light. 'Creature's not going to come if he thinks we've set a trap.' He eyes me. 'You know him; you tell us. What would make him come here again?'

A wave hits the yole and we all brace, sea spray wetting our faces.

'Does he love you?' Ingram asks, pushing his frustration into his arms and forcing his way through the water.

'His beast is growing in her belly. He'll be back,' Hoggan says. I can't bear to look at Ingram. 'If we get him, what then?'

'Father Jessop wants him – *it* – brought back.'

'If a thing like that had fucked my wife, I'd like to get a hold of him and rip off his cock with my bare hands.'

'What's so different between me and you?' I ask Ingram. I keep my hands down in the hull so he can't see that I'm managing to loosen the ties. 'You love someone else. You've fucked her.'

'You're wretched,' he says, stuttering with indignation. 'I would never dishonour my family that way.'

'Doran will find out soon enough, when he looks at his child's eyes. What then?'

Hoggan can't hide his surprise.

'I tried to be your wife and you didn't want me.'

'Tried?' Ingram's scoff sounds hurt; any pretence that he's grown into Doran shatters.

'I wanted to be happy. We could have been. Not here, though. Not like this. Another world.'

'A world for the sick, for sinners,' he says bitterly.

'She's a lying whore,' Hoggan says. 'You're fucked in the head, you and your monster child.'

A wave hits, and we lurch. Hoggan leans over the edge, head lolling, and vomits down the side of the boat and down himself. Ingram tuts.

'Get it together!' he says to Hoggan, thumping him on the back. 'Rain's coming in and I want to find this thing!'

'It's useless,' Hoggan says, biting back on another wave of vomit. 'He's not coming for her. Maybe he has hundreds of whores all around, all growing monsters for him. We should send out a whole fleet in the morning.'

'He'll only come for her.'

Hoggan retches again, and with Ingram preoccupied, I stretch my fingers, worming my hands out of the ties. Free. I don't have much of a plan, only a vague need, an instinctive urge to get away. I rise, leaning heavily on one foot, knowing the boat is tilting, giving way in the same direction Hoggan is leaning. I push and I hold my breath. I see their faces before it happens, the endless black pits of their open mouths, eyes wide.

Their voices are upside down. That's what stays with me as the boat spins, the water pulls me into its grip. I am hollow and nothing once again. All light gone, sound reduced to my own thudding blood. I'm underwater. Gripless, airless, limbs stretching like spiders' legs.

I could stay here. I could close my eyes, let the air die out. But there's a child to think of now, Cal's and mine, and I feel her waking me. I push out my feet and kick my way back to the surface.

My mouth rises above the water and I take in enough air to stretch my lungs. The yole is some distance away, upturned, carried like a hollow casket. I concentrate on the lessons Cal taught me, frustrated with myself for thinking this was going to work without him. I need his calm reassurance, his direction. Instead there's just me and her, looking out at this endless water, not knowing where to start. I don't let myself think of the worst, my useless body dragged away by the current. I imagine myself as a fish – no, says my unborn child, a Seawoman. Legs morphing into a tail, hands turning into the webbed tools of her father.

I look back at the capsized craft, seeing two dark figures struggling to latch onto it. Their bodies sink, arms flailing. I watch them, their spluttering, their choking, and I do not feel a thing. It's freeing to feel nothing. They scream, the fear of drowning sounding so different from a man's mouth. They slump heavily over the boat's hull now, exhausted and terrified.

'Where is she?' I hear Ingram shout. He sounds defeated. He must be thinking how he couldn't even do this right. 'Esta!'

In my head I can hear Cal's voice as clearly as if he's with me. I am free, for the first time. I look across the endless water, thinking: please take me away.

Breathe.

I have to keep going. Fight the tightness of my chest, fight the cold. Splashing, uncoordinated, directionless, but I keep going. The current gulps at me, pulling me down with effortless force.

'Fuck! Look! She's there! The bitch is swimming away. I told you! I knew it!' Hoggan shouts at Ingram, shrieks, convinced of what I am, of what I have become. I picture Ingram's horrified face.

I hear Father Jessop's voice, a fragment of the past: *She's one of them.* I beg silently for Cal to come for me. I wonder if he can hear my heartbeat and hers too. Will he hear that and know?

Kick. Small movements. That's it.

I'm already tired, but I won't let it win. I think of his voice, urging me on. I think of the stars, the place he promised could exist for us. Our child, growing in a new world with no borders, no restrictions. I'd let her run free, I'd let her swim.

Arc your arms over your head. Up and over.

A shallow tide. An ocean ridge. Me on land, him in the water, our child in the in-between. I can see it, I can see us. I can feel her. Keep going.

Good. Neck straight. Chin up.

Swimming. The island further and further away. I push on, purging the water in my path, fighting back the bite of cold, the mist blinding me, the salt trying to choke me.

Push up. Tense your body.

I power forward, legs kicking, arms sweeping out in front of me. I find a rhythm. I want to laugh; my energy feels suddenly bottomless. I think of my girl in my stomach and I think: yes, you and me, we can do this. We can carry on to freedom. The words from the past come back to me: *Foula. Sumburgh. Hollandstoun. Atlantic.* We will get there. I imagine what I look like to Ingram and Hoggan. They've never seen anything like it.

Then a noise, a drilling in my head, a fly in my ear. I don't look around, I keep swimming, but the noise is getting closer. The sea is suddenly lit in yellow and gold, beams from the patrols cast across the water. They've changed tack. I keep going, fighting against the horror of not escaping. My name is shouted. The noise now is a din, electric, a wasp caught in a jar.

'Pull up right beside her,' I hear a voice say. It's hard to make out the words over the whirring noise. I keep going. Nearly there, I tell her. I lie to both of us.

It's Father Jessop. It has to be. He's clearer now, booming, directly above me. The boat ploughing the water beside me has motors, can outrun me without even trying. These aren't our boats; these he's imported, kept hidden, advancements we're meant to shun for simple living. The bow cuts through the waves without a stutter, hardly a jolt.

He barks orders to his men. Letting me go would be a show of weakness. What would it teach the women of the island? That freedom is possible, that authority can be overthrown? Every muscle burns as I swim faster, refusing to believe that this is the end.

I feel something fall around me. A mesh, a cage. A net. I feel the drag of it, the tangle as I try to fight it off. I slip under, choking, hands trying to rise and getting caught in the strings of the netting. I fight again. The water thrashes as my head breaks the surface.

'Give me that. Get closer.'

I glimpse him snatching a fishing pole, one with a hook on the end.

I see the tip of it shine in the wan light, and then it cracks against the side of my head, smacks into the water. I taste blood. I hear a piercing sound. Agony. When I twist my head, I see a harpoon sticking out of my thigh. I almost pass out. He hits me around the head again, and my nose and mouth fill with water, arms limp, face down. The world shutters black.

Twenty-Seven

This limp fold of my lifeless body is fishlike, thrown from a haul. I don't know how long I've been here on the floor, but I haven't moved, haven't spoken in what feels like days. I feel a fever drumming from the corners of my skull. Hot, cold, shaking. There was no rescue, no Cal, no swimming to freedom. These are my limits; this is what they trap me with.

The door opens and I hear my first visitor in a long time. They falter, linger outside, hold a torch like a weapon to their chest. It cannot be a Minister. I look up and see a woman. I see Mull. She stands close to the door, casting the torch cautiously around the room, jolting when the light hits me. I'm not the woman she remembers, not like this. The torch slows and she holds it over me.

'She's not . . . is she?' The Keepers flank her, and she looks at them, her voice thick with tears when she speaks.

One of the Keepers moves further into the cell, crouches by my head and pulls it back. My eyes are open, blinking, so he tosses me aside.

'She looks . . .' Mull cannot finish her sentence and swallows audibly. My mouth is so dry from the salt water, I'm even envious of the way her throat functions.

'We had to drag her out of the sea, and she managed to kick and scream all the way out there in the water. She's fine.'

'Has she eaten?'

One of the Keepers hesitates. 'No, ma'am. Her food privileges were revoked.'

'She's being starved?'

There is a sound of hesitation again, a burring, huffing. 'It's the Father's orders, ma'am.'

She steps a little closer. 'She won't harm . . . ? Has she been given something? Something to sedate her? Is it safe?'

So that's why my head feels furred at the edges, why I'm drifting in and out, my body too heavy to move. Mull's fingers splay, shield her belly.

'We'll keep her back.'

She braves a longer look at me.

'I think . . . I want to be left alone with her,' she says, her hesitation turning into something definite.

'Ma'am . . .'

'On my own,' she says, her voice taking on a different tone. She is more of a John woman than I've ever seen, authority and power in her blood. 'If you're here, watching over us, she won't talk.'

The Keepers give a silent agreement after a long and uncertain pause, and leave lamps in the room. They hand her a knife, but she looks at it like she wouldn't know what to do with it. I know why she's here. She is their last hope to get a confession, to extract all the mysteries of the Seawomen out of me.

The door closes behind them, and then it's just me and her, alone.

'Can you hear me?' she asks, and I manage a silent response. 'Can you sit up?'

If I concentrate hard on every movement and not the effort it requires, not the pain, I can sit, heaving myself with my back against the wall. One swollen eye makes it hard for me to look at her properly, so I keep it half lidded, almost shut.

'Can you talk?'

'Yes,' I say, scratchily. She reacts to my voice, her face pinching.

Her hand darts to her face to wipe her tears. She looks around the bare room, stopping at the bloodied blanket. 'You've been here the whole time? But there's no bed.'

'The floor,' I say, touching my throat as the words drag.

She looks around for a cup, a drink, and sees nothing like it. 'Oh, Esta.' My name catches, swallowed up in her sob. She buries her face in her hands. Once, I would have believed I knew her well enough to understand her tears, but now I don't know who she's crying for.

When I look at the shape of her bump, I realise more time has passed than I thought. How long have they kept me in here, hunting for him, scouring the water for threat, spreading more doctrine and fear in the absence of my confession?

'You're getting big fast,' I say. I see her flinch, imagine her thoughts racing.

'Is it true?' she says, looking at my body. 'I know you lied before. But now . . . something's growing inside you?'

I shift, touch my own stomach in a mirror of hers. 'A child.'

Her eyes glisten in the light. 'I wanted so much to be wrong. For everything that's been said about you to be a lie, but it isn't. It's all true.'

'I'm not cursed. I love him.'

She snorts. 'Love! After everything, you still call it that! Aren't you even sorry? Everything you've done, Esta! We were friends. You lied to me for so long.'

'What could I have said?'

'God would have forgiven you! I could have helped you, shown you the right path.'

'You? You're the reason I'm here. Why I've been beaten and prodded, why I look like this.'

'I thought . . .' She turned her head away. 'I didn't have a choice. It was the right thing to do. What you've done—'

'You betrayed me.'

'You betrayed us all! Year after year.' She puts her hand to her forehead, pacing from one corner of the room to another. I wait for her to speak. I know she has more to say; I can see it, pushing from the inside, long buried. There's more than just anger behind her words.

'All those years ago, you told me, you promised me, there was nothing in the water. If you'd been honest, all of this . . .'

'If I'd told you the truth, your father would have slaughtered him.'

'And we'd have been safe.'

'Safe? What do you think your father would have done to us if he knew we'd been in the sea?'

'We'd have been forgiven. In time. If we'd repented, if we'd proved we had nothing dark inside us.'

'You maybe, but me? With my mother?' I have to stop myself from telling her everything I know. I need her to listen, to believe. I try again, taking us back to the cove. 'I wanted to protect you. I was scared what it would mean for us if we admitted to seeing something in the water. I thought that if I pretended to see nothing, then all of it would go away.'

'All of what?'

I shake my head. 'You already think I'm wicked, that I've been possessed.'

'I want to know. I want to hear it from you.' Something softens in her, and she makes the decision to sit on the floor, opposite me. She can't look at me fully, but she's there, as she promised, waiting for me to speak.

'We spent our whole lives being told how dangerous the water was, but we lived by it, day in, day out. When we were there that day in the cove, I wanted to know what it was like. I wanted to swim.'

'What? But you said . . .'

I say nothing.

'So you tricked me into going into the water with you! And you say it's nothing to do with the Seawomen!'

'We were children!' The emotion in my words stops her, but she's primed, ready to leave me to rot. 'Have you never wanted to play in the water? Splash? Sail in a boat like the men do?'

'No,' she says. 'Because I've seen what the water can do. Why would you risk our lives like that? You let it destroy you.'

'I did everything I could to put it out of my mind.'

In the low light I can see her mouth trembling, her hands fidgeting in her lap.

'You don't understand what it was like. You belong here. You're happy. But I wasn't. It was eating away at me. You were able to move on, never speak of it again, but I was different.'

She exhales, voice quivering. 'You think I didn't pay the price?'

I lift my gaze to meet hers, and for the first time it feels like just the two of us, unguarded.

'We said we'd never speak of it,' she says, 'so we went to the festival as normal. But all the while, it was churning away at me, what we'd done, what might happen to us, the island. Everything I ate curdled inside me. Every word of my father's sermons about darkness circled around and around my head. He knew, I was sure of it. I looked at you, with your grandmother, and it was like nothing had happened. You danced, you sang, you ate. I watched on like a dead person. That's what I thought I was. Because what would God want with me now? And my father, he would soon look at me and see me for what I really was. So when we got home and my brothers went to bed, I knocked on the door of his office.'

'You confessed.'

'I told him a version of what had happened, but it wasn't just that. I told him we'd seen something – someone – in the water. A boy. I was trying to ask him questions, because what we'd seen didn't match with what we'd been told. Perhaps there were other sea people in the water? Or perhaps the Seawomen were not as we knew? I said' – she grimaced – 'that maybe he'd got it wrong. Maybe Father Lambert had.'

She was open to it once, the idea of the water being different to the stories we were told. My weak heart races. I tense, anticipating her father's reaction.

'He beat me. With his boots. With his hands. With the legs of his chair. He had to carry me to bed. He even tucked me in. Made me pray before I closed my eyes. I begged God to take the pain away and let me sleep.'

'And did He?' I could hardly get the words out.

'No.'

She wipes her tears away with both hands, her skin looking so pale and translucent it makes me wonder if he left a permanent mark on her. She rights herself, sucking in deep breaths.

'But I've had time to think about it. He was right to punish me. He was right. He did it to protect me and keep this island safe. Suffering happens because we must learn. The pain taught me a lesson.'

'You're his daughter. You were a child!'

Tearfully, she meets my gaze. 'A girl already showing signs of the Seawomen. He did what needed to be done. And it worked, didn't it? I learnt my lesson and now I have God's blessing of life to show for it. I'm not a prisoner. I don't have a curse on my conscience.'

'You didn't go into the water because you were bewitched; you went in to rescue me. You didn't deserve to be punished for that.'

'No, *you* did! You were bewitched and Father didn't lay a hand on you. He said God would show us in time what you were. He said I had to be his eyes. Prove myself. Like when you disappeared, the night your grandmother . . .' She looked every inch a John woman. 'And Father was right. God has shown us what you are.'

Her betrayal, years of it, eats away at me. 'I wasn't bewitched by anyone.'

'But that man, that . . . How do you explain him?'

I think of Cal in the water, his arms around me, the way he rescued me, the way I felt at seeing his body, the strange blend of land and sea, for the first time.

'Aden. When you first fell for him, how did he make you feel?'

I see her baulk. 'How can you even think of comparing that *thing* to Aden?'

'Because it's the same.'

'God chose Ingram for you.'

'I don't love Ingram, you know I don't. I never did. Aden, he made you feel safe and special. Wanted. He was gentle and listened to you. He'd never have hurt you.'

'Stop!' she cries. I was repeating back all the things she'd told me about him when they first met; how she knew it was love.

'I felt that too. With Cal. He told me about the world; not stories, not the past, but the truth. He gave me a taste of what my life could be, where I'd be free, happy. It's all I wanted.'

'To live as a sinner? A life of disease?' she says, incensed. 'I saw him with my own eyes. Don't tell me he's anything like Aden. He's a monster. If you can love something like that . . .'

'I've never been happier than when I was with him.'

She stares at me in disbelief. 'How can you say it so plainly? He filled your head with wickedness. You know what this makes you.'

I found the energy to kneel, to crawl a little closer to her. 'You know me. You've known me for so long. You know what's in here, in my heart, in my soul. Look me in the eye and tell me you can see in me what your father talks about. You can't, because you know the truth.' My voice falters to see her head rise, her gaze make hesitant contact with mine.

'I thought I knew you.' In a quieter, anxious voice, 'He says you'll harm my baby if I get too close. He says you'll mutate it into one of them . . . give it webbed toes, or . . . or you'll make me lose it.'

Hearing her say it like she believes it is more painful than I could ever imagine.

'You know I would never.'

'You have that thing of his inside you.'

'A child. *My* child.' And as I feel my daughter, I know I want to protect her more than anything in the world. 'We always hoped we'd be pregnant at the same time. Only you'll have to live motherhood for the both of us now.'

'Don't.'

'All those times we talked about. Our children growing up together, you and I growing old. I won't get to have any of that,' I say.

For the first time, I think I've got through to her. Her head hangs, her shoulders juddering.

'Why couldn't you have tried to stay away?'

'I did. I did try.'

She sobs, and somewhere from deep inside me comes an instinct to comfort her.

'That night. I knew you weren't ill,' she says. 'I had this feeling. You'd been acting strangely ever since you said you were pregnant. It felt like you weren't excited, that you didn't want to tell me. Seren and I went to the festival, but I didn't say anything. I swear I didn't. But Father realised you weren't there. And he pulled me aside and—'

I stop her, remembering her black eye when she was dragged into Barrett's house that night. She couldn't escape Father Jessop any more than I could. It was obedience or his fists.

'I didn't want this!' she says, throwing her arms out at the squalor of the cell. Her posture petulant. 'I never wanted to lose you. He made me say. He made me! He said if I didn't . . .'

My thoughts go to that night, her red face, eyes streaming. Images come into focus. I see Barrett on the floor, blood leaking into his white hair. I think of him now, something I'd overheard, looked after by his brother, barely able to remember his own name.

I put my hand on the floor between us. Without me realising, Mull has crept closer. The gaunt new shape of my body, the bruises and cuts, the rough stubs of hair growing back easier for her to see.

'When I'm gone,' I say, and watch her tremble. 'I know what you think of me, but please – will you look in on Barrett and check he's all right?'

'I don't . . . I won't be allowed to.'

'Please,' I say.

'The way he hit his head . . .' she says, guilt thickening her voice again.

'Maybe it's better he won't remember.'

It isn't long before the sound of the Keepers outside becomes prominent again. The time will soon come; they will collect her, grill her for any information she's gleaned from me that they couldn't. She hasn't asked anything. She sees my eyes dart up, and hers widen, panicked that our time is almost over.

'I loved you,' she says, tears running down her cheeks. She stretches across the stone floor, her fingertips just touching mine. 'You were my sister.'

I reach forward and grip her hand. She doesn't pull away. 'You'll be a wonderful mother, like the kind I wanted.' I use my free hand to dry my face, and with my lips feeling like they might split, I smile. 'Just please don't try and sing the baby to sleep. Not with your voice. You were awful in the choir.'

She laughs, more of a smile, a breath cut short. But it's there between us, a final moment of proof, what we were, what is ending. She rushes towards me, her arms open, and I'm pulled upwards by the shock of it. Her chest collides with mine, and I absorb her last sob as she embraces me, a touch so unfamiliar now that it feels years old. Then she tears away, almost repelled, too raw, too much, disbelieving what she just allowed herself to feel.

She says my name, timid, pensive again, drawing us both back into the present. 'If these women are not of the darkness, what are they?'

Her question is not one of interrogation. I can see something in her face and I take my chance. 'Free women. What this island fears the most. He controls us, Mull. It's everywhere, even the drink the Eldermothers make us take—'

'What do you mean, it's to . . . prepare us.'

'To control us.' Looking into my eyes has chipped away at those beliefs just slightly, flaking the surface, because she doesn't see evil in me, and I know it. She *doubts*.

The door clanks open and Mull springs back, separating herself from the criminal. Our fingers were touching, but now they're not.

'Time's up,' the Keeper come to get her says. They can't afford to let her stay with me for too long in case I do something to her, twist her, corrupt her. But that's what they don't see when they enter the room, the changes under the surface, her altered mood, her thoughts.

And I pray it will be too late before they do.

'Will I see you again?' The words rush out of me; I'm desperate for her to hear them before I am shut in again.

The Keeper shoots me a dark look, holding the door open for her to depart. I should know better than to call out, to speak when I haven't been spoken to.

She half turns so we can see each other, and swallows before she speaks. 'Tomorrow.'

My heart rises before the realisation hits me. She'll see me tomorrow because tomorrow is the day I will be Untethered.

The Untethering

The Eldermothers wake me. I'm crowded in by their long cloaks. It takes time to adjust, to realise I'm not still asleep. There are two of them, one either side of me, who pull me up by the elbows. I am given one final chance to confess, to purge myself of sin.

'It won't save your life, but it could save your soul from eternal damnation,' one of them says.

Sending Mull failed. Now, without a confession, without answers, they just want rid of me, to start again, to end this rotten family line once and for all, my monster child with it. I can imagine Father Jessop's justification in his sermon. Once the island is free of me, they might never experience misfortune again.

I tried to get away. I wanted another life, to shed the island rules. In the end, that was enough, that was all the reason he needed.

The Eldermothers fold me into a prayer position on my knees. They chant, their voices joining in a suffocating harmony. I am limp as they undress me, my arms unmoving like a puppet's. They lift me into a tub. Water is poured over my head, one bucket, then another, giving me no chance to breathe in between. Inside me, the quiver of my fast-swimming daughter reminds me of her existence.

Father Jessop arrives, flanked by Keepers. He looks to the Eldermothers as they plant me back on the floor. 'Has she repented?'

'No, Father.' This Eldermother is short, jittery like a mouse. She dips her head apologetically.

'Nothing at all? Not even a hint of remorse?'

'No, Father.'

'Very well,' he says, then addresses them all. 'Thank you for your efforts.'

They glide out of the cell, taking the smoky scent of sage with them.

Father Jessop stands before me for the ceremony. His hair slick and combed, his robes clean and neat, his hands clasped, wearing the gold rings of his ancestors. How many bodies has he touched, hurt, in the name of God's work? Was his father the same, stretching all the way back through the John line to Lambert? All those lies told, beliefs manipulated, all for control.

'The Lord could forgive you, and so could I. We could fix this.'

He has to show his men that he gave me the choice. How easy it would be to believe him. How simple it seems to utter the words he wants and have all of this torture disappear. How many women have been forced into confession like this? Given false promises, hope of redemption.

But I'm not sorry for any of it. It was me all along, not the Seawomen, not God. There was no darkness, no evil spirit shuddering from the sea mist. I wanted the water and everything that came with it – pleasure, freedom, Cal. I still do. I would do it all over again. Nothing will save a woman like me.

'We could fix this.' He repeats his assurance.

I raise my head to look him in the eye. 'There's nothing to fix. The only curse here is you.'

I don't even cower as he approaches.

'Everything you've done to innocent women, the violence you've encouraged, all in the name of God. Hurt them, tricked them, raped them, drowned them. God wouldn't choose a man like you to save us. He'd destroy you.'

Father Jessop's face contorts. He snaps, charging at me, his weight knocking me onto my back, my skull smacking against the ground, eyes swimming.

'The darkness has her tongue!' he cries to his men, clambering on top of me, scrabbling for his cross.

His body crushes me to the ground, and he holds me down by the arms, spit flying in my face. His knee pinning my legs apart, cross pushed into my cheek.

'Renounce them!'

I twist away. 'No.'

'Renounce them!'

His weight is choking, and I don't have the strength to move. I stare at the Keepers' boots and manage to move my eyes up to their faces. They are not watching on placid like I feared. Instead they're unsure, a nervous pull in the way they stand. They hesitate. Father Jessop holds me down, shouting scripture. I can see it in the Keepers' faces. They've never seen him lose control like this. One of them falters. I want it all to be over. I am small and invisible. If I try to fight, they might see me as wicked, but like this, it's him they notice.

'Father!'

The weight lifts as the Keepers pull him off. The three of them stand there, charged, panting. Father Jessop shakes down his robes, trying to gather himself. They look at him like the darkness.

'Father . . .' One of them speaks. He's young. Straight out of school. I recognise him. Lennie. Crescent's brother, taller than I remember. Perhaps there was a time when she cried in the dark of night and told him what had happened to her with the boys from the older classes, and he swore that he would never see that happen again. Perhaps he decided to be a Keeper in a naïve attempt to protect women like his sister. I hope. I hope. Hope is all that's left.

Father Jessop wrenches his arm away from Lennie's touch. His snarling face flashes at me, his hair unkempt, the muscle in his cheek throbbing under the skin.

His temper has him flying towards the door. 'Get her ready for the ceremony.'

I don't scream. I don't spit. In my head I can hear the final refrain of 'Little Fisherboy Blue' coming back to me. I don't ask for it, but it's there, like my grandmother never went away. I have the image from the song playing in my mind, the fishermen licking their fingers, sucking the bones from the Seawoman's tail. I change the ending, imagine another verse where these gleeful men are poisoned by her flesh, where they lie in their beds clutching their bellies in agony, wishing they'd never gone near the Seawomen, never listened to the cries from the harbour of 'Little Fisherboy Blue'.

It's unusually cold today I've stopped being able to feel my body. The women in the crowd are wrapped in coats, woollen jumpers, animal skins. They watch, mesmerised, as the Keepers lead me naked towards the boat. I don't need to be drugged. I'm not fighting, I'm walking calmly to my death. In the diminishing light, it's hard to make out every face, but the ones that stand out are the ones I knew best. Vayle beside Seren, Seren looking drawn in the face, eyes averted. It would have been easier for her if this had happened years ago and she could have loved Ingram without anyone else in her way. At the front of the crowd, Norah and her daughters, the women around her wearing pensive expressions. The hood of Norah's coat is pulled tight around her face. It aches to look at her, to know what she might have to endure if her secret is ever discovered.

Finally there's Mull, standing beside a pair of Ministers I recognise as her brothers. Her arms are wrapped tightly around her body. She's dressed in sheepskin, yet she's trembling. I continue my walk, eyes straight ahead. I replay what I saw. Mull isn't shivering, she's sobbing.

As the Keepers take me by the arms and legs, I get my final glimpse of the crowd. Faces fixed in a solitary stare. I wonder, are they disappointed there's no show tonight, no fighting and biting, no need for me to be sedated and slapped into submission? Are they dissatisfied? I haven't admitted to my crimes. I haven't given a detailed account of my allegiance with the Seawomen or my base lust for the man from the sea. They want what they are about to witness to feel justified, earned. They want to know that it is being done with the Lord's blessing.

The Keepers lay me inside the yole. I've been starved for so long, I'm tiny inside the craft. The smell is just like I imagined it would be, tucked inside: a close, earthy scent of wood, the rotten damp of sea. Lennie's hands shake as he ties the ropes between my arms and the thwarts. They're not cutting into my wrists. I test them. Loose. I try again. I'm not dreaming. He's shown me mercy. He gives me the slightest of nods. I could cry if I had any tears left.

He steps back from me and signals that he's done.

A Minister approaches the boat, and I tense my body so that the ropes look tighter. I'm glad it isn't Doran. He is still by Father Jessop's side. This Minister's haste tells me he just wants this done, the boat overturned and me drowned. He raises his hand to Father Jessop in the crowd and I look up at the stars, hearing the golden bell ring.

Polaris. Cassiopeia.

I'm not here. I'm somewhere else entirely. Sharing the same sky with Cal, my mother and Rose. The harder I concentrate, the closer they feel. I don't listen to what Father Jessop says about me, the lies and the twisted tales. I focus on the truth, the life I lived. The life I want. He won't be able to tell the crowd that God has showed them my true nature. He can't say he's following Father Lambert John's decree. They can all see God has not made me barren. Father Jessop must find a new way to convince them of what I am, what I've done.

There are no theatrics. No young girls brought forward, no newly-weds, no pregnant women. Instead Ingram is summoned, and there's a hush.

Footsteps approach, and I brace to see his face looming down over me. I think of the next woman who will be chosen to be his wife. How will her happiness manifest when she stands in Seren's shadow, when she hears the stories about me, his first and cursed wife? He kneels, unmoors the boat. His face, plain and handsome, creases above his eyes. Some day soon Doran will look into his child's face and see Ingram staring back. The time will come when the truth tears the family apart. It will come.

The noise rises in the crowd, but as the boat drifts, I can hear there's something different about it. Ingram has turned back towards the ridge. I wish I could see what's happening. There's a new sound beneath the applause and cheering. A cry, a roar. The boat slops. I'm lightweight, carried quickly, and in the rush I'm sure I can hear my name in the crowd. Something among them turning. Pushing to the front. Shouting.

Away from the island, the sea sweeps the boat up, turns me, gulps me under. I've slipped the ropes loose, my body unfurling. Inside, my girl kicks and fights. Her sea-made blood swirls against mine, and some-how we detach from the boat, kick it away, kick to the surface, hands roaming free through froth and weed and foam. I don't look back at the island. I don't focus on the noise, the pushing, the unrest, the ringing of the golden bell, the men's voices trying to shout over the top.

I kick at the water and push out my arms, and my body is

weightless again, this time not afraid of what the sea wants from me or where it'll take me. I think of Cal, I think of us. Swimming together, him teaching me how, stones thrown as far as they can make it. His voice, our final kiss. I swim frog-legged, head above the surface, the waves growing faster and thicker. There's somewhere out there waiting for me. Even when my body grows tired and the only energy I have left comes from within, comes from my daughter, somehow I have made it. I have left the island. I'm free. And as I slip under, defeated by the sea's cold grip, I feel a swirl of bodies around me, a flash of silver – tails, webbed hands, scales and skin, touching me, pulling at me – and I am no longer afraid.

Acknowledgements

Ever since I was old enough to write, I was folding sheets of A4 paper in half to make my own books and scribbling stories inside. That love of storytelling and imagination has never left me. Few people have the opportunity to realise their dreams, so I feel incredibly fortunate that you're reading my book right now, and I'm very grateful to the people who have helped me get to this point.

To my agent, Nelle Andrew, thank you for being my ultimate champion from day one, for understanding me and this book. For your wisdom, your encouragement, your passion and strength. Thank you also to the rest of the team at Rachel Mills Literary Agency for your hard work and support. I'm so very proud to be on your client list.

To my editor, Kwaku Osei-Afrifa, thank you for your boundless enthusiasm for this book, for taking my characters to your heart and embracing genre-fluidity with me, for soothing my doubts and making my work infinitely better. To everyone at Hodder Studio: Bea Fitzgerald, Lily Cooper, Laura Batholomew, Kate Keehan, Alice Morley, Will Speed and Peter Strain for the beautiful hardback cover, Jane Selley and Sharona Selby – thank you for making this book a reality and my dreams come true.

Thank you to Richard Skinner and the Faber Academy for the scholarship that changed my life. Richard, I learnt so much from you, and you instilled in me the belief that I was capable of writing and finishing a whole book. This novel would not exist without the skills and confidence the course nurtured in me. To my classmates: Alistair, Ben, Charli, Deborah, Hayley, Jane, Kate, Lily, Lorna, Michele, Nicole, Ruth, Sarah and Susannah – I miss our weekly sessions, but I'm forever grateful for your critiques and wise words and of course the friendships we've made. You're such a talented bunch and I love you dearly. Thank you for being there from the beginning of *The Seawomen*, for all the ups and downs and pep talks. For your advice and suggestions about how to make my writing better and for talking sense into me when the self-doubt kicked in.

I'm so grateful to the wonderful people at The Literary Consultancy for all the work you do in supporting and lifting the voices of writers, especially those from underrepresented backgrounds. I owe so much to TLC for helping me develop as a writer. Your Chapter and Verse mentoring scheme introduced me to the brilliant Sally O-J, whose careful and invaluable mentorship made me a better writer. Sally, your belief in me from the first moment we worked together encouraged me to keep writing even when I was struggling. I wouldn't be in this position without you.

To Kirsty Logan, for sharing your wisdom and mentoring me when I was in the early stages of writing this novel. Your beautiful writing is a constant inspiration to me, and your generous, meticulous guidance made me strive to become a better writer. I will always remember the advice you gave me – to be a shark. The only way to keep going is to keep moving, keep writing.

To my tutors at the Open University and the University of Kent, and the friends I made along the way, thank you for giving me the space and support to take writing seriously and for encouraging me to write a novel. And to the teachers earlier in my school life, thank you for showing me how to appreciate literature and for enriching my writing.

A special thank you to those who say the right words when I need to hear them, and whose encouragement means so much: Bekz, Cat, Conor, Emma, Gem, Helen, Kathryn, Laura, Nick, Nikki and Sean. I love you. To all of my hugely supportive friends, thank you for your love and encouragement and for staying interested even though I have been writing the same book for years and there are only so many ways you can ask how it's going!

To the carers who work tirelessly and have helped me get ready every day, thank you for motivating me to keep writing even in the mornings when I don't want to. Thank you for holding me accountable and checking that I've put in the hours I've promised!

And finally, thank you to my family for being so loving and supportive, and for believing in me. For being there on the good days and the bad. To Mum and Dad, Ollie, Jade, Cliff and the rest of the family: I hope this makes you proud.